T0369224

Praise for Marie Treanor and Her Novels

"Wow! Steamy-hot fantasy, sizzling sex, and a story that makes you think. . . . Marie Treanor really packs a lot into these pages."

—Fallen Angel Reviews

"Witty and sensuous." —Romance Reviews Today

"My first impression of this work was *wow* . . . highly recommended read from an author to watch." —The Romance Studio

"A very unique fantasy. The passion and heat . . . was Pure Erotic but with a loving passion that made me feel all warm inside."

—Paranormal Romance Reviews

"A fantastic story . . . superhot sex. I cannot wait for future books."

—Joyfully Reviewed

"A strange and adorable relationship . . . so much more than a mere vampire story." —Romance Junkies

"Funny, sizzling, and tender." —Bitten by Books

"Marie Treanor always delivers a book that you'll be talking about long after reading it." —Love Romances

"Hauntingly beautiful and entirely sensual." —eCataromance

"Clever, agreeable, and very readable." —BookWenches

"A superbly written story filled with suspense, action, and steamy, passionate encounters." —Literary Nymphs

ALSO BY MARIE TREANOR

Blood on Silk

Blood Sin

AN AWAKENED BY BLOOD NOVEL

MARIE TREANOR

A SIGNET ECLIPSE BOOK

SIGNET ECLIPSE
Published by New American Library,
a division of Penguin Group (USA) Inc.,
375 Hudson Street, New York, New York 10014, USA
Penguin Group (Canada), 90 Eglinton Avenue East, Suite 700, Toronto,
Ontario M4P 2Y3, Canada (a division of Pearson Penguin Canada Inc.)
Penguin Books Ltd., 80 Strand, London WC2R 0RL, England
Penguin Ireland, 25 St. Stephen's Green, Dublin 2,
Ireland (a division of Penguin Books Ltd.)
Penguin Group (Australia), 250 Camberwell Road, Camberwell,
Victoria 3124, Australia (a division of Pearson Australia Group Pty. Ltd.)
Penguin Books India Pvt. Ltd., 11 Community Centre,
Panchsheel Park, New Delhi - 110 017, India
Penguin Group (NZ), 67 Apollo Drive, Rosedale, North Shore 0632,
New Zealand (a division of Pearson New Zealand Ltd.)
Penguin Books (South Africa) (Pty.) Ltd., 24 Sturdee Avenue,
Rosebank, Johannesburg 2196, South Africa

Penguin Books Ltd., Registered Offices:
80 Strand, London WC2R 0RL, England

First published by Signet Eclipse, an imprint of New American Library,
a division of Penguin Group (USA) Inc.

LIBRARY OF CONGRESS CATALOGING-IN-PUBLICATION DATA:

Treanor, Marie.
Blood sin: an awakened by blood novel/Marie Treanor.
p. cm.—(Awakened by blood ; bk. 2)
ISBN 978-0-451-23231-1
1. Vampires—Fiction. 2. Women—Scotland—Fiction. I. Title.
PR6120.R325B56 2011
823'.92—dc22 2010040469

Set in Minion Pro • Designed by Elke Sigal

To my editor, Kerry Donovan, who always sees the bigger picture.

And to all my editors from whom I've learned so much—especially Linda Ingmanson, the Adverb Slayer, for all her support, advice, and encouragement over several years and two publishers; and my other "serial" editors, Crystal Esau and Meghan Conrad, for their unfailing humor, help, and patience.

To the Transylvania trio for all the fun and inspiration. May they never know.

And finally to my husband. For the neck thing.

Blood Sin

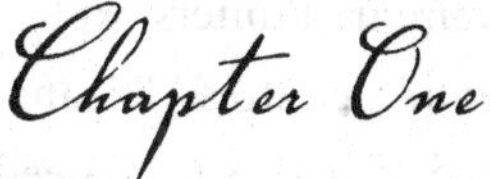

Chapter One

The vampire Saloman had not killed in two weeks. As Luiz Salgado-Rodriguez wandered toward him like a wraith among the shadows, hunger surged and Saloman anticipated the exquisite rush that came from a powerful kill.

And yet, observing the elderly professor shuffle across the vine-strewn courtyard of his Salamanca home, Saloman craved a *harder* kill, an enemy worthy enough physically to make him work. In short, he wanted a fight.

Instead, he stepped off the roof, his black leather coat streaming upward to slow his descent, and landed with impeccable elegance in front of the professor. "Good evening," he said politely in Spanish.

Although the old man was startled—who wouldn't be?—he neither screamed nor bolted, and in his pale, cloudy eyes, Saloman could make out no sign of fear. In fact, Luiz Salgado-Rodriguez smiled, as if he recognized death and welcomed it.

"Are you . . . Saloman?" he asked, his voice as frail and uncertain as his body.

Saloman smiled. "You've been expecting me," he said mockingly. As if he were the host rather than the visitor, he waved one inviting hand at the stone bench beside them, and the professor sat, a little too quickly for grace. "The vampire hunters explained your family history, perhaps? Told you that your ancestress Tsigana once killed me?"

The old man shrugged. "There was no need. I am aware of my own heritage. Although it was interesting to learn that you had been awakened. I didn't expect a dying old man to interest you—not until the others came."

Saloman stirred, closing the distance between them and sinking down onto the bench with his body turned toward the old man. "The others? Other vampires have been here?"

It was the old man's turn to smile, a weak but surprisingly charming gesture. "Not here. I've always known how to protect myself from your kind, so although I see them in the town from time to time, they are not aware of me or my descent." He gazed into the distance, and then, as if rediscovering his thread, back to Saloman. "No, I meant Dante, the American. He wanted the sword."

Saloman sat very still, searching the professor's wise old face. "Did you give it to him?"

"I couldn't. I didn't have it. To my knowledge, it has never been in the Spanish branch of the family." The professor stretched his leg out as if to ease it. "And you, sir. Did you come for the sword, or for my life?"

Saloman liked him. He liked the eccentricity of sitting in the man's courtyard, discussing his death in civilized, conversational tones. In fact, he wished he'd known him earlier.

"Both," he replied. His ears caught a faint sound, like a soft breeze blowing across the roof; his senses prickled and he scanned around the four sides of the little yard. "Although it seems I will have to settle for your life. Who is this Dante who asked you for my sword?"

"An American—charming man. A senator, I believe."

Shadows danced on the roof, dark with menace, too many to be opportunistic. "Thank you," Saloman said politely. "Your masking charm works well—I'm impressed by such knowledge in a human—but I'm afraid I didn't follow the same security. I have a different agenda."

For the first time, the professor began to look bewildered. "What do you mean?"

"I mean sit still and pretend to be dead already." Saloman leapt to his feet as the black shadows all dived from the rooftop in perfect time. Reaching up he grabbed the nearest, plucking him out of the air to snap his neck and hurl him at one of his companions with enough force to fell her too. It gave him the time necessary to deal with the others.

The wooden stake driving for his heart glanced harmlessly off his leather coat. The idiots had come in force but without any clear idea of how to kill an Ancient. Saloman glimpsed the shock and terror in the vampire's face before he swung him up in one arm and snatched the stake from his powerless fingers, tearing at his throat even as he staked the next vampire in line.

They burst into dust at the same time, and Saloman whirled, kicking another across the yard before he staked the female vampire running at him once more. However, he was surrounded now, and the rest provided a harder fight. There were some strong vampires among them. Even now, theoretically, they had the strength to destroy him. With something akin to relief, Saloman let go, embraced the rush of energy and bloodlust, parrying and hitting, taking the blows in stride, staking and breaking with a speed that must have looked like frenzy to the ignored old man who sat still as a stone in the midst of carnage.

At last only the first attacker was left, lying prone on the ground in helpless agony, waiting for his broken neck to heal. Terror glared out of his face as Saloman crouched down beside him.

"What was the point?" Saloman asked him.

"Independence," the vampire whispered. "We do as we please. No rule, not by Juana and not by you."

"No existence," Saloman pointed out with one casual wave around the empty courtyard. A couple of large plant pots had been broken and a tree bent almost to its roots, but the dust glistening in the starlight was the only other sign of the vampire attack. He sighed. "And no understanding." He raised the stake in his hand and plunged downward, and the last of his Spanish enemies turned to dust.

The vampires of the Iberian Peninsula now all answered to him—through the delectable if stern Juana. What a pity that there would be no time for another night with her.

Is it? She's a superb fuck but she's hardly— He shut down the bitter thought. He would not think of Elizabeth. Not here.

Rising to his feet, Saloman walked across the courtyard to the professor, whose eyes were wide in his skull-like head.

"*Madre de Dios*," he whispered. "You really are a demon."

"Did you doubt it?"

"I'm old; I'm dying. I've thought of death for so long and with so much longing that I imagined it would be easy, even at your hands. And now I wonder what my selfishness will cost the world. If you gain strength from my death—"

"I will," Saloman interrupted.

"Has there ever been a more powerful force in the world?" the old man said despairingly. "No one can fight you."

"Not entirely true," Saloman observed judiciously. "But trust me: Death is better from me than from them." He gestured across the yard in the general direction of the place he'd killed the last of his attackers, and reached for the professor. His desire to fight assuaged, he was pleased to give the professor a good death, even as the old man strained feebly away from him.

"I don't want my blood to destroy the world!" he cried out as Saloman drew him inexorably against his chest.

Saloman bit into his throat and the old man gasped, his scrabbling fingers stretching, and then curling into fists on Saloman's shoulders.

Perhaps you will help save the world instead, Saloman said to him telepathically. Blood spilled over his teeth and down his throat, and the old man relaxed in his arms. Bliss had drowned his pain. With fierce pleasure, Saloman sucked the strong, heady blood of Tsigana into himself, and welcomed the rush of power like an old friend.

The old man moved his lips weakly, speaking almost with his last breath. "At least you don't have the sword."

It was her hair that caught his attention. Glimpsed in the tiny space between the moving shoulders of his entourage, it seemed to sparkle like pale red gold in a blink of sunlight. Josh Alexander veered right to see beyond his press secretary, and discovered that the lovely hair belonged to an equally beautiful woman. Caught in the halo of sun from the window above, she looked like a glorious if slightly untidy angel.

She stood at the reception desk, arguing with the immaculately groomed receptionist whom she nevertheless managed to outshine without trying. Her long, strawberry blond hair was tied behind her head in a loose ponytail, from where much of it had fought its way free around a delicate yet oddly determined face. Her beauty lay in her fine bone structure, her appeal to Josh in the fact that she'd done nothing obvious to enhance it.

Pushing past his surprised secretary, Josh propped himself against a nearby pillar to watch her. His schedule was clear and he was ready to play.

"I've already told you, there's no one of that name staying here," the receptionist was reciting in a bored voice.

"How can you tell without looking?" came the dry response, and Josh felt a frisson pass down his spine. Her voice was Scottish—educated Scottish, he guessed from the fact that he could understand her so easily—low pitched and clear. The sort of voice he longed to act opposite, or even just *be* opposite, in any number of romantic scenes on- and offscreen.

"I assure you—" the receptionist began again.

"You can't assure me of anything if you don't use the tools available to you. Please let me speak to your supervisor."

"I *am* the supervisor."

"Then your manager will do perfectly."

The receptionist seemed taken aback by the other woman's quiet determination. Fooled by her casual appearance and something appealingly gentle in her expression, she'd obviously failed to notice the steel behind it. Josh had seen it right away, but then Josh studied faces obsessively. That was what made him so good at his job.

"Josh, what are you doing?" Mark, his press secretary, said urgently, standing right in front of him to block his view. "Hotel security has just warned us to go straight to the elevator. That girl at reception is probably gutter press—she's asking for you and she's about to cause trouble."

"Is she really?" Josh grinned. He'd only just emerged from the press conference a happy man, because the local journalists were eating out of his hand, and because the location filming had gone well, much faster than expected, leaving him time to relax for a few days and see a bit more of Scotland before he had to return to the States. And now here was this unusual and beautiful woman with a voice that sent shivers down his spine, actually looking for him. It was a gift.

Brushing past the outraged Mark, who still hissed after him in protest, he walked toward reception. The receptionist's eyes flickered to him in both alarm and gratification. Presumably it wasn't every day she spoke to a Hollywood movie star. On the other hand, it was bad luck to have this rare opportunity while failing to appease an ill-tempered customer. She almost preened, though, as if glad he'd see her carrying out her instructions so well, even in such a difficult situation.

"Look," Josh's target said, barely sparing him a glance, much to his amusement, as he leaned one elbow on the desk beside her. "I'm well aware he's staying here. Please just give him this note from his cousin."

The receptionist smiled and twitched the plain white envelope from the girl's fingers. At least she didn't put it straight in the bin.

"Madam, Edinburgh is suddenly full of Josh Alexander's relations. Good evening."

Frustrated and clearly well aware that the note was unlikely ever to get near its intended recipient, the strawberry blond sighed. "Your manager, please," she repeated. "As quickly as possible."

"I doubt that will be necessary," Josh said smoothly. "May I read the note now? And *are* you my cousin?"

The receptionist looked aghast under her layers of carefully applied makeup. The other girl swung around in surprise and gave him a long, considering look. Unexpectedly, a breath of laughter sounded and was choked off.

"Ah. Sorry, I didn't recognize you. I was too busy being angry. I'm Elizabeth Silk."

Without affectation, she held out one small but long-fingered hand, free of any rings. Another good omen. Josh took it, smiling, and she let go again after the briefest of shakes.

"Cousin Elizabeth," he said, letting his eyes do the laughing. "How wonderful to meet you at last. Thank you," he added to the receptionist, taking the envelope from her nerveless fingers, before ushering "Cousin Elizabeth" away from the desk—and into the waiting huddle of his bodyguard and press secretary.

Josh took care of their objections before they were uttered with one peremptory wave of the hand, and an extra glare for Mark, who felt orders he didn't like shouldn't apply to him. With reluctance as well as a look of wounded outrage, Mark fell back too.

"What can I do for you, Cousin?" Josh inquired, smiling, when they had a couple of feet of space.

For the first time, she looked slightly flummoxed. A hint of color tinged her pale cheeks. "We *are* actually cousins," she said apologetically. "Very distant, but still related. I've been trying to talk to you for months—so have my friends—but your people never let us near you, even by phone."

"Sorry," Josh said easily. "I'm afraid I get a lot of crank calls and letters. Sometimes genuine ones get blocked with them."

Of course, he still had no way of judging which category she belonged in, and her quick, sardonic smile acknowledged it.

"I understand," she said. "Do you know your family tree? Our nearest common ancestor is Harry Alexander, whose son Daniel emigrated to America in the late nineteenth century. Harry's daughter married Robert Silk and stayed in Scotland."

"Good old Harry," Josh said, but he felt the smile fading from his lips. Cousin Elizabeth Silk had surprised him again. Either she'd done a lot of homework—which made her rather more dangerous than an opportunistic fan—or she really was a distant cousin. "That's a long way back."

"Oh, it goes a lot further, which is what I want to talk to you about. Do you have a few minutes?"

Hell, she was beautiful, and in the sort of way he didn't see every day. She'd worked hard to get to him. She deserved a treat, and after all the difficulties of filming on location under the Scottish weather, so did he. For her beautiful hair and her seductive voice, to say nothing of whatever delights lay hidden beneath her nondescript jeans and jacket, he was prepared to risk it.

"Sure," he said, indicating the elevator, outside which his entourage still lurked, watching them with suspicion. "My schedule is clear. Come on up."

Color flooded her face. She knew exactly what he meant, and the quick flash of indignation in her dark hazel eyes told him he'd made a rare misjudgment. Nevertheless, her gaze remained steady.

"That's not necessary," she said icily. "If we could just sit there . . ." She indicated a nearby sofa in the reception area, with a low table and newspapers. ". . . I'll only take ten minutes of your time."

Josh made a fast recovery. Employing the boyish, slightly rueful grin that had worked for him since childhood, he spread his hands. "I can't be here at all for more than *two* minutes, or the place gets invaded by press. They're probably already on their way. I understand your concern, but acquit me of dishonorable designs! I was only looking for a bit of privacy."

Her gaze fell away, as if she was ashamed, and he knew she'd bought it. Which was a relief, because having started this, whatever it was, he rather wanted to see where it led.

"Of course," she muttered. "I forgot. The life of a film star can't be easy."

"It has compensations. Tell you what, we could go out for dinner and talk. You pick the restaurant. Preferably somewhere small and discreet where we won't attract attention."

A faint smile returned to her eyes. "All right."

She was delightful. There was no mad dash to change for dinner, to repair her makeup—she didn't appear to be wearing any, so far as Josh could tell—or even to comb her hair. She simply walked with him, Mark, and Fenstein the bodyguard, out of the hotel by the discreet side exit and into a cab, which she directed.

Edinburgh was a small city, and it wasn't far to her chosen restaurant. Downhill from the fashionable central part of the city into slightly dingier territory. The driver knew the place she named and dropped them off at the door.

Elizabeth didn't even blink when Mark entered the restaurant with them, spoke quietly with the manager, and handed over the bribe that would facilitate a fast exit around the back if the press got wind of Josh's presence here.

"This is nice," Josh said genuinely, looking around him when they were seated. "Homey."

"The food is wonderful," Elizabeth said, just a little too enthusiastically. As if she understood he was used to more fashionable and expensive haunts and didn't want to be ashamed of the best place she knew.

"You've been here before?" he asked easily.

"A couple of times with a work colleague."

"What do you do?"

"I teach at St. Andrews University. On a temporary contract. I've just finished my PhD, waiting for the verdict."

Ah, she was an academic. He should have guessed sooner, for her appearance gave it away—a little unworldly and scatty, uncaring of her appearance, since her mind, no doubt, lingered in higher planes of learning. He wondered what the hell she made of *Psychics*, despite its commercial success.

But damn, she was a lot prettier than any of the academics he'd ever encountered before. And a lot cooler than most of the women who blatantly sought him out with feeble excuses and downright lies. Her smile was friendly when she met his curious gaze, but no more than that. If she hadn't been kicking up a fuss at the hotel for him he'd never have believed that she was remotely interested in him. A bit lowering for the ego, perhaps, but for some reason it made her all the more intriguing.

He couldn't make up his mind about her age. She might have been as young as twenty-three or -four, or ten years older.

He waited until he'd ordered wine before asking, "What's your thesis on?"

"Historical superstitions," Elizabeth said. There was the smallest pause before she added, "Which is part of what I need to talk to you about."

"Yes? My father would have been more help to you there. He had more superstitions than the rest of us put together."

"Really? What kind of superstitions?"

"All kinds," Josh said. He gave the quick, affectionate grin that the poignant memory of his father always inspired. "My dad was a great guy. A bit eccentric, perhaps, but where's the harm in giving free rein to your imagination?"

"None. Isn't that how you earn your living?"

Surprised, Josh laughed. "I suppose so." The waiter appeared at his side, and while he went through the required ritual of tasting the wine, which was pretty good, considering, he took another quick, appraising look around the restaurant. It was quiet, being midweek, and they had been obligingly placed at the back, near the kitchen entrance, with an empty table between them and the nearest patrons, none of whom were paying him any attention. They wouldn't easily be overheard either. She'd picked just the right place, and Josh warmed to her all over again. A buzz of excitement began to flow through his body at the prospect not just of dinner with this intriguing woman, but the far greater intimacies that would inevitably follow.

Josh kept up a flow of light conversation until their starters arrived, telling her amusing anecdotes about traveling and filming. Many of his jokes were against himself and it was quite fun to watch Elizabeth thaw and warm to his self-deprecation. It wasn't entirely assumed either. In truth Josh still found the whole stardom thing funny. Emily, his wife, had helped keep his feet on the ground when he was younger, and now that she was dead, he couldn't seem to take anything else very seriously, even the catapulting-to-megastardom status that had come with the success of *Psychics*. But he still got a kick out of surprising the enigmatic Elizabeth.

"So," he said over their starters, "what in particular did you want to talk about? Family or superstition?"

"Both."

"Fantastic. Have I inherited a haunted castle in Scotland?"

Elizabeth smiled. "Not to my knowledge." She took a forkful of her lemon risotto and appeared to savor it before she added, "In fact, what you have inherited, you won't want. We have another common ancestor, far older than Harry Alexander. A seventeenth-century Hungarian lady called Tsigana."

"Interesting," Josh allowed. He let the creamy sauce melt on his tongue and swallowed. "Wow, this pasta is good!"

But Elizabeth wasn't distracted. "Have you heard of her? Tsigana?"

"Can't say I have."

"She was very . . . colorful, let's say. In fact, she murdered someone."

"They can't touch *us* for it, can they?" Josh asked in mock alarm.

"It depends on who you mean by 'they.' "

Warning prickles in his neck caused Josh to lay down his fork and pick up his wineglass. He gazed at her over the rim. "Go on."

Elizabeth took a deep breath. "Someone does still want revenge for that killing. And he's taking it out on Tsigana's descendants."

Oh, damnation. Mad as a coot. Josh sipped his wine and set down his glass. "Are the police dealing with this lunatic?" *Are they dealing with you?*

"Not the police exactly. But other authorities are trying to stop him, yes. In fact, I sort of represent this authority."

Josh didn't frown. On the contrary, he kept his face smooth, offering no clues as to his true thoughts. "Some sort of intelligence service?" he hazarded.

"Sort of," Elizabeth said doubtfully, making the corner of his mouth twitch. He hadn't expected doubt so much as self-important boasting. "The point is, this organization has been trying to reach you for several months to warn you and to offer protection. When I saw your press conference announced, I thought this was my last chance to see you in person and pass that warning on before you went home."

"Well, thanks," Josh said, allowing a twinkle back into his eyes. He was sure his original assessment was right—she wasn't dangerous. "But I'm afraid I don't get exactly what you're warning me about. Some madman who dislikes me because I'm descended from your Hungarian lady?"

"Um, yes." She sounded apologetic.

"Doesn't he dislike you too, then?"

Elizabeth smiled into her wine. "We've had our run-ins," she said, and drank a little.

Now, what the hell did that mean? "Okay." Curiously, Josh watched her lower the glass. "I'll keep my eyes open for the lunatic. Thanks for the warning."

"Thanks for pretending you mean it," Elizabeth countered, and Josh let out a surprised laugh. Crazy or not, she was still rather delightful. "There's more," she added before he could get his hopes up too far. "And this is the difficult bit, because I have to make you realize the threat is real and lethal. You said your father was superstitious—do you share any of his beliefs? For example, do you believe in the existence of vampires?"

Josh sighed. "Nope. Nor werewolves, goblins, zombies, demons, or even bad luck." He shifted in his seat and now only good manners prevented him from looking at his watch. He'd plead tiredness and skip dessert. Damn it, he really wanted to get laid, and she was so deliciously layable. . . .

"Taxi for Mr. Alexander," she said with a quick, wry smile, surprising him all over again. Clearly, there was nothing wrong with her observational skills. "It's all right," she soothed. "I'm not insane. A year ago, I didn't believe in any of these things either, but some of them, at least, are real. There *is* a vampire out there—a very strong and ruthless one—picking off all Tsigana's living descendants. And those of the other conspirators in his murder. Not only for revenge, but because they, you and I, carry the blood of his killers, and that blood gives him a kind of mystical power."

"If Tsigana killed him," Josh interjected, seeking an easy victory through reason, "how come he's still running around?"

"He was . . . awakened. By accident." Her eyes flickered away and back, as if she'd briefly lost courage and then recovered it. "His name is Saloman."

Saloman? Where had he heard that name before? Unimportant. "Okay." He sat back to let the waiter take his plate. "I'll bear it in mind."

Elizabeth regarded him ruefully. "No, you won't. You don't believe a word of it, and the worst of it is, I can't blame you for that. Just be watchful. I should tell you that two fellow descendants of ours have died in the last six months, probably at his hands. But at least you have bodyguards and people to look out for you." Again came those warning prickles, but he didn't have time to work out whether they came from her or from her warning, for she was speaking again. "Josh?"

"Yes?"

"Promise me you won't throw away that letter I tried to leave at the hotel. It's got the phone numbers of people who can help you if you're ever in need of it. One of them is mine. The other is for an international organization that deals with threats like this. The one I mentioned earlier. You should contact them, let them protect you."

Josh rubbed one finger across his lips. He wanted to be honest and tell her he'd throw the letter out as soon as he got back to the hotel. Tell her to fuck off because she wasn't the easy-if-eccentric lay he'd believed her to be when they first spoke. But he could never quite shake off the courtesy that formed the foundation of his nature. Nor could he lie, he acknowledged with regret, even to a stranger.

Josh sighed and touched his breast pocket, where he'd stashed the letter. It still rustled. "I promise."

Chapter Two

Returning to the hotel alone hadn't been in Josh's original plan, but he supposed, as he shut his bedroom door, that it could have been a worse evening. Once the crazy talk had been gotten out of the way, he'd rather enjoyed Elizabeth's company. She was intelligent and humorous and happy to listen to his stories. He'd even told her a bit about Emily, and she hadn't pried or annoyed him with outpourings of false sympathy. On the contrary, he'd felt she understood grief and he'd picked up a wave of quiet, sincere compassion. He should have asked her about her own life more, discovered where that understanding had come from, for he doubted he'd ever see her again.

Mind you, away from the crazy talk of vampires and revenge, he realized he wouldn't actually object to seeing her again. After all, he'd accepted his father's similar oddities and still loved him. It struck him now, throwing his jacket on his large, empty bed, that there had been a certain empathy between him and Elizabeth. Or perhaps he was imagining that because he was bored with the rich and self-seeking sirens who seemed to form the bulk of his acquaintances these days.

Smiling sourly, he walked toward the bathroom, only to be distracted by the ringing of his phone. He picked it up from the dresser and glanced at the name on the screen. Senator Dante. One didn't ignore Senator Grayson Dante.

"Senator, hello!" he greeted him with polite enthusiasm. "How are you?"

"I'm great! In fact, I'm in Scotland!"

"Good lord. What are you doing here?"

"Oh, I had some talks with the prime minister in London, and then they wheeled me up here to meet the queen at her Scottish castle—Balmoral."

Josh whistled to show how impressed he was, and began to ease out of his shirt while Dante continued to speak.

"Anyway, I've rented this amazing house for the week, thought I'd throw a party here this weekend."

"Sounds like a plan," Josh approved, removing Elizabeth's letter from his shirt pocket with one hand before tossing the shirt onto the bed beside his jacket. "Is the queen coming?"

Dante laughed. He had a good laugh, which won him a lot of friends, including Josh. "I wish! No, no, but I do have a promise from your gorgeous costar of *Psychics 2*, so I hope you can make it."

Josh grimaced. His gorgeous costar, Jerri Cusack, was a prize bitch and fancied the publicity of an offscreen romance to go with the onscreen passion. Josh couldn't face it. Staring at the letter in his hand, he said impulsively, "May I bring a guest? My Scottish cousin."

"Of course!" Dante agreed wholeheartedly, while Josh tore open the envelope with his teeth. "I hope she's pretty, because I have another guest I'd particularly like to impress. Do you know Adam Simon?"

"No," Josh said without much interest. He was reading Elizabeth's letter, a very brief and stark outline of the crazy talk in the restaurant, together with two phone numbers, one of which was her own. Josh smiled and folded the letter. Refocusing, he repeated, "Adam Simon? Who's he?"

Josh didn't mind Dante using his high profile to impress certain people. He was used to it and happy enough to help out a friend. It had worked both ways in the past.

"European businessman, very young and determined. Popped out of Eastern Europe a few months ago, branching out in the UK and the States. Truth be told, he's stood on my toes a couple of times already. I need the guy onside!"

Josh laughed. "Charm offensive, is it?" he asked cynically.

"Love your understanding, Josh. Be great to see you here at the weekend! Look forward to it. I'll send you details. Oh, and Josh, I don't suppose you've brought that antique sword with you?"

Unbidden, Josh's eyes flew to his suitcase. Uneasily, he remembered exactly why he'd brought the family heirloom, and that was to do with Dante too. He hadn't wanted the senator "borrowing" it, or "buying" it from his people in his absence. He liked Dante, but the man had few scruples about getting his own way, and he'd wanted the sword pretty badly.

"Actually, yes," Josh admitted. "I did bring it. But it's still not for sale."

Dante laughed again. "You're a hard man, Josh! No, the reason I ask is, there'll be some people around this weekend, experts in this field of antiquities, who could give you a proper valuation and maybe even more details of its history. If you bring it up with you, I can ask them to take a look."

"Well, all right," Josh said reluctantly, "but it still won't be for sale, whatever figure your guys come up with."

This was apparently a great joke to Dante, and Josh found himself smiling at the sound of the senator's mirth. But as he rang off, uneasiness tugged at him again. He was not a superstitious man, and he didn't believe in magic of any kind, but the last time he'd touched the sword . . .

He shook his head to clear it. Dante had turned up to visit unexpectedly after learning they had apartments in the same block of New York City; and after a couple of beers, when the conversation had veered toward antiques and heirlooms, Josh had shown him the sword. Something, whether static electricity or imagination, had made Josh drop the weapon, feeling a sharp pain in his hand that couldn't possibly have been there. It was no more real than the weird vision that had flashed in front of his eyes, of a young and bloodied stranger demanding the return of his sword in dark, threatening tones.

Josh shivered and shrugged the memory off. He'd been drunk at the time. But what had really bothered him about the whole episode was the unpalatable idea that the sword was not Josh's own. When it bloody well was. It had been in his family for generations, and was all he now had left of his father—that and the horrible old coat in which it was wrapped. And Josh was damned if he'd give either to anyone for any price.

It was late by the time Elizabeth got home to her flat in St. Andrews, but she knew she wouldn't sleep.

Turning on the gas fire to allay the gloom, she went to the CD player, discarded the classical disk that was already there, and replaced it with a rock one. Hoping the beat would reinvigorate her suddenly dismal mood, she sank onto the sofa and picked up her paperback book. But instead of reading it, she found herself gazing into the fire while her thoughts drifted without permission.

During the journey, she'd hovered between satisfaction at having finally warned Josh Alexander of the danger he faced, and frustration because she hadn't been able to make him believe any of it, let alone to act on it. She just hoped now that he'd never discover he was wrong. He was a nice bloke, for a film star. In fact, he was a nice bloke period, and she wished him well.

After all, she'd no proof that Saloman was responsible for the deaths of the other two descendants in the last couple of months. They'd been old and death was certified as natural causes. But still, Elizabeth doubted.

She closed her eyes, letting the familiar emptiness and loneliness engulf her. Nights were the worst. When she couldn't sleep and there were no distractions, no jobs that had to be done by morning, then her thoughts inevitably turned to him, to memory and need and loss.

A wild guitar solo filled her ears; the relentless rock beat from the CD vibrated softly under her feet and through the sofa into her body. She could almost imagine herself back at the Angel in Budapest, dancing in Saloman's arms with guilty, sensual enjoyment. Or lying here on this sofa watching his naked back as he chose the CD. Rock music had fascinated him, aroused him. . . .

With sudden, painful intensity, she wanted him here, now, to enjoy it with her. She wanted to watch him prowl toward her, his pale, smooth skin gleaming in the dim light, rippling over muscle and sinew as he walked and sank onto the sofa beside her, touching her with his clever, demanding hands, caressing her breasts and hips while the weight of his body pressed into her, and he bent to bite into her throat and drink her blood. She'd love the weird, wicked rush of his touch drowning the instant of pain, but he wouldn't let it go on too long. Instead, he'd heal the wounds with the tip of his knowing tongue, and before entering her body he'd move on to kiss her mouth. Saloman's kisses . . . She'd never know them again, never feel the excitement or the joy of his unique, overwhelming passion. Sex with Saloman . . .

She squirmed against the cushions, drawing in a shuddering breath to banish the fantasy. She couldn't allow herself more than a moment of remembrance. If she lingered on his memory, the loss felt too great.

She sprang to her feet, determined to change the direction of her wayward thoughts, even if just through the familiar routine of clearing up for the night and preparing for bed. Talking to Josh about vampires had brought it all back. Thinking hard about tomorrow's classes would make it all go away again. And tomorrow, in daylight, at the start of her busy day, she'd call Mihaela and tell her about Josh.

It was a good plan, and similar strategies had worked before, but as she lay down, drawing the quilt up to her ears, and switched off the bedside lamp, she imagined she lay in Saloman's powerful arms, as she had done six months ago on the night before they'd parted at her insistence. She turned her face into the pillow, imagining the smell of him lingered there.

I love you. I still love you.

But he couldn't hear her. He'd gone for good.

It was at least a sign of trust that the English vampire Mort invited him freely into his lair. A bleak, uncomfortable home—spacious but with few added luxuries since the days when cars had been manufactured there. As the vampires closed in on Saloman from all sides, the atmosphere bristled with suspicion and hostility.

Only Mort, easily the most powerful among them, made any pretense at welcome; and when he'd made his grudging little speech, the others continued to stare at Saloman in what they no doubt hoped was an intimidating manner. Certainly, their fangs were on display.

In fact, they reminded Saloman of sullen schoolkids being obliged to toe the line and acknowledge their headmaster's discipline.

Saloman introduced his companion. "This is James," he said, and everyone's attention switched to the still human by his side. Youthful and vigorous, if rather shabbily dressed, he happened to be a student of economics.

"What's the matter with him?" Mort asked. "He looks asleep."

"He is."

"Did you bring him as a present for us?" sneered one of the vampires. He was young and arrogant and his name was Del.

Saloman didn't trouble to glance at Del, but looked instead around the bare, echoing east London factory. "No, I brought him as a demonstration. When I'm finished, I'll take him back where he came from. Do you like living here?"

Startled by the abrupt change of subject, Mort dragged his gaze from the sleepwalking human. "It's big and it's safe."

"Don't you ever miss basic comfort?"

"Carpets and sofas and televisions?" Mort snorted. "A two-up, two-down terrace house, perhaps? With the neighbors getting restive as their numbers dwindle?"

Several of the vampires sniggered. Saloman spared each of them a glance, then, in the silence, let his gaze linger on the bloodstains on the floor, the rough resting areas that seemed to have developed in various corners of the factory.

"Well," he murmured, "it seems to me your lives are a little . . . bestial." On the last word, he hooked Mort's gaze again. "And you are better than that. As you swore allegiance to me and I rely on you, I would like to see you more . . . contented."

Surprise ensured the vampires' long silence. A few glanced for guidance to Mort.

"You are strong vampires," Saloman said. "There is no need to live like rats or feral dogs in deserted sewers and condemned buildings, where the most fun you have is when you drag a few humans down here to have a party before you kill them."

"It was only two humans," Mort said hastily, "and we got rid of the bodies. It's not a normal occurrence. We don't wish to draw the attention of the human police or the hunters."

"Very sensible," said Saloman. "And yet you'd find it quite easy to live in more pleasant surroundings without hassle if you just learned not to murder your prey."

"Are you denying us existence now?" Del demanded.

"I might, if you don't stop interrupting me." Although he spoke mildly, Saloman let Del have the full force of his gaze, and the sneer froze on the young vampire's lips. "A vampire needs blood; he does not need to kill. Take my friend James here." Drawing James's unresisting body a step closer, Saloman bent and sank his teeth into the man's throat.

Or rather, Saloman added telepathically, *I'll take James. I met him in a pub and we just happened to leave at the same time.*

His words made it directly to Mort and a couple of others. A few struggled to receive the telepathic message; a couple didn't receive it at all. Saloman felt their bafflement and detached his teeth from James's neck before he'd drunk more than a taste. He glared at the confused vampires who'd heard nothing. One of them was Del.

"Open your minds, fools," he uttered with contempt. "You are *more* than human. Use all the senses you have been given and learn before you perish like the sewer rats you've let yourselves become."

Saloman had no patience with such a waste of existence. Reaching out with his mind, he brutally wrenched open the paths the vampires should have been aware of since their turning. They'd ignored the psychic routes until, like an overgrown track, they'd become impassable. The vampires cried out in shock as he cleared the way in their minds, and Saloman returned to James's throat.

This, he said, showing them, *is how I blocked his mind to what is happening. Some humans can be irreparably traumatized by vampire bites, so unless you have an understanding with your prey, always block them from remembering. Then drink.* He sucked James's blood, and even through his trance, James sighed in pleasure. Saloman made sure the vampires picked that up, let them see in turn the pleasure this gave to him. *And if you feel this*—he paused as James's pounding heart began to struggle—*then you've taken too much.*

Saloman detached his teeth once more, licked the wound to heal it.

"He's going to feel a little weak for a day or two, but he'll remember me as no more than an amiable drinking companion. If I hung around London long enough we might even become friends. In the meantime, I can move among humanity with no one hunting me. I can do more than rot in a disused factory and move on when I need to. I can make my existence more enjoyable and worthwhile."

Releasing James, he looked at Mort. "What you do with that existence is, of course, your own choice. But it is a crime to do nothing. It is a crime to kill without reason. Vampires do not need the kill, only the blood, to survive."

"Killing strong humans can make us stronger," one of them said with a hint of desperation. An end to chaos was not universally appealing.

"A very few humans." Saloman waved one dismissive hand. "Those who've killed strong vampires, or their descendants. But these are rare, even among hunters. You gain nothing and lose everything by killing unnecessarily."

"Saloman is right," Mort said with the sincere determination that had been Saloman's main reason for handling matters in this way. "We will no longer kill as a matter of course. And we *can* do better than this." He waved one hand around his home, indicating not just the bleak surroundings but their whole existence. "Surviving one more day doesn't need to be an end in itself."

"Exactly," Saloman said. "Find occupations that enrich that existence. I have taught this lesson across the world. The lot of vampires has already improved, and it will continue to do so. Under my leadership, the world is changing and you will have an important role to play. You must be worthy of it."

Or else. He didn't need to say the words. They were understood, if not universally liked. Among the sparks of thoughtful excitement the odd trace of pointless, mulish defiance still lurked. But he'd be back to deal with any rebels, and he would not be so forbearing then.

With a sudden swirling motion designed to impress the vampires, he swung around and sat on a disused bench. "Now, tell me about the

American actor who passed through your city recently. I'm anxious to make his acquaintance." He smiled beatifically around his audience. "I believe I knew his ancestor very, very well."

The vampires laughed, as they were meant to. And Saloman thought of Scotland and his sword, and Elizabeth.

The morning dawned fair and sunny. Refreshed, Elizabeth rose and showered and dressed between gulps of coffee. Gathering together the papers and books she needed for the day's work, she stashed them in her backpack and sat down with fresh coffee and a slice of toast, which she ate with one hand while the other held her phone and rang Mihaela's number.

"Elizabeth!" came Mihaela's voice, as crisp and close from Hungary—or Romania or wherever she happened to be this morning—as if she'd been in the same room. "How are things?"

"Good," Elizabeth said enthusiastically, switching to speakerphone mode and laying the instrument down on the table. "Well, pretty good. I finally got to speak to Josh Alexander."

"Fantastic! Well done!"

"Not *so* well," Elizabeth admitted, smearing butter on her second slice of toast. "He's a confirmed skeptic and convinced I'm the stalking nutter from hell. But at least he heard me out. And he's got the numbers, which he's promised to keep."

"Can't do more than that at this stage," Mihaela said comfortingly. "Where is he now? Heading back to the US?"

"In a few days, I think. He said he wanted to see a bit of Scotland now that he's finished filming here and he has some time off."

"I'll have another word with our colleagues in America, get them to keep a closer eye on him when he goes home, even if he never calls them. We still haven't located Saloman."

"How long has he been off your radar this time?" Elizabeth asked, biting into her toast.

"A couple of weeks," said Mihaela. "This time. Almost since he came back here from Spain, in fact. I wish we knew what he was up to. Word is, since Spain has submitted, every vampire community in the world now pays homage of some kind to him. Apart from North America. Opinion is divided there. Apparently the Los Angeles vampire community wants an alliance with him, but the more powerful vampires on the East Coast are still holding out for independence."

"Will they succeed?" Elizabeth asked doubtfully.

"Who knows? It's causing some worrying unrest in the States, but at least the East Coast's stubbornness has to slow Saloman down, postpone whatever his next plan is."

"True. He might even have grown content ruling the vampire world. Perhaps it will be enough for him."

Mihaela snorted. "For *him*? I doubt it."

"Well, you never know." It was hard not to sound as if she were pleading for leniency, so she kept her voice deliberately light. "You thought he'd bring chaos and carnage to the world and so far it hasn't been like that at all."

"True," Mihaela allowed. "In fact, the vampires here are quieter these days. Fewer lethal attacks, fewer fledglings. To be honest, that's what freaks me. No one should be able to control them like that. God knows what he could make them do now, if he felt like it."

Elizabeth shivered. She didn't know if there was more fear than happiness in remembering what he'd made *her* do, what he'd made her feel in his arms, in his bed. . . . *Stop!*

"Anyway," Mihaela continued briskly into the silence, "he could be anywhere by now, so you'd better be especially careful."

"I told you, he won't touch me." Elizabeth tossed down her final crust and reached for her coffee.

"If he doesn't change his mind," Mihaela said dryly. "Vampires are not known for keeping their word. Anyway, what's he like?"

Elizabeth froze with the cup resting against her lips. Shite. Had Mihaela found out? Was she asking for salacious details of her turbulent but passionate relationship?

Elizabeth set her mug back on the table. "Saloman?" she said weakly. How did you describe a man, a being, of so many contradictions and attractions and sheer, unimaginable power? Sexual and otherwise.

Mihaela laughed. "Josh Alexander! Is he as gorgeous in real life?"

Elizabeth, trying not to collapse with sheer relief, gasped. "Yes! I think he is. A tiny bit craggier, maybe, because he's definitely in his late thirties, at least, but I think that improves him. He's got an edgy look, although he isn't at all like that underneath. He's rather sweet, really, very polite and good fun."

"Fun? Did he make a pass at you?"

"Don't be—" Elizabeth broke off and smiled. "Actually he did, at first, but I suspect it was just habit, because we both forgot about it afterward. We went out for dinner and he insisted on paying and then dropped me off at the station. I'm afraid I let him."

"Bloody hell," Mihaela said with awe. She'd learned the phrase from Elizabeth. "You had dinner with Josh Alexander."

"Wow, so I did. Think of the kudos I'm going to have in the staff club now. *And* I can finally impress my students!"

It was good to end the call on a laughing note and go immediately off to work. Talking to Mihaela generally buoyed her if she was down, and she was grateful again for the unusual friendship. It had begun last summer, when she'd been researching her thesis in Romania, and three vampire hunters had come to her door to tell her she'd just awakened the most powerful vampire of all time. Josh's reaction to Elizabeth's warning last night had actually been quite tame compared to Elizabeth's response to Mihaela, István, and Konrad. Until she'd discovered the truth.

Once, she'd nearly wrecked the spontaneous friendships that had begun to form, by storming away because they hadn't revealed all the truth to her; but she was wiser now and appreciated what she had with them, especially Mihaela.

She walked to the department, enjoying the rare sunshine. As always now, when she passed the ruined cathedral, with its tall, distinctive towers, she recalled the disastrous and terrifying showdown with Saloman that had taken place there last Halloween. The fight had been meant to finish him. Instead it had built him another legend on which to base his power in the vampire community. But in the end, this hadn't spoiled Elizabeth's feeling for the cathedral itself. The atmospheric ruins had always moved her. Now they made her physically tingle, because what had happened there with Saloman after the fight—her desperate confession of love and the fierce, urgent passion with which he'd taken her under the east gable arch—had washed away the horror and given her the strength to move on.

Turning her back on it, she crossed the road and walked on to the department building. She was anticipating a difficult morning with her most problematic tutorial group.

On the other hand, she didn't expect to find one of her students already waiting at her office door.

"Hello, Emma, you're early," she greeted the girl, who looked as if she hadn't slept all night. There were dark rings under her eyes and lines of worry around her usually smiling mouth. Emma Forrest, who sometimes reminded her a little of her younger self, had blossomed during this year, both academically and socially, and Elizabeth didn't like to see her upset. "Revision giving you trouble?"

"Um, no, not really . . . I just wanted a quick word with you before everyone gets here. Is that all right?"

"Of course," Elizabeth said, unlocking the door and preceding her inside. She had the distinct feeling she wasn't going to like this. "Come in. Coffee?"

"Thanks, no, I'm fine." Emma closed the door firmly behind her.

Elizabeth threw her bag and jacket on one of the tables and sat down, indicating the seat beside her.

"I have a problem," Emma blurted as she sat. "With Gary Jackson."

It was no comfort that Elizabeth had seen it coming. Gary wasn't an evil lad but he had shown signs of acting stupidly, becoming aware of the power of his size and flexing more than his intellectual muscles, sometimes quite inappropriately. He and Emma had been together for a few weeks until, according to the rumors Elizabeth overheard, he'd slept with her friend and Emma had ditched him. Elizabeth had been pleased about the parting. She'd always felt the dynamic between Emma and Gary was somehow wrong.

"Yes?" she prompted.

"We've split up," Emma explained. "But Gary won't accept it. He's plaguing me."

"In what way?"

"He's too . . . physical. The trouble is, he knows I still like him in, er, *that* way, but I'm damned if I'll go out with him again. I really don't want him back. He doesn't believe me. He waits for me in places he knows I'll be, cornering me, making it hard to get away. This is the only class we share, and I just know he's going to sit beside me and . . ."

"And what?" Elizabeth prompted. There was an uncomfortable parallel here: Saloman's teasing pursuit of her in Romania and Hungary, her rejection of him in her head while her body cried out for a taste of whatever he had to offer. Somehow it had all gone way beyond that, but Emma's words brought those early days rushing back.

Emma's hands twisted together in her lap. "Get in my face, humiliate me in front of the others . . ." She glanced up, a miserable plea in her tired eyes, and with a mixture of relief and pity, Elizabeth knew this was nothing like her own experience after all. Gary Jackson was no Saloman. "Look, Miss Silk, I know this sounds silly, and it's nothing to do with work, but I need to ask you a favor. Make him sit away from me, and if you could find an excuse to keep him back for a minute or two when the tutorial finishes . . . ? You think I'm being an idiot."

"Not at all," Elizabeth said ruefully. She'd glimpsed some of this behavior last week but hadn't realized the extent of it.

"It's stupid." Emma dashed one hand across her tired eyes. "I used to love it here. Now I can't wait for the next couple of weeks to be over so I can get away for the summer. I used to really like Gary, and now all I feel is . . . threatened."

"I'll separate you," Elizabeth promised. "And I'll have a word. Sounds like he needs sorting out."

"You don't have to do that."

"Oh, I think I do." Someone had to, because left to his own devices the bullying would get worse and Emma would certainly not be the only victim. "Don't worry, I'll be gentle with him," she said with a comforting grin.

At least it won a weak smile from Emma. "I've heard you do judo."

And that's not all.

As the clump of feet on the stairs sounded, Emma twitched with obvious alarm. Elizabeth gave her arm a quick pat and stood up. "Sit where you are," she advised, and went to take her usual seat at the short end of the table farthest from the door.

Gary was not the first to arrive, and the seat to Emma's left was not available by the time he wandered in. However, the one on the right was, and, watching carefully, Elizabeth saw his eyes gleam. He was, she allowed, a very good-looking bloke, tall, broad shouldered, and carelessly handsome. Clever too, but beneath the clear intelligence, his gray eyes were a trifle bloodshot. Hangover, Elizabeth recognized. Which wouldn't make him easier to handle.

"Ah, Gary," she called as he began to pull out the chair next to a rigid Emma, and crooked her finger.

Insolently, the lad stood still, gazing at her. "What?"

"A word, please," she said dryly. Since he picked up, as he was meant to, the fact that he might not like what she had to say to be overheard by the others, he moved reluctantly toward her.

Elizabeth gestured casually to the chair beside her. "How's revision?" she asked as he sat on the edge of it, as if not planning to stay.

He shrugged. "All right."

"You think so? You left too quickly for me to talk to you at the end of the last session, but your responses then led me to believe your understanding of constitutional issues is still not deep. If you want to shine, Gary, you need to put in the hours."

She caught the flash of resentment with some pleasure before she looked up and asked the last in to close the door. James MacQueen obliged and dropped into the vacant chair beside Emma.

Satisfied for the moment, Elizabeth began the revision discussions. While the others talked and argued with occasional gratifying surges of enthusiasm as well as inevitable clashes of personality, she watched Gary, who watched Emma. Oh, yes, the bastard was aware of the effect he was having on her. He rather liked the element of fear he was inspiring, and knew she was still physically attracted to him, however reluctantly. Elizabeth could see it in his body language, his casual, open-legged crotch display as he sat back from the table. And he was unrepentant when he caught her observation, merely grinned at her.

Oh, yes, they needed a chat.

"Okay, I think we'll stop there," Elizabeth said, bringing the class to a close. "I'm sure you'll all do fine. Good luck with Friday's paper! Not you, Gary," she added as he leapt to his feet, no doubt to get to Emma on the stairs. "I need to talk to you."

"I'll be back," Gary said, walking purposefully away.

"I don't think so."

Although she didn't shout, she put every ounce of steel she had into that phrase, and it cut through the cheerful departing babble like a knife. Everyone glanced between her and Gary. Watching, wide-eyed, Emma edged toward the door. Elizabeth didn't blame her. She had no idea whether Gary would obey. If he didn't, she'd need to find some other way of dealing with him.

Slowly, he turned back toward her, his gaze flickering around the interested stares on its way to Elizabeth. Their eyes locked and Elizabeth saw exactly why Emma was afraid of him. His face was blatantly intimidating, his gaze hard, almost glaring into hers. It didn't help that he was far taller than she. A year ago, even less, Elizabeth would have been petrified. As it was, she wanted to smack him and tell him to grow up.

Restraining herself, she held his gaze, even gave a condescending smile. "I'm sure you can spare me five more minutes from your important schedule."

A derisory snigger from one of the students greeted this. Someone else said, "Five less in the coffee bar, Gary—how will you cope?" And Gary, presumably realizing what a complete arsehole he'd look by leaving now, raised one hand in farewell to his friends, and Elizabeth knew she'd won the first round.

However, he began almost as soon as the door was closed. Taking a step nearer her, he said mockingly, "*Another* talk? Miss Silk, how *have* I managed to attract so much of your attention?"

"By sloppy work and ill behavior," she returned at once. "We've already discussed the first. Now I'm coming to the latter."

He leaned closer, definitely in her personal space, large, male, and overwhelming. At least, he meant to be overwhelming as he said with open mockery, "How do you want me to behave, *Miss Silk*?" He managed to speak her name in a tone that crossed insult with caress.

"With courtesy and respect," she replied as calmly as she could.

Gary smiled, a young man who believed himself irresistible both physically and sexually. "Oh, I respect *you*, Miss Silk."

"No, you don't," Elizabeth snapped. "Right now the only respect I see in you is for the immature and hungover adolescent I'm looking at. Sit down," she ordered before the shock in his eyes gave way entirely to anger. She guessed it was a long time since anyone had made him feel small, and it wasn't a technique she normally approved of. In this case, however, it seemed necessary.

But she misjudged him. The anger was there, all right, furiously there. But he had an arsenal of weapons. Changing tack, he smiled through his hatred and, instead of stepping back out of her personal space, he actually reached up and touched her hair.

"Aw, Miss Silk," he said soothingly, "what's got you so hot and bothered?"

"Take your hand off me," Elizabeth said evenly.

The boy's smile only deepened as his hand touched her neck. "Or what?"

"Or I'll make you," Elizabeth warned.

"How?" Gary asked with soft derision. Just before she swiped his legs from under him with one flick of her foot and pushed him into the seat behind, keeping him there with one hand hard on his chest.

"I asked you to sit," she said coldly into his stunned face. "And now you listen to me. There's a word for boys like you who discover they like bullying women. Don't make me use it, not to your face, and not to your parents or to the university authorities. You *can't* bully me. Nor can you bully Emma Forrest."

He sat still with shock under her hand, as if his testosterone had melted. But at Emma's name, something flashed again in his eyes.

"Take your dismissal like a man," Elizabeth warned. "True—before you say it—of course your love life is not my concern, but stalking, threatening, or intimidating my students *is*. There's a watch on you, Gary. I've initiated it. For now it's unofficial, but if you step out of line, if you so much as look at her—or anyone else—the wrong way, action will be taken and more than your reputation will be ruined. Do you understand me?"

His mouth twisted. Elizabeth removed her hand and stepped back.

At once he leapt to his feet, breathing like an angry bull. Even now, he hoped to stare her out. There was a lot of pent-up anger there. The question was whether he was prepared to use it against her. She knew without any doubt that it wouldn't do him any good. Although he was bigger, he only imagined he was stronger. She was faster—she was a powerful descendant of Tsigana and the Awakener of Saloman. He couldn't possibly know it but the boy didn't stand a chance.

"Do you understand me?" she repeated. For an instant longer, it hung in the balance. Bafflement began to replace the anger in his face, as if he still didn't quite understand how she had the upper hand. He gave one brisk nod, just as the door opened and her colleague Joanne came in.

"Elizabeth, have you got a—" Joanne broke off, gazing at the confrontation before her. "Everything all right here?" she asked.

"I think so," Elizabeth said.

Gary turned away without a word, snatched up his bag from the floor, and strode past Joanne, barely avoiding a collision in his hurry to get out of the room. Joanne raised her eyebrows.

"Gary." Partly Elizabeth wanted to see if he'd respond. Partly she had one more thing to say. He paused, at least. An instant later, he twitched his head in the direction of his shoulder. It was as good as she'd get, and she thought it was enough. "You're a good student, Gary, one of the best. Don't spoil that."

He didn't answer, just swung out of the room without troubling to close the door.

"At least he didn't slam it," Joanne observed. "What was that all about?"

"Inappropriate male behavior."

"Is that Gary Jackson? I've heard he's becoming a handful. Might have been a good idea to get department support from Richard before you confronted him." Joanne gave her a quick, anxious scan. "Are you all right? Do you need Richard to intervene in this?"

"I'm fine. And I think I've made my point," Elizabeth said. Somewhere, she was surprised that both statements were true.

. . .

"So, what are you doing during the holidays?" Joanne asked as they shared sandwiches for lunch in her office. Feet up on her paper-strewn desk, almost on the computer keyboard, she looked ultrarelaxed, but her gaze was uncomfortably penetrating. "Going back to Eastern Europe?"

"Maybe for a week or so," Elizabeth answered. "I have a few friends out there I'd like to keep in touch with." Mihaela had already offered her spare room. "And Richard suggested I think of expanding the thesis into a book. . . . But I've got no plans. I can't really think beyond the PhD thing right now."

"Well, that's one definite plan," Joanne said with enthusiasm. "The whole department will be out celebrating with you as soon as you hear the result."

"Providing it's the right result," Elizabeth said ruefully.

"It will be. Your thesis is brilliant."

It's a load of bollocks. Or at least some of it is. You wouldn't say it was brilliant if I'd written the truth: that most of these superstitions are based on the fact that vampires have always existed.

"There's a permanent post about to come up at Glasgow University," Joanne observed, reaching for another sandwich without moving her feet. "You should go for it."

"I might." Trouble was, she liked it here at St. Andrews. Unfortunately, her post was for only this year.

"Doesn't mean you can't come back when old Doughty retires," Joanne encouraged. "But you can't wait for that. It might only be a year, but it might be three, or even five if he holds on by his fingernails. Richard will still take you before any other candidate. In more ways than one," she finished with a wicked grin.

Elizabeth threw a paper bag at her, just as her phone began to ring. Although she took some time to locate it in the depths of her bag, and she didn't recognize the number, she pressed the receive key before it rang off.

"Hello?"

"Hello, is that Elizabeth? Elizabeth Silk?" The voice, echoing on speakerphone mode from when she'd called Mihaela, sounded American and vaguely familiar, though she couldn't quite place it.

"Yes, that's me," she admitted.

"Hi, it's Josh here. Josh Alexander."

"Josh!" She jumped to her feet, alarm outweighing her surprise. She'd doubted she'd ever hear from him again. She certainly hadn't expected it to be so soon. What the hell could have happened since last night?

Oh, shite, is he here? Is Saloman here again? Inevitably, the possibility spawned a surge of conflicting delight and fear, longing and dread.

"What's the matter?" she demanded.

"Nothing." Josh sounded amused. "I just wanted to ask you a favor. Listen. I know it's short notice, but I've been invited to this dull party in the Highlands this weekend and I was hoping you'd come with me to save me from boredom."

"Party?" she said faintly. "What party?"

"Grayson Dante's. He's a bigwig senator back home, been visiting—and working—over here. He's invited us to his weekend bash." She could still hear the lilt of appreciation in his voice, because she hadn't leapt at his invitation the way most normal women would.

Josh Alexander had invited her to a weekend party.

Laughter caught in her own throat. "Thanks for asking me," she managed. "Especially when you think I'm insane. But to be honest, it sounds a bit posh for me. I'd be out of place."

"Nonsense. You hold your own in any place," Josh said gallantly. "But you'd be my guest and I wouldn't desert you."

Elizabeth bit her lip. Every personal instinct urged refusal. Social gatherings such as she imagined this one to be were her idea of hell. Plus, she rather thought Josh Alexander's world would be completely alien to her. Gazing at Joanne's uncharacteristically dumbstruck face, she wrestled briefly with her conscience. How could she refuse another chance to convince Josh of impending danger? It might make all the difference to whether he survived.

Conscience, damn it, won.

"All right." She sighed. "I mean, thank you, I'd love to. Where do I go and will they let me in?"

Josh laughed. "I'll pick you up on Saturday, say around twelve? I'll call when I hit St. Andrews and you can give me directions to your place."

"What do I wear?" she demanded, as another pitfall sprang to mind.

"Anything," Josh said unhelpfully. "See you Friday!"

"Typical bloody male!" Elizabeth stared indignantly at the dead phone.

"Elizabeth," said Joanne, who'd been listening in quite blatantly. "Tell me that wasn't *the* Josh Alexander, because you know, it even *sounded* quite like him."

"It was," Elizabeth said smugly. "He's a cousin of mine. Sort of."

"Fuck me," said Joanne faintly. She took her feet off the desk and leaned forward. "Can I come too?"

"I wish you could," Elizabeth said with perfect truth.

Chapter Three

The early morning sun struck the high, tiny windows of the hunters' library in Budapest, dazzling Mihaela as she raised her head to find her colleague.

Konrad, more suited for action than for research, had already put his books away. Like herself and István, he dutifully came here to pursue the ongoing case of Saloman whenever he had a spare moment. But they were heading for the Transylvanian mountains as soon as István got here, and Konrad clearly figured his research time was over.

Apart from the librarian himself, she and Konrad were the only occupants of the library, so Mihaela broke with custom, raising her voice to call, "Konrad, come and look at this."

Her excitement must have leapt through her voice, because Konrad actually brightened as he came back to the table, and even Miklós's frown of disapproval quickly vanished. Shifting position, Mihaela pushed the sixteenth-century book across the table, jabbing her finger at the passage that had caught her eye. "Read that. It's a prophecy supposedly made by the Ancient vampire Luk, Saloman's cousin."

Konrad groaned at the Latin. "Why couldn't these guys write in Hungarian?"

"Read it," Mihaela commanded, and with a sigh Konrad did.

" 'She who stirs the Ancient,' " he began haltingly, " 'will end his power and make way for the rebirth of the world, for the dawn of the new vampire age. She will smite his friends and . . . cleave? . . . to his enemies, who would end all undead existence. To see the new age, she must give up the world.' "

Konrad raised his head, frowning at Mihaela. "It's contradicting itself. Someone will end an Ancient's power, and yet will cause an era of vampire domination? Doesn't make any sense to me."

"Prophecies rarely do," Miklós observed, peering over Mihaela's shoulder. "What book is that?"

"Memoirs of Szilágyi Gabor, the sixteenth-century hunter. He had a few run-ins with both Saloman and Luk, and lived to tell the tale. Seems to have been during one such encounter that Luk suddenly sat down and made this pronouncement. Although Luk was apparently vulnerable during the time he was speaking, Szilágyi was too 'awed' to attack him."

"Interesting," Konrad allowed with a hint of impatience. "But what makes you think it's important?"

" 'She who stirs the Ancient.' " Mihaela stabbed her finger at the gothic line of text as she spoke. "What if the Ancient is Saloman, and 'stir' means awaken?"

Konrad's eyebrows lifted. "Elizabeth?" he hazarded, and Mihaela sat back watching him read it again. His breathing quickened, but his expression remained calm as he raised his gaze to Miklós.

"Prophecies are bunkum, right?"

"Not necessarily." Miklós straightened and took off his glasses to rub his eyes. "Their problem is in the interpretation, and it's only too easy to make a later event fit some old and vague prophecy. The early texts are full of them, though, showing that both vampires and humans took them seriously at the time."

He bent and carefully picked up the book, supporting its spine in both hands. "This one is intriguing. I've never seen it before. And I thought we'd checked through everything surrounding Awakeners last year. I think it's never been filed correctly, but you could well be right, Mihaela, and it does refer to a future Awakener, possibly Elizabeth."

"Then Elizabeth really could be destined to bring him down?" Mihaela heard the eagerness in her own voice, and yet behind that, fear for her friend rose up and drowned the excitement.

"Let's hope not," Miklós said dryly, "since it seems she would be doomed to leave this world—to say nothing of the new vampire age she would apparently facilitate!"

"It doesn't make much sense," Mihaela agreed. "If she can defeat Saloman and smite his friends, you would expect that to curb vampire activity."

As the library door opened and István slouched through, she turned her worried gaze on Konrad. "I don't think we should tell her about this. It might make her take risks if she believes in some dubious destiny thing."

"It might also," Miklós pointed out, "cause *you* to urge her toward a path she isn't capable of taking. Prophecies are fickle and vague and should never be accepted at face value. They should certainly never form the foundation of hunter strategy."

"Then we shouldn't tell her," Konrad said decisively, and stood up as István approached the table.

"Tell who what?" István asked.

Mihaela rose to her feet. "We'll explain on the way. But if any of this stuff can be believed, Elizabeth might have been prophesied."

"Cool," said István.

Inevitably, despite the warning phone call for directions, Elizabeth was nowhere near ready when her doorbell rang on Saturday. Mostly because Joanne had come over and hung around the flat asking questions about her "date," as she insisted on calling Josh. On the other hand, when Elizabeth had invited her to stay and meet him, Joanne had grabbed her coat and fled, intoning, "No, no, my dear. Far be it from me to stand in the way of love's young dream. I'm off." She turned and winked. "Just get his photograph for me. The more intimate the better."

Elizabeth shooed her out the door, laughing, and went for her long-delayed shower. At least she was dressed in decent jeans and a newish green shirt by the time Josh arrived. And although her hair was still damp, it was combed and loose about her shoulders.

He smiled when she opened the door, and strolled in. Dressed casually in designer jeans and a loose sweater, expensive sunglasses dangling from one manicured hand, he looked remarkably glamorous for her humble abode. Elizabeth wished Joanne had stayed to appreciate him.

Vaguely, she knew she should be more fazed by Josh Alexander's walking into her home. But she had switched into what she thought of as "hunter" mode. This weekend was not about socializing and certainly not about dating, whatever Joanne chose to imagine. It was about hunter business and making Josh understand he was in danger before it was too late.

"Cup of coffee while I sling some things in a bag?" she offered, ushering him into her living room.

Josh glanced around him. Although her modest flat could hardly have been what he was used to, he took the trouble to look appreciative, even murmuring, "Nice place," before politely refusing the coffee.

"Sit down," Elizabeth invited. "I'll just be a couple of minutes."

Bolting through to the bedroom, she jumped up to grab her old traveling bag from the top of the wardrobe. She wrenched open the zipper and tossed it on the bed before throwing in the toiletries she'd already collected from the bathroom, and her only decent pair of dress shoes.

Opening all the dressing-table drawers at once seemed the quickest way to grab what she needed in the way of underwear, night things, tops, and jeans, although even so, she rummaged so much for her favorite sweater that the clothes began to spill out of the bottom drawer and it wouldn't close. She ignored it and spun around to the wardrobe, examining her poor collection of dresses and skirts. Most of them came from charity shops, or were at least five years old.

The only decent clothes she possessed were the outfit she'd bought from Jenners last year and the emerald green evening gown acquired in the spring sales for the graduation ball. She'd refused to buy it at first, insisting to her encouraging colleagues that it was bad luck to make the assumption that she'd get her PhD this summer. Richard had ended the argument by inviting her to go as his partner. Much to Joanne's barely concealed amusement.

Josh's voice from across the hall dragged her out of the memory.

"Sorry?" she called back, grabbing the evening gown off the hanger and tossing it on top of everything else into the bag. With a slightly irritated sigh, because she didn't know or care much about clothes, she turned back to the wardrobe and took the other outfit too.

Josh's mild voice came from the doorway. "I said, do you need any help?"

Elizabeth glanced up to see him scanning her bedroom with appreciation. Annoyance prickled her skin. Although she was happy to invite friends into her home, she didn't feel comfortable with strangers in her bedroom.

"It looks just like you," he observed. "Pretty and untidy."

"Well, thanks for the pretty," she muttered, folding the dress so that it wouldn't get too crushed and closing the zipper. "I'm ready."

But Josh's roving eye had landed on her bottom drawer and all the clothes spilling out. "Hey, that's gorgeous," he said, crouching down without embarrassment for a better look.

Irritated further, she followed his attention and felt her heart lurch. It was the jeweled fastening of Saloman's cloak.

Without thought, she strode around the bed and brushed past him, dropping to her knees to hide it from him.

"Looks like an antique," Josh observed. "Why don't you take it with you? Dante's got some antiquarian experts coming this weekend."

Damn it, why couldn't she have taken more care? What was the point of hiding the thing at the bottom of her drawer if she then churned everything up so that it sprawled over the top?

"It's not valuable," she said hastily. "Except to me."

Josh moved slightly out of her way as she seized the cloak and began to fold it. "Ah, you have a family heirloom too," he said.

"No. Just a gift from a friend."

He'd wrapped her in it when she was unconscious and nearly dead from his bite, and carried her in it across Budapest from his palace to Mihaela's flat. Whether it was the memory of that, or some magic that came from simply touching something of his, emotion flooded her.

She'd tried to give it back to him before he left her at dawn on the first day of last November. He'd taken it from her and gazed at it a moment, as if remembering the three hundred agonizing years he'd spent wearing it before she awakened him. It couldn't have inspired many fond memories in him. And yet he'd smiled and swung it around her shoulders, carefully fastening it at her throat before, still holding the clasp so that his fingertips brushed the sensitive skin of her throat, he'd bent and kissed her mouth with slow, thorough sensuality.

"I wore it when you awakened me, and for that reason, that value, I give it to you."

She'd covered his hand on the jeweled clasp, threaded her fingers through his. "I don't need this to remember you," she'd whispered.

"Then take it to comfort you."

He'd known, more clearly even than she, that she'd need every ounce of strength, every comfort she could find to survive their parting. And when he'd gone, swooping through the window into the gray mist of the dawn sky, she'd sat in the corner for hours, huddled in his cloak, resting her cheek on the folds that lay across her drawn-up knees while her tears stained it.

She'd wept all day, and then stopped.

Carefully, she laid it in the drawer, smoothed it out, and covered it with another old, tumbled sweater.

"Ready?" said Josh lightly.

"Ready." She smiled brightly, rose to her feet, and reached for her bag.

"Let me take that," Josh offered.

Elizabeth was almost surprised not to discover any of his entourage in the unassuming car parked outside.

"I've escaped." Josh grinned, opening the door for her before walking around to stash her bag in the boot. She gathered, from the scrape of luggage rearrangement, that she was traveling rather more lightly than he.

"Okay," Josh said, sliding into the driver's seat and fastening his seat belt. "Sat nav on; Highlands, here we come."

Elizabeth couldn't help smiling. "You sound excited. Weren't you filming up there already?"

"Actually, we did most of it in the Borders. Only one day at Glencoe—wow, that is one spectacular place!—just enough to give me a taste for the country. I'm really looking forward to seeing more." He glanced at her as he changed gear. "Your turn. Spill."

"Spill what?" she asked, amused.

"Why did you agree to come with me to this party?"

"Josh, women must fall over themselves to go to parties with you."

"Yes, but those women want me. Either me or my money or whatever influence they imagine I have in the industry. You don't give a shit about those things, do you? For the record, that's why I invited you. You might end up falling for me after prolonged exposure."

Elizabeth gazed at his sharp, handsome profile for a moment. "I hoped prolonged exposure might convince you I wasn't insane." Then, before discomfort could set in, she added, "But what I want to know is why *you* agreed to go to the party at all if it's so boring you need someone as annoying and insane as me to liven it up."

Josh laughed. "Dante and I always go to each other's parties when we can. His presence lends me gravitas, and apparently I supply some glamour to his serious affairs. I've known him for years, on a superficial level, but recently—since his wife died, I suppose—we've become better friends, do each other favors when we can."

"Like turning up to dull parties?"

"Exactly." Josh grinned, checking out the car behind in his rearview mirror. "I think he wants me to impress someone. I have to be charming and splendid and tell the guy how helpful Dante can be. In return he gets his antiques experts to value my sword."

"Your sword?" Startled, Elizabeth stared at him. "Is . . . is that what you meant by heirlooms? You mentioned something at the flat."

"Yes. It's a beautiful thing, been in my family forever."

My God, it can't be. . . . But of course it could. According to legend, Saloman's sword, which had been missing when she first awakened him, and which she had read about in the hunters' library last year, had remained in the possession of Tsigana's family for generations. It was more than possible that this was Josh's heirloom.

Not quite sure how she felt about that, she managed to ask, "How old is it?"

Josh pulled out and overtook a lorry. "To be honest, I don't know a damned thing about it. I've brought it with me to let Dante's experts give it a poke."

Elizabeth blinked as they sped along the clear road. "You brought it from the States for that?"

"Nah, I guess I'm paranoid about theft," he said ruefully.

"But not about airlines losing your luggage?"

"Everyone has their foibles," Josh said easily. So easily that she wondered if there was a deeper reason behind his traveling with the heirloom.

Leaving that for the time being, she asked instead, "So who's the guy you're meant to impress? Some British politician?" God, she really was going to be out of her depth, dining with government ministers, rich actors, and industrialists. . . .

"No, some foreign business rival. Simon Adam? No, Adam Simon! Ever heard of him?"

"No," Elizabeth said apologetically. "I don't know much about that kind of thing, and I'm afraid I don't move in wealthy social circles."

Josh shrugged, slowing down to round a bend in the road. "Even if you did, I doubt you'd know this guy. Apparently he's Eastern European."

"Yes? Whereabouts?" Elizabeth asked eagerly, then added apologetically, "I did most of my thesis research in that part of the world—I have a fondness for it."

"Well, that's good—gives you something to talk about. I've never been there in my life."

"*I* have to impress him too?" Elizabeth asked wryly, holding on to her seat with both hands as Josh broke the speed limit. "You didn't say that was part of the deal."

Josh cast her a quick smile. "It isn't. But if opportunity knocks, schmooze the guy."

Elizabeth laughed. "Josh, I couldn't schmooze a pussycat. Don't you want to go left here?"

"Maybe I should put the voice on the sat nav. . . ."

Josh was easy company, and as they drove through Fife and Perthshire and on up into increasingly spectacular scenery, Elizabeth began to think the weekend might not be so bad after all. In fact, if she could just have had the weekend in his company without the party and the senators and the business rivals, she'd have been quite happy—although that might have given Josh the wrong idea.

"Why aren't you taking some glamorous actress?" she blurted out, as the thought came into her head.

"Don't want to," he said simply. Then, with a boyish wink: "Actually, you're my protection from them too."

Elizabeth raised one skeptical eyebrow. "I doubt anyone will mistake me for serious competition."

"Of course not. You're my cousin."

And that, she thought, admiring the flow of steep-sloping hills into the glen they were driving through, was probably the truth. He wanted a break from his reality, and she was the comfort of family. It didn't matter that they hadn't known each other a week ago. Blood often was thicker than water, and in fact, she felt far more comfortable with Josh Alexander than she should, considering his fame and standing.

The house Senator Dante had rented for the week was a great Victorian folly of a place near Loch Tummel. Even the inevitable rain and gray skies that had followed them for the last two hours couldn't spoil its splendor. All romantic towers and turrets, it had clearly been built at the height of Queen Victoria's love affair with the Scottish Highlands, and the resulting popularity of the region with rich and aristocratic families from all over Britain.

Although they'd made good time for most of the journey, the last part was covered on mainly single-track, muddy roads with even more bends and bumps and hills than Josh must have grown used to in the preceding hours. To make things worse, it began to rain and visibility grew tricky. But at least they met few cars coming in the opposite direction.

As Josh finally pulled up outside the impressive front door, a man leapt off the steps to come and park the car. Someone else would, apparently, fetch the luggage. Another man in a suit stood by the open door. Too young to be Dante, Elizabeth thought, although Josh appeared to recognize him, greeting him by name.

Inside, despite the daylight, the entrance hall was lit by a blaze of electric light shining down on splendid parquet flooring, faded tartan carpets, and polished wood paneling.

A man strode across this gracious space, his hair glinting silver from the chandelier above. He moved with such spryness that Elizabeth was surprised to see, as he came closer, that he must have been around sixty years old.

"Josh!" Holding out both hands, he patted Josh on the shoulder with one and, with the other, clasped Josh's. "Glad you made it! Wonderful to see you!"

"Hey, Senator! How are you? I'd love you to meet my Scottish cousin, Elizabeth Silk. Elizabeth, Senator Grayson Dante."

Dante turned to her, offering his right hand, while his left just touched her elbow with a well-used gesture of sincere welcome. Elizabeth took his hand almost numbly. This man with the silver hair and the craggy smile and the firm, vigorous handshake had amazingly bright blue eyes through which shone a huge and powerful personality. It almost seemed to strike her like a blow, and for some reason, although nothing but good-natured if overpracticed welcome shone from his eyes, a shiver ran down Elizabeth's spine. It might have been anticipation.

Josh liked the house. He wondered if the senator planned to buy it, because if he didn't, Josh might well be interested on his own account. He rather liked the idea of a home in Scotland now that he'd discovered the reality of his roots.

Since he'd left Elizabeth in her own room—next door to his—to bathe and dress before dinner, he set off to explore on his own. Leaving the upper floors, which seemed to be devoted to bedrooms, he confined himself to the bottom two levels, where the public rooms were located, and found nothing to dissuade him from his new fantasy of becoming a Scottish laird.

Wandering into a dim room with the curtains drawn, no doubt to protect the green baize of the huge snooker table that filled most of it, he idly lifted a cue and cast an admiring eye over the paneled ceiling and walls before his gaze came to rest on an elegant chaise longue and its occupant.

He thought at first that the man was asleep, he lay so still. He wore dark chinos and a cream shirt that was probably silk, open at the throat. With the envy of a man approaching middle age and his constant battle with weight already begun, Josh acknowledged that the young stranger had not one ounce of spare fat. And yet not even the unkind could call him scrawny. Beneath the casually pulled-up sleeves lay muscle and sinew. His stomach was flat, his chest and shoulders broad. Strength was obvious in the pale column of his throat, in the set of his slightly pointed chin.

In fact, the stranger was a handsome devil whatever way you looked at him. Long, unruly black hair fell half across a face that was just about as attractive as it could be without detracting from its undeniable maleness. Cheekbones an actor would die for. A nose that might have been a little too prominent for classical perfection lent him an attractively predatory air that must have had women throwing themselves at his feet. Long, thick lashes curled away from eyes that, in the dim light, were so dark that they looked black. And, of course, they were regarding him with interest.

In spite of himself, Josh's stomach gave a jolt that might have been guilt or just surprise, but at least he didn't jump.

"Hello." The stranger's voice was deep, low, well modulated, reminding Josh of someone or something elusive.

"Hello," Josh returned. "Sorry, didn't mean to disturb your sleep."

"I wasn't asleep, merely meditating." Though his English was perfectly enunciated, Josh guessed it wasn't his first language.

Josh grinned. "Yeah. That's what my dad used to say too—when I interrupted his snoring."

The stranger sat up in one enviably graceful movement, swinging his legs down to the polished wood floor. His feet, long and slim, were bare. "Flattered as I am by any resemblance you perceive to your esteemed parent, I feel compelled to point out that I was not snoring."

Josh laughed and took a step nearer to offer his hand. "I'm Josh Alexander."

The stranger rose to his feet, which made him several inches taller than Josh, taking Josh's outthrust hand in a firm, cold grip.

Unexpectedly, Josh shivered, as if someone had walked over his grave. The stranger had intense, almost opaque dark eyes, and yet as Josh gazed into them, strange lights like yellow flames seemed to dance in their blackness—a bizarre fantasy, and even so, Josh couldn't lose the feeling that he already knew this man. Despite the fact that he clearly wasn't someone one could easily forget.

"Adam Simon," the exotic stranger said.

Adam Simon, whom Dante wanted him to court. It was a surprise. The man looked less like a businessman than a rock star not yet completely given over to the debauchery of drink and drugs.

Adam Simon broke the handshake first. Josh had to restrain himself from rubbing his hands together for warmth. Regarding his "target" with increased interest, he remarked, "Pleased to meet you. The senator told me you were coming. I hear you're setting the world of international business alight."

"The senator is a very interesting man," Simon observed. His gaze dropped briefly to the region of Josh's throat and rose again to his face. "As are you."

It came again, a twinge of unease mixed with a recognition that was almost . . . attraction. Shaking it off with a laugh, Josh said, "Interesting? Hardly! I merely act out other people's fantasies. They're the creative ones."

"Always so modest, Josh!" Senator Dante said, bustling into the room. Josh didn't know whether he felt more relieved or annoyed by this interruption to his odd tête-à-tête. "You guys want to play?"

"You *know* how to play this ridiculous game?" Josh joked.

"Sure, it's just like pool, only more complicated. I'll teach you."

"Maybe later," Josh said easily. "I'd better make sure Elizabeth's all right. My cousin," he added to Simon, who merely bowed politely, although his steady gaze never left Josh's face.

"Delightful girl," Dante approved. "Adam, want to play before dinner?"

Josh didn't wait to hear the reply. Over the years he had learned to accept most people and find a level on which to feel at ease with them. But it had been a long time since someone had inspired such strongly conflicting emotions in him as Adam Simon did. At once intrigued, attracted, and repelled by the strength of the personality that leapt out of Simon's handsome face, Josh wanted to know more and yet felt some kind of relief when he finally left the room.

As he ran lightly up the stairs to his own bedroom, it entered his head that Dante might finally have met his match, and the thought amused him so much, he began to laugh.

In spite of her knowledge that there were so many other vastly more important matters in the world, Elizabeth couldn't quite rid herself of the uncomfortable butterflies that seemed to have lodged at the pit of her stomach.

"Are you sure this is right?" she asked Josh, stepping out of the bathroom to examine herself by a different light in the bedroom mirror.

Josh, sprawled at ease on her bed, glanced up from the society magazine he was idly thumbing through and sat up, still staring. He looked very handsome and angelic in a cream dinner jacket with matching silk shirt and bow tie. "Wow, you look fantastic!"

Elizabeth flushed, noting the surprise as much as the sincerity of his comment. She wore the evening gown she'd bought for the graduation ball and had tied her hair up behind her head in a style she knew suited her, but otherwise, she felt she looked as she always did—except for the added discomfort.

"I feel overdressed for dinner," she confessed.

"Trust me, in this company, you won't be."

"You're not making me feel any better! Who's here, anyway? Apart from Jerri Cusack and this Simon person you're meant to impress?"

"I met him," Josh volunteered. "Adam Simon. Asleep in the snooker room. Not at all what I expected."

"Stuffed shirt?" Elizabeth inquired, delving in her semiunpacked bag for the necklace that was the only decent jewelry she possessed.

"The opposite," Josh said. "He reminded me more of a rock star, but not quite so wasted. He's kind of charming—doesn't take himself too seriously, although I have the feeling he makes sure others don't make that mistake! Anyway, he's a handsome devil—I doubt you'll find it a chore to talk to him. In fact, I'll probably be jealous."

"No point," Elizabeth said without thinking. She was concentrating on fastening the tiny clasp of the necklace behind her neck.

Josh met her gaze quizzically in the mirror. "Is that a put-down or a compliment?"

"Neither." Elizabeth hesitated, then turned to face him. "I feel stupid saying this to you, but you don't need to pretend. I'm well aware there's no chance of romance between us."

Josh stood up. "Who says I'm pretending?"

It seemed he was too honest to take the ego-preserving way out she'd just given him. Which was frustrating, yet made her all the sorrier she couldn't fall in love with him like any normal woman would.

Josh said quietly, "There's an empathy between us that's rare. You must feel it too. I know you like me."

"I do," Elizabeth admitted. "I think the empathy's to do with our shared heritage. Blood really is thicker than water. For the rest, I *do* like you as a friend, a friend I'd hate to see come to harm."

A quick frown formed and vanished on his face. "Harm. That's why you agreed to come. I didn't believe you when you told me that. How egocentric is the human male."

Uncomfortable, Elizabeth looked away.

But Josh only took her hand and swung it lightly in the air without obvious resentment. "It's the man who gave you the cloak, isn't it?"

Elizabeth's stomach jolted. "What?"

"He's the reason you reject romance with me or anyone else. And I think that whatever happened with him is the source of the grief I sensed in you when we first met."

Elizabeth swallowed. "Partly. One grief, perhaps. But I prefer to think of it as the source of my strength." She gave a quick, awkward smile to banish any pathos, and walked toward the door. "You're bloody perceptive, aren't you, Josh?"

"I'm good at faces. And yours, when you touched the cloak, was an open book."

Elizabeth paused, stricken. How could she regard herself as strong when she gave so much away so easily?

"Hey, your secret's safe with me," Josh said, reaching past her to grasp the door handle. "And don't be uncomfortable. I don't need a crazy woman in my bed anyway."

Elizabeth couldn't help laughing, as she was meant to. She felt a renewed rush of liking for Josh.

"Um, one more thing before we go down for drinks," he said. "Jerri Cusack, my costar in the new movie. Don't be upset if she's a little . . . odd."

Elizabeth scanned his face for clues. There was a rueful twinkle in his eyes.

"She might think you're my date," Josh explained. "And she won't like that."

Elizabeth's spirits fell further. "Oh, bugger. Are you and she . . . ?"

"No, no, but she thinks it would be good publicity if we were, and she doesn't like being thwarted."

"So she'll hate my guts." Elizabeth held up her hand to count points off on her fingers. "Okay, I have to avoid Jerri Cusack and seek out Adam Simon. Anything else?"

"Just enjoy yourself," said Josh blithely.

"Ha," Elizabeth returned without gratitude, and, laughing, Josh opened the door.

As they descended the staircase, sounds of lively jazz music and the buzz of many-voiced chatter and laughter drifted up to them.

"Seriously," Josh murmured. "Dante's parties are always fun. None of the other stuff really matters. Everyone will be nice."

Which might have been his way of saying that however much Jerri hated her presence, she wouldn't get too nasty. Elizabeth didn't really care. She'd met a lot nastier creatures than bitchy movie stars. Squaring her shoulders, she concentrated on getting through the evening as pleasantly as possible, and hoped for a few opportunities for a friendly tête-à-tête with Josh. By the time the party ended, she was determined to have convinced him of his danger, and his option of hunter protection.

As they entered the big, impressive drawing room where predinner drinks were being served, Elizabeth's first thought was that it wasn't as bad as she'd expected. There weren't as many people as she'd feared, maybe around twenty. The men all wore formal evening clothes, some traditional black-tie, some a bit more individualistic. The women wore formal dresses too, of all lengths and levels of daringness. Elizabeth allowed herself a quick sigh of relief that her own gown did indeed suit the occasion, and then she noticed that despite the formality of the dress, the guests themselves didn't seem to be in the least stuffy. Several looked over and smiled. Some actually waved, and one man called out, "Hey, Josh!" from the other side of the room.

And then Dante, standing just inside the doorway with a group of traditionally garbed men, welcomed them with a big smile. An instant later, a waiter was before them with a tray of drinks. Elizabeth took a glass of champagne while Dante introduced the men around him. Their names passed right over her, although she smiled and shook hands with each.

"These guys are all expert antiquarians," he explained. "I was telling them about your sword, Josh, and how you'd be glad for them to take a look."

"Sounds a most interesting piece," one of the men said. He was American. "How long has it been in your family?"

"Hundreds of years, so I'm told." Josh sipped his champagne.

"And do you have documents to show its provenance?" asked another, with a definitely English accent.

"Nope. Just the sword. I'll show it to you after dinner if you like. Just don't let the senator convince you I'm prepared to sell it, because I'm not!"

"Whatever the price?" one of the men joked.

"Whatever the price," Josh agreed.

If it really was Saloman's missing sword, the price was probably rather higher than they knew. Elizabeth said lightly, "May I see this amazing sword too?"

"Of course," Josh agreed at once, explaining to the others, "Elizabeth's a historian, so she might well have some valuable knowledge."

"How come you've never tried to find out about it before?" Elizabeth asked, curious.

Josh shrugged. "Never really thought about it, because it was always around when I was growing up. Just recently I've become more . . . intrigued by it. No doubt because of the senator's interest!"

Dante laughed and toasted Josh with his champagne. Over the top of his glass, his piercing blue eyes twinkled, and yet Elizabeth caught a hint of hardness there that might have been acquisitiveness or distrust. Possibly the latter, because for the first time since she'd met him, she had the uncomfortable feeling that Josh wasn't telling the entire truth. She began to wonder whether there was more to his relationship with Dante than he'd let on.

"So, are you gentlemen all in the antiques trade?" Josh inquired. "Or are you just enthusiastic amateurs?"

"I have an auction house and Bill here owns a chain of shops," the Englishman volunteered. "But for most of us the interest is pleasure rather than business."

Elizabeth let her gaze wander away from the antiquarians and around the other guests, who all looked in good spirits. She spotted Jerri Cusack, stunningly glamorous in a risqué white dress, laughing up at a tall, black-haired man—with his back to Elizabeth—whose arm she playfully shook. The woman on his other side didn't seem very pleased, judging by her rigid body language, although she kept smiling.

"Actually," one of the antiquarians was saying, "my interest began with the paranormal and paranormal artifacts, and it was from there that I moved on to more general antiques."

Elizabeth's attention swung back to the speaker, the American whose name she thought might have been Bill.

"What in the world," she asked, "are paranormal artifacts? Sharpened sticks for staking vampires?" Or a cloak that had once belonged to the most powerful vampire ever to have walked the earth . . . Or the sword belonging to that same vampire.

What a coincidence, she thought with a sudden chill, that one of Dante's antiquarians was interested in the paranormal. If Josh's sword really was Saloman's, would Bill recognize it for what it was?

Although a ripple of laughter had greeted her words, Bill's response was immediate. "Hardly! Merely objects reputed to be imbued with supernatural powers," he stated.

"*Are* there such things?" That was Josh, taking the words out of her mouth.

Dante laughed. "The star of two *Psychics* movies needs to ask that?"

"You know perfectly well *Psychics* is complete bunkum," Josh said dryly. "However much fun it is."

"But certainly there are such things," Bill said. He smiled thinly. "With the emphasis on 'reputed.' "

"But you won't deny you've found things with inexplicable powers, will you?" Dante urged.

"Of course not. But rarely, very rarely. I *have* come across one or two objects with magical properties. One was a human skull, with horns."

"With horns?" Josh interjected. "Then it can't have been human, now, can it?"

"Yes, it can," Dante said, surprisingly. "Go on, Bill."

"Another was a golden mask—a pagan object older than Christ. And trust me, the power that emanated from these objects was intense."

"Yes, but what did they *do*?" Elizabeth asked, keen to get to the point. However, she wasn't so focused that she didn't notice the warning cough or the frowns that came from Bill's colleagues.

"Well, the skull seemed to increase one's strength when one touched it, while the mask—"

"Josh! Darling!" interrupted a gushing voice. An instant later, Jerri Cusack embraced Josh, and everyone fell back to give her room. Her movements were all quick and dramatic, and she seemed to have released him almost before she'd grabbed him, reaching behind her in high excitement to exclaim, "I've just *got* to introduce you to Adam Simon!"

The name alone would have made Elizabeth turn in the direction of her grasping hand, but the speed of Josh's spin to meet the man interested her far more. She stepped aside to get a better view, and almost dropped her glass.

He walked toward her, his black hair flowing loose over his shoulders. Alone of the men present, he wore no dinner jacket, just a black shirt that might have been velvet or crushed silk, with a matching tie that looked more like a cravat. He moved with all the grace and threat of a panther.

All this she absorbed in the first instant before his beauty blinded her, as it had always done. Yet it never even entered her head to doubt her own sanity, or to wonder whether her recognition was faulty. His mask had fallen.

He gazed only at her. She took a step toward him without meaning to, and he smiled, the rare, full smile that haunted her dreams. Shock overwhelmed the emotions struggling for release.

Then joy broke through like a tide, propelling her forward and into his arms, her face already raised for his kiss. Amber flames danced in his black eyes, burning her with the force of his desire. His mouth no longer smiled as it covered hers.

Elizabeth, he said silently. *Elizabeth.*

Saloman.

It was an instant, a very small instant of bliss. The powerful arms she'd never thought to feel again closed close around her, while his mouth, his incredible, wonderful mouth, moved over hers with tenderness, accepting all her need and all the uncomplicated happiness of her kiss.

But it wasn't uncomplicated. And they weren't alone. A fact that Saloman, clearly, had never lost sight of for a moment. Even as she gasped into his mouth, trying to force herself to draw back, to ask questions that had only half formed in her brain, he was already releasing her. Her stunned lips felt cold, her body rebellious as his arms fell away. Although the tips of his fingers trailed over her naked back and lingered, so that she stood in the circle of his arm, being inexorably turned as if to be shown off to friends.

She shivered, desperately reaching for what dignity or even sense she could muster. They were being watched by several people with varying degrees of surprise, interest, and disapproval.

As if from very far away, Josh's voice said, "I didn't realize you two were acquainted."

"Neither did I!" Elizabeth hoped she didn't sound as hysterical as she felt.

"We met in Eastern Europe," Saloman said, and God, yes, his voice still sounded the same. A little more modern in its intonation, perhaps, but it still reached right inside her, turning her outside in. "I expect Elizabeth remembers the Hungarian form of my name."

"Oh, yes," Elizabeth agreed, fighting the urge to laugh.

"What would that be?" Jerri asked eagerly.

"You couldn't pronounce it," Saloman said blandly.

Elizabeth, who, incredibly enough, was still clutching her champagne glass, hoped she'd spilled some of its contents over his mocking, arrogant person. Lifting it to her lips with fingers she prayed didn't shake too visibly, she took a sizable gulp and tried to think.

What the hell was he doing here? And why was he posing as Adam Simon? Shit, what had he done with the real businessman? Was he after Dante?

No, you blind, blithering fool! He's after Josh! Josh, whom you came here to protect, remember? To warn him against this very vampire? Well, Silk, now's your moment!

Instinctively, she moved nearer to Josh, an act that Saloman acknowledged with a bland smile.

Dante, listening to the servant murmuring in his ear, nodded once and called, "Dinner is served, everyone! Let's go to the dining room and eat!"

In the general happy exodus from the drawing room, Elizabeth found and gripped Josh's hand. "Don't trust Adam Simon," she implored. He glanced at her, frowning, but there were too many people around them. "Just don't," she warned. "I'll explain later."

And what else should she do? Warn Dante that he was entertaining a vampire? Tell him this wasn't Adam Simon but a dangerous impostor? Although the senator did seem more open to paranormal possibilities than she'd expected, her mind boggled at his likely response to being informed his favored houseguest wasn't his troublesome business rival after all but a vampire. Not just any old vampire, either, but the most Ancient and powerful left in the world, the prince to whom all other vampires knelt, cringing.

Perhaps she should just stick to the impostor element. Explain that she'd met Adam Simon and this wasn't him? Except she'd already denied knowing him to Josh.

Shit, what she really needed to do was talk to Saloman, warn him off Josh. After all, he'd promised to spare Konrad because she'd asked.

Because she'd asked . . . Her heart beat even faster, drowning the talk around her. Was it possible he hadn't come here for Josh after all, but for her?

She arrived at the table still in a daze of speculation and anxiety, blindly following Josh. Gradually she became aware that there were little name cards at every place, and that Josh was making straight for the top end of the table as if he already knew where to go. Dante stood at the head of the table, smiling benignly while his guests seated themselves. On his left sat Jerri Cusack, and, almost inevitably, Josh halted at the seat beside her. Glancing at the table Elizabeth saw Josh's name beside Jerri's, then hers—and on her left, Adam Simon's.

Her heart somersaulted.

It will never be over. That was what he'd said to her on their last night together. Was this his way of proving it? Or had he come simply for Josh? Either way, how was she to get through the agony of sitting so close to him in public?

Use it, she told herself fiercely as she sat down. *Take the opportunity and tell him he can't have Josh.*

She tried not to watch him sauntering up the room, nodding to the waiter, who directed him to his place, just as if he were used to servants pandering to his every whim. He probably had been in the past, whatever his life was like now. Did he have an army of vampire servants to do his bidding? Oh, shite, were they here?

"How fortunate," Saloman murmured, dropping into the velvet-upholstered chair beside hers.

Was it? How the hell could she talk to him, ask him useful questions, with Josh listening in to every word? The obvious answer came to her almost like a cartoon lightbulb switching on in her head.

It was hard to concentrate through the laughter and several conversations going on around her, but she managed to gaze into her gently steaming soup bowl as if debating the recipe with herself and calm herself enough to initiate a connection. It wasn't hard to think of him when he sat right next to her, his black silk–clad arm almost touching her elbow.

Saloman, she sent to him.

The word bounced harmlessly back to her. Silence greeted her and she knew she hadn't reached him. Because he'd blocked her, damn him. What the hell did that mean? That he wasn't yet ready to say anything that no one else should hear?

"Hi, you must be Elizabeth!"

She almost jumped as the voice cut through her abortive attempt at telepathy. She looked up into the smiling face of an attractive, dark-haired young woman leaning in front of Saloman to shake her hand.

"I'm Nicola Devon."

"Pleased to meet you," Elizabeth said faintly, rousing herself to shake hands with civility, and Nicola sat down on Saloman's other side. Across the table sat the United States consul to Edinburgh and his wife, the antiquarians, and a couple of glamorous women she hadn't yet met.

Dante sat down and everyone began to eat. With a feeling of numb helplessness, Elizabeth picked up her spoon.

"So you're Josh's Scottish cousin!" Jerri flung at her without warning. The woman was smiling, her teeth white and perfect between full, sculpted lips, but her gaze didn't seem to be on Elizabeth. Instead, it switched continually between Josh and Saloman. "Wow, what's it like to live in this amazing country all the time?"

"Wet," Elizabeth said vaguely, which won an unexpected ripple of laughter, not least from Nicola on Saloman's other side.

"You've got that right," Nicola said fervently. "I've found myself deliberately choosing work in warmer countries. What is it you do, Elizabeth?"

"Research," Elizabeth replied; then, realizing she was sounding rather monosyllabic, she added, "I've had a junior, temporary post at St. Andrews University while I finished my PhD, but it's about to expire."

"How is the thesis?" Saloman inquired. He raised the spoon to his mouth. Elizabeth tried not to stare. He seemed to be eating the soup, but she wondered what he'd do with the main course.

"Under consideration," she managed.

"What's it on?" Nicola asked.

"Historical superstitions," Saloman answered for her. He glanced at her, one eyebrow twitching upward to acknowledge the shared joke none of the others would understand. "With special reference to my country." Where reality had blown her theory sky-high, and yet she'd still held it together.

"Fascinating," Nicola said. "Have you met Bill and Gerald over there? They're into that kind of thing."

"But they prefer objects to go with their stories," Saloman pointed out.

Objects like you? She hurled the thought at him without looking, and this time he chose to catch it. She felt his presence slip into her mind like a warm, familiar drink.

Oh, I think I might be a little too strong for their palates, he returned, faintly amused, and when she sneaked a glance at him, he smiled and added, *Of course, they wouldn't be too strong for mine.*

Elizabeth almost choked on her soup, and Saloman, his smile widening, took another delicate spoonful. Elizabeth had to drag her gaze away. She remembered only too well the feel of those firm, knowing lips on her skin, caressing her throat and breasts, lingering to tease and torture her sensitive nipples. . . .

Her whole body flushed at the memory, from her cheeks to her thighs and all points between. Worse, she was sure he'd sense her heat and use it, whether for his own amusement or to advance whatever plan had brought him here.

She laid down her spoon. *Why did you come, Saloman?*

He appeared to consider, while the waiters smoothly removed soup bowls and the second course was brought in. She found herself answering Josh, making automatic contributions to the general conversation while the larger part of her focused and strained for Saloman's answer.

To take what is mine, he said at last.

It could have meant anything. It shouldn't have brought the surge of desire and pleasure shooting to her core. She wouldn't allow it, of course, but the idea that he had come to claim her, despite all her objections, was insidious, intoxicating. Trying to quash it, she reached for the more likely meaning. Josh.

You can't have Josh. I won't let you harm him.

Can't I? He sounded merely amused. *Why not? Is he your lover?*

Of course not!

No need to sound so indignant. I didn't accuse you of adultery. Then he's just one of the lucky few you happen to feel responsible for? Like the unspeakable Konrad. At this rate, I shall run out of other descendants and be forced to consume you. Again.

She gasped. Flame licked through her, burning.

"Are you all right?" Josh asked in quick concern.

"Oh, yes, I'm fine. Thank you," Elizabeth murmured. "I just swallowed the wrong way."

"So, Elizabeth, you live in St. Andrews?" Dante said jovially. "Love that town. Great golf. Do you play?"

"No," Elizabeth said apologetically. "Though over the years I've learned to avoid flying golf balls."

From the corner of her eye, as she spoke, she could just make out Saloman's long, pale fingers curled around the stem of his crystal wineglass. It was full of bloodred wine. He lifted it out of her line of vision, drinking as she tried to concentrate on the spate of golf stories that sprang up.

Saloman's glass reappeared on the table, still held in his long fingers, but this time his forearm just touched hers. The tiny hairs on her naked arm seemed to stand up to meet him. Electricity sparked, as it always did to his touch, and yet she couldn't withdraw her arm without making it too obvious.

There came an inevitable burst of laughter at Josh's golfing story. Elizabeth, who'd barely heard a word, forced herself to smile. Saloman shifted in his seat and suddenly his thigh was against hers too.

Oh, God, don't do this to me, Saloman. . . .

She shifted her arm, at least, away from his touch and turned to see him pronging a small piece of fish with his fork. Beyond him, the friendly Nicola laid down her glass. Behind the perfect grooming, she looked thoughtful and intelligent, with tiny yet deeply etched lines of character, or perhaps humor, at the corners of her eyes and mouth.

"What is it you do, Nicola?" Elizabeth asked, covering her desperation for distraction. Saloman's thigh, firm and muscular, moved against hers in an obvious caress.

"Advertising," Nicola said. "Which is how I know Adam here. My company's doing some work for him."

Involuntarily, Elizabeth's gaze flew back to Saloman, in time to see him lower his fork with the fish still attached. He seemed to be hacking up the rather delicious sole without eating it.

This doesn't make sense. Why does she think you're Adam Simon? Where is he? How long have you been—

Meet me outside later. I'll call you.

Saloman . . .

But his presence had withdrawn from her mind. It would have

felt like a loss if his leg hadn't been pressing against hers, if she didn't have the promise of a meeting with him, alone in the dark. She knew it would be a mistake to let this happen all over again, and she knew that when they met, she'd have to be strong enough to assure him of that. And yet she couldn't prevent the surge of excitement, of pure hunger just to talk to him, just to be in his arms for one more minute.

Well, if she was honest, the hunger went well beyond a minute in his arms, but she couldn't, she really couldn't afford to be that honest.

As the evening wore on, it occurred to Elizabeth that she was being played. Waiting to speak to Saloman, she delayed warning either Dante or Josh. And although she couldn't actually imagine Saloman doing anything as crazy as killing everyone in the house, she knew it wasn't beyond his capabilities. The hunters had told her a few weeks ago about a rumor from Spain, according to which, in one of the few violent confrontations of his "reign" so far, Saloman had killed ten strong vampires in less than five minutes—before going on to drain the wily old professor who was Tsigana's descendant. Legend said Saloman had no help in the battle, but then, legend probably said the same thing about the fight in St. Andrews. Saloman had written the book on self-propaganda. He'd taught Vlad the Impaler and no doubt his detractors too, to devastating effect.

All she could do was stay close to Josh after they left the dining room—the meal had been delicious and Elizabeth regretted being far too anxious to do it justice—and wait for Saloman's call. The worst part came after they gathered again in the large drawing room, where Dante entertained them with an eclectic mix of rock, country, and jazz music. People inevitably split up into groups, and Josh chose to carry out his promise to the senator by seeking out Saloman and falling into some story about how Dante had saved his business interests.

Elizabeth had cringed for him, but couldn't halt him without rudeness. Saloman listened with apparent interest, even remarking on what a "player" the senator was. Inspired, Josh told an amusing story that served to show just how powerful the senator was, since it brought in all sorts of important people, including a former president of the United States.

Relieved when Dante himself came to join them, Elizabeth happily followed the conversation to more neutral ground and ignored Saloman's hooded gaze when she felt it burning her neck. She drifted away with Josh after that, watching Jerri and a couple of others dancing an enthusiastic Charleston.

"I had to learn this for my last film!" Jerri crowed, showing off her long, elegant legs.

"She can dance," Josh allowed, and Elizabeth had to agree. In fact, she got so caught up in it that by the time she remembered to look around again, Saloman was no longer in the room.

Her nerves tightened as she waited for his voice in her mind, which would summon her. Somewhere, she hated herself for it, but she knew she had to go, to find out what was going on, since Saloman wouldn't talk to her any other way. And the hunters had no leads on what he planned next. It would be another battle of wits and sex that she was damned if she'd let him win. And if Saloman was with her, then he couldn't be harming Josh.

If Saloman was with her, if he had come here for her . . .

He didn't, idiot. He had no way of knowing you'd be here.

Didn't he? Saloman always had ways of knowing things he couldn't possibly know.

"So, Josh." Dante came up behind him and placed a fatherly hand on his shoulder. "We're about to go on to the smaller sitting room upstairs so I can show these fellows some of the pieces I collected in the UK. Do you want to bring down your sword?"

"Sure," Josh agreed. "Want to come, Elizabeth?"

Before Elizabeth could agree, her phone rang. Although various phones had gone off all evening, the sound of her own seemed so mundane in this room full of film stars and foreign dignitaries—to say nothing of visiting vampires close by—that for an instant she couldn't think where it came from. Then, hastily retrieving it from her purse, she cast Dante an apologetic smile.

"Sorry. I'll follow you up, if that's all right." If it was Mihaela or one of the other hunters, she certainly didn't want the conversation overheard by any of the "paranormal object" collectors.

Dante gave her a wave of approval on his way out. Josh patted her shoulder and winked. Elizabeth moved toward the door in their wake, acknowledging that the number on the screen was new to her. She took it anyway.

"Hello?"

"Elizabeth."

She froze. "What the . . . ?"

"I said I'd call."

"I didn't think you meant—"

"I'm outside, on the terrace."

Where the hell was that? She'd just have to go out the front door and walk around the house until she found it.

"There's a French window," Saloman said from the phone, as if he'd read her thoughts, "behind the closed curtains. Just keep talking. No one will think it strange that you choose to take a call in private."

He was right, of course. Mumbling something, still holding the phone to her ear although he'd already rung off, she changed direction and slipped behind the red velvet curtain. The French door was open a crack, and she slipped easily out into the cool darkness, closing it firmly behind her.

The long northern evening had almost turned into night. Rain pattered on the canvas awning that covered the terrace and its few wooden tables and chairs. Beyond stretched a well-kept garden, rising outward and upward into the black, misty hills. In spite of herself, the beauty of her surroundings distracted her, and she was almost startled when a shadow detached itself from the wall of the house.

She caught her breath and moved to meet it. Her heart hammered in her breast; her stomach twisted in familiar pain and longing at the sight of him. A hundred questions tried to burst from her lips at once, but as soon as he was close enough, Saloman simply took her in his arms and kissed her.

Saloman's kisses were like a drug. And she'd been deprived of them for so long that surely she wouldn't have been human if she hadn't thrown her arms up around his neck and kissed him back.

The phone fell from her fingers to the ground with a dull thud. Elizabeth didn't care. His mouth delved deep, his tongue exciting hers to dance while his palms pressed on her back, drawing her closer in to his body. His full-on erection pressed into her abdomen, making her gasp into his mouth with triumph and longing. She seized his head between her hands, smoothing his soft hair, relearning the contours of his cool, distinctive face with her fingertips. She opened her mouth wider under the force of his kiss, welcoming the ferocity of his hunger because it matched her own.

She pressed against him, licking at his sharp, wicked teeth, sucking on his tongue, kissing him as if she could absorb him into herself. Between her thighs pooled warm, lustful wetness.

"Saloman," she whispered against his lips, and went back to kissing him. "I've missed you so much."

"So I see." He took back her mouth, more slowly now, but with a deliberate sensuality that devastated her.

"Oh, God," she said, trying to get a grasp on reality before she slid back into the haze of no return when sex, raw, exciting, and blissful, would be her only option. "What are you doing here, Saloman?"

"I'm kissing you. Caressing you." His hand slid around to close over her breast and a low moan escaped her.

"Why?" She gasped. "Did you come for Josh? Why do so many people think you're Adam Simon?"

Saloman paused, although he didn't release her. "I came for lots of reasons. To meet Dante, and Josh; to take what is mine; to kiss you again." Suiting the action to the word, he grew bolder, sliding his hand inside her dress to feel the aching, tender peak of her nipple. At the same time, he moved his groin against her, letting her feel the shape and hardness of his erection. Releasing her mouth, he added, "And they think I'm Adam Simon because I am. At least, I stole his papers to become him. The real Adam died as a baby around the time a man of my appearance might have been born."

Clutching his silk cravat for support, she stared into his face uncomprehendingly. "Why?"

"I needed to be someone. The way to power in this age is wealth. And so I am amassing it. Legally."

"So quickly?"

"It helped to have some stashed away. Gold is very valuable these days."

It shouldn't have hurt. She hadn't expected anything else. "So you haven't given it up. You still want to rule the whole world, not just the vampires."

"I never pretended anything else."

She pulled away from him, and yet was perversely sorry when he let her. Pushing her fingers through her hair, she tugged, and most of it tumbled loose around her neck and shoulders.

"Bugger," she muttered, seizing it and rolling it back up under the elastic ribbon. Saloman bent and picked up her fallen phone, reminding her of another question. "Since when do you have a mobile phone?"

"Since Dmitriu gave me one. He's right. They are very useful."

Dmitriu, the enigmatic vampire who had caused her to awaken Saloman, Saloman's own "child," one of the only two vampires he was known to have created. "Is he here too?" she asked.

"Dmitriu? No, he's back in Hungary."

"Do you have . . . support here?"

"Do you? Are there vampire hunters skulking behind the garden shed?"

"You know there aren't. You'd smell them at fifty paces."

"More." He held out the phone to her. She considered asking how he found out her number, but in the end there were too many more important issues, so she simply took it and dropped it back into her bag. "I am alone," he said.

"It makes no difference, does it? I can't warn anyone against you. They wouldn't believe me. I can just picture the senator's face."

"Our genial host," Saloman observed. "Very interesting man, but I certainly wouldn't trust him farther than Josh could throw him with one hand tied behind his back."

"He wants you on his side."

"I know he does. I don't suppose you do?"

Elizabeth frowned. "What?"

"Want me on your side," he said patiently. "Or by your side. On top of you, perhaps. Inside you, definitely."

"Saloman!" She had to stop him before her desire got the better of her and she hurled herself at him. She didn't know whether to run, or to seize him up against the wall and impale herself on him. Pride forbade the former; and fortunately, the remains of her common sense prevented the latter.

His mouth twisted at her half-angry, half-anguished cry. "I'll take that as a no."

She stared at him, her lust fading slowly back to the old, painful longing, barely understanding yet that she'd refused him again. His dark, knowing eyes bored into hers as if he could see her soul and all its conflicts. The bastard had always known exactly what he did to her. Except the love. He hadn't guessed that until she told him, thus casting and losing all her chances in one throw. It had won her a night of joy and a lifetime of sorrow.

"God, I hate self-pity," she said bitterly, and saw his lips curve into a smile, just as the French door moved with a creak, releasing a surge of talk and music from the drawing room, and Nicola Devon stepped out onto the terrace.

"Darling," she said at once, going right up to Saloman and taking his arm to reach up and kiss him briefly on the mouth. "We're about to play some poker. Are you in?"

Nicola's attention was all on him, but Saloman must have seen what her simple act did to Elizabeth. It seemed to be a day for those cartoon lightbulbs, for the belated discovery of things that should have been obvious from the start. Nicola was here as Saloman's partner, as Elizabeth was here as Josh's. But that familiarity, that kiss, told her everything else. He didn't even look surprised, just accepted it as his due. Because they were lovers.

It felt like a knife in her heart, twisting and twisting.

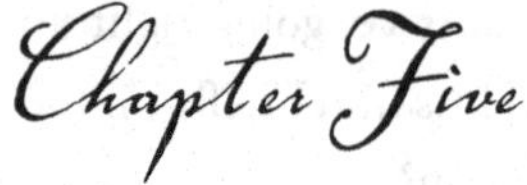

Chapter Five

She'd already fled the unbearable scene, and was back inside the house before she realized that what she wanted to do was run to the hills, away from everyone. Smiling, making some inane comment to the revelers and poker players who caught her eye as she passed through the drawing room, she escaped from there too. Only halfway up the staircase did she freeze in midstep, remembering that she should protect Nicola, not run away like a betrayed teenager.

Only, how the hell did she do that? *Oh, Nicola, you really should dump this guy—he's a vampire.*

Perhaps she knew and didn't care. Shit, perhaps she was one too.

I'd have felt that, sensed it. . . . Wouldn't I? Or am I too busy wallowing in my own stupid emotions to see what's under my nose? Again?

More slowly, Elizabeth continued upstairs. No, Nicola wasn't a vampire, and if Saloman wanted to drink from her, there was nothing Elizabeth could do to prevent it. She doubted he would kill anyone here and risk the Adam Simon identity he'd taken such trouble to build.

The hunters had to be told about Simon. If nothing else, it would make it easier to track him. And yet if she told them now, if local hunters arrived here to eliminate him. . . . They would probably fail, as the Hungarian hunters already had, but in any case she didn't think she could bear being the one to betray him.

Voices broke into her chaotic thoughts. With relief, she recognized Josh's among them, coming from behind a door on the first-floor landing, and remembered the antiques evaluations. She'd promised to be there, to see Josh's sword. Aside from her very real curiosity, it was probably also just what she needed, something else to think about for an hour. Maybe then she'd know what to do about Nicola and Saloman and Dante. And the sword itself, if it was truly Saloman's.

When she knocked lightly, the voices stopped immediately. Poking her head around the door, she saw six male heads all turned toward her. Although Josh grinned and at once stood up to welcome her, she could have sworn some of the other faces had expressed annoyance or even . . . anxiety.

Senator Dante's, however, was not one of those.

"Just in time!" he said jovially. "Come in and see my goblet. What do you think?"

They were seated at a round table—which would probably have been better for poker than the small occasional tables they were setting up downstairs in the big drawing room—in the center of which stood a gold goblet encrusted with gleaming stones and jewels.

"It's beautiful," Elizabeth said with awe. "It looks Anglo-Saxon."

"It is," Dante said modestly. "I bought it from a private collector. Apparently it was used in medieval times as a communion chalice, and really did turn wine into the blood of Christ."

In front of Dante, Josh's eyebrows flew up in comical disparagement.

Dante clapped him on the shoulder as the others made way for Elizabeth to join the proceedings. "Josh here doesn't believe a word of it," he said tolerantly.

"Well, I'd quite like to know how one identifies Christ's blood from anyone else's," Elizabeth remarked.

"I suspect that part of the story was assumption," Dante allowed. "At Holy Communion, Christ's blood would be expected."

Elizabeth looked closely at the cup. "But you believe the rest of the story?"

"I don't disbelieve it." He smiled as she cast a quick glance at him. "You find that odd?"

"Forgive me, it's none of my business," Elizabeth said lightly. Perhaps she was suffering from too many shocks this evening, but she decided to speak bluntly to her host. "I just find it strange that so distinguished a man as yourself—famous, I would add, for your Christian principles—is so interested in, and so open to, magical superstitions."

"It's not strange at all," Dante argued, although he didn't appear to be remotely upset. "I'm a spiritual man." Reaching out, he picked up the goblet and placed it in a box one of the antiquarians lifted from the floor onto the table. "Okay, Josh, bring on the sword!"

Josh shrugged and sauntered across the room toward the wall, where an untidy bundle lay. He picked it up as though it were a lot heavier than it looked and, as everyone made space, he dumped his burden on the table and began to unwrap it.

The wrapping was an old and musty woolen coat, an incongruous setting for the treasure that lay within. As Josh opened up the garment, careful not to touch the gleaming object thus revealed, Elizabeth gasped.

The sword was big, far larger and longer than the modern rapier she used in fencing lessons. Its ornate hilt was carved from shining gold and silver intertwined, forming an intricate pattern that looked like interlocking letter "S"s. A large, bloodred ruby embellished the very top of the hilt. The blade was clean, almost new-looking. Certainly there was nothing to show that the weapon had ever been used in anger. Or if it had, it had been very well cleaned and cared for afterward.

Like Elizabeth, every occupant in the room gazed at the object in stunned silence. Even Dante seemed overwhelmed by it. Josh, more inured to the sight, gave a lopsided smile as he scanned his companions.

"Yeah, it still gets me that way too," he remarked. "And I was brought up with it in the house."

"May I?" Dante asked reverently.

Josh waved one hand in permission, though he made no effort to touch the sword himself, even to push it nearer the senator.

"This," Dante said, gripping the hilt in both hands and raising it with obvious effort, "is the most beautiful piece I've ever seen."

Without taking his gaze from the sword, he held it up in front of his face, then let the sword fall back a little until the flat of the blade just touched his forehead. Elizabeth could understand that—she often got the urge to touch old objects, as if they could somehow bring her closer to the past, but Dante made it look almost religious. Then he passed the sword to Bill, who also stood to receive it.

"So what do you think?" Josh asked. "How old is it? Do you know where or who it came from originally? What's it worth?" He cast a quick grin at Dante. "Though I'm not selling."

Beyond him, Bill touched the upright sword to his forehead, just as Dante had done. To Elizabeth, it looked uncomfortably like worship. In fact, as Bill passed the weapon to the man beside him, it struck her that they were performing some bizarre ritual, and a tingle of unease passed down her spine.

"Old," Bill said vaguely. "Impossible to date accurately. This work on the hilt looks almost Byzantine, and yet not quite. I would say it's even older than that, and yet the carving is so fine. . . ."

"And the value?" Dante asked.

Bill shrugged. "Priceless." Then, presumably since Dante looked slightly annoyed, he added more carefully, "If Josh agrees to sell, he could ask any reasonable price. Its value is simply whatever it's worth to the individuals concerned."

Josh, watching it progress around the table, said dryly, "So basically, you know no more about it than I do?"

"It's definitely the one in the book," said the man who held it now.

"What book?" Elizabeth and Josh asked together.

The man touched it reverently to his forehead while Dante said, "One we saw in a private library. Your turn, Josh." His voice was clipped, as if not quite pleased.

"I'll pass," Josh said quickly, pushing his chair back.

"Do you want to hold it, Elizabeth?" Dante asked.

"Sure." Elizabeth stood up, reaching across Josh, who made a quick movement as if to prevent her, then shrugged with a half-embarrassed smile.

"It's heavy," warned the man who offered it to her.

Elizabeth nodded and wrapped both hands around the beautiful hilt, heaving it upright. Instantly, a thrill shot up her arm, excitement she could never suppress at actually touching something so old and so incredibly beautiful.

And yet the tingling didn't fade as it should. Instead, it galloped through her whole body like an electric shock. The force of it jerked her backward and she fell, knocking over her chair. Her hands around the hilt seemed to burn and yet she couldn't open her fingers. Josh's anxious face swam in front of hers, flanked by Dante's and Bill's. The noise of their questions grew momentarily louder, as if they were yelling in her ear.

"Elizabeth, what is it?"

"Are you hurt?"

"What's wrong?"

"Are you ill?"

And then they blended and faded into a different noise, the cry of a thousand voices, scraping metal, and screaming horses. A blur of motion filled her eyes. There was only blood and a hand she knew all too well, wielding the sword in front of her. Another face swam before her, dark and beautiful and terrifying in its familiarity.

I am Saloman. Give me my sword.

Elizabeth cried out. The sword seemed to be wrenched from her fingers, and Josh was saying her name over and over.

He held both her hands, anxiety and guilt almost splitting his pale, handsome face. Behind him, Dante held the sword, but was looking at her with a bright, piercing gaze that went far beyond inquisitive or even speculative. In her shock, she imagined he wanted to consume her.

Josh was opening her tightly closed fist, and at his indrawn breath she glanced down at her red, blistering palm. No wonder it hurt like hell, she thought vaguely.

"Too far, Dante," Josh said, and she'd never heard him speak like that before—icy, harsh, full of barely suppressed rage. "Much too fucking far." He put his arm around her waist, urging her onto her trembling feet. "Out of my way," he snarled at someone, and then as they made their stumbling way across the room: "Open the door.

"I'm sorry, Elizabeth," he ground out as they began to climb the stairs. "I never thought he would do that, not to you."

Neither did I. Ungrateful bastard. I awakened him, too. . . .

Elizabeth shook herself, shooting a quick glance at Josh to make sure she hadn't spoken aloud. Too late, it came to her that they were blaming different people.

"Come on, I'll dress your hands, and then I'll take you to the hospital."

Elizabeth frowned. "I have to talk to you, Josh."

"In here," he said, opening her bedroom door, and not releasing her until she sat on the bed. "I'll get some water."

"No, wait." She grabbed his hands to stop him from rising. "Josh, you have to listen to me." She closed her eyes to shut out his anxiety and her own. *I've come to take back what is mine.* "That sword, your sword, belongs to Saloman, the vampire I told you about in Edinburgh."

"Oh, for God's sake, this is no time for—"

"Josh, you saw what it did to me!"

"I saw what Dante did to you," he said grimly. "He did the same thing to me the night I first showed him the damned sword. I thought at the time I was just drunk and imagining things, because in the morning there was no sign of any burn marks. But now I know it was Dante. He wants the sword and he'll go to any lengths to get it, even doing this to you."

Elizabeth opened her eyes to stare at him. "You think it was some conjuring trick? Even though the same thing happened to you?"

"Dante was present on both occasions," Josh said dryly. "And trust me, I've held that sword many times, and only when Dante was present has anything like this ever occurred!"

"Because he's awake," Elizabeth whispered.

"Who's awake?" Josh asked helplessly.

"Saloman. I wakened him. Before that, the sword didn't care where it was. Now he's awake and he wants it back. . . ." She focused on him. "When it burned you, when was that?"

Josh dragged his fingers through his hair. "Last year. Autumn, maybe."

"And before that, when was the last time you'd touched it?"

"God, I don't know, years ago, possibly."

Elizabeth nodded. "And between last autumn and now, how often did you touch it?"

Josh's gaze fell away. "Actually touch it with my bare hands?" When Elizabeth nodded again, he sighed. "Never. To be honest, my experience with Dante left me with a dislike of touching it. I carry it, wrap it, and unwrap it in the coat without ever laying hands directly on it."

"There you are, then," Elizabeth said flatly. "Don't you ask yourself why all those other people can touch it, yet you and I can't?"

"Because Dante wants it!" Josh exclaimed. "He tried to tell me in New York that it's some kind of warning, that it's not right for the sword to be with me. As if it 'wants' to be with him!"

"Or any of those other men. It's not like that at all. The sword attacked us because we're the descendants of Tsigana. Her blood, the blood of Saloman's killers, flows in our veins. The sword recognized that. We're its enemies."

"Elizabeth, *please* don't talk such bollocks, not tonight. Just let me see to your hands."

As he spoke, he turned them over in his and opened the palms. A few of her fingertips were still red and there was a sore-looking patch on her right palm. But there was no sign now of the blister she'd seen forming right after the incident.

Josh said, "It doesn't look as bad as I thought."

"I heal quickly. So do you. You must have noticed that."

"I've been lucky enough never to hurt myself very badly."

"Stop fighting it, Josh. It doesn't change what you are. Be grateful that Tsigana's crime brought you some good. Even if the worst does outweigh that somewhat."

"The worst being?" Josh inquired, with the air of merely humoring her.

"That Saloman will drink your blood and kill you. As I said before, your blood is particularly valuable to him. And, Josh . . ."

He'd leapt to his feet with more than a hint of impatience, but at her plea, he did at least glance back to her. She gazed helplessly back at him. When it came down to it, she just couldn't give Saloman away, even to a man who didn't believe in him.

"Dante," she said aloud, frowning. "Does Dante know what it is? Why does he want the sword so much?"

Josh shrugged. "He's an obsessive collector. And in case you didn't notice, although he's a nice guy most of the time, he doesn't like to lose. Men don't get to be as powerful as he is by losing."

"Does he know about Saloman?"

Josh frowned, as if trying to remember. "I told him what my father called it—the Sword of Solomon—and he got quite excited."

"Solomon, Saloman. It's the same name, really. I expect it just got corrupted over the many generations the sword's been in your family.

But seriously, he doesn't know what he's dealing with here." She needed to speak to Mihaela. And Saloman himself.

Her stomach twisted as she remembered their last encounter. But she couldn't go there. This was about more than hurt pride.

She said abruptly, "I don't think you should have the sword anywhere near you."

His lips twisted. "You're not going to tell me to give it to Dante, are you?"

"No, I don't think he should have it either, but at least he isn't a descendant." *So far as I know* . . . "Couldn't you keep it in a bank vault or something? Or maybe *I* should look after it, just until I find out what we should do about it."

Josh sighed, looking at her fixedly. After a moment, he came back and sat down on the bed beside her. "Elizabeth, I like you, insane and muddled as you are, but you'd better understand this at once. It's not up to you to decide what to do about the sword. It's mine."

No, it isn't. You only think it is. She said abruptly, "You saw him too, didn't you? Saloman. When you touched the sword. Didn't he say his name? Didn't he remind you of anyone?" *Like Adam Simon?*

"He reminded me I shouldn't drink so much."

She regarded him. "Has anyone ever told you you're just thrawn?"

He grinned. "Can't say they have. Is it good?"

"In these circumstances, no. It means a particularly annoying kind of stubborn. I wish you'd trust me on this."

"Trust *me*, it's Dante," he countered. "And first thing in the morning, we're leaving. I meant what I said; he really has gone too far, and I'm damned if I'll have anything more to do with him."

"It wasn't Dante," she said, almost automatically, but he'd stood up and didn't seem to be listening.

"Have you got some burn cream for your hands?"

"They'll be fine by the morning. I'll put a wet cloth on my palm overnight. Let's sleep on the rest."

"Good night, Elizabeth." At the door, he paused again and glanced back over his shoulder, almost apologetically. "You and Adam Simon, are you—"

"We're not even friends," she interrupted. "Good night, Josh."

"Where's the sword?" Josh demanded. Discovering the smaller sitting room empty and his sword gone, he finally confronted Dante, about to enter the drawing room on the ground floor.

Dante paused, his hand resting on the door handle. "I put it in the safe with my own stuff. How's Elizabeth?"

"As shocked and injured as you might expect."

"One phone call and I can get her a nurse or even a doctor to look after her."

"Yeah I know, you probably could." Reluctantly, he added, "It doesn't seem to be as bad as I first thought. But that doesn't alter the fact that you were *fucking* out of line."

"Don't swear, Josh. Maybe I was remiss, considering what it already did to you, but it seems I didn't have all the facts. Who is that girl? Is she really your cousin?"

"Sort of. Distantly. Don't change the subject!"

"Oh, I'm not, believe me. I'm as anxious as you are to get to the bottom of this. Does *she* want the sword?"

"No, she doesn't want the damned sword!" Frustrated, Josh dragged his hand through his hair and glared at the senator, whose face displayed only concern and an anxiety Josh could have sworn was genuine.

"Good," Dante said, nodding. "Because I don't think either of you should have it."

"Why the hell not?" Josh demanded.

"Because it hurts you," Dante said dryly. "Or had you forgotten that?"

"No, I haven't forgotten that, or the fact that you were there on both occasions!"

Dante shrugged. "Luck. And Elizabeth, what does she say happened?"

Josh waved an impatient hand. "Some nonsense about our descendant killing the original owner of the sword and the sword recognizing us. Have you been talking to her? Shit, you haven't set me up, have you?"

Josh froze with his hand halfway to his hair again, staring at Dante as the suspicion rose and spread.

"Of course not. I wasn't aware of her existence. But she intrigues me. She appeared to be a skeptic earlier, and yet now she's attributing magical powers to the sword. Who did she say it belonged to?"

"Saloman," Josh said reluctantly, letting his arm fall to his side.

Dante's eyes flashed. "That's close to what your father told you. And how does she know about Saloman?"

Josh shrugged. "Research. It's her specialty. She believes he really was a vampire." As soon as he spoke the words, he wished them unsaid. It felt like betraying Elizabeth's little eccentricities. Dante, even now that Josh was so angry with him, just had a habit of calming you down and making you talk. Of making you believe he'd done nothing wrong. And yet in this case, if Dante hadn't done it, then who had?

"And why," Dante asked softly, "would she think that?"

"Oh, this ridiculous fantasy that she awakened him. She'll have met some other trickster like you."

"Josh, Josh, the world is not so full of tricksters." The senator patted his arm, and yet Josh could see his mind was elsewhere, on something that excited him far more than this conversation. Irritated, Josh jerked away from him.

"It doesn't matter," he said flatly. "We'll be leaving early in the morning and I'll need the sword."

Dante sighed, turning the handle of the door. "If you insist. I'm always up early. Why don't you come and play some poker? Adam's taking us all to the cleaners."

. . .

Saloman. Saloman, speak to me!

It was no good. Although the house was quiet and she had no difficulty at all in filling her mind with the ancient vampire, he was blocking her efforts to reach him telepathically. Well, she had no time for his games.

Scrambling off the bed, still fully dressed in her elegant evening gown with her favorite sweater pulled over the top for warmth—it was a drafty old house—she left her room with grim determination to track him down. Part of her knew she was wasting her time—unless he chose to "broadcast" his presence, she hadn't a hope in hell of finding him, especially if he was outside, hunting. However, by eliminating the bedrooms she knew to be occupied by other people, because they'd told her in idle conversation that evening or because she'd seen people coming and going from them, she managed to narrow Saloman's down to one of four.

A couple of pale night-lights shone from the ceiling. At the end of the corridor, a tall window with open curtains let in what feeble starlight could wink between the clouds. Elizabeth padded the length of the hall and back again, wishing she had a vampire's ability to "sense" presence. She tried to build on the warning of danger she'd felt just before the vampire attacked her in St. Andrews last autumn, letting her mind search out a similar presence. But this was Saloman. . . .

In the end, she chose the old-fashioned method and simply put her ear to each possible door. She eliminated another bedroom immediately, since she could hear outrageous snoring, and she couldn't imagine Saloman making so uncivilized a noise—supposing he ever slept.

At the second door, she heard nothing at all. At the third, two women talking, amid the clink of glasses and the odd giggle. She thought one of them might have been Jerri Cusack. And at the fourth, which she had already guessed to be the largest, corner room, she heard Nicola Devon saying, "How's that?" in a low, teasing voice.

Elizabeth drew back at once, clutching the sweater over her heart, where it felt as if someone were twisting a knife. It wasn't Nicola's room; she already knew hers was on the next floor. But Dante was "courting" Adam Simon; he'd have given him one of the largest bedrooms. Could even Saloman go straight from kissing her to screwing Nicola?

It didn't matter. She should be more concerned about him *biting* Nicola, about what the hell was going on with that sword that had blasted her across Dante's sitting room. And yet she was physically and socially incapable of reaching out to open the door.

She closed her eyes. *Saloman, I need to talk to you. Come out.*

The words bounced back at her. She stepped back, waiting, but all she heard was a very real feminine squeak and a creak of the bed. Defeated, Elizabeth turned and trailed back to her bedroom.

She felt as if she were letting everyone down. What if she was wrong about Saloman behaving in a discreet and circumspect manner? What if he decided he didn't care and went on a feeding frenzy?

The image of a shark with Saloman's face swam into her mind, bringing a sour, unhappy smile to her lips. For now, she'd phone Mihaela in Budapest, see what was known about Saloman's sword. At least then she might gain more insight into his plans and work out what the hell she could do to combat them.

She turned the handle of her bedroom door and walked in. Immediately, her heart plunged in fear. In the shadows behind the bedside lamp, which was the only light in the room, stood the tall, dark figure of a man.

Saloman.

Saloman knew she was there, on the other side of his bedroom door. In spite of everything, including the fact that the seminaked Nicola was doing her very best to seduce him as he lay on the bed, he willed Elizabeth to come in. He even unlocked the door with his mind, careless of the consequences of her discovering him like this. Part of him wanted her to see, to suffer. Part of him just wanted her with him.

Nicola's hand slid under his silk robe and swept down his body. In the passage outside, Elizabeth waited, hesitating. Saloman rolled Nicola off him and she squeaked with delight as he pinned her underneath him. He felt Elizabeth calling, but didn't answer, didn't let her in. Instead, he reached out to her in secret, and felt a wave of desolation and anxiety so powerful that it shocked him.

He rose from the bed, as if he'd always meant merely to clamber over Nicola to the other side. Perhaps he had.

"Go back to your own room," he advised. "You're tired."

He opened and closed the bedroom door so quickly that it would have been a blur to Nicola, if she could see through her outrage. Saloman didn't much care. At the other end of the passage, Elizabeth walked the last few paces to her room, her shoulders drooping as if with defeat.

Saloman ran after her and, when she opened the door, slipped past her to stand by the window in the lamp's shadow. A boy's trick, but it did no harm to remind her of his power. And it gave him ample opportunity to watch the play of expressions across her face—shock and fear, relief, and then fear again, all mixed up now with the emotions she refused to give in to. Saloman wanted to make her acknowledge them; he wanted to throw her on the bed and lose himself in her heat and softness.

"Never lurk outside a vampire's door," he said mildly. "It's taken as an invitation."

She swallowed. "Good," she said, closing the door behind her and leaning on it. "I need to talk to you. There's a sword here. It's been in Josh's family for generations and I think it's yours."

Saloman waited.

"Is it?" she snapped, with a hint of impatience.

"Of course it is."

"And that's why you're here? To take the sword?"

"I told you there were many reasons. I even recited some of them."

"You missed Nicola."

He admired the dry tone she managed, mixed even with a hint of humor. If it weren't for the pain in her lovely, too-open hazel eyes, he might even have believed her.

He walked toward her, soaking up the alarm in her face, the stiffening of her shoulders as she prepared to resist him. But he didn't touch her, merely halted a foot from her.

"What's the matter? Did you think because you sent me away I should remain celibate for the rest of my very long life? Or at least for the length of yours?"

She stared at him an instant longer, before her eyelids closed, hiding the pain. "I have no right to expect or to ask anything of you. But I need to know about the sword."

"It's mine. That's all you need to know."

"How dangerous is it?"

"You know."

Her eyelids snapped up again, revealing wide-eyed indignation. Slowly, he reached out and took both her hands. They jumped in his, as if she'd pull them free; then she was still, letting him turn the palms upward and gaze on the raw, red skin. Tsigana's blood flowing in her veins healed her quickly, and yet she must still have hurt.

He lifted her right hand to his lips and kissed the palm, running his tongue delicately across the injured skin. It was good to taste her again, to inhale the scent of lemon flowers and vanilla and something intangible that was peculiarly Elizabeth.

She gasped, tugging away from him once more, but he held her firm and took the first injured finger into his mouth, swirling his tongue around the burned tip.

"I don't need your help!" she raged.

He released her finger and turned to the next. "Yes, you do. You're already angry that I didn't offer it earlier. For what it's worth, I thought you'd come to my room to ask."

"Then it's fortunate I didn't, since you were otherwise engaged!" She bit her lip, obviously angry with herself.

Saloman smiled around her third finger, then licked the fourth. He could hear her heart pounding, took pleasure in watching the rapid rise and fall of her breasts under the sweater that should have looked ridiculous with her evening gown and yet didn't. He could smell her sweet, heady blood, wanted to draw it into his own watering mouth. He contented himself with licking her skin.

Without releasing her right hand, he lowered it and raised the left instead. The burns were less severe here; only her fingertips seemed damaged and a tiny patch on the base of her wrist.

"Nicola," she said, gasping, as if trying to focus on something other than his mouth. He twisted his tongue around her middle finger, licking far more than the injured spot, and sucked it into his mouth before releasing it.

"What about her?" he asked without interest.

"She's besotted with you. I saw it in her face. Let her go; don't hurt her."

Saloman smiled and closed her fists. "Don't worry about Nicola. Dante hired her to spy on me."

He loved the way her lips parted in shock. He wanted to kiss them, pull her so close against him that he could feel those beautiful breasts pressing into his chest. He wanted to lay her on the bed and undress her with exquisite care before seducing her and fucking her and biting her to pliant, willing insanity.

So when he felt the drifting of the sword, he didn't move.

The sword had been in a downstairs room when Elizabeth had touched it. A little later, it had been moved, but not very far. Now Saloman could feel the distance between him and it increasing.

"Dante? Why would Dante spy on you?" Elizabeth demanded.

"To find out my next move. Adam's next move."

"And Nicola . . . Why don't you just send her away?"

"Because I might get hungry."

"Stop it!" She dragged her hands free and tried to push past him, but he wouldn't let her, just stood immovably in her path until she gave up. "Something's off about Dante. He knows too much, believes too much of this stuff, and his friends are like some sort of cult. Does he know about you?"

"Not yet." Saloman considered. "But you're right. Dante is a most interesting person. He has incredible power, in the human sense of the word. All the power of money and success, of political and social connections. Some people say he's the most powerful man in the world because he holds sway over the president of the United States. Whichever happens to be in office."

"Then what's he doing here? What does he want? Apart from your sword."

"That's what I'd like to know." Saloman's sensitive ears picked up a car starting in the distance and then the sword began to fade fast from his senses. Instinctively, he stepped past Elizabeth to the door and laid his fingers on the handle. The sword was being stolen, which suited him just fine. He could catch whoever it was on the road and retrieve it and no one would ever connect it with Adam Simon.

"Saloman." The quick, desperate word was wrung from her, forcing him to turn. She looked so beautiful and so lost that his heart seemed to break all over again. "I thought it would be different," she whispered. "I used to dream of meeting you again, some chance encounter that would give each of us a moment of happiness. I never thought—"

She broke off and turned away from him. The sword was disappearing into the misty night. He could barely maintain the connection.

He said, "You never thought what?" He closed the distance between them, turning her back to face him. "That things between us would not be exactly as they were when we parted? That life would not have moved on?"

She closed her eyes, as if she could thus hide the tear squeezing out of one corner. Saloman took her face between his hands, brushed the tear with his thumb. "You have to live with the decisions you make. Pain does not invalidate them."

"I know. I was prepared for pain, just not . . ." *Jealousy.* The word hovered between them, unspoken. "Indifference," she finished.

Saloman listened to the beat of his own heart. It was much slower than hers, and yet for several moments, they seemed to beat in perfect time. Because he couldn't help it, he brushed his lips across her smooth forehead, inhaled the perfume of her skin and her hair. He knew he could take her now, bury himself in her soft, passionate body until dawn, granting release and joy to them both. He ached for it, burned for it with an intensity that drove him nearer, pressing into the sweet contours of her body.

"There was never indifference," he said low. Her eyes opened wide, staring deep into his with yearning and blind, powerful lust. Oh, yes, he could take her, thrust into her now before their bodies even hit the bed and she'd wrap herself around him and pull him in with rapture.

But it would change nothing.

Her gaze dropped to his lips. He smiled, because he couldn't trust himself to kiss her and still leave her. But not for the first time, she surprised him. She stood on tiptoe and kissed him, just as she had the instant after trying to kill him, the instant before she confessed to loving him.

But that had been a kiss of desperation, a spontaneous outpouring of emotion. This was one of hot, blatant seduction. Her lips brushed his and fastened fiercely. Her tongue swept into his mouth, as if trying to absorb all of him. She sucked on his tongue until he snapped and took control, bending her backward with the force of his lust, plundering her mouth as his hands possessed her body, roving over her breasts and hips and thighs.

His robe came undone with her writhing and she moaned into his mouth as her hands encountered his naked flesh. She was his, as she'd always been his.

And his fucking her would not make her happy. Not for longer than the fucking lasted.

He straightened, drawing her with him, still kissing her, but more slowly now, until he could part their mouths and give her air.

Gently, he laid his forehead against hers. "Even valid decisions can be changed."

She stared into his eyes, hope and temptation chasing each other across her expressive face. Slowly, longing gave way to the determination he'd seen all too often before.

She swallowed and stepped out of his arms. "Only for valid reasons."

Saloman inclined his head. Whatever conclusion she reached, at least she would think again about their parting.

And his sword, damn it to hell, had gone well beyond his tracking range. "You'll excuse me," he murmured, walking across the room to the window and pulling back the curtains, "if I use the alternative exit."

"Why? Are you leaving?" she asked, bewildered.

"I'm hunting," he said, opening the casement wide and leaping onto the sill.

"Saloman," she began warningly, then seemed to run out of words. Saloman launched himself through the window into the cool night air. Before his feet touched the ground, he was running in the direction he'd last sensed the sword.

"Can't I even give you breakfast before you leave?" Dante pleaded.

"No, thank you," Josh replied, still with that grimness he'd used last night after the sword incident. "Just the sword. We need to get going."

Josh had roused her so early that she felt she'd never been asleep. She'd lain awake for hours, listening for any sounds that might indicate Saloman had come back to the house. She knew she should be anxious about whatever or whoever he was hunting out there, but in reality she was just pleased he wasn't going after anyone she knew. Like Josh. Or Nicola. And selfishly, secretly, she wanted to sleep under the same roof as Saloman, wallowing in the heady mixture of excitement and perverse security his presence always brought her.

And now, as Dante led the way upstairs to a study where he said the safe was, she became conscious of even more conflicting emotions. She was both glad and sorry to be leaving here early, before she encountered Saloman again—or worse, Saloman with Nicola, whom he'd accused of spying for Dante.

Just inside the door of the study, Dante stopped dead. Josh actually bumped into him before apologizing with a hint of irritation.

"That's weird," Dante said, striding across the room. "The door's open."

Following them in, Elizabeth saw that the door of a large safe stood wide-open.

Dante almost fell to his knees, rummaging inside. "My God," he said in tones of disbelief. "It's gone! I've been robbed. . . ."

"What's gone?" Josh demanded harshly. "Where's my sword?"

"Gone." Dante sat back on his heels. "It's gone, Josh. Along with my goblet."

"Impossible!" Josh exclaimed. "Who could possibly have stolen them? This isn't New York City! There isn't even a village here! Who the hell would rob you?"

Who the hell, indeed?

Quietly, Elizabeth slipped out of the room and hastened along the passage to the stairs. Her heart drummed like a rabbit's as she ran up and along the hallway to Saloman's room. This time, uncaring whether Nicola was there, she entered without knocking.

"Come in," said Saloman's deep voice in some amusement.

Although the curtains still shut out the bright, early morning sunshine, there was more than enough light for her to appreciate the sight of him lying on top of his bed like some large, predatory cat, watching her with one hand tucked behind his head. At least he wore more than last night's black silk robe. In fact, apart from socks, he appeared to be fully dressed in black trousers and a loose-sleeved shirt.

Elizabeth, ignoring the leap of lust in her stomach, swung the door closed behind her. "You took it, didn't you?" she said without preamble.

"Took what?"

"Josh's sword!"

"You mean my sword." He crossed his legs, acknowledging her irritation only by a faint twitch of his lips. "Actually, I didn't. Someone made off with it while I was talking to you. By the time I, er, gave chase, it was too far away. I couldn't track it."

There was no way to be sure he was telling the truth. Except that he generally disdained to lie.

Slowly, she sank down on the bed beside him. "Really?"

"Really." His black, opaque eyes gazed steadily into hers. Just looking at him made her heart turn over. In the half-light he seemed more beautiful than ever, his dramatic black hair tumbled around his almost-sculpted face with its broad bones and shadowed hollows. Without even raising his head from the pillow, he managed to look sexier than any other man she'd ever seen, on- or offscreen.

Trying to focus, she said, "Then who did take it? Where is it?"

"I haven't a clue," he confessed.

She frowned. "Aren't you angry?"

"I think your Josh is angry enough for all of us."

"I think he suspects Dante himself."

"He's almost certainly right." Saloman sat up with one of his sudden, graceful movements and swung his legs off the bed. Elizabeth sprang to her feet to avoid being too close to him. She wanted to hold him too much, was afraid to get too near him.

"I've got to go," she muttered, almost running toward the door, where she paused and turned. "Saloman? You won't hurt Josh, will you?"

His lip curled. "What in the world makes you think that?"

On a bleak piece of waste ground in Queens, the vampire Severin faced his rival in the darkness, and laughed.

"You really don't have a clue, do you?" he said, sweeping his gaze from Travis to the bodyguards and followers lined up behind him. "I've spoken to him, and trust me, our differences no longer matter. Saloman has more power in his little finger than you and I will ever muster between us."

Travis, who'd looked slightly irritated by Severin's laughter, now pushed his trilby hat farther back on his head and grinned. "So, what, you've come to me for protection?"

Travis's followers hooted. Severin's vampires growled in response, and Severin realized afresh the risk he'd taken in coming here to New York. Probably it was this obvious risk that had brought Travis to meet him so quickly. Jacob, the unaligned vampire who'd carried his civil message to Travis in the first instance, now sat quite literally on the fence some distance away, picking his teeth while the levels of posturing and aggression increased. As if he were hanging around to watch the inevitable fight.

Well, it wasn't inevitable, and the stakes were too high for him to be drawn into a senseless battle that could ruin everything.

Severin strove for calm. "You couldn't protect yourself," he insisted. "Not from him. I came from LA to suggest we lay our differences aside and welcome him to America."

Travis stared at him. "*Welcome* him? Like some bloody messiah?"

"Yes," Severin said eagerly. "He's got vision, Travis, and he's been making changes all across Europe and Asia. Things could be so much better for us—"

"Trouble is," Travis interrupted, "I like things fine just the way they are. You want to hand your operation over to me, that's good. But I'm not giving anything to this Saloman."

Maggie stepped forward from behind Severin, exclaiming, "He's an *Ancient*! How exactly do you propose to stop him?"

"I'll think of something if and when he gets here," Travis drawled.

He really was a stupid shit. Severin dragged his hand across his forehead, just as Travis, with a more enthusiastic glint in his eye, added, "Unless you actually came to propose an alliance *against* him?"

"Not against him," Severin said evenly.

"Too scared, huh?"

The vampires behind them began to mutter aggressively. Again, Severin stilled the rumble with an impatient wave of his hand.

"Of Saloman? Maybe *you* should be scared, Travis. I didn't have to come here; I could just have let Saloman wipe you out."

"So, what, you want to impress the new boss by our cordiality?" Travis said disbelievingly. "Get kudos from him by talking me around? Exactly how much of an idiot do you take me for?" He strode forward and his vampires immediately came after him. "An Ancient isn't a *god*. He *can* be beaten!"

"But he shouldn't be," Severin argued. "At least, not this one."

"So you're just going to lie down for the guy? Shit, I never liked you, Severin, but I never thought you lacked backbone before!"

He should have known better, Severin thought savagely, than to have come here and expected a sensible discussion with this fool who couldn't see past the nose on his face, who cared for nothing except his stupid gambling joint. And now there had been too many insults for Severin to overlook in front of his followers. Already, Maggie was gazing at him with a mixture of outrage and worry.

"That's funny," Severin said deliberately. "I never thought you lacked quite so much brain before."

That should do it, he thought resignedly. Maybe they could talk after the fight instead.

Travis smiled and pushed at his hat once more. It was so far back now that Severin couldn't see how it still clung to his head.

"Then get the hell off my territory," Travis said softly, taking another step forward. One more and he'd be in Severin's face. To avoid that, Maggie placed herself squarely in Travis's path. Travis raked her luscious body with his eyes and he grinned. "Though you can leave your whore, if you like."

Maggie hit him. Or at least she tried to. Travis was too fast and managed to duck, laughing. Severin yanked her away. "Take that back, you piece of shit," he said between his teeth.

"All right," Travis said, straightening, a grin just dying on his careless lips. Only a malevolent flash in his blue eyes betrayed his intention. "*All* of you, *including* your whore, get off my territory."

The growl of discontent among the vampires on both sides quieted for an instant as Severin and Travis glared at each other. No one gave the order in the end; no one needed to. In a single motion, Severin and Travis leapt into the air and crashed together. Over Travis's shoulder as each tried to tear ritually at the other's neck, Severin watched with a sort of resigned anxiety as the other vampires flew at one another.

Only as he and Travis fell back to earth, already disengaging for the more serious fight below, did he notice Maggie, in the midst of it, swinging her stake with a vicious accuracy that turned one of Travis's followers to dust.

But Severin's pride in her was short-lived. She staggered under the blow of a fist, and as she fell, a stake stabbed downward and Maggie exploded into nothing. Severin cried out in grief and fury. Kill the bastards!" he yelled. There could be no talking now. "Let the streets of New York run with blood!" For Maggie, his lover, who'd believed in Saloman.

After the bizarre weekend among the rich, famous, and influential, Elizabeth found that marking a couple of late essays on Monday morning was something of a welcome relief.

Promising to stay in touch, Josh had dropped her off in St. Andrews with no more than a cousinly kiss on the cheek, and she was aware that only good manners had prevented him from ranting about the stolen sword for the entire journey. Abandoning his proposed holiday in Scotland, he was flying down to London today, no doubt to be nearer Senator Dante, whom, despite all evidence to the contrary, he still suspected of the theft.

Elizabeth had e-mailed Mihaela a request for information on the sword, together with a brief description of recent events and a stark announcement that Saloman was in Scotland in probable pursuit of it and of Josh. By now, the British hunters should be aware of Saloman's presence in the UK, though she doubted they'd know any more than she did about his precise location.

Apart from that, she was making a determined effort to move on from the weekend. When the knock came at her office door, she expected one of her students and called, "Come in!" at once.

The figure who stepped over the threshold was a complete surprise.

"Senator." She almost gasped, springing to her feet. Annoyingly, she felt like a schoolgirl whose formidable headmaster had just walked in the door.

Senator Dante smiled as he crossed the room to her, hand held out. "How are you, Elizabeth?" His handshake was as firm and warm as she remembered it. "I hope I'm not interrupting anything. I'm on my way back to London—decided to take a quick detour here for a round of golf. Can I talk you into a game?"

"Oh, no! No, thank you. I'm working."

"Of course you are," he said regretfully, looking around her untidy office with its scattering of books and papers and coffee cups on the tables, and the shelves of books that lined the walls. "Quaint," he observed.

"Messy," she corrected, and he laughed. "I've got time for a coffee, if you'd like one," she offered.

"Oh, no, thank you. I'll get one at the clubhouse after my game. I really just called in to say hello again. It was great meeting you at the weekend."

"And you," Elizabeth said politely. "Thanks for inviting me."

"My pleasure. You're a most intriguing young woman."

Elizabeth blinked. "I am?"

The smiling blue eyes were steady. "You know you are. I'm in the presence of the Awakener, am I not?"

Elizabeth sat down slowly, heart and mind racing. She played for time while trying to straighten her thoughts. "I'm not sure what you mean."

"You told Josh you awakened Saloman."

Straight from the hip. They did say the senator was a straight-talking man. She said, "I didn't realize Josh paid attention to anything I said on that score."

"Josh can always surprise you. How in the world did you do it?"

She dropped her gaze, wondering if she could avoid the question. But it was too late for that. Dante was a believer. Worse, he seemed to know of the legendary Saloman.

"By accident," she managed to say ruefully. "My finger was jagged by a thorn and I dripped blood on his so-called tomb. If you believe that sort of thing, it worked because I'm descended from his original 'killer.'"

"You must have been terrified."

"I've never been more frightened in my life." That, she could say with complete candor.

"He didn't kill you," Dante observed.

"I think," Elizabeth said, "he was too weak at the time. I bolted."

"A wise precaution." Amusement as well as admiration seeped into his smile. "So where is Saloman now?"

You mean since he left your house? "I haven't the foggiest idea. Probably Eastern Europe, where most of his kind are found."

The senator continued to gaze into her eyes, blinking so seldom that it made her thoroughly uncomfortable. Worse, his eyes were sharp and perceptive, and Elizabeth had too much to hide. She went on the offensive.

"You amaze me more at each encounter, Senator. You should be calling me batty, not believing what I tell you about vampires—which I'll have to deny in public, by the way. I have a very precarious reputation as a serious academic to preserve."

Dante's smile came back. "I'll keep your secret, if you keep mine."

"Sure," Elizabeth agreed, relieved that the senator seemed ready to leave.

"I'm sure we'll meet again," he observed. "Interests such as ours are rare. We have to stick together."

Elizabeth smiled and offered her hand again. "Good-bye, Senator. Thanks for dropping in. Enjoy your golf."

"Oh, I will, I will."

From the window, she watched him climb into his large, sleek car and be driven off down South Street.

"Now, what," she murmured to herself, "was that all about?"

. . .

From the roof of his London hotel, Saloman was irritated to witness the young vampire, Del, stalking the waitress who'd served Saloman earlier in the evening—in more ways than one. Having accepted the wine she'd brought to him and his new business associate in the hotel bar, Saloman had followed her into the quiet passage between public and staff entrances. She'd seemed glad enough to be accosted, and her blood was good. Saloman had taken care, as he always did, to seal both wound and memory, and the girl had still been smiling at him in a coquettish sort of way when he'd finally left the bar.

Although young, Del was more than a fledgling, perfectly capable of controlling his hunger to the point where he didn't kill the girl. On the other hand, by now he should also have smelled Saloman on her and backed off to look for other prey. And so Saloman watched him leap on the girl, clap his hand over her mouth, and sink his fangs into her throat, no doubt right over her other healing bite. The girl struggled, her legs kicking uselessly, trying in vain to scream for help.

Saloman had seen enough. Although it was easy for him to access the thoughts of most beings, he generally didn't, partly because reading everyone's thoughts all the time was a quick road to insanity, and partly because he generally respected people's rights of privacy. In this case, only one thought could save the attacking vampire's life, and Saloman was pretty sure he wouldn't find it. He didn't.

Saloman stepped off the roof. Before the idiot vampire had even registered his presence, Saloman landed on the ground behind him and jerked him away from his victim, who stumbled back into the wall, falling onto her weakened knees.

Del's eyes were wide with more than fear. It wouldn't save him.

"Saloman," he whispered. "I didn't kill her! I didn't!"

"She's barely alive. You took her to defy me, to make some display to the others because you thought I'd gone. I'm never gone. Learn the lesson." The last was for the local vampire community, whom he was admitting to the show telepathically. It was too late for Del to learn anything, for Saloman, ignoring his demented struggles, dragged him close and bit into his flesh until the body exploded to dust in his hold.

That done, he went to the almost unconscious girl. Her head lolled when he moved her, but though she whimpered with fear, she gasped in welcome when he covered her wound with his mouth. It was harder to find and oust the frightening memories from her traumatized and untidy mind, but rummaging deep, he healed the worst of them and left her sleeping in relative peace in the doorway. One of the hotel staff would discover her soon enough.

Next time, Saloman announced to the awestruck community he'd made his own, *police yourselves. I trust I've made my point.*

There was no dissent, not even in the recesses of the stronger vampire minds. Satisfied, Saloman leapt onto a third-floor windowsill and made his way around to his own room.

Stepping inside, he registered the insistent knocking on his bedroom door. Nicola Devon's scent drifted in to him, and he sighed as he brushed the dust off his clothes. He considered ignoring her, since in his mind he had already moved on. But in fact, it would do no harm if the business community got to know that you couldn't put one over on Adam Simon. So he called a negligent, "Come in," while he continued his interrupted task of throwing clothes in a suitcase.

Nicola entered, wearing her favorite smart business suit and carrying a newspaper. She scanned the living area quickly, then caught sight of him in the bedroom and walked toward him.

"Sorry to drop by so late, Adam. At least I didn't wake you. This was outside your door." She laid the newspaper down on the bed and her gaze dropped to the suitcase. "Are you leaving London?"

"Tonight."

"Oh." She sounded deflated. "Where are you going?"

"Here and there."

She'd come close to him, as if plucking up the courage to embrace him. Obviously she didn't find it, for she swallowed and said in an oddly small voice, "Have you time for a drink?"

"No."

She sank slowly down on the bed, watching him close the suitcase lid and zip it. "I need to talk to you, Adam. I . . . I haven't been entirely straight with you."

"I know."

Her gaze flew up to his. "You know? How?"

"You're too inquisitive, and Dante's people always learned the things I fed you."

A spark of indignation mingled now with what was probably genuine shame. "You've been feeding me false information?"

Saloman picked up the early-edition newspaper. "It's been very useful. Thank you."

"Don't thank me yet," she said bitterly. "I didn't tell him about the oil shares. I thought *that* was doing you a favor."

"Made no difference." Opening the newspaper, he scanned it quickly for anything of interest, and found his gaze halted on the name Bill Cartwright.

Nicola said, "Dante's furious. He told me you now have the controlling share in his pharmaceutical company."

"I do."

"What do you want with a drug company?"

Saloman shrugged. "Humans need drugs." Bill Cartwright, an American antiquarian, had been found stabbed to death in Glasgow's city center. "I don't want to be rude, Nicola, but I have to leave tonight."

"You're not even angry at me, are you?" Now she did seize his arm, gazing up into his eyes with miserable intensity. "Adam, I agreed to do this for Dante before I'd even met you! I thought pleasing him could only be good for my career, for my company, but I never lied to you!"

"Er—good."

"Did you always know? Didn't you mean any of it?"

"Any of what?"

"You and me!"

Saloman folded the newspaper. "There is no you and me, Nicola. We used each other; that was all. I just happen to be better at it."

"I can work for you," she blurted. "I can do it the other way around, let you know what I can about Dante. . . ."

He didn't even need to reply to that. Her gaze and her hand fell away from him.

"You don't trust me, do you?"

"No."

"And that's it? Wham, bam, thank you, ma'am?"

"That's it, certainly. So long, Nicola. Stick to the advertising. You're good at that."

He was aware, as he watched her defeated exit from the room, that he hadn't been entirely fair to her. He'd taken her without love, as he'd taken many women in the last six months. And the fact that she'd been betraying him hadn't really made any difference to his feelings. Her only importance had been in scratching his sexual itch. Elizabeth would call that unkind at best. And she'd be right.

Saloman moved to his laptop, calling up sites and files with a speed that would have bewildered any watching humans. When he found what he wanted to know, he postponed his flight to America and booked a different one for tonight.

Elizabeth woke before dawn, as she often did. But before she even thought about making coffee—normally her first act of the day—she reached for her laptop to see if there was any reply from the hunters about Saloman's sword.

Settling back on the pillows with the computer on her knees, she downloaded her e-mails and saw at once that there was one from Mihaela. Excitedly, she clicked on it and began to read.

The beginning of the e-mail was mostly a reiteration of the information she'd found digging around for herself last summer: that the sword had been taken by Tsigana and passed on to her descendants, and that the sword was reputed to have special powers.

"If you believe everything you read," Mihaela wrote, "then this sword could do everything from winning you a battle to making your dinner. Very little of this stuff is substantiated, but what is clear is the importance accorded the sword by Tsigana's descendants. And the fact that they were largely left alone by vampires because of it. It's also mentioned in prophecies, although its purpose isn't. What facts there are do point at some genuine power in the sword. Most important, it is reputed to make the wielder invulnerable to any attack. And I've seen repeated in several different places that if a human is killed by this sword and subsequently turned into a vampire, then this vampire will be stronger than all others. No evidence of the latter so far, but I wouldn't discount it.

"I'm busy tomorrow; got a lead on some business connection of Saloman's. But I've asked Miklós to keep researching this for you and if he finds anything else, he'll be in touch."

There followed what looked like a more personal paragraph, but before Elizabeth could read it, some soft, unusual sound from the kitchen distracted her. Her head snapped up, and she listened intently.

Damn, do I have mice?

Not unless they opened windows for themselves. That was definitely the creaking sound of the window being pulled down. Her heart thudding, Elizabeth wriggled out from under the laptop and reached for her phone. But she held it in her left hand. With her right, she picked up the sharpened wooden stake from her bedside table.

Burglaries were comparatively rare in St. Andrews. So were vampire attacks on her person, but neither was unheard of. She moved softly, every sense straining to determine which threat had invaded her house. Pausing in the hall outside the kitchen door, she could hear nothing except the rapid beating of her own heart. No movement, no breathing. Her fingers tightened on the stake and she pushed open the door.

She didn't see it coming. She didn't even see the stake being snatched from her grip. But the next instant arms seized her and she was gazing up in bewildered shock at Saloman. His black hair tumbled forward across his face; a sardonic smile curled his lips and vanished.

For a moment she couldn't think, let alone speak. She swallowed. "What's the matter?" she managed at last. "Did I finally manage to frighten you with a stake?"

"There's a history of that particular combination," he observed, his gaze dropping to her lips and lower. "It makes me nervous."

"Liar." Why was she wearing the scabby old T-shirt instead of a sexy nightdress? Why did she care? She took a deep breath. "What are you doing here?"

"I'm delivering your newspaper," he said, releasing her to indicate the paper that lay on the kitchen table.

Elizabeth felt cold. He hadn't come just for her. She moved nearer the newspaper and saw that it was folded to show a particular article on the second page.

" 'Bill Cartwright, antiques . . .' " she read, raising her gaze back to his. "Is that Dante's Bill?"

Saloman nodded once and she quickly scanned the rest of the short article.

"Mugged in Glasgow, died of his injuries . . . His car was discovered a few miles away. He was in Glasgow for an antiques convention." Elizabeth sat down at the table. "How awful . . . It always seems worse when something bad like this happens to someone you know."

"I think Dante happened to him," Saloman said wryly.

She blinked. *"Dante?"* Though the senator was a little stranger than she'd expected of such a distinguished political figure, blaming a mugging on him seemed a step too far for sanity.

Saloman was gazing around her kitchen, as if remembering the last time he'd been here—the longest and yet the shortest night of her life. Almost casually, he said, "I think Bill took the sword on Dante's orders, and when Dante got it back, he killed him to keep him from telling."

Elizabeth closed her mouth. "Bill can't have taken the sword," she objected. "Josh made Dante check up on all the guests before we left that morning and they were all still in the house."

"But Bill was tired. I doubt he'd had any sleep. I think he hid it somewhere—I can't sense it beyond the range of a mile or so—or got someone else to carry it on to Glasgow while he hurried back to the house. He'll have gone on to Glasgow later, where either Dante or another of his followers met him."

"Do you *know* this? Do the police?"

His gaze came back to her, oddly serious behind the mockery. "Don't be silly. Dante was officially in London on Tuesday, at the time of the murder. And now he's gone back to America. I'm sure the sword went with him."

"Then it wasn't discovered among Bill's things?"

Saloman shook his head and sat down at the opposite side of the table. It seemed a ridiculously mundane setting for so exotic a creature, and yet she liked to see him there. She liked it too much.

She said, "You came here to tell me this? Why?"

"Because I think, at last, we have a common enemy that we both need to eliminate."

Elizabeth stared. *"Eliminate?"*

Saloman shrugged elegantly. "Neutralize. Stop. Oppose. Whatever."

She drew in her breath. "You mean Dante? He's a respected politician, not a crook."

"You know very well one does not preclude the other. But I believe Dante's gone way beyond 'crook.' I think he's risking everything in a play for ultimate power. And judging by his business interests and his political methods, you don't want him in that position any more than I do."

Elizabeth stood up and began to fill the kettle, more for something to do than because she actually wanted coffee.

"I've read that there are whispers against him in America," she confessed. "Complaints that he's too powerful, has too much influence; but most of it seems to come from the conspiracy theorists, not his political opponents."

"Dante is so completely rooted in their political establishment, it doesn't really matter whether he represents Republicans or Democrats. His connections are so wide, he can influence just about any decision, whether that's political or commercial. And he has so many friends in foreign governments that his personal reach extends well beyond the United States. Wealth and connections are what rule this world, and Dante has far more than his fair share of both."

Elizabeth reached for the coffee, regarding him sardonically over her shoulder. "You mean he has what you want?"

"In a nutshell." Saloman sounded pleased by her understanding.

"So you want to bring him down." She shoveled coffee into the cafetière. "I understand that. What I don't get is why in the world you imagine I might want to help you. At least Dante is part of a democracy."

"He's aiming well beyond that."

"Same as you," she shot back, pouring boiling water over the coffee with unnecessary force.

"On the contrary. I aim at benevolence. Dante . . . doesn't."

Picking up the cafetière, she plunked it down on the table and grabbed two mugs from the cupboard. She couldn't work out why she was so angry, unless it was his complete failure to understand anything she'd said last autumn, when, her heart breaking, she'd sent him away. She knew then, as she did now, that she couldn't find happiness with an ancient vampire.

"What sort of benevolence does Dante fail to appreciate?" she demanded. "Toleration of murder, coercion, and tyranny? Does he dislike the idea of vampires rampaging through his country, openly drinking the blood of his people?"

She threw herself into her chair, glaring at him. He didn't appear to be remotely angry. He merely raised one eyebrow. "Actually, I don't think he objects to any of those things."

With the grace and delicacy he brought even to the most mundane tasks, he pushed down the plunger on the cafetière. Elizabeth remembered those long, clever fingers on her body, caressing, stroking. At the very idea, her whole body began to burn and tingle. It made it hard to appreciate the outrageous nature of Saloman's last remark.

He said, "That's the reason I went after him. When I first began to look into the business world, too many roads led back to him. I looked deeper, and the further I went, the less savory his dealings. The vast majority of his wealth comes from oil, pharmaceuticals, and arms. He's struck deals with some of the most brutal regimes in the world in order to harvest their oil. His companies sell drugs to the poorest countries at prices so huge they'll never afford enough of them. He supplies arms to governments he professes publicly to despise, and to rebels and terrorists of all persuasions. The latter is not generally known, but it can be found out."

"All right, I get you." She poured coffee into the mugs and sloshed some milk into one before picking it up like a shield. "He's not a nice man. He has no morals or integrity in his business dealings. He's hardly the only man in a position of power at whom we could level such accusations! Either now or throughout history! Why pick on him?"

"Because he's the biggest. And because I suspect he's about to take a step that even you will feel compelled to prevent." Saloman picked up the free mug and lifted it to his lips. It was always fascinating to watch him drink, to see those sensual lips draw liquid into his mouth. She had a sudden, shocking desire to see them fastened on her neck as he drank from her. She could watch in a mirror. . . .

Involuntarily, her hand flew to her neck and she shivered. Desperately, she drank from her own cup and tried to think instead about what he'd just said.

"What step? Why should you think he's not perfectly happy as he is? He has everything he wants, it seems to me."

"Not everything. He'll die."

Her gaze lifted again to his. "Why does he want the sword?" she said slowly. "Why does he collect paranormal objects? To find even more power. To make it last."

"Exactly. He wants the sword to make him invincible."

She caught her breath, staring at him as Mihaela's e-mailed words came back to her. "If a human is killed by this sword and subsequently turned into a vampire, then this vampire will be stronger than all others. He *wants* to be a vampire!"

Saloman said nothing, merely drank his coffee.

"Would he be stronger than you?" she whispered.

"Don't be ridiculous. But he does have the kind of forceful personality that would quickly overcome the problems of most fledglings. With that and my sword, he is liable to draw a following that will interfere with my plans. Particularly in America, where I am not yet paramount."

"Bringing the war and carnage that the hunters have been waiting for . . ."

"They must be terribly disappointed," Saloman mocked.

"Surprised," she retorted, picking up her phone from where it lay on the open newspaper. "I need to warn them about this." She paused, suddenly uncertain. "But this is a huge leap of faith, Saloman. You have no evidence of any of this, except that he wanted the sword from Josh."

"Then come to America with me and we'll find the evidence. And the sword."

Her breath caught, and as her gaze flew to his, everything in her yearned to go with him, to work with him.

But he hadn't come here for her. She was being used. She said flatly, "You want the hunters to get rid of Dante for you."

Saloman gave a beatific smile. "Oh, no. I just want my sword back. You and the vampire hunters can do what you like about Dante. Although I would recommend stopping him before he actually persuades one of my brethren to turn him."

Elizabeth pushed back her chair and stood up. "Then go and get your damned sword. *Josh*'s sword! I've got no time to jaunt across the Atlantic."

She didn't want to storm out. She wanted to be dignified, and she succeeded pretty well. Until he said provokingly, "When he's a vampire, Dante's going to want the blood of the descendants." Then she couldn't help slamming the door.

Work was slow. It was exam season, so there was little teaching. And since her post was about to expire, there was little point in preparing work for next year. Nevertheless, she made herself stay in the department all day, apart from one foray to the library to return some books. The flat drew her like a magnet, but she wouldn't give in. She wouldn't go back to see if he was still there, and yet the thought of him sitting in her living room, reading her books, lying on her bed, twisted her insides with excitement.

She spent most of the day going through her thesis, working out where and how it could be expanded to make a readable but scholarly book. Eventually, she left at five o'clock, turning down the offer of an impromptu departmental drink.

Her heart seemed to thunder as she walked closer to the flat. She wanted him to be gone, to stop tempting her, and yet she longed for that temptation, even for the chance not to give in to it. Just to see him in her home again, to talk to him, argue with him. She'd thought she was managing all right, moving on with every aspect of her life—until he'd turned up again and made that full, busy life seem empty.

Just be gone, she prayed, turning her key in the door.

He was gone.

Something of his scent lingered in the air, but his presence, the overwhelming knowledge of his nearness, was gone. She couldn't even hope he was masking—the flat was too small to harbor many hiding places.

Throwing her jacket on the kitchen chair, Elizabeth glared unseeingly out of the window. The calm she'd fought for and worked so hard to maintain had vanished as if the last six months had never been. He'd come back, churned everything up, and left, and now it was all to be built back up again.

How often do I need to keep doing this?

As she breathed deeply, the view of the sea and the beach came back into focus. Turning away from the window, she got a couple of eggs from the fridge. Scrambled eggs on toast would be nice. Wouldn't they?

Halfway through beating the eggs, she stopped and reached for her phone, suddenly desperate to hear Mihaela's voice, as if to remind herself why she needed to keep rejecting Saloman. Besides, she needed to warn her about the possible danger presented to the world by Senator Dante. She found the hunter's number and pressed connect.

"Elizabeth." Mihaela managed to sound both distracted and apologetic, as though she were still working and it had already been a trying day. "Sorry; I haven't been able to get back into the library today."

"I know. You were chasing leads."

"I meant to, but in the end we've all wasted most of the day quarreling with various American hunters." Her frustration felt palpable even through the phone.

"Why?" Elizabeth asked, glad of the distraction and the opportunity to soothe her friend, if she could. She pressed the speakerphone button and laid the handset on the table so she could continue beating her eggs with a little more enthusiasm. "I thought you guys always had the same aims, whatever country you operated in."

"Same aims, different means," Mihaela said ruefully. "There's been an incident in New York."

"What sort of—" Elizabeth began, then broke off as another, more distant voice on the phone spoke Mihaela's name in a distinctly warning manner. It sounded like Konrad.

"It doesn't matter," Mihaela said, muffled, as if she'd turned away from the phone. "It's only Elizabeth." Her voice became clearer again. "Big vampire street fight between the locals and an invading horde of West Coast vampires. Two humans died by being in the wrong place at the wrong time. Another is recovering in hospital, complete with 'hallucinations.'"

Elizabeth dropped the egg whisk into the sink. "Hallucinations about people tearing at one another with their teeth? And stabbed people exploding into dust?" she said wryly.

"That kind of thing. There were other witnesses too. The American hunters have had a hell of a job covering this one up."

"It isn't usual, is it?" Elizabeth asked, grabbing a pan out of the cupboard and setting it on the cooker. "To have public fights of that magnitude."

"Highly *un*usual. The Americans are, not unnaturally, scared shitless. Frankly, so are we."

"But I thought you said things were actually quieter since Saloman took control?" Elizabeth dropped a knob of butter into the pan before turning on the gas.

Mihaela sighed. "I knew it couldn't last. I knew it would come to this somewhere, somehow."

"What set it off?" Elizabeth asked, watching the butter melt and sizzle.

"Saloman," Mihaela said with loathing.

"But Saloman isn't—" *Saloman isn't in America.* The betraying words that would have begun her confession were drowned out, for Mihaela was talking again. Elizabeth closed her mouth with guilty relief and listened.

"There's a rumor that he's expected in the States any day," Mihaela said. "I suppose it's inevitable, since he's in control of everywhere else.

The LA vampires seem to have been trying to get advance kudos with Saloman by defeating Travis for him—Travis leads the New York community that opposes Saloman. Anyhow, no one expected a fight on this scale. The American hunters called us for an update on Saloman's whereabouts. We passed on your info that he was in Scotland at the weekend."

"He still is," Elizabeth blurted. "Or at least, he was this morning. But I think he might be on his way to America."

"How—" Mihaela's baffled voice began, before Elizabeth interrupted with a hint of desperation.

"How come you're quarreling with the Americans?"

"What? Oh, they don't seem to *get* the issue of Saloman. They don't realize how dangerous he is. And they didn't like our advice on how to deal with their little vampire war."

"What advice?" Realizing the butter was about to burn in the pan, Elizabeth hastily turned down the heat and poured the egg on top of it. At the same time, she stuck a slice of bread in the toaster with her free hand, and reached for a wooden spoon.

"Eliminate Severin at all costs."

"Severin?" Elizabeth hazarded. "Saloman's supporter in LA?"

"They won't do it. For much the same reasons we *all* tolerate certain vampire leaders. Stability, the devil you know, all that. This is different, and they can't see that. Severin's gone rogue, and last night's fight is just the beginning of the chaos. They'd rather eliminate Travis, for God's sake."

"Why?" Elizabeth asked. "If Travis is against Saloman?"

"He's a much more dangerous character, apparently. Severin rarely gave them any trouble before now. And they're determined to stand by him until something better comes along. Even though we explained that letting Severin survive would increase Saloman's chances of winning the whole of the United States. And with it, the world."

A slightly bitter laugh echoed down the phone. "Sorry to sound melodramatic, but there it is. They're unlikely to get to Travis; they won't touch Severin, and in the meantime, battles will rage. God, if I were there, I'd take him out myself."

Elizabeth smiled lopsidedly and grabbed the toast as it popped up. "No, you wouldn't. You'd be in trouble for encroaching on other hunters' territory."

Mihaela sighed. "True."

A sudden rustle of commotion sounded through the phone, a quick babble of male voices in which the only word Elizabeth could distinguish clearly was her own name. As she poured the scrambled egg over her toast, Mihaela's voice said impatiently, "Don't be ridiculous! You can't ask her to do that. . . . For one thing, she can't afford to go to America. For another it's far too bloody dangerous! Besides, I thought we'd agreed not to—"

Elizabeth picked the phone off the table. "Are you talking about me?"

"Afraid so," Mihaela replied, barely veiled anger spilling out of her voice. "Konrad had this bright idea that although we, as hunters, couldn't go after Severin, *you* could go to America and do it for us. *Un*officially."

"Single-handedly?" Elizabeth said, only half amused. "I really don't think I'm quite up to that."

Or is it really that I'm not up to opposing Saloman with more than words?

"Maybe I could go and take a look, though," she blurted. "See what's possible."

"Elizabeth—" Mihaela broke off. Elizabeth could hear the rustling of paper through the phone, as if someone had plunked a book in front of Mihaela and was turning the pages. Mihaela swallowed audibly. "Have you got the time and the money?"

"Sure," said Elizabeth. "Anyway," she added, warming to her theme, "isn't there another descendant over there who wouldn't speak to the American hunters? A car mechanic?"

"Rudolph Meyer," Mihaela said doubtfully. "Descended from the nobleman Ferenc, who joined the conspiracy against Saloman. Maybe *you* could get through to him. After your success with Josh Alexander—"

"What success?" Elizabeth demanded. "Josh doesn't believe a word I say."

"Well, you can follow up with him again too," Konrad's voice said in the distance.

Elizabeth laughed. "All right. And maybe you could look into Senator Dante? I'm afraid he's chasing immortality by any—"

"Sure," Mihaela interrupted. "But I don't like your being in America with no backup. Not if you're going near Severin . . ." There was a short pause; then she added defiantly, as if someone, perhaps Konrad, were gesticulating at her for silence, "Look, Elizabeth, why don't you sleep on this? Let us know in the morning."

Sleep. She needed to sleep to clear the jumbled thoughts from her head, but she was too restless, too churned up even to manage it. Somewhere, she recognized that at least part of this discomfort was guilt.

As dusk began to fall, she grabbed her jacket and left the flat, determined to walk or even run on the beach until she was physically exhausted. At least then she'd be able either to sleep or think.

Sleep would be best, she told herself as she strode off the road and across the soft, powdery sand to get to the damper, harder stuff that was easier for walking. Thinking would bring her back to Saloman and Dante and Josh.

Josh, her very distant cousin, the megastar whom she barely knew, and yet who already seemed like a *real* cousin, someone she should look after and protect from the vampire and the vampire wannabe who were closing in on him. And even if they weren't, she knew he wouldn't leave the issue of the sword alone. For someone so easygoing he had a very determined streak—a little like her own, she supposed ruefully—

that inspired him to hang on to something that's only value to him was the fact that his beloved father had given it. If Dante didn't seek him out, then Josh would look for Dante.

And both of them would be walking into the middle of a vampire war.

Saloman was going to America to assert his authority and to retrieve the sword. Would that stop Dante? Did she really believe all that stuff Saloman had told her? Some of it was undoubtedly true. She'd read up on it. And Dante's interest in the occult was self-confessed. It wasn't proof. But Saloman believed it.

Alerting the hunters was a cop-out. She knew Josh and Saloman as none of the hunters did, and in spite of everything, when it came down to it, she knew she was the best protection from Saloman that Josh had.

It was turning into a clear, starry night. The breeze was just enough to blow the hair back from her face rather than blasting her into the sea, as it sometimes seemed to attempt. In the distance a few students were celebrating the end of an exam with a shared bottle. A couple of dog walkers moved like pinpricks across her vision. Elizabeth strode in the opposite direction, wanting no companion but the salty wind and the sound of her own brisk footfalls crunching softly in the sand.

Gradually, the knots in her stomach unraveled and her mind quieted. There was only the gathering darkness and the winking of stars, the lapping of waves and the smell of sea and salt. In peace, however brief, she let the thought of Saloman fill her until she almost felt his presence by her side, his long, predatory strides shortened to match her own.

It took several moments to realize he was there in more than her imagination, and for once she simply accepted without question or fear. In silence, she absorbed his company, with no sense of waiting, and he seemed content to leave it so.

At last she said, "Dante knows about you. He and his friends knew about the sword. They'd seen pictures in a book."

"It's possible," he allowed. And for a time, they said nothing more. There was pain in his presence, as there always was, but gladness more than made up for it, because he was here by her side when she'd thought he'd gone. He didn't touch her, didn't even take her hand—which was a pity. Ever since she'd first come to St. Andrews as a naive and romantic student, she'd imagined herself walking on the West Sands at dusk, hand in hand with a lover whose face was as vague as his name. It had never happened, and she wouldn't make the move to let it now.

Saloman said, "We could leave tomorrow night."

She gazed up at the growing number of stars in the sky, as if hoping the right answer would be there. It was as likely as anything else.

She had little to lose by accompanying him. Her job here was more or less finished. She owed the hunters some research, even some effort to halt Saloman's seemingly inexorable march toward world domination; and she owed Josh some protection. And if Dante was all Saloman said he was, then perhaps she owed the world some small effort to halt him. If those were the only reasons urging her to go to America, then she'd be on the next plane.

But more urgent than all of those things was her desire for the man—the vampire—walking silently at her side. If she didn't want to go with him so much, it would have been easier to say yes.

"I can't work out," she said, "whether I'm perverse, or the world is."

"Does it matter?"

She thought about it. The world mattered. Responsibility mattered. And beside those things, the peace of mind of one not very important woman didn't really count for much.

She said, "We'll leave tomorrow night."

Chapter Eight

It wasn't a cold night. In fact, after Scotland, the New York weather was pleasantly balmy. But sitting still for so long seemed to freeze up Josh's bones. He wanted to get out of the car and jog back to his own apartment for a soak in the tub and a shot of the excellent Scotch he'd brought home with him. Despite the gangland street fights that had broken out across the city the other evening, he was sure this neighborhood would be safe enough on foot. But he was damned if he'd leave before the detective showed up.

Josh checked his watch again, then eased himself out of the car and began to stroll along the sidewalk. In the apartment building on the other side of the road, Dante's lights were still on. Josh had been watching his apartment for the last two evenings, without seeing anything more interesting than the odd familiar visitor, or the senator leaving to step into his car to go to some function or other. But he could see no harm in provoking him a little.

Josh had a double plan: either to find the sword himself, or badger Dante into returning it with whatever pretense the senator cared to make about recovering it from fictitious villains. Although he was aware that some, including Elizabeth Silk, would call his determination obsession, it didn't stop him. He needed this keepsake of his father.

Josh crossed the road, darting nimbly between passing, hooting cars, and strolled into Dante's building. The man on duty in the hall lost his supercilious expression almost immediately and goggled at Josh. "Could you see if Senator Dante's in?" Josh asked amiably. "I'm Josh Alexander."

The man pulled himself together enough to make the call and a second later was ushering Josh into the elevator. "Straight to the top, sir."

Josh nodded and smiled again as the doors closed. He'd have to sign autographs on the way out.

The senator was alone and appeared delighted to welcome him. Josh had never been in this apartment before and guessed by the bare, unlived-in look that the senator wasn't here much either. Blatantly, Josh looked about him for signs of the sword or the old coat it had been wrapped in. Not surprisingly, there weren't any.

"I was just wondering," Josh said, "if there was news of the sword?" The only point they'd agreed on was not to involve the police. For one thing, neither of them wanted to advertise their treasures, and for another, they were both well aware that in this particular crime, Dante's reach went well beyond that of the Scottish police.

"None, I'm afraid to say," Dante replied, walking toward a cabinet on which stood a crystal decanter and four clean glasses. "Or of my goblet. But did you hear about poor Bill Cartwright?"

Josh frowned, waving away the drink the senator was silently offering while he poured one for himself. "Bill? Your antiques guy? What about him?"

"He was mugged in Scotland—died of his injuries."

"Shit," Josh said, sitting in the stiff leather armchair and trying to work out what that meant. "Shit, that *was* bad luck."

"Scares the hell out of me," Dante said heavily, taking the seat opposite him. "I know these things can happen to anybody in any city, but don't you think the timing's a little . . . strange?"

Josh closed his mouth. "You think it had something to do with the theft?" He sounded too incredulous, but he didn't much care. He was damned sure Dante had taken the sword. But the theft itself seemed almost honorable compared to the crime of trying to blame it on your tragically dead friend. He'd expected Dante to blame an entirely fictitious thief. Although if it meant the return of the sword . . .

"It strikes me he was keeping bad company." Dante sipped his drink and set it down on the polished table beside him. "Bill was in financial trouble, you know. I think to solve his problems, he might have made a deal with some unsavory people and then stolen from you and me upon their order. Something went wrong when he tried to deliver, and they killed him, taking the sword and goblet with them."

Uneasily, Josh regarded the strong, open face opposite, and almost believed. Dante was frowning with anxiety, a hint of shame in his piercing blue eyes for thinking and passing on such suspicions. Unhappiness lurked around the lines of his thinned mouth. Either the senator was genuine, or he was a bloody good actor.

Josh already knew he was a bloody good actor.

"I suppose you have more evidence than conjecture?" he said.

Dante inclined his head. "I have. Although it's not conclusive."

"Care to share?"

Dante smiled slightly. "Actually, no, Josh, I wouldn't. But I haven't given up on this. I'll let you know at once if I discover your sword. You know how bad I feel about such a thing happening in my house."

"Yes, I believe I do," Josh said ambiguously. He stood up. "Surprised you're still in New York," he observed. "I thought you'd have gone straight back to Washington."

"I've got a few things to attend to here first. Keep in touch, Josh."

Josh nodded, deliberately turning away before the senator could offer to shake hands. He doubted he'd ever forgive Dante, either for the trick on Elizabeth or for stealing the sword. Not unless the bastard gave it back.

Josh descended in the elevator, signed the doorman's autograph, and headed outside. A man sheltering in the doorway said, "Evening, Mr. Alexander."

"Ah. Good evening," Josh returned politely. He glanced about him to make sure they weren't being overheard. "He's up there now. I need to know every visitor he has, and everywhere he goes."

"Yes, sir. You said."

"Thanks," Josh muttered with a nod, and strode on toward his car.

Elizabeth didn't think she'd sleep at all on the long transatlantic flight. With Saloman at her side, she needed all her wits about her all the time. And in any case, sitting so close to him that they almost touched, she felt a constant zing of electricity, keeping her in a permanent state of excitement. But somehow, the hum of the engines and sheer tiredness must have gotten to her, for she woke from one of those light, dreaming half dozes to feel the slow, powerful beat of his heart under her arm.

Her cheek lay on cool silk over hard flesh. She'd fallen against him as she slept, her head tucked under his neck, her arm across his chest. How long had she been like this? It didn't matter; she should straighten immediately and apologize. . . . Except it felt so good. She could allow herself this moment of secret happiness. If he thought she was asleep, she could soak up his familiar, distinctive scent, the hard strength of his lean, muscled body, the sheer joy of being close to him.

His hand stroked her hair, settling on her nape, and pleasant little tingles ran through her head and down her spine. She opened her eyes, drinking in the sight of him, even if all she could see was his shirt buttons and the long, pale hand resting in his lap.

I could get used to this. Oh, but I could . . .

It wasn't just the present moment that caused the upsurge of yearning. It was being in his company so long. He'd stayed in her flat since their encounter on the beach. She'd slept in her own bedroom while he played music and watched television, and even used her laptop in the living room. She'd maintained the distance between them so well that he made no effort to join her.

And the next day, when she'd come home from work after negotiating with Richard for early leave, he'd still been there. Since she had no idea what to say to him, the silences were long, and yet gradually they'd ceased to be uncomfortable and talk had begun to flow naturally, talk of things that had nothing to do with vampires or swords or ruling the world.

For long periods, he'd lain on the sofa with his eyes closed, and she had the impression he was communicating telepathically. She didn't ask who with. She didn't want to know.

She realized it was dangerous falling into this . . . *comfort* with him, but she had hoped that so long as she maintained the physical distance, perhaps she'd survive taking this risk.

And now she'd let that slip too. His hand moved over her hair and settled on her back, lightly holding her. As if he cared. As if she still meant more than the love of a moment in a very long life.

She closed her eyes. *Why do I need to believe that? Many women must have lived and died loving Saloman. I wonder how many he actually noticed. Will he care when I die?*

Appalled by the direction of her thoughts, she sat up, mumbling, "Sorry." His hand slid away. Fortunately, the stewardess passed, offering drinks, and by the time her orange juice was delivered, she was able to look him in the eye again. She could even stretch out her legs and say with appreciation, "First class is good."

"Glad to help," he said, a hint of humor gleaming in his dark eyes. To all intents and purposes he'd existed for only a few months in the modern world, and yet nothing seemed to faze him. Not high-powered business or transatlantic flights. He looked completely at home.

She sipped her juice, watching him over the rim of her glass and counting the times she'd ever seen him disconcerted.

Once. Only once, when she'd thrown down the stake with which she'd meant to kill him and kissed him instead. It had lasted only an instant, but she treasured it as much as the fierce, urgent loving that had come after.

Heat began to spread through her body. Before it could reach her face and betray her, she said with a hint of desperation, "Is this *really* the first time you've been to America?"

"Since I awakened, yes. I'm sure your hunter friends have told you that is the case." He spoke in Romanian, no doubt in consideration of his fellow passengers, who could conceivably overhear.

She wondered if he knew the hunters "lost" him for long periods. But of course he did. It was entirely deliberate, to give his "character" of Adam Simon a head start. Elizabeth ignored the twinge of guilt about not yet telling them about his new identity. She had a feeling Simon was the business connection of Saloman's that Mihaela was pursuing, and she should have saved her friend the trouble by just informing her outright that Simon was Saloman.

This weird double-loyalty thing worked only if she and Saloman stayed apart. Otherwise she was always betraying somebody. So she went on the attack. "They told me the North American vampires don't acknowledge you. Is that another reason for going there?"

"Of course," he said serenely.

She set her glass on the table and cast him a dubious look. "You're not going to start a war here, are you?"

"I rarely start wars."

"I hear one is under way already."

Saloman shrugged elegantly. "A foolish little skirmish with too much collateral damage. I visit and I reason."

"Is that what happened in Spain?"

"There are always some who don't listen to reason."

"Are you expecting the American vampires to listen?"

"Eventually." He smiled, a faint curl of the lip that vanished almost as soon as it formed. "It's not so easy to tell me to fuck off when I'm actually right in front of them."

In spite of herself, Elizabeth gave a little crow of laughter. "Is that what they say to you?"

"Dear Travis," Saloman said fondly. "I'm looking forward to making his acquaintance."

Elizabeth wandered around the spacious blue and gold suite, touching the backs of chairs, the polished wood of the stylish tables, the thick fabric of the curtains framing the full-length windows. She'd never stayed in such a luxurious hotel in her life.

But there was only one bed.

"It's yours," Saloman said, as the door clicked shut behind the departing porter, and she swung around to face him, almost guiltily. "I don't sleep."

"I wish you'd stop reading my mind," she said ruefully.

"In this case, I was only reading your face."

As he walked toward her, she turned her gaze to the window, drinking in the stunning view of Central Park's dark greenery below, and beyond it, the famous New York skyline, lit up against the night.

"This is amazing," she murmured. "I don't know whether I should thank you for this luxury or scold you for however you managed to afford it."

"Neither is necessary. Why don't you sleep?"

"I might have a quick shower in this extraordinarily beautiful bathroom first."

Although the shower wasn't quite as quick as she'd intended, it served the purpose of making her genuinely sleepy. Emerging from the steam in her nightdress—the elegant one—with the hotel bathrobe clutched in front of her like a shield, she padded quickly through to the bedroom and slid between the cool sheets of the huge bed.

Through the open door, she could see Saloman moving along the windows of the living area, touching the glass. He seemed to be murmuring to himself, as if talking on his phone. But he wasn't.

Intrigued, she watched him until he moved out of her sight. Again, she heard the murmuring without being able to make out the words. Then he strolled into the bedroom, and she was struck all over again by his overwhelming presence, large, solid, and almost ridiculously sexy. She loved the way he moved inside his dark jeans, the subtle, catlike sway of his hips that seemed to speak straight to her own loins. His handsome face wore an expression of serious concentration, made all the more appealing by the lock of raven hair that fell forward over his cheek and forehead.

"What are you doing?" she asked, curious.

"Making us safe," he said unexpectedly. "Adding a few more secure locks to the windows and doors."

Unease twisted through her surprise. "*You're* afraid?" she said, unable to keep the wonder out of her voice.

His lip twitched. "I'm cautious. I'm alone in a city where a large number of vampires want me gone, and together might be capable of making it happen."

Fear surged so fast it felt like panic. She'd gotten into the habit of thinking him invincible, invulnerable. But he wasn't. Saloman could die all over again.

"Why did you come here?" she demanded, hearing the anguish in her own voice. "If the risk is so great—"

"It's worth the risk. I'm prepared and you're protected. Nothing will harm you." He moved toward her and a fresh, quite different panic gripped her.

"I'm not frightened for *me*," she objected, and he smiled. Her heart turned over, for his whole face had softened as she remembered it in her most intimate dreams. The way he'd looked in his palace in Budapest, in her bed the night before they parted. And she realized she hadn't seen him as unguarded since they'd met again. As if he'd grown harder and colder without her.

He sat down on the bed, and, swamped with memory and a sudden rush of lust, she found it difficult to breathe.

"Why is it," he wondered, "that your anxiety moves me more than another woman's most passionate seduction?"

She gave a shaky laugh. "Because you know how rotten I am at seduction."

Something flamed in his black eyes. "I'm willing to let you try again. Just for the practice."

"You think I need practice so badly?"

"No, but I do."

She swallowed, trying not to drown in his eyes, in her own need. "I have no idea what you're talking about."

"Yes, you have." He leaned toward her and her heart seemed to stop. He reached out and touched the pulse beating at the base of her throat. "I've set out to seduce you, and yet been the one seduced. I've set out to kill you, and been seduced again." His fingers trailed around her neck to the vein at the side, where they softly, sensuously massaged. "It never felt like losing, but I know it happened."

She swallowed. "It never seemed that way to me."

"How did it seem to you, Elizabeth? That you tamed a monster? Or resisted temptation?"

His gaze followed his fingers, and with wicked excitement, she recognized the hunger in his eyes. It was more than sexual. He wanted her blood. The monster was far from tamed, and God help her, the fear of him only fed her own hunger.

"That I shouldn't love you and did," she whispered. *That my soul dies when we're apart.*

As if he heard her silent thought, his gaze shifted back to her face, and the bloodlust slowly died, leaving his eyes black and opaque. Yet still she was afraid to move. He could always move faster.

He said softly, "We're not so far apart, you and I. And we're here together." His hand slid free of hers to stroke the hair back from her forehead. "Sleep. And then we'll do what we came to do."

It was dark in the bedroom when Elizabeth woke, because although it was midmorning, the curtains were closed. She rose and pulled them back, letting in the New York sunshine and the amazing view. She couldn't help smiling. Turning, she padded through the rest of the suite in search of Saloman to share it with her, but she was alone.

With a sigh, she went back to the bedroom to finish unpacking and get dressed. She was distractedly brushing her hair in front of the mirror when Saloman entered without warning. He wore a smart business suit and a snow-white silk shirt, open at the neck, and although his hair was loosely confined behind his head, he still managed to look just a little bit wild and dangerous. His beauty made her throat ache.

He walked across the room to stand behind her chair, and met her gaze in the mirror.

"You *do* have a reflection," she said faintly. "I never noticed before."

"Of course I do. Bram Stoker wasn't right about everything."

"It's a myth I've heard from several sources," she said defensively.

Abruptly, his figure disappeared and she jerked her head in alarm to see him standing several feet to the left.

"Speed of movement," he observed. "If I move fast enough, you might think I still stood behind you and had no reflection."

Elizabeth closed her mouth. "What a pity I couldn't use that in my thesis. What's with the suit? Going to see the bank manager?"

"Almost. I'm going to visit Edward Dante."

She frowned and laid down her brush. "*Edward* Dante? Not Grayson?"

"Not Grayson," he agreed, wandering toward the window. "It's time to consider what will happen to the Dante wealth when Grayson dies."

She should have been prepared for disappointment, but she wasn't. It felt like a pain corroding her stomach. "'The way to power in this age is wealth,'" she quoted bitterly. "You don't really give a damn about Dante's threat to the world, do you? Was any of that even true?"

"Every word," he said mildly. The curtain moved, apparently of its own volition, blocking the sunlight, which had threatened to move directly on to him. "But the money won't go away. I can make excellent use of it."

Oh, God, oh, fuck, why did I agree to come with him? "What are you planning to do with Edward Dante?" she said hoarsely, dragging her gaze away from the self-closing curtain.

Saloman turned from the window and met her gaze. His eyes were black as coal. "Sup on him slowly. Like a gourmet meal."

She sprang to her feet, to do or say what, she wasn't sure, and before she could decide, he was already speaking again.

"Or I could just talk to him. You can come, if you like, and see."

She stared at him, and slowly convinced herself to relax. She could almost imagine she'd hurt his feelings. At any rate, she discounted the "supping" jibe. He was dressed, she imagined, as Adam Simon, and was going to conduct business rather than death. There was relief there, and yet the tiny incident served to remind her all over again how irreconcilably different were their points of view.

She turned away. "I don't want to see. Do you really imagine the accumulation of money will bring you power?"

"It worked for Dante."

"Along with family connections that stretch back generations. Dante is pure American establishment. You are anything but." She drew in her breath. "You despise Dante. Can't you see that you're actually just like him?"

His long black lashes swept down over his pale cheek and lifted to reveal his dark, mocking eyes once more. He walked toward her with such deliberation that it took every ounce of self-control not to panic and bolt. He came right up to her, so close that his jacket brushed the swell of her breasts. Her breath caught as he bent his head, but his lips didn't touch hers, not quite. There was no warmth, no breath to stir her skin, and yet she was aware of every movement of his mouth almost gliding across her jaw to her neck, and up to her ear.

"No," he whispered. "I'm not."

Elizabeth closed her eyes, as terrified by her own upsurge of fierce, desperate lust as by the knowledge of his anger. Had she ever angered him before? Weird triumph warred with fear and regret.

Nothing happened. When she opened her eyes, he was already across the room. "Don't go out," he advised. And the next instant he was gone. She didn't even hear the door close.

Elizabeth let her breath out in a rush and grasped at her throat as if for comfort. Part of her wanted to laugh; the rest was far too angry with him, both for pursuing wealth and power—*just* like Dante, whatever he said—and, more trivial, for daring to tell her not to go out. *Stuff that.*

Marching across to her bag, she rummaged until she found the scrap of paper inscribed with Rudolph Meyer's New York address.

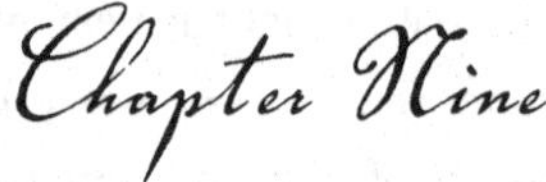

Chapter Nine

Driving through her home country of Romania for the second time in a week, Mihaela found it difficult to appreciate the scenery. They were going to talk to a couple of tourists who'd been asking questions about vampires, in order to find out how serious their interest was. Such tourists not only put themselves in danger by drawing the attention of vampires, but they upset the precarious balance that kept vampires secret from the mass of the population. Although Mihaela understood the importance of the task, her thoughts lingered on the similarity between this mission and the one that had first led them to Elizabeth. When they'd set out from Budapest then, Elizabeth Silk had just been a researcher; by the time they'd caught up with her, she'd become the Awakener and didn't even know it.

And now, having awakened Saloman, it seemed she could be the one destined to destroy him. Certainly, she'd been willing enough to go to America and "smite" Saloman's friends.

"We shouldn't have let her do it," Mihaela said abruptly from the backseat.

Neither of the men pretended to misunderstand her. “Couldn’t stop her, once we’d brought the subject up,” István pointed out.

“Why *did* we bring the subject up? We’re using her to do our job!”

“She’s *helping* us do our job,” Konrad corrected. “She volunteered, and it’s our duty to use every available opportunity. She knows the score.”

“We’ve sent her into the same country as Saloman, into the middle of a vampire war, with a mission *we’d* struggle with.”

“If the Severin thing is too dangerous, she knows to back off. Just contacting the descendant Rudolph Meyer will be a big help now that Saloman’s in the States. Besides,” Konrad added comfortably, “if things get rough she can call the American hunters.”

Mihaela leaned forward between the front seats. “Why don’t we tell them she’s there already?” she suggested.

“Because then she won’t be able to kill Severin.”

Mihaela sat back and eyed the back of his head with hostility. “Do you know what I hate about you, Konrad? Your pragmatism.”

“It keeps us alive and makes us the most successful hunter team in the world.”

Mihaela gave a short, humorless laugh. “Let’s hope it keeps Elizabeth alive too.”

Rudolph Meyer’s apartment was in an old, run-down building. The elevator was out of order, so Elizabeth took the vandalized stairs to the second floor and, along a short, bare corridor, discovered the door with *Meyer* scrawled in black crayon on a piece of card and stuck over the previous nameplate with tape.

Music came from inside the apartment, so at least he was in. Elizabeth rang the bell and, after waiting several moments without any response, knocked loudly. After another half minute, she rang and knocked again.

Oh, God, has Saloman been here already?

Protecting Josh, had she condemned the unknown Rudolph as the only one still available to him?

But no, she was sure she could hear voices over the music. A man's and a woman's. Crouching down, she put her eye to the old-fashioned keyhole, just as the door flew open.

"Ah," said Elizabeth. It hadn't been part of her plan to antagonize the descendant by so obviously spying on him. A white man with iron gray hair, aged somewhere between forty and fifty, stared at her. So did the young woman beside him, a black girl still in her twenties, dressed in the same well-worn type of combat gear as the man who was, presumably, Rudolph Meyer.

"Who the hell are you?" he said, pushing past her as she sprang to her feet. He turned to slam and lock the door.

"I'm Elizabeth Silk," she said numbly.

The girl barged past too, and the pair strode off toward the stairs. With some amazement, Elizabeth realized they were just going to ignore her and leave.

"I'm looking for Rudolph Meyer," she said, hurrying after them.

"You've found him," the man flung over his shoulder. He and the girl both wore well-stuffed backpacks, and their pockets looked bulky as their jackets swung around their hips.

"Could I talk to you for a moment?" Elizabeth asked, keeping up as they ran downstairs.

"Busy," said Rudolph Meyer.

"Then could I come back later?"

"No. I'll still be busy."

"Mr. Meyer, this is important!"

"So is this," he said with odd grimness, and beside him, the girl laughed.

Emerging into the street, they marched straight to a beat-up old pickup truck. Clearly, they were going to climb in and drive away without hearing a word she had to say. It was as frustrating as dealing with the hotel receptionist in Edinburgh.

Lunging forward, Elizabeth inserted herself between Meyer and the driver's door.

"Mr. Meyer, you have to listen to me," she announced, as impressively as she could. "Vampires exist, and you are in extreme danger."

She knew the risk. She was prepared for a verbal string of abusive ridicule, poised to avoid a fist or even a knife, to surrender at once to any gun threat. What she didn't expect was the mocking grin that broke onto Meyer's face.

"No shit, Mrs. Sherlock," he said. It took Elizabeth a baffled moment to realize he was holding open one of his jacket pockets.

Slowly, she lowered her gaze, ready to back off as soon as she saw whatever weapon he was warning her with.

He had a pocketful of short, sharpened wooden stakes.

Minutes later, Elizabeth found herself squashed in the front seat of the truck between the girl and the door—mainly because she'd jumped in when no one forbade her—bumping over city streets.

Leaning forward to see past the girl to Rudolph, Elizabeth said, "So you already *know* you're the descendant of a vampire killer?"

"Got attacked by a vamp two years ago—right outside my apartment. If it hadn't been for Cyn, here, passing at the right moment, I'd have been a goner. She stabbed it with the wooden point of her umbrella and it turned to dust. We've been hunting the damned creatures ever since. Then, a few months ago, I started getting calls telling me I was descended from someone who killed a bigwig vampire, and now this vampire was awakened again, so I should look out. Ignored them, but figured it could be the reason this vampire picked on me in the first place."

"You would have the scent of a strong kill," Elizabeth agreed. She glanced at the girl, Cyn. "How did you know how to kill the vampire?"

Cyn's large, curiously hard brown eyes met her gaze. "I guessed. I'd seen them before, knew what they were, though people called me crazy if I mentioned it. That's why I had that particular umbrella, and that's why I sharpened it."

"Wow . . ." For a moment longer, Elizabeth regarded her with open admiration, before she asked, "Do the American vampire hunters know about you?"

Rudolph and Cyn both grinned. "We *are* the vampire hunters," Rudolph said with a hint of pride.

Elizabeth elected to leave that discussion for later, opting instead for the more immediate point. "Is that where you're headed now? Vampire hunting? In broad daylight?"

"Best time," Rudolph said. "They're holed up and resting. We found a whole nest of them last night. Should be able to clear out the lot before noon."

Elizabeth blinked, taking that in. "Need any help?" she offered.

Rudolph and Cyn exchanged glances. Rudolph said, "No offense, lady, but if you can't fight, you're more hindrance than help. The chances of them all being asleep are remote."

"I can fight a little," Elizabeth said humbly.

"Against vampires?" Cyn demanded, already unbuckling her seat belt as Rudolph brought the truck to a screeching halt outside a disused office block with boarded-up windows and posters bearing the name of some construction company.

"Mainly," Elizabeth said ruefully. "You should know that I'm the one who awakened this Ancient vampire there's all the fuss about. Also, he's here in New York and he's stronger, much stronger than anything you've yet had to face."

Rudolph had already jumped down, but he turned now to stare at her through the open door. "You think our nest includes him?"

"No, I don't." *Not unless he's visiting at the wrong moment.* "But you'd better be prepared."

Rudolph gave a brisk nod and turned away.

"You're in," Cyn said dryly. "If you can stand it."

Rudolph led the way swiftly around the back, and through a window board he'd apparently loosened the previous evening. Elizabeth followed, jumping lightly to the dirty floor, and drew her stake as she ran with them to the stairs.

On the second floor, they paused, pressing themselves against the wall and indicating the door on the left. Its window was boarded too, so Elizabeth couldn't see inside. In the silence, she could hear only the beat of her own heart. Her companions' chests rose and fell rapidly, but they made no sound. Nor did anyone on the other side of the door, or anywhere else in the building.

Cyn was frowning. Slowly, Elizabeth drew nearer to the door, sure, somehow, that nothing and no one lurked on the other side.

"They've gone," Cyn said flatly, and Elizabeth gave her another curious glance. When you came in frequent contact with vampires, you got a sense of them. Like Elizabeth, Cyn clearly hadn't felt any prickles that warned of danger.

Undeterred, a stake in each hand, Rudolph burst through the door.

The big office was empty. No partitions, no furniture or equipment beyond a couple of wires lying loose on the floor. And definitely no vampires.

And yet, as Elizabeth touched the door handle, a frisson stirred her spine. She believed Rudolph and Cyn *had* tracked vampires here. She imagined she felt some distant echo of their presence.

"Who were these vampires?" she asked. "Do you know?"

"We think they were involved in the big street fights the other night," Cyn said, touching the wall with the tips of her fingers and running them along as she walked forward. "Incomers, challenging for territory."

Or for Saloman's favor. "From Los Angeles?" she said aloud. "Severin?"

"We're not on first-name terms," Rudolph said, kicking the wall with frustration. "Damn!"

"I don't think they've been gone long, Rudy," Cyn said, eyes closed. "Maybe as little as an hour."

"Can you *sense* that?" Elizabeth asked her, fascinated.

Cyn looked at her. "Yes. And so could you, if you tried."

Elizabeth took a step nearer her. "Cyn, are you a descendant too?"

The girl shrugged. "Not to my knowledge. I just *feel* things, you know?"

A genuine human psychic? Elizabeth couldn't discount it, but intriguing as it was, she couldn't afford the digression.

"I'm looking for these vampires too. Particularly Severin, if he's with them."

"We'll be damned lucky to catch up with them again," Rudolph said bitterly. "The homegrown vamps will chase them out."

"Maybe not. I think they're hanging around to meet Saloman. The Ancient." Unless they'd met him and were already leaving? Her first mission accomplished, however unnecessary it had turned out to be, she was going to have to move fast if she was to have any chance of achieving the second. "Where would I go to meet vampires in New York?" she asked abruptly, hoping for some equivalent of the Angel club in Budapest.

"Central Park after dark," Cyn said. "If you don't value your life." She began to walk back toward the door. "Want a lift?"

Although Josh welcomed her when the elevator opened directly into his apartment, he looked uncharacteristically flustered. He wore a short leather jacket over a T-shirt and designer jeans, and sunglasses dangled from his fingers.

"Elizabeth," he said, giving her a distracted kiss on the cheek. "How did you get here?"

"In a pickup truck and one of your famous yellow taxis."

His smile looked automatic. "I mean, what brings you to New York? I had no idea you were coming."

"It was a sudden decision. But I think I've picked a bad time to call around. Again. I should have phoned first. You look as if you're going out."

"Well, I was." A slightly sheepish grin curved his lips. "To be honest, I'm still chasing the stolen sword."

"Really?" Elizabeth, who'd been casting quick glances around his ultramodern and spacious apartment, brought her gaze back to his. "And you've found something out?"

"Not really." He shifted his feet and then, as if he'd caught himself shuffling, stood still. Elizabeth merely continued to hold his gaze until he let out a breath of laughter. "Damn it, don't look at me like that! If you must know, I hired a private detective to watch Dante, find out who visited him, if anyone left with a large, swordlike bundle, that sort of thing. Also, to follow him, see where he goes, because he's got no official engagements left in New York that I know of."

Josh swung the sunglasses between his fingers. "I just heard he's gone to this club in Queens."

"Is that bad?" Elizabeth asked, baffled.

"Well, it's a gambling club," Josh said uncomfortably. "Strictly illegal. And this is Dante's second visit in two days."

Elizabeth frowned. "But he has a reputation as Mr. Squeaky Clean Christian. Why would he go to a place like that?"

"Either because he has a secret gambling addiction, or because he's meeting someone unsavory there. Probably to reclaim my sword. I was on my way to find out."

"I'll come with you," Elizabeth decided, swinging back around to face the elevator doors.

Josh rubbed the back of his neck doubtfully. "Not sure you should. It's not the most salubrious venue in the city."

"Then how come you know of it?"

"Everyone knows of it. Well, everyone who's rich enough." The elevator doors slid open and Elizabeth stepped inside, Josh at her heels. "It's become the haunt of the rich and reckless, rock stars and rich kids who want to be bad, celebrities who like a bit of risk with their fun. I went once and never went back. It's hardly Dante's scene."

"You have a point," Elizabeth said eagerly as the elevator came to a smooth halt. "But it's only midday. Will we be able to get in?"

"If he can, we can," Josh said, stepping out into the reception area and shoving on the stylish sunglasses.

"And blend in?" she asked more doubtfully.

"Right now, I don't care about that. Elizabeth, are you sure you want to do this? It could easily lead to police trouble. Although," he added thoughtfully, "the police must know about the place and turn a blind eye, for whatever reason."

"I'll risk it," Elizabeth said.

The excitement of the chase rose higher as they drove through New York in Josh's large, flashy sports car. Elizabeth amused herself by imagining she was in some television cop show, especially as they left the cleaner, wealthier streets around Josh's apartment and sped through much poorer, bleaker neighborhoods.

"I hear there was some trouble in New York the other night," Elizabeth said casually. "Gang fights breaking out all over the place."

"Exaggeration, probably," Josh said without much interest. "Or mass hysteria. Several people described suspiciously similar fights in different parts of the city at more or less the same time."

"Then you were nowhere near any of it?"

"Nope."

There was relief in that, because the vampires didn't seem to be paying Josh any attention. However, she had no lead from Josh to Severin. *Central Park it is, then.*

Josh didn't say much more during the journey. He seemed deep in thought, and it struck her that he was a little too obsessed with getting the sword back. She wondered for the first time whether that was some property of the weapon itself—if it had some kind of supernatural hold on him, like the ring in *Lord of the Rings*. She wished she'd asked Saloman more about it, but he seemed to avoid discussion of its actual properties, concentrating on the more forthright statements that it was his and he wanted it back.

She glanced uneasily at Josh. If he did retrieve the sword, it would only put him in worse danger from Saloman. Somehow, she'd have to persuade one of them to give it up. And considering the power he'd already amassed, that one should be Saloman. God help her . . .

Near a kind of road flyover above them, Josh's car swung around into a dark tunnel that led into an underground car park. Josh slowed as two men in 1920s-style suits and trilbies approached from the shadows. Winding down the window Josh said something in a low tone to the man who stood there.

Elizabeth glanced at her own side window and only just smothered a squeal of shock at the closeness of the curious-looking face that peered in. Pale skin, red lips, gleaming white teeth, dark shadows under eyes that were blue and expressionless.

Then the car was moving again, running forward and through an open gate that she hadn't noticed, to park in one of the many empty spaces.

"That's Dante's car," Josh said with grim satisfaction, jerking his head to the right. Elizabeth barely glanced. She got out of the car warily when Josh did, probing with every screaming sense she possessed. She could almost swear the two who'd spoken to them were vampires. Which didn't bode well for this club. Would it turn out to be something like the Angel in Budapest? Could she rely on the vampires to behave according to the same rules that applied at the Angel?

Trotting after Josh, her mind spinning, she rummaged in her shoulder bag until she felt the comfort of the stake she always carried with her. She hadn't needed it on the outing with Rudy and Cyn, but now she wished she'd brought more. She wished there were a way of talking Josh out of this.

"Josh," she said urgently. "I'm not sure this is safe. Stick close to me. . . ."

"Sure," he said comfortingly, putting one arm around her, presumably to make her feel secure. He'd misunderstood. But of course, there was no way he could know that if this place turned out to be what she feared, it was *his* security that would depend on her.

Grayson Dante was not a man who frightened easily. In a long and varied career that included distinguished service in the US Marines, he'd dealt with more than his share of trouble. Nor did the paranormal frighten him. Rather it drew him, like a moth to a flame. And yet he couldn't prevent the shiver that passed down his spine when he first saw the vampire Travis.

On this, his second visit to the gambling den, he'd come by appointment especially to meet Travis. On the first occasion, he hadn't gotten past the hoods who sprawled around the nearby table playing cards and watching him as if they'd rather eat him for lunch. Which they probably would.

He called them hoods in his mind because they were dressed that way, like 1920s gangsters, in sharp suits and trilby hats—some even toted machine guns, whether or not they were real. In reality, he was aware that they were vampires. It just helped his nerves not to acknowledge it.

Travis, however, had presence that must chill the spine of the most seasoned vampire hunter. A shock of angelic fair hair poking out from under the hat he wore pushed back on his handsome head did not fool Dante for a moment. He awaited the approach of evil.

Dante almost jumped when Travis kicked the chair beside him.

"Sit down, Senator," Travis drawled, slouching into a chair close by and grinning to reveal perfect white teeth. "It's not every day we get such distinguished visitors. What can I do for you?"

There were several ways to approach this. Despite all the information he'd received, Dante had left the decision until meeting Travis in person, and now, gazing into the sharp, intelligent face, and eyes that somehow seemed to see everything while looking as dead as a corpse's . . . Damn, someone else had eyes like that—who the hell was it?

Dragging his wayward thoughts back to the point, Dante smiled, sat down, and made his decision. Cards-on-the-table honesty.

"Mr. Travis, I'm honored to meet you." He held out his hand, as he always did, but Travis only smirked, making no attempt to shake it. Dante let it fall to his side. "I should tell you at the outset that I am aware of your operation here and your, er, condition."

Travis laughed and stuck one foot up on the table. "Hey, do you hear that, boys? We have a condition!"

"Would you prefer 'status'?" Dante inquired. "You'll have to excuse me; I'm afraid I'm not familiar with the correct terminology."

"Oh, you can just call us vampires." Travis smiled, and in spite of himself, Dante felt panic rise up from his stomach, threatening to choke him. He fought it down, reminding himself that he had something Travis needed. At the moment he was safe through Travis's curiosity as to why so distinguished a senator would have anything to do with him. But such precarious safety wouldn't last, and the sooner he came to the point, the better.

"I understand you might need to defend your position here," he said in a rush.

Travis spread his hands wide. "From whom?" he said incredulously.

"Saloman."

The smile died on Travis's insolent lips as if someone had wiped it with a cloth. He sat so still he might have been a wax model. At last, when Dante had almost forgotten to breathe, he said, "You come from Severin? Or from Saloman?"

"Lord, no," Dante said with an effort at heartiness. "But I do come with an offer of Saloman's sword."

Travis's lips curled. He put his other foot on the table and crossed his ankles. "Do you, now? Interesting. Care to tell me where you got such a valuable item?"

"From Josh Alexander, descendant of Tsigana."

"He gave it to you?" Travis asked incredulously.

Cards-on-the-table honesty. "Hardly. I stole it."

"Okay," Travis allowed. "Let's assume you have it, and are prepared to give it to me. Why? You want money?"

It was Dante's turn to smile. "Money, I have. On the other hand, it is in your power to give me something I desire. If you'll give it to me, I'll lend you the sword, which will, I understand, enable you to defeat Saloman. When he comes for you. As I'm told he will."

"Who told you that?" Travis asked at once.

Dante shrugged, leaving it open, and it seemed Travis didn't much care anyway, for he said immediately, "What do you want for the, ah, *loan* of Saloman's sword?"

Dante drew in his breath and held Travis's dreadful gaze. It got easier with practice. "I want immortality."

Travis laughed and pushed back his chair, letting his feet drop from the table to the ground. "Just immortality? You want to be a vampire? I don't think you do, Senator. I don't think you know what that means—blood and killing by night, never seeing the daylight except through filters."

"I am prepared for those things," Dante said calmly.

"Are you, by God? And you the Christian senator too."

"I'm open to all beliefs."

"Yeah? But I doubt you'll like going from top of the human heap to the bottom of the vampire hierarchy." Travis stood up and grasped the tabletop before leaning over it to bring his face close to Dante's. "If I make you a vampire—leaving aside the pain of whatever death I choose to inflict on you first—you'll rise again a stupid, brainless monster, going after blood and human death by sheer instinct. There'll be years of that, living like an animal at the mercy of every vampire who's stronger and more intelligent than you. And for a long, long time, that's going to be just about every other vampire in the world. Apart from the odd stupid fledgling like yourself, who'll fight with you over every scrap of blood. And I haven't even started on the vampire hunters, to whom you'll be easy meat. Sound appealing, Senator? Two weeks of ugly undead existence instead of the, what, twenty years plus of the good life?"

"Not when put like that," Dante allowed, trying not to let his stomach shrivel at the prospect.

Travis curled his lip and sat back down. "Immortality only lasts as long as you can keep it. You can still be dead after you're undead."

"With the sword," Dante said, just a little desperately, "with Saloman's sword, I believe I can avoid such a vile beginning to my new existence. And gain power to equal that of the Ancients. Which I would share with you in return for the gift of immortality."

Travis leaned his head to one side, watching him without blinking. "Go on."

Dante drew another breath. He felt as if he were counting them, as if each might be his last. "How much do you know about the sword?"

Travis shrugged. "Not much. A bit of rumor, a bit of legend."

"It is said that a human who's killed by the sword and subsequently turned into a vampire will have power equal to that of the sword's original owner."

"Saloman," Travis said, almost in a whisper.

"Exactly." For the first time since he'd entered this place, Dante felt he was in control, and his confidence soared in response. Leaning forward across the table, he said, "You have quite an operation here. You answer to no one, go your own way, and you're respected far beyond the vampire world. I know these things. And I don't want you to lose them."

"Why should you give a damn?" Travis threw in.

"Because I think we can work together, in cooperation, without interfering with each other or stepping on each other's toes. Here's my deal, Mr. Travis. You kill me with Saloman's sword, and make me a vampire. Whatever power I gain through the strength of that, I'll share with you. And, more immediately, you'll have the use of the sword to defeat Saloman."

Travis gazed at him. In the sudden silence, Dante realized the other vampires at the next table had heard everything. Did it matter? Probably not. The door through which he'd entered an hour ago creaked open and someone he couldn't see walked in. Travis's gaze flickered toward the newcomers, and two of the other hoods rose and walked across the room to them.

Dante asked, "What do you say?"

Travis considered. "I say your proposal requires a lot of trust on both sides. Now that I know you have it, I could take the sword anytime and still kill Saloman."

"But you wouldn't then have such a powerful ally as I would be in the human world."

"How can I trust you to honor that part of the bargain once you have what you want?"

Dante shrugged elegantly. "I guess I wouldn't have such a distinguished vampire as you to be my ally. As you say, trust—and good sense—is required on both sides."

Travis's gaze continued to travel back and forth, from one of Dante's eyes to the other. Dante could almost hear him mulling over pros and cons. Then the vampire smiled and parted his lips to speak.

"Senator!" The shockingly familiar voice cut across the room, filling Dante with an annoyance that amounted almost to rage at the interruption. "What an unlikely place to find you."

Dante jerked around, and there, strolling toward him between two hoods, were the figures of Josh Alexander and Elizabeth Silk. Beside him, Travis sniffed the air and then leapt to his feet. His gaze was fixed on the girl with such rampaging hunger that even Dante felt the pain.

"Shit," Travis said softly. "What the hell do we have here?"

As soon as she entered the large gaming room, Elizabeth knew. She didn't need the hunters' detectors to tell her. Every tiny hair on the back of her neck stood up like a stalk. Every sense recognized their stillness, their appearance, their sheer threat. The men who came toward them, those who continued to sprawl at the table they'd just left, and no doubt the man who sat with Dante, were all vampires.

Elizabeth's confidence in her own abilities had grown in the last six months, but she knew when she was overwhelmed. Her instincts had screamed against coming in and they'd been right. They needed to get out as fast as possible.

Only Josh wouldn't come, and now there was Dante to look out for as well. . . .

"There he is," Josh breathed, nodding toward Dante's back.

"We've got to get him out of here," Elizabeth said grimly. "And, Josh? Don't even think of fighting them. Any of them. They're all vampires."

"Oh, for the love of . . ." Josh cast his eyes at the ceiling, muttered something under his breath, then spoke between his teeth. "Elizabeth, I do not need this right now." And, just as the two vampires in their suits and trilbies reached them, he raised his voice and called to Dante.

Elizabeth kept her hand on her shoulder bag, her fingers inside it grasping the stake. Her heart hammered; every sense was alert as they walked with their vampire escort toward Dante, who looked anything but pleased to see them. For an instant, there was no sign at all of the benevolent, amiable host of last weekend. His eyes were bleak, his mouth a thin, forbidding line. And then the smile came back, but by then Elizabeth had lost interest, because his companion had stood up and she realized that this being was the biggest threat they faced.

Worse, his gaze devoured her, hot and hungry. *Oh, shite, oh, Saloman . . . Saloman, are you there?*

It was too hard to concentrate with vampires surrounding her. She wasn't surprised she couldn't reach him. So she'd have to manage on her own, get herself, Josh, and Dante out of there alive. . . . *Some bloody hope!*

As for the senator, was Saloman right? Had he come here looking for immortality?

Josh was speaking with false bonhomie. "What brings you to this neck of the woods, Senator?"

"Business, my dear Josh, business."

"Won't you introduce us to your friends?"

Dante rose to his feet, as courtesy presumably won out over annoyance. "Of course. Mr. Travis, I'd like you to meet Josh Alexander and Elizabeth Silk."

Travis? Oh bloody, bloody *hell . . .*

"My," Travis said, moving around the table toward them. "My, oh, my. What *do* we have here?" He sniffed the air around them, and Elizabeth was suddenly reminded of her first encounter with the Hungarian vampire Zoltán, who had behaved in much the same manner and then laughed, as if he'd recognized her by the very smell of her blood. Although Travis didn't laugh, there was no doubt of his recognition.

"Powerful human blood," he observed, his mouth so close to Elizabeth's ear that she wanted to scream. She held herself rigid, unmoving. "Elizabeth Silk, the Awakener . . ."

Josh yanked her away from him, staring down his nose at the vampire, who paid him no attention whatsoever.

"Okay, boys," Travis said. "Two descendants to play with, and the victim was Saloman, so no gulping. Share the boy and hold the Awakener for me."

Josh, who seemed to have finally picked up that the "men" surrounding them were dangerous, took a step backward. Before he could draw too much attention, Elizabeth glared at the vampire who grasped her arm.

"Gulping?" she said. "Without an introduction, I don't even allow biting." And she whipped out the stake, plunging it into his heart. At the same time, she spun in the cloud of his dust and kicked the vampire nearest Josh hard enough to knock him into the table. "Josh, run!" she yelled, and lunged at Dante, grabbing his wrist and yanking him after her. "Go!"

It was desperate; it probably required a miracle to make it work; but at least its suddenness gave them a chance. Unfortunately, Elizabeth had reckoned without Josh's recent skepticism, which she'd just blown sky-high with the vampire. He stood rooted to the spot, blinking at where the creature had last stood. His lips moved, making no sound.

"Get them," Travis snarled. Elizabeth gave Dante one last tug after her to make her point and grabbed Josh's arm instead. She couldn't drag both of them and fight at the same time.

"Josh!" she cried. "Move!"

He stumbled in her wake, but she had to punch the vampire who had hold of him and dragged him to the ground. As Elizabeth leapt and staked the fallen vampire, she could see that their moment had passed. The vampires were closing in on all sides. More were emerging from the office beyond, from the doorway to the car park. Wildly, she scanned the room for an escape route, holding fast to Josh's arm. He was breathing like a steam engine. Dante backed away toward Travis, who, however, ignored him. The vampire leader's attention was all on Elizabeth.

"Sir, do we have an agreement?" Dante shouted.

"Not now, Senator." Travis smiled and walked forward into the circle. "It's feeding time."

Dante strode the length of the room toward the exit, and began to run, shoving past the vampires who were not remotely interested in him when the blood of two descendants, one of whom was also the Awakener, was up for grabs.

"I'll fight, Josh," Elizabeth said shakily. "But I can't win. If you can manage it, get out—they want me more. Find Adam Simon and tell him what happened here. Do you understand?"

There was no time for any reply. The vampires approached, beginning at a walk and advancing quickly to a run. Elizabeth raised her stake and released Josh in order to have both arms free.

"Straight ahead," she breathed, and launched herself at the first vampire with a scream of pure rage.

But something was louder than her cry—the crashing of falling masonry as the ceiling began to cave in. Her chosen victim's distraction gave her an easy kill. Whirling, she spun to face the vampires closing behind her, and found their backs to her. They were watching in stunned amazement as someone fell—no, *stepped*—through the hole in the ceiling as if descending a staircase.

He still wore the business suit, minus the constricting jacket. From his long, loose black hair to his shining shoes, he was dazzling. He advanced on those who stood between him and Elizabeth and Josh. "I'm Saloman."

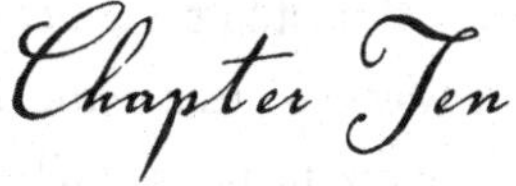

To Josh, the advent of a man who resembled Adam Simon via the club roof merely added to his sense of nightmare. None of this could be real: not the bizarre fight, not the murders committed by Elizabeth Silk, of all people, and certainly not the exploding bodies. His subconscious was merely dragging all his acquaintances into his dream.

And yet somewhere Elizabeth's last words nagged at him. Even in a dream, surely it wasn't right that she should be prepared to die to save his skin? But Elizabeth's mood seemed to change abruptly. The desperate tension he could almost feel as his own suddenly vanished. He even thought he caught a breath of laughter.

The men between him and the door began another rush, and Josh acted from pure instinct. Apart from childhood scraps, he'd never been much of a fighter, but as two men ran at Elizabeth, he struck out with a fist at the nearest. No doubt his sudden action after prolonged passivity helped, but as his victim fell back under the punch, landing flat on the floor, Josh felt a fierce sense of satisfaction.

He whirled to discover that Elizabeth had dealt with the second immediate attacker. She stood now back-to-back with the man who looked like Adam Simon. It couldn't have taken long, maybe only seconds, but Josh found himself watching with fascination as together they performed maneuvers almost like a dance, drawing and repelling attacks until suddenly the way was clear to the door.

Dante's friend Travis sat on the floor as if he'd been flung there, observing through narrowed eyes. The man who looked like Adam seized a chair and crashed it over someone's head. In the same fluid movement, he caught one of the chair's broken, jagged legs and threw it over his shoulder. Elizabeth caught it deftly and without a word passed it to Josh. Almost numbly, he grasped it.

Elizabeth nodded, as if in agreement to something he hadn't heard. "Let's go," she said breathlessly, and Josh registered that there was no longer the same desperate grimness in her voice. It was almost as if she were *enjoying* herself.

On autopilot, Josh ran with her the length of the room. She kicked open the door, scanning for any new threat; then, for the first time since this began, she seemed to hesitate. She looked over her shoulder, and Josh glanced with her.

All Travis's men—or at least those of them who hadn't disappeared in clouds of dust—still dressed in their ridiculous gangster outfits, were crowding in on the man who looked like Adam. Elizabeth made a tiny movement, as if, after all, she intended to go back, but in the end, with a sound like a strangled sob, she wrenched herself straight and ran on toward the parking lot.

Josh loped after her, clutching his broken chair leg more like a talisman than a weapon, and when they all but ran into two more men rushing from the parking lot toward the club, it was Elizabeth who stabbed one and kicked out at the other. But her kick never connected. The man was more interested in whatever fight was still going on inside.

As they ran to his car, Josh noted that Dante's vehicle had gone. But there was no time to debate what it all meant. If this really wasn't a dream, the most important thing was to get himself and Elizabeth as far away from here as possible.

At least he'd found his key and sprang the lock in time for them to leap inside as soon as they reached the car. Without any pause to fasten seat belts, he started the engine, threw it into reverse, and screeched around to speed out of the parking lot, crashing through the closed barrier and out into the road.

Beside him, Elizabeth said low, "Are you all right to drive?" She was tense again, like a coiled spring, and the fear had returned to her rather beautiful hazel eyes.

Josh dragged his gaze back to the clamorous traffic, took a deep breath, and forced himself to slow down.

"Shit," he breathed, rubbing one still-shaking hand over the back of his sweaty neck before replacing it on the steering wheel. "This isn't a dream, is it? What the hell just happened, Elizabeth?"

"I'm sorry," she said quietly. "I tried to tell you. But some things you just can't believe until you see them for yourself. It was like that for me too. We just met Travis, the strongest leader of the North American vampires, and his bodyguard. And we were recognized as Tsigana's descendants. Like I told you, our blood is valuable to them."

She dug the back of her head into the headrest. "Bugger, I should have listened. I shouldn't have gone out."

Josh had no idea what she meant by that. But an instant later, she seemed to pull herself together, replacing her wooden stake carefully in her bag before she rummaged for her phone.

Josh concentrated on driving. What he'd just seen, what he'd seen Elizabeth do back there, needed a lot of processing.

"Mihaela, it's me," she said into her phone. There was a pause, then: "I'm in New York now. Can you find me what you have on the American vampire Travis? With particular reference to a possible relationship with Senator Grayson Dante."

Curiously, her matter-of-fact words soothed Josh. Then Elizabeth said, "Maybe, but the American network wouldn't necessarily give me the info—they don't know me. You'll have to do it for me. . . . Yes, I'm afraid it is important, Mihaela, bloody important." She smiled faintly. "Thanks, you're wonderful," she said, and broke the connection.

Josh began to laugh. Elizabeth glanced at him in alarm, as if afraid he'd cracked. Maybe he had.

"What?" she demanded. "What is it?"

"I've just realized the really annoying thing about this . . . adventure. We went through all that, and I still don't have my damned sword."

They all had stakes of some kind, many made after Saloman's own example of a broken chair leg, and Travis was strong enough to pierce his skin. There was no doubt that together they could take him, weaken him with bloodletting where his skin was less tough than over his heart, while gaining greater strength from drinking his blood, pushing a stake farther and farther into his heart until, eventually, he would be sent back into the agonized sleep from which Elizabeth had awakened him less than a year ago.

They might not know it, of course. Ancient-killing had become something of a lost art in the last three hundred years or so. But Saloman didn't care to bank on it. He could fight, rely on his greater strength to keep them all at bay while he talked them out of a mutual killing spree, if he could. But their bloodlust was up. Elizabeth and Josh had seen to that, and now, without some kind of powerful jolt, they were unlikely to pay much attention to talk.

A display of his superior power was clearly necessary. It would weaken him, sap his strength and his ability to fight for much longer, so if his ploy didn't work, he was, in modern parlance, fucked.

What is life without risk?

"Enough!" he roared. He used his thundering tone, the godlike one that echoed around the head as well as the atmosphere. It garnered enough surprised attention. Saloman parted his lips and blew out a howl of rage, sending every vampire in the path of his "breath" flying across the room. Several hit the wall on the far side; the rest crashed into them. Saloman turned his head to ensure that every vampire from Travis down got his fair share.

"Good," Saloman said into the stunned silence. "Enough fighting for one day." His roving gaze, which he made as stern as possible, found Travis, who was picking himself somewhat shakily off the floor. "Forgive the unconventional entrance, but the Awakener is mine, not yours. Fortunately, I don't bear grudges. Shall we talk?"

Travis's gaze flickered around the room, taking in the piles of injured and demoralized vampires around him. Clearly he was a realist. "In my office?" he suggested in the tones he might have used to a favored salesman. "Al—two beers."

Saloman's lips twitched, but he inclined his head with politeness as he preceded the American vampire into his office. At least here the desk and chairs were still usable.

"I hope your operation is not inconvenienced," Saloman said, taking the visitor's seat. It was a relief to sit. The loss of the power used in his little demonstration had left him dizzier than he'd been since Elizabeth awakened him. He needed to feed and rest. But not yet.

Travis straightened his gangster tie and adjusted his hat to a preferred angle on the back of his blond head. "I don't mind them having to work. I pay them enough. In dough as well as blood."

If he thought to flummox Saloman by his use of old-fashioned slang, he must have been disappointed when Saloman merely smiled.

"I didn't expect you," Travis said, sprawling in his chair. "I guess I wasn't paying attention."

"I guess you weren't. I unmasked some time ago, since I had no wish to startle you when I visited."

"So you planned a courtesy visit before you smelled the Awakener in my vicinity?"

"Something like that."

"I trust you found my friend Severin quite well."

"I found him serene, and his welcome a little more traditional than yours."

Something like annoyance flickered in Travis's blue eyes and vanished, as if he was irritated rather than impressed by Saloman's openness. Or perhaps he'd wanted to impress Saloman by his powerful sense of smell.

Travis's brow cleared again. "Well, now you're here, what can I do for you?" he asked almost jovially.

Travis clearly was a vampire who liked to play games. It was no accident that he'd chosen to host an illegal casino. His thoughts were closely shielded, his amiable expression revealing very little. But although he lounged in his chair as if perfectly at ease, the still, tense set of his shoulders gave him away. Travis was suspicious and on edge, as he should be. And as Saloman gazed into his dense eyes, he was pretty sure anger simmered. Travis saw no reason to give up his power, no reason it should be expected of him. He was a modern vampire, living with minimum order only so long as it suited him. His heart was as chaotic as Zoltán's, as those of the Spanish rebels Saloman had killed in Salamanca.

But Travis had considerable power here. He was intelligent; the theme of his club as well as his speech proclaimed a hint of humor. In fact, in time, Saloman might even like him.

"What can you do for me?" he repeated. "You could tell me what Senator Dante wanted with you."

Travis's eyelids didn't flicker. "He's looking for a sword." He smiled. "Your sword."

Saloman tapped his lips with one finger, contemplating the other vampire's dishonesty until Travis shifted in his seat but still didn't break eye contact.

Saloman smiled. "A wager would seem to be called for. You like games?"

Travis shrugged elaborately. “What else is there?”

“Good. You are aware of the powers attributed to my sword? Why it is that Senator Dante wants it?”

Travis inclined his head. “Of course.”

“Very well. Then let us race to find it. Since the sword is mine, as you acknowledge, the sword itself will be my stake, which you win if you find it first.”

Travis smiled as if amused, but this time he couldn’t hide the sparkle in his sharp blue eyes. “And my stake?”

Saloman smiled. “Overlordship of the North American vampires, of course.”

If Saloman “died” again, she wondered if she’d know. He’d been so firm in his telepathic instruction to go, so amused by the very idea that he could not deal with the American vampires, that despite the jagged fears in her heart, she’d left him in order to look after Josh. Shying away from the very idea that Saloman could be killed, she wondered instead what the consequences of his victory would be. Would the conflict spread out across the city, like the “gang fights,” leaving human as well as vampire casualties?

Elizabeth’s throat closed up in horror. Perhaps it would simply mean Saloman now controlled all the American vampires? Which might be more peaceful in the short term, but was the very thing she’d come here to prevent. Had she actually handed him more power on a platter by going to Travis’s? And doomed the human world to whatever rule Saloman chose to inflict?

“Was that Adam Simon?” Josh said abruptly, breaking into her bleak thoughts. They were back in his apartment, where Josh was ignoring the constant messages coming from his phone in order to make tea. Since his hands had stopped shaking, Elizabeth was happy to let him. He needed mundane tasks to counteract the weirdness of the day.

Elizabeth shook her head. “No.” It was the truth, looked at one way.

Josh frowned, handing her a mug of tea. "But you mentioned him. You said I should tell him what happened if I got out. Why? In Scotland, you told me not to trust him. What's he to do with any of *this*?"

Elizabeth turned away from him to walk back into the spacious living room, where she took a seat on one of the leather sofas. "Nothing, really," she said vaguely. "He's just a man with a finger in lots of pies, useful to have on your side to get you out of a scrape." *Like the one we were in.*

Another thought occurred to her. In the heat of the moment, she'd sent Josh not to the hunters who should have been his first line of defense, but to Saloman, who wanted his blood. What sort of crazy instinct was that?

But Josh had moved on. While she absently sipped her tea, he said, "You couldn't hurt them. No matter how hard you hit them, they just got back up. Except when you stabbed them, and then they disappeared."

"That's vampires for you," she said flippantly. She became aware of his gaze on her, steady, fascinated, but no longer containing any trace of attraction. It wasn't even friendly. Rather it was as if he were studying a particularly rare if ugly insect.

"You have hidden parts, Elizabeth Silk," he said slowly. "Is anything I've seen before today actually real?"

"It's all real. It's all me. I just can't marry it all up." She set down her mug and jumped to her feet. "Look, Josh, I have to go. I'll call you later. Don't worry about this stuff; it gets to feel normal after a while. Mostly. For now, just remember you're quite safe here." *If Saloman isn't dead. Or if Saloman doesn't elect to go his own way and kill you anyway . . .*

But she wouldn't believe that. Any of that.

"We've alerted the local hunters and they've promised to watch your apartment," she reminded him, as a half-anxious, half-annoyed frown re-formed on his brow. "Contact me anytime, Josh, but for now, can you call me a cab?"

. . .

He wasn't in the room when she got back to the hotel. Telepathic queries bounced back at her. Restlessly, she walked to the big full-length window and gazed down at the greenery of Central Park. It would be dark soon, but tomorrow, whatever else she did, she'd walk in Central Park, maybe even go to the zoo.

Finding the remote control on the table beside her, she pointed it at the television, just to have some background noise while she paced. After a few circuits of the entire suite, she gave up and went for a shower. Staking vampires was a sweaty business. She'd just emerged from the bathroom in the hotel robe and slippers when the sound of a name brought her attention back to the television and she walked quickly through to the living area to see a close-up of a familiar face on the screen.

". . . Dante has canceled his appointments for the next several days. According to his aides, the senator has been unwell since returning from his UK visit earlier this week. On to sports now . . ."

The suite door opened and closed behind Saloman, once more wearing the jacket that went with his suit. Where had he kept that while he battered his way into Travis's casino and took on a dozen vampires?

She felt giddy with relief, with the surge of helpless desire that always swamped her in his presence. Yet she blurted only, "The news says Dante's sick. He looked pretty fit to me as he legged it out of Travis's place."

Saloman walked toward her. "He's giving himself time to act, and a cover story ready if he needs to bow out of the public arena for a longer period."

"Do you think so?" Elizabeth asked doubtfully, hiding her perverse disappointment when he walked right past her into the bedroom. "Did he really go to Travis to ask for immortality?"

"Undoubtedly."

"Did Travis tell you?" she asked, following to stand in the doorway.

"No." He sank onto the bed and it struck her, almost with awe, that Saloman was tired. "I heard him. From above."

Elizabeth walked toward him. "How did he know, Saloman?"

"Know what?"

"Everything! About the sword, about your awakening. How did he know where to find Travis?"

He smiled faintly, but appeared to be more intrigued by the shine on his smart black shoes. "I told you he was an interesting man."

"Saloman, are you all right?" With sudden anxiety she dropped to her knees in front of him to peer up into his pale, handsome face. Although there was surprise in his dark eyes when they met her gaze, she could see no signs of illness, no shadow of exhaustion or flush of fever. But that meant nothing. He was a vampire. "Were you hurt back there?"

His eyes seemed to lighten, softening in the way that melted her heart. "Don't be silly. I merely spent a little too much energy in a manly display of power."

Her breath caught. "I hope it was as you left."

"Not entirely," he said, after a pause, and without meaning to, she caught his arms as if she meant to shake him.

"You stayed among them like that? Could they have killed you then?"

"Actually, they could have killed me anytime," Saloman said, slipping his arms free, though only to take her hands. "Fortunately they didn't know how. And now Travis and I are the best of friends. We're even playing a game together. I didn't know you worried about me."

She tugged her hands free, as much in protest at his risk taking as at his accusation. "I'm not worried," she muttered. "But what took you to Travis? I thought Severin was your best friend."

His right eyebrow lifted. "Did you? I don't recall telling you that."

So he would know the hunters had. She didn't think it mattered, and if it did, right now she didn't care. "Are you playing them against each other so you can pick up the pieces?" she asked, eyes narrowed. Another thought struck her like a blow. "Saloman, you didn't order Severin to come here and attack Travis?"

Saloman curled his lip. "Any attack under my orders is carried out with considerably more efficiency. Not to mention success."

"Then Severin lost the fight? From what the—" Under Saloman's sardonic smile, she broke off. "I thought he was still hanging around New York," she finished defiantly. "Which doesn't indicate defeat."

"He stayed on in order to meet me, of course."

"You've met him already? I thought you were visiting Dante Junior this morning."

"I did that too. He and his sister were quite shocked about some of their father's dealings, and quite amenable to my suggestions for the future." His fingers gripped the bedclothes as if to anchor his thoughts. "I'm surprised no one told them before. I did some other things too, before your presence grew too close to Travis's." His eyes glinted. "As you know, I don't care for other vampires stealing my dinner."

"You're trying to rile me," she observed, though she couldn't prevent her lips from curving into the faintest smile.

"Oh, no." He lay back, stretching his long, lean body on the bed, and closed his eyes.

The smile died on Elizabeth's lips. She swallowed. "Do you need to . . . drink?" she asked awkwardly.

"No. I drank on my way up."

She frowned. "How did you do that?"

"I bit the parking attendant."

Shockingly, she wanted to laugh, and the smile forming and fading on his lips betrayed that he knew it. Watching him, she asked, curious, "How did you get into Travis's place?"

"Like Rumpelstiltskin, I stamped my angry foot."

One stamp of his foot had done that? His power was terrifying, and yet now he looked no stronger than she. That was scary too, so she found other questions. "But how did you even get onto the roof in daylight?"

"It's under a bridge—a flyover? I had to park very close. I'd have gotten a ticket if anyone were brave enough to police the neighborhood."

He was silent and Elizabeth knew that he was waiting for her to ask where and how he'd learned to drive. She'd already resisted the same pressure as he'd driven her here from the airport in a hired car with blacked-out windows. Although curiosity niggled at her, she refused to ask, just because he wanted her to. Instead, she let her gaze drop from his calm face to his broad, muscled chest, the contours of which were quite clear through his shirt, and his stomach, then down his narrow hips to his thighs. At the juncture of his legs was a bulge she recognized, one that made her pulse race.

"Elizabeth."

Guiltily, she dragged her gaze back to his face to find his eyes open and a smile playing on his sensual lips.

"We had fun at Travis's, didn't we?"

Outraged, she glared at him, her mouth already open to deny any such thing. Then she remembered the relief of his arrival, the blind faith that had lifted her spirits at the very sight of him, the certainty that now she and Josh were safe. And after that, it had been easy to fight, to feint and maneuver, back-to-back with him in perfect understanding of his next move and the purpose behind it. Like some intense, exhilarating game.

Something that was half laughter and half sob fought its way out of her throat.

"Yes," she admitted. "We had fun."

But his eyes were no longer laughing. The tiny flames she sometimes imagined burned there flickered yellow and amber in the darkness. "We should face the world together more often."

Excitement leapt at his words, along with a surge of longing to make it happen. To enjoy all the new abilities of her body and the confidence of her mind side by side with him, fighting battles they could both believe in.

Only there weren't so many of those. Her next battle would be as his enemy.

The truth was, the most powerful—and feared—vampire in the world had little common ground with her. Wishing for it wouldn't change that. He wouldn't falter in his pursuit of power, whatever the consequences for anyone, for the world itself. So she forced down the yearning, and the pain.

"No," she said firmly. "We shouldn't."

Before she could change her mind, she stood up. Rudy and Cyn had offered to meet her in Central Park much later on, when, Elizabeth had hoped, Saloman would be out hunting. But she'd never have a better chance than now, when he was too weak to follow her. "I thought I might go down to the bar, maybe go for a walk. You can rest while I'm gone."

"Thank you," he said politely. "Are you going to dress first?"

"Of course," she muttered, reaching for the jeans and T-shirt she'd laid out already on the chair.

Shouting from the bathroom seemed easier. Because she couldn't see his face while she did her best to betray him.

"If Travis is based in Queens," she called casually, zipping up her jeans and thrusting her feet into comfortable sneakers, "where is Severin hanging out?"

"I'll take you," Saloman said, his voice so unexpectedly close that she jumped and spun around to face him. "If you're desperate to go."

Elizabeth stood still. Saloman offered the quickest and safest way of locating her prey. He was the only lead she had, and Severin could leave New York at any time. Did Saloman suspect she had a mission from the hunters? It didn't really matter. Whatever the greater good, she couldn't bear to use Saloman in this way.

"Hardly," she muttered, brushing past him to pick up her bag from the table.

. . .

Travis waited until the Ancient had left, by the same means he'd entered, until he could no longer hear the retreating engine of his car. Then he sprang into action, turning on his still subdued underlings with a snarl that barely hid his glee.

"Clean this shithole up! I want the ceiling repaired and new furniture in here by the evening. Al, you'll be in charge. I have a little business to take care of." Which should get the dangerous Ancient off his back once and for all, and send Severin scuttling back to LA. Provided, of course, that Saloman was an honorable vampire. It was hard to tell on short acquaintance, but at any rate it would take the arrogant bastard down to size.

Leaving his minions sweeping up, Travis strode off toward the parking lot.

He'd had a special semitransparent blind fitted to the side window of his car, so that he could leave it open and still keep the sun off himself. It was useful for smelling out enemies and, in this case, friends. The scent of Grayson Dante was still in his nostrils. It was easy to track him, even among the busy traffic, easy too to find the parking garage under his apartment building, just by following the senator's trail. And there, keeping his eye on the senator's car, he settled down to wait for darkness. He'd had bad experiences before, visiting humans in daylight—he still had the burn scars to prove it.

The waiting was easy for a patient vampire. The hardest part of the expedition turned out to be persuading the doorman to let him into the lobby. In the end he had to use a mesmeric stare to get the man near enough the glass door to mouth through it, *Senator Dante.*

Fortunately, the man then released the lock; Travis had no desire to kick in the glass and cause an incident for his new ally.

"Sir, the senator isn't at home."

"Yeah, yeah," said Travis. "His car's down there. Just call him up, will you? Tell him I'm here. My name's Travis."

"Ah, Mr. Travis. One moment." Under Travis's irate gaze, the man dived back behind his desk and produced an envelope, which he held out placatingly.

Travis snatched it and ripped it open.

"Dear Mr. Travis. I'm pursuing other options in Budapest. Will be in touch. D."

"Shit!" Travis crumpled the paper in his fist. He wasn't stupid enough to imagine that Dante had left the sword in his apartment, so how the hell was he to get it now?

He began to think that making a deal with Saloman had been a big—a very big—mistake.

Chapter Eleven

Sitting alone on a bench in Central Park after dark was not, Elizabeth knew, generally advised. Perhaps she was overconfident after her escape from Travis's vampires, but for some reason she didn't feel afraid. She was a little tense, certainly, and her fingers curled constantly around the stake hidden in her bag. Every sense reached out for the faintest signs of approach, but she had no real fear of attack, either by muggers or hungry vampires.

Interestingly, two youths in hooded tops, whom she might have suspected of criminal intent, gave her a wide berth, and she wondered if she actually looked too suspicious—like a decoy for some serious professional muggers. The vampires, she was sure, would come very soon, drawn by the scent of her powerful blood. Rudy and Cyn had claimed it was a haunt of vampires by night, and word would have circulated around the vampire community from Travis that the Awakener was in New York. Surely someone would notice her and be tempted to bite.

But it seemed she was wrong, and the native vampires were in no great hurry either to drink from her or to "gift" her to Saloman. As the hands crawled around her watch face, tiredness dragged at her eyelids. Five more minutes, she told herself, and then, for her own safety if for nothing else, she'd have to give up for tonight. She shook herself to stay alert.

She didn't hear it, or even feel it. There was just the tiniest prickle at the back of her neck, and then the thing flew at her from behind, knocking her off the bench. Before she hit the ground, she'd twisted to face it, so when it jumped on her again, it half impaled its shoulder on her stake. Elizabeth glimpsed a youngish woman with furious yet surprised red eyes and long, sharp incisors, before the vampire reared up with a yell of rage and wrenched the stake out of her own shoulder. Hurling it at Elizabeth's head, where it bounced side-on with a sharp smack, she lunged again for Elizabeth's throat.

The vampire was a snarling, wriggling mass of bestial anger. Elizabeth felt saliva dripping on her neck as she pushed desperately at the vampire's chin with one hand, and with the other scrabbled to find the discarded stake.

As her fingers finally closed around the sharpened stick, the vampire jerked her chin free and raised her fist to smash it into Elizabeth's face. Elizabeth dragged up the stake and plunged. Her first wild blow caught the vampire's punching arm, distracting her long enough to let Elizabeth take better aim. The second stab was true, and in midyell, the vampire exploded into dust.

"Damn," Elizabeth muttered, picking herself up. She'd meant to ask questions before killing. Even instead of killing, but the option just hadn't presented itself. Her skin prickled again and she gripped the stake tighter, whirling to face the trees on the left of the bench.

A shadow stepped into the moonlight. A young man in jeans and a dark T-shirt.

"Well," he observed, apparently watching the particles of dust disperse into the night. "She didn't last long."

"Fledgling," Elizabeth said briefly. She didn't move, aware that for the first time ever, she didn't know what she faced here: vampire or hunter. He had to be one of the two.

The young man came closer. "Only a week old," he agreed. Lifting his head, he sniffed the air, giving her the clue she needed. "Your blood is strong," he observed. "No wonder she didn't wait for my order to strike. Are you a hunter?"

"Not exactly." But none of this was going according to plan. Shouldn't he know from her scent who she was? Travis had known. "Who are you?"

The vampire smiled and halted a couple of feet away from her. "Jacob."

"I met your leader this afternoon. Travis."

"Strong vampire," Jacob allowed, "but not my leader."

Bull's-eye. Elizabeth's heart beat faster. "Then you came with Severin from LA?"

Jacob smiled. "Hardly. New York born and died. Are you going to use that thing?"

"What?" Disappointed with his answer, Elizabeth took a moment to realize he was talking about her stake. "I haven't made up my mind."

"Neither have I," Jacob admitted. "I want your blood very badly, but I've a feeling you'd stake me before I could take it."

"I would," Elizabeth agreed, fortunately sounding far more certain than she felt. She hadn't encountered a vampire quite like this one before. "You're very honest," she observed, dividing her attention between his face and his hands, alert for the faintest threat.

"I'm not known for it," Jacob said. "In this town, a vampire who holds apart from Travis has to make money where he can."

She began to understand. "So you hang around Central Park to mug the muggers?"

"I wouldn't like you to mistake my morals." Jacob sounded amused. "I'll mug anyone, scam anyone, kill anyone who can't kill me first. Why are you so strong for a human, Miss Not-Exactly-a-Hunter?"

Saloman, she thought in sudden, furious understanding. Only luck, not the scent of Awakener, had drawn Jacob and the fledgling to her. Her question about Severin had been too pointed. Saloman was tracking her and masking at least some of her identity—whether for her own safety or because he'd guessed her plans. She hadn't known he could do that, even at full strength.

"It doesn't matter," Elizabeth said hastily. And in fact, neither did Saloman's interference. "Would you like to make money from me?"

"If it doesn't involve coming close to you while you're armed."

"It doesn't." The vampire, she suspected, was a con artist, among other things. She had absolutely no intentions of dropping her guard, or of trusting him. But perhaps they could use each other. "Do you happen to know if the vampire Severin is still in New York? And if so, where he's hiding?"

"No," said Jacob. "But for the right price, I can find out."

Elizabeth smiled. "Good answer."

Elizabeth woke to darkness.

Still heavy with sleep, she struggled for a moment to orient herself, to realize someone else was moving in the bedroom with her. She tensed, remembering the stake in her bag beside the bed, but as her senses reached out, she knew it was Saloman by his faint yet distinctive scent, his silence, his quickness, and then his stillness.

He hadn't asked her where she'd been when she'd returned to their room. He'd simply risen from the bed, informed her of the room service meal on the table—which proved he knew she hadn't done more than pass through the hotel bar—and sat down by the computer. Elizabeth hadn't mentioned Jacob either, or questioned him about masking her identity. In his company, the whole idea of trying to locate and kill his supporter seemed absurd. Saloman was always one step ahead of her.

Now no one moved; no one breathed except her, and yet she was aware that he stood at the bedside. She kept her eyes closed, pretending to be asleep, even while her heart hammered in her breast.

Saloman wouldn't tolerate more betrayal. She'd put herself in more danger than she'd bargained for with this mission.

With his fingertips, he touched her cheek, her lips, so softly it could have been her imagination, except for the instant tingle of her skin in helpless response. She was afraid to breathe; she wanted to weep because of his tenderness, because it was clear to her he sought nothing from this. He wanted to touch without waking.

Shame filled her, along with the gnawing pain she'd brought on herself by trying to choose two opposing sides. It wasn't just idealism either. She *wanted* to help the hunters, to ease Mihaela's burden.

She felt Saloman's gaze on her face for a moment longer, and then the air shifted as he walked, almost glided, away from the bed toward the window.

Elizabeth opened her eyes, so moved by the incident that she began to wonder if she was right to keep herself from him. But the reasons that had parted them hadn't changed. Saloman hadn't changed and neither had she. But that tiny sign of affection seemed to intensify her love for him. The ache of need spread through her like wildfire and she wondered if she dared to call him back. What difference could it make, after all? She was beyond help, long past the time when staying away from him could prevent her hurt. What difference would one night in his arms make to that? To the world? One snatched night of happiness couldn't worsen the pain of parting; it could only ease the present, for him as well as for her.

For this moment, this night, Elizabeth, I love you. That was what he'd said to her in Budapest. Seven weeks later, in St. Andrews, she couldn't doubt that that precious flame of affection still burned. *I will never kill you,* he'd promised, because it was too hard to kill what you'd loved.

Memory of the unexpected meeting in Dante's Highland house

swamped her. She remembered the passion of his kisses and wanted more, wanted to be in his arms so much it frightened her.

She couldn't make decisions in such a state. He was here with her, and that would have to be enough. She closed her eyes firmly and reminded herself she'd come to New York for good reasons: to warn Rudolph Meyer, to find and kill Severin, to investigate Dante and protect Josh, who at least believed her now.

After Elizabeth left, Josh spent a lot of time on the phone to his agent, two producers, and a director, negotiating a short postponement of his commitments. He also had to fend off Mark and Fenstein, who wanted to come around and cosset him and didn't take kindly to being told to go on paid vacation. But Josh was growing too used to the pleasant independence of life in New York, where it was much easier to keep a low profile and slip into anonymity. It reminded him of the old days, when he and Emily had been young and working in theater. Except, of course, that he hadn't been attacked by vampires back then. And no one had stolen his sword, which he now needed to reclaim more than ever, since he'd discovered his unworldly father had been right about so many impossible things. The sword was more than a keepsake now; it was an icon, a justification of his father to everyone who'd ever laughed at him.

As darkness began to fall, Josh closed all the drapes and blinds in the apartment, shutting out the night because Elizabeth had told him that was when vampires roamed at will. He had to trust her that none of them would seek him out, especially not when he was under hunter protection, but he didn't understand it. That Travis had seemed pretty determined to get him this afternoon, even if he'd fancied a bite of Elizabeth even more.

And Elizabeth! Now that the shock was wearing off, he could remember her defense against the vampires with pride as well as astonishment. Never in a million years had he expected the quietly spoken academic to turn into such an efficient killing machine, more like Buffy the Vampire Slayer than any other label he'd pinned on her. As he retrieved his frozen dinner from the oven he realized that he hadn't even told her how much he admired her for what she'd done; he hadn't even said thank-you.

Josh sat down in the living room with his dinner on a tray and opened a bottle of beer. He'd call her tomorrow, say all the things he should have today. And ask her all the questions that had been occurring to him since she left.

Just as he turned the television on, and began to enjoy his unaccustomedly down-market meal, his cell phone rang. Cursing, he set his tray on the sofa beside him and fished out the phone. It was Garrick, the detective he'd hired to watch Dante.

Dante! Shit, I forgot all about him!

"Hi, Garrick, what's happening?" he asked breezily, covering up his weird feeling of guilt.

"Got some news on our friend," Garrick reported. "While you took over at the club, I waited back at his apartment building until he came home. But he wasn't there for long. Left in a cab just after five o'clock and I followed him to JFK. And I'm afraid that's where I lost him. I know he made a private charter, but I couldn't find out where to, not by wheedling, cajoling, or bribing."

"Shit, you mean he's left the country?"

"He could have. I went back to his apartment, saw his people shutting it up as if his stay in New York is definitely over. He could have just flown back to Washington, of course. I'll get in touch with my contacts there."

"Okay," Josh agreed. "Let me know if you hear anything."

"Will do," said Garrick, and rang off.

Josh scrolled down to find Elizabeth's number, then hesitated. Since the poor girl was probably jet-lagged on top of all today's excitement, perhaps he should just send a text. He made it brief, since he planned to call her in the morning.

. . .

It was hard to sleep knowing he was there, knowing what she wanted more than anything. In fact, it became impossible even to lie still. Restlessly, she shifted her head on the pillow, then turned over onto her other side.

Risking it, she opened her eyes slowly. He stood with his back to her, his dark silhouette against the tall full-length window. One hand rested on the pulled-back curtain as he gazed out at the night.

He'd said he wouldn't go out, that he didn't need to, and certainly by the time she'd gone to bed, leaving him in front of the computer, he'd looked as if his full strength was fast returning. But she realized all over again that although he'd taught himself how to make the most of daylight too in this modern world, he was at heart a creature of the night. *Eat your heart out, Bela Lugosi. . . .*

She wondered if it called to him, or if he saw the darkness much as she did. She wondered what he did out there when he wasn't plotting and planning and exerting his will over the ever-growing numbers of his minions. Aside from feeding.

She tried to shy away from that thought. He drank a lot of blood, although he rarely killed. It didn't make the idea of him feeding from humans much more palatable to her. Unwanted, an image swam before her eyes of a young woman—she looked a little like the girl who'd brought her room-service dinner—clasped in his arms as he buried his fangs in her neck.

Shocked, Elizabeth realized that her feelings weren't merely distaste. Between her legs trickled the wetness of sexual arousal, because part of her, a ridiculously large part, was jealous of each of his victims, real and imagined.

And yet she'd hated him in Budapest after he'd fed from her.

She licked her dry lips, banishing guilt as well as jealousy. "Go out if you want to," she said quietly.

He didn't turn. In fact, he answered with so little surprise that she suspected he'd always known she was awake. "I don't want to. I like to stand here, listening to you breathe behind me. It gives me the illusion of companionship."

Elizabeth closed her eyes. In that moment, she understood him so completely it hurt. She knew his loneliness as if it were her own, and this was all there would ever be for them, snatched nights when circumstances beyond them dictated they could be together for twenty-four hours. For a being thousands of years old, that was less than a drop in the ocean.

This is all there is. Don't waste it, Silk.

She rose from the bed before she could change her mind, padding the few feet across the soft-pile carpet to his side. Still he didn't turn from the window, but by the city lights reflected on his face, she glimpsed his faint smile.

"Is it all illusion with us, Saloman? Is none of it real?"

"It's all real, just . . . fleeting."

He wanted more; he still wanted more. It should have appalled her; it should have sent her scurrying back to bed with the sheets drawn up to her chin in protection. She should not have continued to stand there in her sexy nightdress, and she certainly shouldn't have taken his hand, threading her fingers through his as she gazed with him across the blackness of Central Park. The sounds of traffic and partying were faint, but audible.

"I never expected New York to be this beautiful," she observed.

"It has its own charm, as all places do."

"You *have* been here before!"

The smile came back briefly and vanished. "Not since it was like this. A long time ago, before it was called America."

She accepted that. One day, perhaps even tomorrow, he would tell her about it. Tonight, it seemed, he didn't want to talk. So she lifted their joined hands to her cheek.

"I wish it was different, Saloman," she whispered, and then, before the tears came, she dropped his hand and turned away.

But she moved too slowly. Before she had even taken a step, he'd seized her wrist and swung her against him. His arms were hard around her and his head swooped like some bird of prey. There was no time to protest before his lips crushed hers.

Her mouth opened wide in shock; she might even have intended to object, but as he took possession, she gave up and sank into his embrace with a muffled moan of relief and joy. He bent her body backward, grinding the hardness of his erection into her abdomen, and she flung her arms up around his neck, grasping his hair between her fingers. As he deepened the kiss, she welcomed his tongue with her own, and when she felt the graze of his dangerous fangs, she licked them greedily.

Saloman spoke inside her head, presumably so that he could keep kissing her. *Did you come to offer me your blood or your body?*

Either. Both.

I wish I'd thought of showing you weakness before.

At that, she tore her mouth free, tugging at his hair in a feeble attempt to prevent him from doing exactly as he wanted to. "You think this is some kind of weird, misplaced pity?" she whispered.

He didn't answer, simply took her mouth back, and her tugging fingers relaxed in his hair, holding him to her. *You don't like pity*, she reminded him.

I like sex with you. One hand caressed her shoulder, pushing down the strap of her nightdress, then slid down over her exposed breast. Elizabeth moaned, pressing into his hand, into the bone-hard erection nudging between her legs.

Saloman jerked down the other strap, and her nightdress pooled around her ankles. At last he released her mouth, drawing back a little so that he could look at her. "Naked in my arms," he whispered. "That's where you should be."

She couldn't disagree with that, especially not when he bent his head to take one elongated nipple into his mouth. She held his head to her breast, her eyelids falling in bliss as his sucking seemed to draw on some invisible pleasure cord running between her nipple and her womb.

"But you're not," she gasped out. "Naked, I mean."

He smiled around her nipple, then lifted his head to take back her willing mouth while his hand closed on her breast once more. *I don't need to be.*

Elizabeth disagreed there. Sliding her hands down his back, she tugged at the loose silk shirt he wore, trying to draw it free of his trousers, but it seemed Saloman's needs were more urgent. With a surge of fresh excitement, Elizabeth felt his fingers pushing between their bodies, working at the fastening of his trousers. She gasped into his mouth as the immediacy of his desire infected hers. He raised his head and lifted her by the waist. From instinct, she wrapped her legs around his hips. Amber flames shot through his black eyes and he lowered her slowly. His naked erection nudged between her legs, drove along her slit, making her gasp and jerk with the sharpness of the pleasure, and then he found her entrance and let her slide down his shaft.

Elizabeth moaned long and low. She'd dreamed of this, yearned for it since she'd last known it—making love with Saloman. He filled her, stretched her with such exciting sensation that she thought she'd come at once. But he held her still, his cool cock slowly heating and twitching inside her. She was drowning in his eyes, in lust and love.

The movement seemed to grow very gradually from his throbbing inside her. When it morphed into a slow, sensual thrusting, she began to undulate very slightly, soaking up the additional delight it gave her. Increasing the pace, she lifted herself and fell on him in slow, sensual strokes that made him groan and throw back his head. She smiled, reaching again for his mouth, kissing him deeply while their bodies gyrated and thrust together, grinding in such exquisite pleasure that she wanted it never to end.

Over his shoulder, she became aware that the curtains had drawn themselves fully back, that Saloman made love to her against the background of New York's beauty. Upright in his strong, steady arms, she had the illusion that they floated above the city, the only two beings who existed there. And as their bodies thrust and writhed and strained with ever-increasing urgency, the lights of the city lost focus, became confused with the glittering of his burning eyes and the unbearable ecstasy building inside her and clamoring for release.

Like all of this loving, the orgasm came slowly, rising higher with each stroke inside her until she thought it would never stop and she wouldn't be able to bear any more. Her own moans and cries echoed in her ears as she convulsed on him, clinging to him, burying her face in his hair as he kissed her neck in a long, sucking kiss. She felt his teeth like shards of ice on her skin, and with an abruptness that made her jerk, he bit her and sucked before she was properly aware of what was happening.

As if the blood were being drawn from her delirious, convulsing core, each powerful suck was like a fresh pulse of ecstasy, holding her in orgasm while he fed. His deep, howling groan told her he'd released his own climax, intensifying it with her blood.

She felt as if she were spinning through air, half fainting from sensation she could no longer bear. And then, with a jolt, she realized he'd laid her on the bed, still buried between her thighs as he loomed over her. He detached his teeth from her throat, pressing his tongue to her wound.

"More later," he promised huskily. "I could drink from you forever."

So long as he didn't take it all and kill her.

Rearing up on his knees, he tore off his shirt and slid out of her to remove his trousers and underwear together. He threw them all on the floor with such force that Elizabeth struggled through her haze of joy to say, "What are you doing?"

"Preparing to make love to you again."

. . .

When the knock sounded, Severin gazed bleakly at his hotel room door. The new future he'd begun to envision with such eagerness seemed to have crumbled with Maggie's dust. It wasn't his first loss of a beloved female companion, but it was the deepest, and he struggled now to make the necessary decisions.

Saloman, who'd been everything he'd hoped for and more—powerful, impressive, commanding—had also been surprisingly sympathetic at their meeting early yesterday morning. He seemed to understand both the loneliness of Severin's position ruling his unruly people, and the blow of Maggie's loss. Saloman had said he'd deal with Travis, that Severin should take his vampires home to safety. And he was right.

Except part of Severin demanded revenge for Maggie. Another part disliked being quite so submissive, even to so powerful an ally. Especially when this ally was also talking to Travis. Travis had made sure he knew about that, sending him a mocking, if brief, telepathic message that he and Saloman were gambling for the leadership of America.

Where exactly would Severin fit in? Disgruntled as he was, he found it hard to care. He missed Maggie, whose enthusiasm for Saloman's new world had convinced him to come here.

And so here he still was, surrounded by his restless followers. And the unaligned vampire Jacob now stood patiently on the other side of the flimsy door. Severin's senses could pick up no other vampire presence in the vicinity, so he jerked his head at his minions to let Jacob in.

With vague distaste, Severin watched him swagger across the room.

"Glad I found you," Jacob said. His pleasure appeared to be genuine. "I met someone who's looking for you."

"Who?" Severin asked, without much interest.

"A girl. Human, but very strong. Not a hunter. She wants to know where you are."

Severin curled his lip. "I presume she paid you for the information."

"She will when I give it to her. I was wondering if you'd care to pay me to make the introductions on your terms instead."

Severin let out a contemptuous laugh. "Do you really have nothing more on your mind than making money?"

"No," Jacob said candidly.

Severin regarded him. "Does she have a name, this girl?"

"Presumably. But I don't know what it is. She's not American—British, I'd say. And I had the impression her interest was not friendly."

Severin narrowed his gaze, thinking of the two humans who'd followed them to the office block after the previous night's hunt. "There've been people sniffing around us since the fight. What does this girl look like?"

Jacob shrugged. "White. Red-blond hair. Pretty. Looks fragile as antique china."

Severin frowned. "That's not the one." Standing up, he walked over to Jacob and sniffed. He hadn't touched this human woman, for none of her smell lingered on him. Knowledgeable and strong and not a hunter. And British. A suspicion began to enter his head. Could this girl be trying to use him to get to Saloman himself? Could she be the elusive Awakener whom Saloman had failed to kill? Trying to lead the hunters to the Ancient before Saloman got to her?

Seeing his way at last, Severin felt his inertia fall away. He swung on his followers. "Anton, you and Frederick stay with me. Louis, you take the rest home. We'll catch up."

"Now?" Louis objected. "It's nearly dawn and I—" Under Severin's glare, he broke off and shut up.

"What are we doing, boss?" Anton asked eagerly.

"We're going to catch a present for Saloman," Severin said with relish. "Which should give us a little more leverage in this relationship. Jacob, you may arrange it."

Gamble with that, Travis.

. . .

It had happened before—slipping into this cocoon of happiness and sensual pleasures that excluded the world and every notion of right and wrong that she knew. There was only Saloman.

Eternally fascinating, he held her in thrall once more. The remains of the night disappeared in the blissful excitement of lovemaking, punctuated, or even accompanied, by lethargic talk and laughter. She'd almost forgotten his wit and how he could make her laugh, even when she least wanted to.

Only as dawn broke, and she sprawled naked against the pillows within the circle of his arm, did she remember why he'd come here, and what he'd said in his tiredness yesterday evening.

"What game are you playing with Travis?" she asked lazily, running her fingertips along the veins of his hand.

"Hunt the sword. Winner takes America."

She blinked and stopped caressing to stare at him. "Isn't that a bit of a risk?"

"Not when I know where the sword is." His hand moved, finding her breast and idly rolling the nipple between his fingers as he spoke. It made it harder to be angry.

"Where is it, then?" she managed.

"At Dante's apartment."

"You're guessing," she accused, wriggling under the growing pleasure of his relentless fingers.

"At this moment, yes. But it was there yesterday. In fact, if you hadn't fallen into Travis's clutches just at the wrong moment, I would have,.er, reclaimed it. That's the second time you've distracted me from that particular quest."

Elizabeth couldn't resist a crow of triumph, which made him smile, so she teased, "You don't seem to regard it as a very urgent quest. Shouldn't you have gone to get the sword last night? Even if just to keep it out of Travis's hands?"

"I had better things to do last night," he said, and when she glanced at him provokingly, his hand stilled on her breast and he added by way of explanation, "Fucking you and drinking your blood."

The flush of heat rose swiftly into her face. "You used to say those things because you thought they would shock me."

"Now I say them because I know they arouse you."

Indignantly, she tugged at the hand, which had begun to torture her breast once more. "I'm not so shallow!"

"I didn't say you were shallow, but you are damnably fuckable."

"Saloman!"

"What?" he said, rolling her under him and stroking the sensitive wound on her neck, which he had broken and healed twice in the night.

"Aren't you afraid Travis might have taken the sword?" she said, rediscovering her thread with some difficulty under his distracting fingers, which slid from her throat back down to her breast.

"One more little drink," he said huskily, "just because you recover so fast. And no," he added against her skin. "Someone has taught Dante an object-masking enchantment. I doubt Travis could see through it."

"Where can Dante have learned . . . ? Oh, Jesus," she whispered as he pierced her skin and she felt again the blissful pull of her blood into his cruel, tender mouth. But this time, it lasted only a moment, just long enough for him to push himself inside her once more, thus distracting her from her perverse disappointment as he healed the wound so soon after making it.

"It isn't natural to make love this often." She gasped, holding on to him as he rode her.

"It is for me. And you don't appear to object."

She didn't. Her body soaked him up like an addict, although she couldn't imagine it even tolerating this amount of attention from anyone else. She was also aware that at some point she really would need to sleep.

"I can't," she whispered. "Even when everything hurts, as soon as you touch me it turns back into pleasure and I want you all over again. That isn't natural either."

His eyes darkened impossibly as he moved above her, his face pale and shadowed in the shifting dawn light. "It is for me."

When she woke, the travel clock beside the bed told her it was just after nine o'clock, which meant she'd been asleep for only a couple of hours. And yet she felt almost luxuriously refreshed as she stretched alone in the large bed and saw Saloman through the open doorway, sitting at the desk in the living area with his back to her.

Perhaps she needed less sleep as her physical strength grew. She'd killed several vampires yesterday and some of them had been strong.

Or perhaps she was just happy.

Between her legs was a dull, pleasurable ache that became more than part tingle as she gazed at Saloman. Impossible to want more sex. She'd shatter.

Smiling at the ridiculous thought, she rose from the bed and padded across the room, pausing to pick up her green nightdress from the floor and drop it over her head as she walked through to the living area.

Saloman, dressed in a loose white shirt and dark trousers, glanced up and smiled, the rare, full smile that warmed her heart. She'd seen it a lot in the last twelve hours.

"What are you doing?" Elizabeth asked.

"Researching paranormal sources," he replied unexpectedly, reaching one arm around her.

She blinked. "I thought you knew more than all the books put together!"

"I do, but Dante doesn't. You made a good point last night. He must be getting his information from somewhere."

"Yes, but would you find those kinds of books online? The hunters' libraries aren't available," Elizabeth pointed out.

"I'm looking for other sources. Rare books in private or public collections. But I'm not finding much that could have given Dante the knowledge he has."

"Maybe his relationship with Travis is long-standing. Travis could have told him everything he knows."

"Possibly."

Elizabeth slid reluctantly out of his arm to go to fetch her phone from the dressing table. Mihaela might well have discovered some connection between the two unlikely allies. Or some clue as to Severin's whereabouts that might make the dubious Jacob redundant. But the only message waiting for her was from Josh.

"Oh, dear," she said ruefully, and when Saloman glanced across at her, she almost wanted to laugh. "Dante's left New York. Do you suppose he's taken your sword?"

Chapter Twelve

Having decided to go together to Dante's apartment to allow Saloman to "feel" for the sword, they took longer than expected to finally get out of the hotel—largely because the sight of Elizabeth fresh from the shower inflamed Saloman all over again. With her sunny hair toweled and rumpled and glistening with dampness, the snowy-white bathrobe that was too large for her drooping across one graceful shoulder, she looked adorable in a completely different way from the compassionate, almost hesitant siren of last night.

He couldn't watch her padding across the bedroom without touching her, and her reaction to being touched—an oddly delightful one of mingled surprise and pleasure as she turned in his arms—made him kiss her. And after that, the rest was inevitable.

However, as he took her to bed once more, arousing her further with hands and lips that knew her body increasingly well, he surprised himself by his powerful urge to care for her. He was aware he'd exhausted her last night, had taken more from her body than was good for a human, and not just in terms of the blood she regenerated so quickly now. And so he took his pleasure in pleasuring her, always a joy and now given an exquisite edge by his deliberate restraint.

Ignoring the clamor of his own body, he did not enter Elizabeth's, but made love to her only with tender hands and lips, teaching her new rapture that she welcomed with gratifying wonder. And when he finally took his lips from her convulsing sex and moved up her body to kiss her mouth instead, she clung to him in a way that made his heart soar and ache at once, especially when she shifted to make her body more available to him.

"I think you've had enough for now," he whispered.

Her eyes were both soft and deliberately tempting. "Have you?"

"I'm teasing myself by waiting for the night."

Her eyes searched his, as if for some dissatisfaction, and then, presumably finding none, she pushed him with a mischievous grin, rolling him over to straddle him. But he lifted her off and set her on the floor.

"I want my sword," he said with mock severity.

Laughing, she ran back into the bathroom, although this time she left the door open, like a symbol of their new intimacy, while she called through the doorway with spontaneous curiosity, "Don't you ever need to shower?"

"My body cleanses itself from the dirt of the air. And since I produce no bodily toxins or sweat, I have no need of water."

"That's bizarre." The sound of the shower spraying her naked body once more added to his suppressed arousal. Over the splashing, she added, "It used to bother me—how you always smelled so good when I'd never once seen you wash!"

"You humans concern yourselves too much with trivia."

"Comes of having bodily toxins," she said dryly, "and an attraction for dirt that isn't too afraid to cling to our bodies."

The shower was switched off and she reemerged in the decidedly damp bathrobe, rubbing herself dry. This time he kept his hands off her, but entertained himself by lounging in a chair and watching her dry and dress. There was an intimacy in it that almost frightened him, but, having begun it, he refused to forgo the pleasure.

Clearly deep in thought, she didn't talk as she dressed and combed out her hair. Only as she set down the comb and turned to him did she say abruptly, "What will you do with the sword when you find it?"

Saloman stood. "Treasure it," he said flippantly. "And keep it safe from others. Much as I do with you, in fact. Shall we go?"

He walked into the living area and toward the door. Keeping up with him, she parted her lips to ask more questions, as if well aware she wasn't being told the whole truth. Which, of course, she wasn't. He couldn't tell Elizabeth that. He couldn't tell anyone.

He didn't even need to get out of the car. He knew before they entered the parking garage under Dante's building that the sword wasn't there.

"You don't seem to mind too much," Elizabeth observed as he restarted the car.

"I expected it to be gone with Dante."

As he drove toward the exit and pulled out into the traffic once more, he felt her intense gaze on his face. "Do you suppose Travis has it after all?"

"No, but I'll drive past his lair to make sure."

"He could have hidden it somewhere else."

Saloman smiled at her innocence. "Nowhere I couldn't find it. Besides, if he had it, he would be waving it in my face—no doubt before as many witnesses as he could drum up, including Severin—to show that he had won our wager and that I should now slink off with my tail between my legs."

"Would you?" she asked curiously.

"Slink? I'm not sure I know how. I would have to find another way to win his submission."

By this time, her gaze almost burned him, so he spared a moment's attention from the hectic road to glance at her. For an instant, her clear hazel eyes seemed to pierce him, as if she were trying to examine his very soul. Then she gave a quick, deprecating smile and dropped her gaze.

"You're afraid to ask," he observed, slowing to avoid a collision with a large truck in his path. "But you're wondering why I don't just kill him."

"It crossed my mind," she confessed. "I even wondered if you *could* kill him."

"I could," Saloman said, overtaking the truck and speeding up in order to make it to the next traffic light before it changed. Driving in a large city was like one of those computer games Dmitriu had first shown him in an arcade in Bistrița. "But where would be the fun in that?"

Again, she surprised him, seeing behind the flippancy of his words to the deeper truth beneath. "It *is* fun for you, isn't it? Gathering power and territory, pulling the strings."

There was no point in denying it, so he merely shrugged. "Yes." After a moment, skidding through the lights the instant they changed, he added, "More fun than killing, although I'd be lying if I said I hadn't enjoyed that too. It's a trait of my race that humans find contradictory—we enjoy the exhilaration of the hunt and the kill, and yet value all forms of existence."

There was a pause, then, "So speaks the vampire Saloman."

"You don't believe me," he observed. It shouldn't have hurt. He was well aware she still regarded him as the enemy. In fact, she regarded herself in much the same light, just because she loved him.

But unexpectedly, he felt the brief, brushing caress of her head on his arm. "That's the trouble," she said ruefully. "When I'm with you, I believe everything you say. I don't think you ever lie, but I know you can be economical with the truth. I have to think of every possible meaning behind everything you say. And don't say."

"I don't want death and destruction," he said. "Still less do I want to rule over these things. Do you believe that?"

He glanced at her again and saw a faint smile on her lips. "Yes," she said. "Although I refer you to my previous caveat."

"Always the academic," he murmured, giving in to the next red traffic light.

"I'm just trying to understand," she said intensely, and he believed she was.

"It's not so hard," he said gently, "when you add it to what you already know of me. Existence embraces *all* of life, good and bad, the most extreme emotions, and physical feats as well as the lesser events and the quiet times. What is the point of any existence if you don't experience all of it?"

"If you don't enjoy it," she said slowly, still watching his face. "Like you made me enjoy my life in Budapest, even though you meant to take it from me."

"Yes," he admitted. "Believe it or not, my people regard it as a responsibility. Used to regard it. Now I carry it alone."

Her breath seemed to catch. "But who are you to choose?" she burst out. "It isn't up to you! Why should I get to live when Professor Salgado-Rodriguez didn't? On your mere whim, Saloman!"

He loved her anger, her opposition. It made him all the more determined to win her. And he had no objection to explaining his point of view.

"A whim, if you insist," he allowed, "but there was nothing mere about it. I make choices for the greater good, and that demands that I be strong—emotionally as well as physically."

Again, her eyes burned him. "I make you strong? Even alive, I make you strong?"

He couldn't help smiling at her tone, which managed to mingle disbelief with pleasure and downright astonishment. But he didn't want her immolating herself for the hunters. So he rephrased it. "You add to my existence." He hesitated, then added, "And there is potential in you that goes beyond the personal."

"Potential for what?" she demanded.

"I don't know. It's still, er . . . potential."

Almost as if they were married, he dropped her off on Fifth Avenue to do some window-shopping while he went to a business meeting. First of all, she found an ATM and withdrew money she could ill afford in case she needed to pay Jacob that night. Then she relaxed into tourist mode.

It felt weird. As she gazed into windows full of glamorous clothes and fashionable shoes, she was chiefly conscious of the desire to meet up with Saloman again. And yet the very prospect of it added an exciting luster to her expedition. Although she couldn't afford the fabric she let slide between her fingers, or the handbags she admired from a safe distance, it was fun to look, to soak up the ambience of New York, and know that soon she'd see him again, talk to him again. Make love with him again.

For Elizabeth, the future was a blank canvas, and she took care to keep it that way. In her heart, she knew this fragile happiness couldn't last, but she refused to think of it as an illusion, because for this moment, it was real. And she grasped the moment with eagerness.

I'm beginning to think like him. . . .

When her phone rang, she grabbed it from her bag like a teenager waiting for her boyfriend to text. But this was no love note. It was from Jacob.

Stupidly, shock brought her to a halt on the pavement and someone walked into her heels. Muttering apologies, Elizabeth slunk up against a shop window to read the brief note.

"I have it. Bring money. J.," followed by an address off Fifth Avenue. The closeness made her blood run cold, sent her gaze scanning among the crowd and up on the rooftops. But that was ridiculous. Jacob couldn't walk under the sun.

He could have human accomplices. He's the type who would. They wouldn't even guess what he is.

Dropping her phone back into her bag, Elizabeth pulled herself together. She hadn't been afraid of Jacob last night, alone in the dark; she was damned if she'd give in to fear in broad daylight. This was *her* world.

She paused only long enough to surreptitiously conceal a second easily accessible stake, then turned on her heel and walked back the way she'd come until she reached the first crossing. Jacob must have been driving behind her to know she would recognize the street easily and join him quickly. And if he was in one of the shops, he wouldn't risk attacking her.

But the address he'd specified appeared to be a deserted shop. Dark blinds covered the windows and the glass door. A sign read CLOSED FOR BEREAVEMENT. Elizabeth only hesitated a moment before, right hand on the stake in her bag, she pushed at the door with her left. It opened easily.

Warily, she stepped inside. The shop was gloomy, with most of the sunlight blocked by the blinds, but she could still make out racks of coats and jackets and dresses. Too many places for a vampire to hide. If Jacob decided he wanted her blood as well as her money, she'd have to rely on her reflexes and hope they saved her from losing either.

She moved slowly inside, glancing around, deliberately brushing into the clothes to disturb anyone skulking beneath them. Halfway across the shop, a staircase ran up to a gallery full of hats, bags, belts, and other accessories, modeled on shadowy mannequins.

As she reached the middle of the floor, checking to the right and left, another shadow detached itself from under the stairs. Elizabeth halted, curling her fingers more tightly around the stake in her bag.

"Miss Not-Exactly-a-Hunter," said the mocking voice she remembered. "I have your information. I hope you have my money."

"If you lie to me, I'll have your description spread around every hunter network and police force in the country. You'll lose more than you've earned."

"I get you," Jacob said patiently, halting a respectful—or circumspect—two feet away from her. Slowly, he lifted one hand, palm upward in an unmistakable request.

With her left hand, Elizabeth drew the sheaf of money from her bag to let him see it. "Where?" she asked.

"They move around to make sure Travis's boys don't find them. But right now Severin and his bodyguard are at the Sheraton Hotel on Long Island. All together in room two twelve."

She scanned his steady eyes. She'd never know if he was lying until she went there. If it was true, would she have time to get there and kill Severin before Saloman found her? Then at least it would be over; she'd have completed her mission.

Slowly, she extended her left hand with the money. "Thank you."

Jacob smiled. "Thank *you*," he said, closing the distance and reaching for the cash. But as he took it, his fingers touched hers, giving her an instant's warning before they twisted, snaking up to seize her hand along with the dollar bills.

She expected it. At least she'd get her money back. She whipped the stake free of her bag and plunged it unerringly toward Jacob's heart.

Something clobbered her from above and wrenched the stake from her right hand, while Jacob snatched the money from her left. With a grunt of pain, she fell to her knees, and realized she'd been jumped from the gallery above. *Stupid, stupid, stupid . . .*

"It's been a pleasure doing business with you, ma'am," Jacob said with a mocking tug at his forelock as he wandered to the door with his money. The being who yanked her head back by the hair to see her face was a stronger vampire. She could feel it. And he was not alone.

"I'm Severin," he said with a curl of his lips as two other vampires emerged from the back of the shop. "I hear you've been looking for me, Elizabeth Silk."

She had little choice but to let him draw her to her feet by the hair and turn her in his rigid hold to face him. He was tall, black, and well dressed, his head shaved and his face unexpectedly thoughtful.

"I want to make a suggestion," she said, relieved her voice didn't shake. Her shoulders throbbed from the blow she'd taken.

Severin released her hair, but not her right arm. "Go on."

"You don't need to submit to Saloman. Ally with Travis against him."

Severin grinned with undisguised contempt. "To stop him from killing you?"

Elizabeth inclined her head.

"You must be very clever to have evaded him for so long," Severin observed. "Though, of course, he likes to play cat and mouse. I hear he's playing with Travis now too. Pay him," he added to his followers with a jerk of the head, and Elizabeth realized Jacob still lurked at the door.

As one of the vampires walked in Jacob's direction, Severin turned his gaze back to Elizabeth, who was afraid to breathe. The door opened and closed behind Jacob. One less vampire. If anything, Severin's immovable grip on her arm tightened as he said softly, "As either a gift or blackmail, Saloman's Awakener is extremely valuable to me."

Which, Elizabeth thought, was only too true. Although Severin clearly didn't have all the facts, with her in his power he could make Saloman do anything. For many reasons, Saloman would not risk her. She didn't doubt that if Severin took her to Saloman right now, the Ancient would save her.

She would have failed both the hunters and Saloman.

Before Severin could drag her, she jerked her head to one side, drawing his attention to her throat. "My blood is valuable too," she said huskily, and even as hunger flashed in his eyes, she gave one subtle shake of her left arm, as if she shivered. The hidden stake dropped from her sleeve into her palm and she thrust upward, fast and sure.

Severin's scream of fury cut to silence as he exploded into dust.

Elizabeth leapt back, catching the falling stake that he'd taken from her earlier and holding both in front of her against the vampires who leapt toward her. Severin's power rushed into her like a tidal wave. She felt exultant, invincible.

"I'm the Awakener!" she cried. She sounded insane and she didn't care. Instead, she laughed with triumph, because she'd succeeded. She'd done the right thing and won. Both vampires skidded to a halt, staring at her. One glanced uncertainly at the other. Elizabeth took a purposeful step forward, and they fled.

Although Grayson Dante hadn't ever visited Budapest before, he had good feelings about the city. This place would be the setting for his acquisition of the ultimate power—he knew it, and the knowledge gave him added confidence as he walked alone in the dark along the gloomy, narrow streets of the old part of town. Although he'd been given directions, he almost missed it. He'd walked to the end of the street and back again before he took to staring with extreme concentration at each building.

To the trendily dressed young couple who passed him, giggling, he must have looked a trifle weird, studying architecture in the dark. He didn't care. He suspected some kind of masking spell and was determined to see through it. Whether he would have without help, he never discovered, for the young couple disappeared into a doorway in front of him.

Now, why would such a young pair, dressed up to the nines as if for a party, be visiting such a run-down building that resembled nothing more than a warehouse? Pausing in front of the grimy, firmly closed door, Dante glanced around the building above him—and saw the angel carved above the door.

Eureka.

Smiling, he pushed at the door, which gave instantly. He had time, on his journey up the long and dirty staircase, to wonder if he'd gotten it wrong. A bare lightbulb dangling from a wire near the top of the building barely illuminated the shabby walls with the paint peeling off. The steps beneath the handmade leather soles of his shoes felt gritty with dirt and fallen plaster. However, at the head of the staircase, he was greeted by a large young man dressed in black who showed no particular surprise to encounter him.

"Hi," Dante said amiably. "Can you help me, sir? Is this the Angel Club?"

Although he spoke in English, the expressionless young man appeared to understand him, for he nodded once and even opened the door for him. Dante felt a little thrill run up his spine, a spark of danger, because the doorman could be a vampire.

Inside was massively different. Everything was clean and well lighted, although tastefully so, lending to an array of booths around the walls an illusion of cozy privacy. The walls were painted with bright, baroque murals, and a large dome in the center of the ceiling with an open window at the top provided an impression of light and space and fresh air. Under it, a few people were dancing to loud, modern music. Not Dante's taste, but he was happy to tolerate it for the night.

The wall nearest him was taken up with a long bar counter, at which sat one or two men and a beautiful woman in a black dress. Since it would appear the most natural thing to do, Dante took up position on the stool next to the beautiful woman in black.

A smart young man behind the bar spoke to him in Hungarian. Guessing, Dante said, "Bourbon, please," and turned to the lady beside him with his most winning smile. "Hi. I don't suppose you speak English, do you?"

"Actually, yes, I do. A little."

"Fantastic! I have absolutely no Hungarian, which is a little bit daunting when I don't know the city either."

The lady smiled. She had the sexiest dark eyes Dante had ever seen, and for the first time in many months he felt the stirrings of lust. If she was a vampire, she was by far the most attractive of his admittedly limited experience. He found himself wondering if vampires fucked.

The beautiful woman who might have been a vampiress watched him pay for the drink, saying lightly, "And yet you found your way here."

"That was easy. I had directions. Can I buy you a drink, Miss . . . ?"

"Angyalka. Thank you, no."

He stuck out his hand. "I'm Grayson. Pleased to meet you."

She took his hand in a brief, cool grip and released it. "Someone recommended the Angel to you?"

Dante smiled. That had caught her attention. The rest would be easy. "Absolutely. I was hoping to meet a friend here."

She inclined her head.

Dante let himself hesitate, then said, "I don't suppose . . . Do you come here a lot, Angyalka? Do you know the regulars?"

"I recognize some faces," she admitted mildly. "Who are you looking for?"

"A guy named Dmitriu. Do you know him?"

"Indeed," said Angyalka.

"Is he here?" Dante asked. Shit, he sounded too eager. He had to hold himself back. It was just that he hadn't expected this to be so easy.

"No," said Angyalka.

So much for easy. "Any idea where I could find him?"

"No." It wasn't encouraging, and perhaps he looked as crestfallen as he suddenly felt, for she added, "If I see him, I'll tell him you're looking."

"Could I try again tomorrow night?"

She shrugged and slid off the stool. "You could," she said, and, lifting the flap, she walked around behind the bar. Dante understood that their interview was at an end.

Saloman stood by the hotel room window with his back to her. He knew. He'd have known as soon as Severin died.

Elizabeth's whole body shook. She closed the door with a short, sharp click and lifted her head. "I killed him."

He didn't turn or make any response. After what she'd done, it was madness to have come back here to him. But her pride and defiance had insisted. And she wasn't defenseless. She grasped the stake in her pocket and, forcing her trembling legs, she strode toward the bedroom.

Before she was halfway there, he caught her, holding her chin between his strong fingers. She glared into his opaque, unreadable eyes, refusing to be afraid or ashamed; and yet inexplicable tears prickled at her throat.

"I killed Severin!" she raged.

"I know you did." He didn't even sound angry, just curious, which made everything worse. He should at least care enough to be angry. "You went after him for the hunters and you killed him. So why are you crying?"

"Because I'm happy he's gone!" She gave a futile jerk against his hand, and a sob rose up in her throat, choking her. She closed her eyes, but she couldn't shut out the images of Saloman or Severin. "Because I feel like an assassin. Because he wasn't a ravening beast."

Saloman drew her against him and the tears flowed faster, soaking his shirt as she inhaled his scent, his strength, and gripped the stake tighter. His lips touched her neck.

Her breath shuddered. She opened her fingers wide, releasing the stake, for there was no point in fighting, not against Saloman. She had nothing left to give him. He'd said he'd never kill her, but she couldn't blame him if he changed his mind. Another betrayal by someone who loved him.

His teeth grazed her skin. His words vibrated along her vein. "I mourn Severin's passing. But it was never Severin I needed most. It's Travis."

Without biting, Saloman raised his head and gazed into her stunned face.

"I'm grateful for your care and your distress," he said softly, taking her face between his hands. "You walk a difficult path, Elizabeth Silk, and it will only get harder. Take heart from the strength that has brought you through this."

Her lips parted and closed again. "You *aren't* angry," she blurted.

"I could have stopped it. I could have kept you by my side, masked you as I did last night. But you wouldn't be who you are if you didn't go your own way, make your own choices. As Severin made his."

Slowly, she let her head fall forward onto his chest.

It seemed she'd managed to do the right thing, and still kept her happiness for another day. There would be time, later, once they'd parted, to come to terms with all the emotions surrounding her killing of Severin. For now, the fact that Saloman forgave her was too awe-inspiring to leave room for anything else.

Josh, who'd negotiated a week's grace to sort out his sword and vampire problems, now didn't know what to do with himself. He called Garrick, his detective, who knew no more than he did last night, except that Dante hadn't yet appeared in Washington. He thought of calling Elizabeth, but kept putting it off because the bizarre events of yesterday seemed increasingly like a dream, and he had no idea how to talk about them, or even if he should.

Eventually, around dusk, he drove to her hotel, the Mandarin Oriental, and asked for her at reception. While the girl rang Elizabeth's room, he left his sunglasses on, but she kept glancing at him until, with a big smile, she said, "Hey, you're Josh Alexander."

Josh grinned and lifted one finger to his lips. At once the receptionist nodded enthusiastically, keeping his secret for at least as long as he was there to watch her.

"I'm sorry, sir," she said at last. "There's no answer from Miss Silk's room. Would you like to leave a message for her?"

Josh nearly laughed in her face. *Sure, tell her this vampire business is completely freaking me out. . . .* "No, that's all right. Thanks."

He turned and walked smartly out again, riding the elevator back down to ground level. He decided on a quick walk around Central Park before it got completely dark, and then he'd try the hotel again.

But the first person he saw in the park was Elizabeth.

Josh stopped dead and stared. She wore a bright, Gypsy-style skirt and top, neither new nor fashionable, and yet she looked stunning. Her magnificent hair fell loose around her shoulders, shining in the half-light like a memory of the setting sun. Relaxed and smiling, completely oblivious to his observation, she walked hand in hand with a tall man he recognized. Adam Simon.

Find Adam Simon and tell him what happened here. . . .

He's just a man with a finger in lots of pies, useful to have on your side to get you out of a scrape.

Adam Simon, who knew her well enough to kiss her on the lips in greeting at Dante's house party, whom she then told Josh not to trust. But with whom she now walked hand in hand looking . . . looking happier than Josh had ever seen her.

Well, he didn't begrudge her that. Whatever attraction there had ever been between him and Elizabeth seemed to have simmered down to mere empathy on his part. On hers, there had never been anything more. He'd known that as soon as she'd lifted the cloak that had fallen out of her bedroom drawer back in St. Andrews. Adam Simon had given her the cloak. He knew that now as well as he knew anything at all. What it didn't explain was what he had to do with Elizabeth being in New York now, with Senator Dante, with his sword, or with the vampires who'd attacked them. And shit, if Simon wasn't the man who saved them from that little escapade, then he had a brother with a damned close family resemblance.

Could Elizabeth have been lying to him? Elizabeth, his cousin whom he barely knew and yet had trusted out of some mere instinct, simply because he thought he understood faces?

His fists curled tight at his sides. Why the hell would she lie? What did it achieve?

The answer took his breath away. She wanted his sword.

Ahead of him on the path, Adam Simon turned his head and looked straight at him. Josh's stomach flipped in sudden, inexplicable fear. The man's eyes seemed to flash like lightning, reminding him unbearably of that vision he'd done his damnedest to forget. *Give me my sword.*

"It's mine," Josh whispered.

After a late room-service dinner, Elizabeth guiltily opened her computer for the first time since her arrival in New York. There was an e-mail from Mihaela, but before reading it, she got her own news off her chest. Since this was likely to be seen in some form by many people, she kept it dispassionate, and somehow that made it easier to tell—her encounter with Rudy Meyer and Cyn, and how the vampire Jacob had led her to Severin, whom she'd managed to kill that afternoon.

She hit send with a feeling of relief, and then opened Mihaela's message. It was disappointing. Basically, apart from his discreet interest in the spiritual and the paranormal, Mihaela had been able to find no connection between the vampire world and Senator Dante. However, tomorrow in the Budapest headquarters, they were expecting to entertain the visiting Grand Master of the American hunters, so Mihaela promised to pick his brains if she could.

"Not," Mihaela added, with her typical disrespect for authority, "that the Grand Masters necessarily know anything more than the man in the street, but at least it's worth a shot. *Some* of them prefer to be more than figureheads." Which was a sideswipe at the Hungarian Grand Master.

"By the way," she finished, "Seen anything of Josh Alexander? ☺"

Elizabeth smiled and scanned the rest of her e-mail. No word yet on her thesis. Surely it wouldn't be long now. What if they wanted to interview her again and she was still in America?

Oh, well, she'd deal with that if she had to. Right now, it was difficult to care. Elizabeth closed the lid and glanced across at Saloman, who was busy with his own computer. For a while, she watched him in silence, feeling the ache of love grow stronger. He was going to live forever, and yet the fact that he chose to spend a day with her, to love her for one night or two, still stunned her.

His long, elegant fingers flew across the keyboard faster than she could comfortably see; his dark eyes darted across the screen, a faint crease of concentration between them. He still wore his suit trousers, but with his silk shirt pulled free of the waistband, and his feet under the desk were bare. With his hair tumbling loose about his shoulders, he looked like some improbably handsome computer-geek hero from a futuristic hacker movie. Or something. She smiled at the thought, and as if he sensed it, he glanced up, his hands stilling on the keys an instant later.

"What?"

"I was just wondering what you're doing with such industry. Wheeling and dealing?" She rose and walked toward him.

"Undealing."

"What does that mean?"

"Canceling arms deals with some very unsavory characters."

Her breath caught in sudden pain. "You're arms dealing now?"

"Undealing," he repeated gently.

"But you're deciding again!" In distress, she dropped to her knees, peering up into his face as if pleading with him to see this her way. "You're deciding who's worthy to receive your arms! I wish you had nothing to do with stuff like this!"

"But you want the world to be made better. Someone has to make a start."

"With arms dealing?"

"Controlling it, policing it, if you like. I've begun in a small way, and in time, as my influence spreads, I'll be able to make sure no one else sells where I refuse. Dante has a huge stake in this industry, and once I have control of that . . ."

"God knows where it will end," she whispered. Was he not powerful enough without a vast array of weapons at his command? "No one person should have power like this. . . ."

"That," said Saloman, "depends on the person."

She took hold of his knees. "No, it doesn't," she said seriously.

His face softened. He stretched out one hand to smooth her hair from her cheek. "Trust me. There are so many things I can do for the world, that vampires can do for humanity. It can be as it was before, that we care for you."

She caught his wrist. "We're not pets, Saloman! We need to be in charge of our own betterment."

"Then would you consider working together?" His lips quirked. "Like you and me."

She searched his eyes, her fingers tightening on his wrist. "You're serious. You really imagine humans could work with vampires? Travis for state governor, perhaps?"

"Open your mind, Elizabeth," he urged. "I said 'care for,' not govern. My people had an affinity with the earth that gave them senses way beyond those of humans. Some of that blood runs still in the veins of modern vampires, however corrupt. The world could use that."

She swallowed, fighting her instinct to believe his plausible yet impossible words. "Humans couldn't live with the knowledge that vampires exist. They'd slaughter you without compunction, and in the inevitable war, they'd be destroyed."

Saloman sniffed the air. "I smell hunter," he mocked, and when she jerked her hand away from him in protest, he caught it back and pulled her up on to his knee. "Think for yourself, Elizabeth. You're a clever woman," he said, as once before, and kissed her mouth.

She wasn't prepared to surrender, not yet, but she couldn't maintain her rigidity in his arms for long, not when everything in her body leapt to meet the demand of his lips and the deliberate, wicked sensuality of his hands. There was an odd, intense sweetness about being so seduced, and in the end, it didn't matter what he said, what he believed, what he did. She couldn't prevent herself from loving him.

It was a weakness she couldn't even hate anymore, although somewhere she remembered how she had once despised women who loved and stood by their men through the most horrendous crimes. Loving Saloman gave her a new understanding, and yet she knew there would come a time, very soon, when she could no longer stand by him. After Dante and the matter of the sword were dealt with, she would have to leave him again.

"Not yet," she whispered into his mouth, throwing her arms around his neck. "Not yet."

He stood, lifting her in his arms and strode with her to the bed. "Yes, right now," he commanded, and what was left of her bodily resistance burst into fire. She opened her mouth wide under his, fought him for control of the kiss, even as she gasped out, "Yes, oh, yes," and when he laid her on the bed, she dragged him down with her, wrapping her legs around his hips and thrusting up to meet his exciting hardness.

Another night of bliss with Saloman. There had never been more than one night at a time before this, and she was aware of the danger as she writhed under him, dragging at his clothes and wriggling to feel all of him against her desperate body. She was sinking deeper into the darkness and it felt increasingly like light.

Chapter Thirteen

Dante's morning appointment suited his mood perfectly. The discreet but impressive old building, efficiently masked, seemed a perfect setting for the next stage of his plan. He just had to hold his excitement in check, put to the back of his mind the knowledge that by tonight the ultimate power would most probably be his.

The Hungarian Grand Master of the Order of Vampire Hunters greeted him in the foyer with flattering respect. Keeping to protocol, they didn't use each other's names, and in fact, Dante was unaware of the Hungarian's. An impressive array of staff was lined up behind him too, and Dante's spirits soared again to know that here he was in the most densely vampire populated area of the world. These hunters were the best because they had to be. And tonight, Dante needed them.

Therefore he was exceedingly gracious when the Grand Master turned to his team, saying with barely a hint of pomposity, "And all of my staff join me in the honor of welcoming to Budapest the Grand Master of the American Order. Your Excellency, allow me to present to you my deputy and chief librarian, Miklós."

A thin, almost unimpressive man of middle years bowed to him. He didn't possess enough muscle to be Dante's prime interest of the day, but since one never knew when more information would be valuable, he shook Miklós's hand heartily, and moved with the Grand Master to be introduced individually to his hunting teams.

Like the Americans, these guys also hunted in threes. The senior team consisted of two fit-looking men and a young woman who stared at him with flattering intensity. Dante noted them in his head as possibles while the Grand Master introduced them by first name only, beginning with their respectful leader, Konrad. Dante missed the other man's name because of the way the girl, Mihaela, continued to stare at him. It was almost unnerving, particularly since her cheeks looked slightly flushed in the cool of the drafty old foyer, and as he shook hands with her, giving her a special pat on the shoulder to show he thoroughly approved of her spunk in doing such a rough job for a female, he realized she must have recognized him.

It wasn't impossible. Despite his deliberately low profile, he figured in the American news from time to time, and even abroad he was mentioned occasionally. He wondered if it was worth catching her later to ask her to keep his name under her hat, although after tonight, would it really matter?

The other hunters all looked equally fit and strong, and Dante decided any one team would serve his purpose. Together with the sword, they'd ensure Dmitriu was his.

When he broached his special mission in the reception hall, where cold drinks and a rather magnificent breakfast feast were set out, the Hungarian Grand Master was pleased to give his gracious consent and asked for volunteers among the hunters.

They all stopped talking and eating to glance at one another, clearly hoping for the honor. But the Grand Master looked at Konrad, the leader of the senior team, who smiled and parted his lips, no doubt to accept. Then, without warning, his expression changed to one of pain and indignation.

"Unfortunately, it's impossible for us," Konrad said smoothly in perfect English. "Tonight, we have a duty that cannot wait."

Dante wondered if he'd only remembered it when the girl, Mihaela, stood on his foot.

Saloman said conversationally, "Travis has gone."

Elizabeth, lying across his naked chest with her chin on her folded arms to watch him, frowned. She wasn't sure she wanted this night interrupted with talk of external events, and yet it didn't bother her as much as she expected—because he was still here, with no obvious plans to change that in the immediate future. She roused herself to ask, "Gone where? When?"

"A couple of hours ago. And I don't know exactly. East, toward Europe."

Elizabeth didn't ask how he knew. He could sense the presence of other vampires, track them over vast distances without moving an inch himself.

"Then he hasn't acted to take over Severin's little empire? Even though he must know that Severin's dead. What do you suppose that means?" she wondered. "Has he gone after the sword?"

"Probably. Which means he's gone after Dante."

Elizabeth smiled. "So if we sit tight here for a little longer, you'll know where Dante is through Travis?"

"Exactly." He stroked her hair, spreading it out across his chest. It was a quiet, precious time after a long, delicious loving. Although Elizabeth was tired, she refused to sleep and lose the moment, the feel of his tender hands and his relaxed, powerful body.

She moved her arms to drop a lazy kiss on the smooth skin of his chest. "So which do you want to find most? The sword or Dante?"

"The sword," he said at once. His lip twitched, but it wasn't quite a smile, before he added like a mitigation, "One will come with the other."

It seemed she knew him now, for she could tell he'd revealed more than he meant to. "But it's the sword that drives you," she prompted. "In fact, I wouldn't be surprised if pursuit of the sword hadn't led you to him in the first place."

His fingers tangled in her hair and gently tugged. "You are too shrewd. I'd already run across him in business and marked him. But you're right, the Spanish professor—yet another distant cousin of yours—told me Dante had been to him looking for the sword. Which means he was on the trail of Tsigana's descendants."

"But I could almost swear Dante didn't know who I was until I touched the sword at his house party."

"He probably stopped looking for descendants once he discovered Josh had the sword. The question, as you already noted, is how he knew where to look in the first place."

"Actually," Elizabeth said, giving in to the pull of his hand to slide up nearer his questing mouth, "I've moved on to a different question." Her lips parted, hovering over his.

"And what is that?" he asked. The words stirred her lips, spreading new sparks through her sated body.

"Why you want the sword. Is it so very powerful?"

His lips curved, brushing against hers so faintly it might have been an accident. "You mean more powerful than I?"

"Yes."

His gaze lifted from her lips to her eyes. There was a pause, as if the question meant more than she knew, and suddenly she was afraid to breathe. Their lips didn't move to separate or to join, and when he finally spoke, she felt the words slide into her like a secret never before revealed.

"I place a different value on the sword. Because . . ."

"Because?" she prompted when his words dried up.

"Because it was a gift."

Not from Tsigana. Oh please, not from Tsigana . . . Although sudden, pointless jealousy filled her, piercing like a knife, she held his dark, stormy gaze, kept her lips where he could take them at will, and waited.

"My cousin Luk gave me it when I died."

Her lips parted. "Luk? Your cousin whom you . . . ?"

"Killed. Yes."

"You want a keepsake of your enemy?"

"I want the keepsake of my friend." Abruptly, he took her mouth, as if that made it easier to tell, and his words formed in her head to the rhythm of his deep, sensual kisses.

I'd known Luk all my life. When I died, it was he who led my revival, he who became my guide in my new existence. He was strong, clever, just rebellious enough to appeal to my youth. His profound wisdom and understanding of all earth's races was second to none. He was respected and admired, even by the elders who frequently disagreed with him. And yet he usually got his way because of his other gift. . . .

He released her mouth, allowing her one quick, gasping breath before he returned to it, almost fiercely. Passion soared higher, making it difficult to concentrate on Saloman's story. Elizabeth felt torn, wanted to concentrate on one or the other, and yet she couldn't stop him now. For some reason, he needed to talk and to lose himself in her at the same time. So she drank him in like wine and urged him on.

What other gift? she asked.

Prophecy. Foresight. The gift that is more of a curse. Most of my people had it to some extent, even I; but in most of us it is little more than a feeling, a tingle, a mostly forgotten dream associated with an object we touch, a place we see, a person we meet. Luk, however, had true visions, and no one but I could see how they tore him apart and drove him toward madness. . . .

He opened her mouth wider, deepening and hardening the kiss, as he rolled her under him and continued it, holding her head steady and winding his tongue around hers like a lash.

I loved Luk more than any being, and it broke my heart when he began to lose his mind and turn against me. He grew jealous of my increasing power, and in the end he could not see beyond Tsigana, beyond taking her from me.

His kiss became desperate, and his wicked incisors grazed the inside of her lips. Elizabeth welcomed the pain with the pleasure, and yet she ached for the deeper, far more corrosive pain that still ate him up. His hands slid under her buttocks, kneading.

Tsigana fed his lust, of course, hoping to gain immortality from one of us. I'd known for a decade that I should kill him before his madness brought us all down, endangering humans and vampires alike. I put it off, hoping he'd recover. But then, when Tsigana went to him . . . I wanted *to hurt him, for her, and I hated—*

His words broke off. His knee parted her legs and he pushed himself inside her with a force that made her gasp in as much astonishment as pleasure. Somehow, she hung on to the thread through the devastating assault on her senses, afraid he'd tell her no more. Afraid that he would.

You hated yourself for that, she managed at last. Sorrow for him, for herself, had somehow blended with the sexual bliss. Together they surged higher, overwhelming her.

He gave me the sword, Saloman said, moving above her, inside her, hard, fast, and relentlessly. His dark eyes glittered with inhuman power. *And I will have it back. As I have you. Possessed. Come.*

As if at his command, she came with a speed that shook her, pounded over the edge as he reached his own savage climax. She wanted to weep through the shock of physical pleasure, because she understood that he hadn't meant to tell her this; Luk was his own, hidden pain that he'd intended should remain so. Moved to her core, she arched under him, kissing him now in compassion and love and gratitude. She could only be proud, profoundly glad, if the use of her body had eased some of his pain.

He broke the kiss slowly, still lying over her, still hard inside her as he gazed down into her face. "I've waited more than three hundred years and I've let it slip away from me twice now, but never doubt that when the time comes I will take it back."

She opened her mouth to reply, but he gave her no time. He thrust once more inside her, a lazy, sensual stroke that caught the fading embers of her orgasm and made her gasp. "And never doubt that I can take you too."

Oh, Jesus, do it. Give me no choice, no thought; just do it, just let me be with you. . . . Everything in her leapt to meet his unspoken demand, and yet her sane, thinking self knew even then that it was not a temptation she could follow.

She hugged him to her, her palms flat against his hard back. Then she dragged her hands up to touch his face with her fingertips. "Saloman," she whispered. "Saloman."

The fierce passion in his eyes began to fade, leaving them lighter and softer. He rolled off her, pulling her to lie facing him. Much more urbanely, he said, "However, I wouldn't like you to think I'll tolerate Dante as a vampire either, with or without my sword."

"Good," she said faintly, and his face broke into a full smile that she couldn't help but return.

The sound of her phone ringing on the bedside table interrupted the moment with all the force of a fire alarm. Reaching over him, she picked it up to switch it off and saw that it was from Mihaela.

Oh, bugger, how far gone am I? Catching her breath, she pressed receive. "Mihaela? I got your e-mail. . . ."

"It doesn't matter now," came Mihaela's voice, low and urgent, as if she were speaking in front of others she didn't want to overhear.

Elizabeth pushed herself up on her elbow. "Mihaela, what's—"

"Dante's here," Mihaela interrupted.

Elizabeth's heart jolted. "In Budapest?" she asked eagerly.

"Yes, but I mean *here*," came the impatient response. "At headquarters. He's the Grand Master of the American hunters!"

Elizabeth's gaze flew to Saloman, lying still and silent by her side. She remembered to breathe again. "So that's how he knows so much. . . ." She sat up, her mind racing through possibilities. "Has he mentioned the sword?"

"No." There was a pause, a shuffling sound, as if Mihaela were moving position. Then, in an even lower voice, she continued. "But I'm sure he's up to something. He's asked for a team to help with a special job tonight."

"You don't know what?" Elizabeth said at once.

"No," came the rueful reply. "There's something about him. . . . I wanted no part of whatever he's up to, and knowing your suspicions . . . Shit, every instinct is against having anything to do with him, so I talked Konrad out of volunteering. He's not very pleased with me, and maybe he's right, because if Dante took us at least we'd all know what he was doing."

"No, your instincts were right," Elizabeth reassured her. "I very much doubt his loyalties are with the hunter network." *Are mine?*

She pressed her head back into the pillow. Saloman's hand found her shoulder, kneading the suddenly tense muscles there, and her eyes flew to his. Opaque, unreadable, watchful. *Saloman, Saloman.* They'd go to Budapest together and then . . . There was no point thinking beyond that.

"Thanks, Mihaela. I'll come over as soon as I can get on a flight. In the meantime, will you call me if you find out what this mission of his is?"

"Sure. I'll have a word with my colleagues if I can. It'll be good to see you," Mihaela added warmly.

Will it? Like this? In bed with the enemy? Her eyes closed in shame, for hearing Mihaela's voice brought home to her that she wasn't just betraying some impersonal ideal that the hunters stood for. She was betraying her friends. She was betraying Mihaela.

Saloman's arousing hand on her shoulder stilled. *Saloman.* She opened her eyes again and smiled, because she knew that whatever happened, she couldn't regret the last two days any more than she regretted their previous encounters. If she could choose again, she wouldn't do it differently. "We can meet you at the airport," Mihaela was offering.

"No, that's all right," she said hastily, and Saloman smiled, running his lips along her shoulder. "I'll call you when I get there."

As she ended the call, Saloman lifted his head and met her gaze. "He's in Budapest," she said unnecessarily. "What in God's name took him there? He's meant to be sick, so it's not an official visit. . . ." She frowned. "What the hell is there for him in Budapest that he couldn't find here in America?"

Her breath caught. "You?" she said doubtfully. "He doesn't know he's met you. He'd run from Travis's before you arrived. Could he be looking for you?"

"I doubt that," Saloman said slowly. "Not for me."

In one sudden, impossibly fluid movement, he unwound himself from her and rose from the bed. Saloman was always splendid; naked, he was magnificent, and Elizabeth couldn't drag her gaze away from his long, powerful legs, the graceful, economical movement of his hips, the undulation of muscles across his back and shoulders as he straightened and turned to her. His sheer sexual beauty overwhelmed her, and, in spite of everything, her heart began to drum once more.

"Not for me," he repeated, his eyes blazing with sudden, frightening fury. "For my blood. He wants to be turned with the blood of an Ancient, however diluted, to give him greater power." He grabbed up his clothes from the floor. "He's gone for Dmitriu."

Chapter Fourteen

Dante's only fear as he walked into the Angel on his second night in Budapest was that Dmitriu wouldn't turn up. He'd laid his plans well, with his volunteer hunter team in hiding, just waiting for his word. The men he'd brought from America for protection, mindless thugs even in his own estimation, were farther back but ready to be called in if necessary—duly primed, of course, that they might see some weird sights. He didn't want them freaking out and fleeing just when their muscle was required.

The club was busier than on the previous evening. Angyalka, serving behind the bar, gave him a sultry smile of welcome as he approached. "Good evening, sir. What would you like? Bourbon?"

He'd guessed last night she was a vampire. The Hungarian hunters had confirmed that suspicion, and also told him she was the owner of the establishment, and the main reason the club was tolerated. Like Travis's place in New York, it had been known to the hunters for several months and at one point almost closed down. But they'd decided to leave it in the end, mainly because they'd have had no idea where the next such place would open up if this one vanished. And so the Angel remained, a documented haunt of vampires who could thus be watched. And Angyalka herself tolerated no violence on the premises. The only known fight had erupted during an abortive raid by the hunters to capture the Ancient Saloman.

"Yes, please," Dante said, and she reached for the bottle. The knowledge of her power, a power he would soon surpass, sent a delightful little frisson through his body.

"Good to see you back," Angyalka said, but although Dante waited, she said nothing about Dmitriu, merely presented him with his glass and turned to the next customer.

Dante didn't want to call her back, to show too much eagerness by asking again about Dmitriu. He decided to wait awhile, and turned on his stool to watch the dancers, who, this evening, had a live rock band to gyrate to. Dante hoped he wouldn't have to wait too long—the music did his head in.

"Too loud, eh?" said the man sitting next to him.

Dante smiled. If he said yes he had no excuse for hanging around, and yet his expression must have been pained to elicit the comment. "I'm getting used to it." He glanced at his companion, unsure whether he had been there when he'd first arrived.

Dante spoke sharply to himself. He mustn't, he really mustn't let his guard down in this place. If he let overconfidence in his future mess up the present, then God alone knew what that future would entail.

The man beside him was youngish, maybe in his thirties or very early forties. He had spoken in English and had an intelligent look about him, and since he oozed comfortable amiability rather than threat, Dante figured there were worse ways to pass the time than in conversation.

"You Hungarian?" he asked in his best friendly-stranger-in-town manner.

"Romanian," the man responded. "I'm Dmitriu, and I hear you've been looking for me."

Everyone's self-esteem should be given a slap now and then. It woke a person up, kept him on his toes. Unfortunately, in this case, it also made his stomach twist with unexpected nerves.

Fighting it, he stuck out his hand. "Hey, Dmitriu, great to meet you at last. I'm Grayson."

Dmitriu took his hand in a cool, brief grip and waited. A five-hundred-year-old vampire must have learned a lot of patience.

"You've been recommended to me," Dante said, aiming at forming some kind of trust.

Dmitriu's dark brows twitched upward. He looked distinctly skeptical. "By whom?"

"Lots of people," Dante said vaguely; then, as the vampire's lip curled, he added hastily, "Look, Dmitriu, I won't beat about the bush here. The bottom line is I have a proposition for you."

Dmitriu continued to look at him in silence. Dante allowed himself a rueful glance at the band.

"We can't talk here," Dante said. "Shall we go somewhere quieter?"

For a moment he thought Dmitriu wouldn't even answer that, wondered if he'd have to bring the hunters and his own men in here.

Then Dmitriu pushed himself off his stool, clearly waiting for Dante to do the same. Dante smiled. He even remembered to call good night to Angyalka while, under pretense of checking in his pocket for wallet and phone, he pressed the "buzzer" the hunters had given him to attach to his phone. Now they'd know he and Dmitriu were on their way.

Dante's heart thundered with excitement as they made their way down the dingy staircase to the street. Beside him, the vampire Dmitriu, in whose veins flowed the rare and powerful blood of the last Ancient, the owner of the sword himself, walked in careless silence.

Although Dmitriu wasn't flamboyant and cocky like Travis, Dante wasn't fooled. He knew Dmitriu was strong and something of an enigma to the hunters; and in fact, his very negligence in leaving the bar with a complete stranger on a such a flimsy pretext spoke of a belief that he couldn't—or wouldn't—be harmed. Dante was happy to foster that belief for the next couple of minutes.

And then he'd strike. With the sword and the hunters, he couldn't lose.

"There's a quiet café down here," Dante said, turning left at the door. On cue, a solitary hunter turned the far corner and walked toward them. Dante's skin prickled as he prayed the other two were already approaching from behind. Despite his largely honorary position as Grand Master, he'd had no actual dealings with vampires apart from his two not entirely successful sorties to Travis's in New York; but he was aware Dmitriu was likely to sense danger, and to react with faster reflexes than any human could hope for.

But so far, at least, he could detect no concern in the body language of the silent vampire beside him. The hunter was maybe ten yards away and closing. And there were only about two more yards to where his inconspicuous car was parked.

Deliberately, Dante shivered. "I'm just going to get my coat from the car, if you don't mind. The night's turned a bit chilly."

Dmitriu inclined his head and halted while Dante unlocked the doors of his car. Casting a surreptitious glance in the direction they'd come from, he saw the two hunters walking smartly behind Dmitriu. Dante bent and felt yet another thrill as he touched the sword, even through Josh's dad's old coat, and dragged the bundle toward him.

His heart hammered. Timing was everything here. The hunters' footsteps were drawing closer. Three, two, one.

Dante yanked the sword free and spun to face the still passive Dmitriu, just as the hunters sprang.

Dante should have known that in a vampire, stillness did not necessarily betoken unpreparedness. And Dmitriu, it turned out, was perfectly prepared. Dante barely saw him move, and yet the two who jumped him from either side were sent flying across the pavement toward Dante, and the third, who managed to dodge Dmitriu's fist, was felled instead by a vicious kick.

The vampire walked purposefully toward him, and Dante saw that his blazing dark eyes were not amiable at all. The hunters, still stunned, scrabbled sideways out of his path, clearly trying to regather their energy for another attack.

Dante held the sword in front of him with both hands. The thrill of it helped counteract the desperation, the failing hope that the hunters could fight this being without the wooden stakes Dante himself had forbidden. He needed Dmitriu alive. Or at least still undead.

"You can't kill me with that," Dmitriu observed.

"I don't want to kill you," Dante said. With renewed excitement, he realized Dmitriu's gaze was riveted on the weapon. He recognized it, surely, knew its power.

But for several heartbeats, nothing happened. The sword did not compel Dmitriu to surrender. Perhaps it needed blood. Wildly, Dante thrust it into the vampire's shoulder. He didn't see Dmitriu move, but realized at once that the blow had been deflected to a mere graze. And that Dmitriu continued to gaze at him with curiosity but absolutely no submission in his dark face.

Shit. What the hell do I do now? How does this damned thing work?

"Three!" yelled the lead hunter, and once again all three of them launched themselves at the vampire, who shook them off like fleas.

Dante gave in and yelled for backup. He had a couple of moments to feel proud of his thugs, for Dmitriu clearly hadn't expected them. As Dmitriu wheeled to face the new threat piling out of the car across the road, the hunters managed a few good blows that sent the vampire staggering backward. And by then the four thugs were upon him.

The scene degenerated into a confused mess of flailing limbs. Dante had to shake his head to try to regain focus, to make out what was going on. Bodies began to fly into the road with such force that Dante knew, sickeningly, that there would be broken limbs. And they weren't Dmitriu's.

He could make out the vampire now, holding one of his thugs in both hands. With monstrous ease, Dmitriu broke his neck and hurled him to the ground. Dante, gripping the sword hard, moved forward, and Dmitriu advanced once more to meet him. His fists flew, knocking the still-game hunters cold beside his fallen thugs, and unbelievably, Dante knew he'd lost.

At the same time, his heart soared with excitement, because of the sheer strength in Dmitriu. He couldn't prevent the freezing, mind-numbing fear, but that didn't change the surge of longing, his desperate knowledge that this *was* what he truly craved, this power, which would never die but only grow with the passage of time.

Dmitriu's gaze dropped to the sword, which he wrenched from Dante's grip without further warning.

"That," said Dmitriu, "does not belong to you."

"I have a proposition for you," Dante croaked, just as one of his thugs lying at Dmitriu's feet rolled into the vampire's legs, trying to knock him off balance.

Dmitriu sliced down with the sword and the thug screamed. Dmitriu bent, dragging the man upright with his free hand. Under Dante's appalled but fascinated gaze, Dmitriu yanked the thug's head back by the hair and bit into his throat.

It was over with dizzying speed, the vampire dropping the drained body to the ground as if it were a finished beer can. The point of the Sword of Saloman pricked Dante's throat.

Yes! The desire for this death, anticipated so long and eagerly, filled him, almost smothering the need to negotiate.

Dmitriu's brow twitched into a frown. "Interesting," he murmured, searching Dante's eyes.

"My proposition . . ." Dante began desperately.

But inexplicably, Dmitriu lowered the sword. "Oh, no. You want this too much. I won't oblige you. But I thank you for the sword."

And the vampire turned away, stepping delicately over his victims as he sauntered off down the road with the sword swinging from one hand.

"Dmitriu!" Dante yelled pleadingly. "Wait!" He tried to run after him, but his legs shook too much and he'd never felt so old in his life. By the time he'd cleared the last of his fallen henchmen, Dmitriu was out of sight, and Dante was left alone with at least two dead bodies and several unconscious victims of violence.

He wasn't a politician for nothing. He averted his gaze and walked away.

Saloman. I have something of yours.

At the sound of the familiar voice, Saloman smiled. *I thought you might.*

He was with Elizabeth in the airport departure lounge, waiting for their flight to be called.

You might have warned me, Dmitriu complained.

I had faith in you to deal with him, Saloman responded blandly.

I'm touched. What do you want me to do with it?

Keep it for me. I'm on my way. Saloman sank into the seat beside Elizabeth, who was drinking coffee and turning the pages of a newspaper. *Where is Dante?*

Fled the carnage. He had hunters with him, and American bodyguards.

Saloman glanced at Elizabeth. *Did you kill the hunters?*

You know I like a peaceful life, Dmitriu said reproachfully. *Why would I kill them?*

Self-defense.

Well, that was the interesting thing. They had no stakes. And your man Dante has a death wish. Or is that undeath?

Elizabeth nudged him. "You're in the newspaper," she said sardonically, pointing at a photograph of him and an American businessman that had been taken at yesterday's meeting.

Don't grant it, Saloman commanded Dmitriu. *Under any circumstances. And by the way, watch out for a visiting vampire from America. He's called Travis and he's strong.*

His senses prickled, reminding him of someone he'd almost forgotten. Breaking the connection with Dmitriu, he reached over and folded the newspaper trumpeting Adam Simon's spectacular rise into the world of international business, and placed it in Elizabeth's open bag.

She regarded him over her coffee cup.

"Your cousin is here," he said, by way of explanation, and her gaze shifted with his to the door of the departure lounge, through which strolled Josh Alexander, stylish and handsome in dark glasses. He appeared to be alone, without any of the entourage of staff and hangers-on expected of a film star. Clearly, he was traveling incognito.

"Josh!" Elizabeth exclaimed, jumping to her feet and drawing his attention. His lips fell apart in obvious surprise when she all but ran to meet him. What had he imagined? That she wouldn't recognize him in shades? That she wouldn't be pleased to see him because she was with Adam Simon? Possibly. Certainly, suspicion oozed from his every pore as Elizabeth spoke to him, and took his arm to urge him to walk with her back to Saloman. Which was interesting too. She would have been forgiven for leading him in the opposite direction.

"Josh is going to Budapest too," she said flatly.

Josh looked him in the eye. "I figure you go where my sword is."

Saloman allowed himself a smile of delight. "You're following us."

Josh looked slightly disconcerted by this response. Then he sighed and, as if tired of pretending such distant dignity, took off his sunglasses to reveal the shadows of sleeplessness. He rubbed his eyes. "You don't even object, do you?"

"No. In fact," Saloman said, "I have no objection to our, er, pooling knowledge. At this moment, I think that would be to your advantage, since I know where the sword is."

Elizabeth paused in the act of retrieving her coffee to stare at him. "You do?"

"With Dante," Josh said at once.

"It was," Saloman allowed. "A friend of mine has just taken it from him."

Josh's eyes widened; then his gaze dropped in what might have been no more than a blink. He replaced his sunglasses.

"Is Dante dead?" Elizabeth demanded.

"No," Saloman said regretfully. "On the other hand, neither is he undead."

Josh said, "Is this a trustworthy friend?"

"Is there another kind?"

"Yes," said Josh fervently.

"Then, yes," Saloman said, and abruptly, Josh laughed and flung himself into the seat beside him.

"So what's your story, Adam? What have you got to do with the sword, with any of this?"

"Everything," said Saloman.

When Dante finally opened the door of his modest hotel room, his feet were dragging and his head spinning with the speed of his defeat as well as with desperate efforts to think what this meant for his plans. After everything he'd done to get it, he'd managed to lose the sword. And he figured alienating the vampire Dmitriu was another mistake. He didn't know whether it would be worse for Dmitriu to keep the sword for his own ends, or for him to return it to the legendary if shadowy Ancient Saloman.

And where in the hell *was* Saloman? Sooner or later, surely, the Ancient would enter the game to reclaim his sword. That was one reason Dante had wanted this done quickly, for once he had the immortal power and the sword, surely even Saloman couldn't take it from him?

However, Saloman's creation Dmitriu had taken it from him as easily as taking candy from a baby. As if it could sense his lack of power, the sword would not fight for Dante. Because he was not yet undead? Perhaps he should send the hunters out to catch him some slavering, bestial fledgling to do the turning.

But Dante had aimed high, once he'd understood something of the hierarchy of the immortal undead. And now, mere bestial vampirism wasn't enough for him. He wanted to be reborn at least at Dmitriu's level, with enough status and self-control to use the sword to his best advantage. Otherwise he couldn't hope to present any meaningful challenge to Saloman, who would simply kill him when their paths eventually crossed. He needed to be turned with some form of Saloman's blood—otherwise the whole endeavor was pointless.

There had to be another way to reach Dmitriu.

Closing the door, Dante leaned back against it and shut his eyes. In that instant, he felt the other presence in the room with a certainty that had him reaching, trembling, for the light switch.

Not Saloman! Oh, please, not Saloman. Not before he had time to think, to plan . . .

The vampire Travis swung gently in the swivel chair by the desk, spinning his hat on one finger. "Evening, Senator," he said amiably. "About your proposition . . ."

And suddenly, with the rush of relief came a wave of understanding. Whatever his earlier ambivalence in New York, Travis now wanted the sword enough to have followed him here. And Dante didn't underestimate the difficulties involved in long-distance vampire travel. In fact, when he'd left the note for Travis, it had been intended as a polite dismissal rather than an invitation, to show him in a placating sort of way—after all, he was a vampire—that negotiations were over.

Dante felt his shoulders straightening, and the lost smile reforming on his lips. "Travis, my friend. What a welcome surprise. I have a slightly different proposition for you now, but I know you'll like this one too."

"What about Josh?" Elizabeth said suddenly, as they settled into the connecting flight at Zurich airport. She'd spent most of the transatlantic crossing asleep, as if the excitement and sleeplessness of the last several days had finally caught up with her. She'd slept curled into Saloman's shoulder, although a couple of times she'd woken sprawled across his chest, as if clinging to him in sleep because the New York couple fantasy was about to end.

In Budapest, where Saloman had first seduced her, also resided her friends the vampire hunters, who would tolerate no alliance, let alone an affair, with the vampire who had defeated them in St. Andrews and eluded capture on two occasions since; who had drunk from Konrad as well as Elizabeth. *And killed neither*, she reminded them in her head, as if pleading his case. There would be no opportunity for that.

A Hungarian vampire now had the sword, and he would give it to Saloman. Elizabeth had to decide what to do about that. Loving him, and understanding the lonely, vulnerable side of him that missed the cousin he'd eventually killed, she wanted him to have it. But she couldn't allow the massive increase to his power that it would bring. What chance would humanity have then? Already, apart from America, he had almost the entire vampire community at his beck and call; more slowly but no less surely he was building wealth and influence in the human world. She had no idea how it would eventually occur, whether he planned to keep his kingdoms separate or use one to rule the other, whether he planned to rule humans covertly through puppet leaders, or to engineer some violent coup. Neither was acceptable. But with the additional power of the sword, surely either was increasingly possible.

She would have to give the sword to the hunters for safekeeping, to hide it forever from all vampires. And from Josh.

And as her cousin entered her head, she wondered what the hell to do with him in Budapest. And ridiculously, she spoke aloud to Saloman, whom she was planning to betray again, because she couldn't shake the recently formed habit of alliance with him.

"What do you want to do with him?" Saloman inquired, not even troubling to watch as Josh took his seat farther up the plane.

"Well, we can't have him blundering about Budapest demanding the sword back. If Dante doesn't kill him, one of the vampires will. A descendant who's also your enemy is a desirable kill, and he has no protection whatsoever."

"Give him to your hunters."

Elizabeth glanced at him uncertainly. It was the obvious answer, of course, but it meant an early visit, which she wasn't quite ready for. And he must have understood that without being told. He always understood too much. Deflecting his perception from herself, she spoke challengingly inside his head. *You've given up on killing Josh?*

The hunters can't protect him from me.

How safe are the hunters? The question tumbled out to him only because she couldn't stop it. Konrad, as a descendant of Tsigana's partner in crime, was valuable to him, as was the propaganda value of killing a hunter. On the night of the battle in St. Andrews, she'd violently stopped him from finishing Konrad off, and later, in closeness, she'd pleaded for the hunter's life and been granted it. She'd understood then that he spared all three hunters because she asked it. But how far would that promise stretch if she stole his sword?

The dangerous, alien being at her side was totally unpredictable. She'd always known that. He could make love to her exquisitely one night and kill her the following morning without seeing anything wrong in either. If she was honest—and she tried to be—his very strangeness added to her fascination; the very real risk brought addictive excitement. But just occasionally, like now, these points were rammed home with all the force of a hunter's stake to the heart, and the fear took her breath away, curling around her stomach and gripping until she wondered how she'd ever borne him to touch her.

Until he touched her again, as he did now, threading his fingers through hers between the seats, and then she melted once more.

As safe as they need to be. The hunters chose their own path. But as I told you, decisions can be changed and new choices made.

She closed her eyes, letting her head fall back on the seat as the familiar pain and longing welled up. A choice to stay with him. Unthinkable. And yet how easy had it been in New York? There was more too, a knowledge that had been struggling for recognition since the fight in Travis's gambling club, one she still refused to look at.

"I chose to protect Josh," she said quietly, "and he didn't choose any of this stuff."

"Then keep him with you."

Chapter Fifteen

As it turned out, there was no difficulty keeping Josh by her side when they arrived in Budapest. Having ignored them for most of the long, exhausting journey, he attached himself to them at baggage claim and clung like the proverbial limpet. Elizabeth, torn between her desire to stay with Saloman and her duty to steal from him, between her wish to see Mihaela and the hunters and her need to protect Josh, wrestled with her conscience until they walked into the front hall of the airport and Saloman went to arrange pickup of the hired car he'd ordered.

Then, with a distinct feeling of sacrifice, she began, "Josh, I'll take you to friends of mine—"

"Is *he* coming?"

"God, no."

"He's going to get the sword from *his* friend."

Elizabeth grasped his arm and shook it until he looked at her. "Josh, he won't give you the sword. And despite its connection with your father, you really, really don't want it. You and I both had a glimpse of its power. I know you didn't believe it then, but you've seen things since then, things that must make you realize that sword is more than it seems."

The cold disdain with which he'd regarded her since entering the departure lounge slipped slightly as he scanned her face. Perhaps her earnestness was finally getting through to him.

"Josh, my friends can explain all this so much better than I can. You probably think I lied to you—"

"I *know* you lied to me. The man who jumped through the roof at Travis's *was* him."

There was no way of knowing whether Josh had also clocked him as a vampire. Elizabeth said ruefully, "Yes, but Adam Simon isn't really his name. I'm sorry; I was playing with words to keep you as far out of this mess as I could. I should have known that was a lost cause. But you must see that you can't have the sword back now. Every fiend in hell and on earth would fight to take it from you, and shit, Josh, the sword *was* Saloman's. There's no way you can keep it from him, not on your own."

Some of that penetrated his stubbornness. His eyes grew thoughtful, a serious frown marring his brow.

"Come with me?" she pleaded.

Then, as Saloman came to stand silently beside her, Josh's gaze shifted to him and hardened. "He knows where the sword is. I'm going with him."

"By all means," Saloman said graciously, waving the car keys in his hand. "Let us all visit Dmitriu. He will be charmed."

Elizabeth closed her lips. "Dmitriu's in Budapest? *Dmitriu* took the sword? My God, Dante got so close. . . ."

"Dante could not trouble Dmitriu," Saloman said with a hint of pride that made Elizabeth want to laugh or hug him or both. "Not even with hunters at his back. Shall we go and find my car?"

As they piled into the large car whose windows were inevitably blacked out, Saloman laid his documents on the dashboard and put the key in the ignition. Elizabeth, in the front seat beside him, waited until they were clear of the airport and onto the main road into the city before she reached out and picked up his driving license.

It was an empty wallet.

Saloman smiled at the road.

"You don't have one, do you?" she murmured in Hungarian.

"No, but it's easy to make anyone who looks at it see what I want them to." Under her astonished eyes, the blank wallet suddenly looked like a Hungarian driver's license in the name of Adam Simon.

She blinked until it showed blank once more and then, with a sigh, tossed it back on the dashboard. "Is your passport like that too?"

"Oh, no, it's perfectly legal. I paid for it."

"Congratulations." She gave in. "All right. Where did you learn to drive?"

"In a disused industrial estate," he said. "I used to race the local hooligans in their stolen cars."

"Where does your friend live?" Josh's voice interrupted from the back.

"Dmitriu? He has a secluded penthouse in the city," Saloman said so blandly that Elizabeth knew there was some joke. She "got" it immediately when Saloman drew up outside a disused warehouse near the river.

"Your friend lives *here*?" Josh said, as he got out and gazed up at the ugly building, with its broken windows and the graffiti of several decades. For the first time, he actually looked daunted. "How the hell can he keep *anything* safe here? Let alone a priceless antique!"

"You'd be surprised," Saloman said, closing the car door with a casual swing and leading the way into the building.

Elizabeth touched Josh's arm. "Dmitriu is a vampire," she said quietly, and when Josh's head jerked around in panic, she added hastily, "He won't attack you. Trust me, I wouldn't lead us into another mess like Travis's. I know this city a little better than New York." *And we're under the protection of the strongest vampire of them all.*

Saloman led them through the bare, empty building, picking his graceful way over the rubble and broken glass to a dirty stone staircase. They began to climb.

"You've brought company," a voice observed from the top. He spoke in English, which meant he'd recognized Elizabeth. Although she and Josh both paused and glanced upward from instinct, Saloman merely smiled, continuing to climb with long, steady strides.

"Only the best," he said to Dmitriu. "I hope you've cleaned up."

It seemed he had. Although the windows were all boarded, someone had painted bright, swirling pictures on them. There was even a thick rug on the swept wooden floor, and a comfortable dark leather sofa. An incongruously pretty glass shade covered the dim lightbulb hanging from the ceiling and spreading a curiously cozy glow around this part of the bleak, grim building.

"Dmitriu, let me present your guests," Saloman said graciously. "Josh Alexander from America; and Elizabeth Silk, I believe you've already met."

Dmitriu didn't offer to shake hands, for which Josh looked heartily grateful, but merely inclined his head and shoulders in the sort of old-fashioned bow he might once have exchanged with his social equals.

"And, Miss Silk," he said smoothly, in his precise English, according her a similar bow, "I am, of course, delighted to see you again. Please make yourselves comfortable."

As they passed him, moving in the vague direction of the sofa, Dmitriu addressed Saloman in Hungarian. "*Two* descendants? You brought dinner for me too?"

"Dmitriu," Saloman scolded at once. "Have you forgotten Elizabeth is proficient in Hungarian as well as Romanian?"

Of course he hadn't. He'd said it deliberately to provoke some kind of reaction. Dmitriu, she suspected, did that a lot: dropped the hunters a piece of information to see what they'd do with it; sent the skeptical academic to Saloman's crypt, pressed a thorn in her hand to see if she bled all over his tomb to wake him; turned up to do battle at Saloman's side after the Ancient had discovered his betrayal, to see if Saloman killed or welcomed him.

Elizabeth cast him a brief, sardonic glance, looking him straight in his dark, gleaming eyes.

"The sword." Josh gasped, distracting everyone. He started toward the sofa, where lay the long, golden sword. Elizabeth, struck afresh by its beauty, almost forgot to breathe. After two swift paces, Josh halted, remembering, no doubt, that he couldn't touch the sword with impunity. Dmitriu brushed past him and lifted the weapon with a casualness that seemed plain wrong.

"Here," he said negligently, and threw it to Saloman. It cut through the air with a whiz, close enough to Elizabeth that she felt the displaced air ruffle her hair. Light sparkled on the blade and the glinting golden hilt as it flew, to land squarely in Saloman's reaching hand.

Oh, yes, there was some huge, untapped power in the sword. It seemed to electrify Elizabeth's spine.

Saloman's fingers closed around the hilt like the hand of an old friend.

"Thank you," he said mildly, but his fingers showed white where they gripped it, and as he turned away, swiping the air with one clean, graceful stroke, Elizabeth's heart ached for him. For the first time that she could remember, his shoulders looked tense and rigid. He would have given a lot to be alone.

Do vampires weep?

She hadn't meant him to hear the stray thought, but after the faintest pause he replied, *Yes. But I won't.*

He turned back to face them, lowering the point of the blade to the floor while he looked at Dmitriu. "Thank you. Now I have another favor to ask."

Dmitriu sighed, waving one resigned hand. "Ask and it's yours."

"Look after Tsigana's descendants for me." His lips twitched. "That means they eat. You don't."

Josh made a noise somewhere deep in his throat and coughed to cover it.

"I remember the days when you used to be fun," Dmitriu complained. He shrugged. "It doesn't matter; I've eaten already."

"Ignore them," Elizabeth said to Josh. "It's their perverse sense of humor." And then, looking at Saloman, she demanded, "Where are you going?"

"To lay a false trail. And to do a little urgent business." He walked toward her. "First, come here."

She took one curious pace forward, and he lifted the sword between them before coming to a halt almost toe-to-toe with her.

"Give me your hands."

"No!" Josh exclaimed, starting toward them before he came to an abrupt halt, stopped, it seemed, by the repulsion in Saloman's eyes. "It hurt her before!"

"I know," said Saloman, turning his gaze back to Elizabeth and waiting. Slowly, Elizabeth raised her hands. Holding the sword in one hand, he took Elizabeth's right and began to speak low, incomprehensible words as he laid it on the hilt, covered entirely by his own larger hand. Although Elizabeth imagined some enormous power vibrating through the weapon, there was no pain, no sense of burning, no vision.

Without taking his gaze from her, Saloman took her left hand and clasped it also to the sword hilt, still intoning the foreign, half-familiar words that made no sense. Elizabeth's throat constricted, because he was doing this; he was allowing her to touch the sword with impunity. He was trusting her.

Saloman stepped back. His hands fell away, leaving her to support the weight of the huge weapon.

"It *was* you," Josh said hoarsely. "It was you I saw in the vision."

Saloman didn't spare him a glance. Elizabeth couldn't. Held by

Saloman's dark, burning eyes, she was drowning in love and gratitude and the pain of a new betrayal she hadn't yet committed.

She swallowed, slowly bringing the heavy sword nearer to Saloman. Perhaps it was just her arms that hurt. He took it and placed it against the wall, point down. Nodding curtly to the watchful if expressionless Dmitriu, he said wryly, "Don't lose it."

"Take it with you if you're bothered," Dmitriu retorted.

"I wish I could. But in this weird modern world, there are some places where even a masked sword is just too noticeable. Not to say unwelcome."

"Then it's no use to you, is it?" Josh interjected.

"On the contrary, the problem is easily overcome—in time, which I don't have right now."

Then he strode across the room toward the stairs and disappeared. Elizabeth suspected he jumped, for she never heard his footsteps clattering downward.

"I thought anything or anyone could be masked," Elizabeth remarked.

Dmitriu shrugged. "They can. It's a question of degree. Something one wouldn't expect to see, like a sword on a sauna bench, for example, requires much deeper, more time-consuming layers of enchantment to hide than, say, a particular sword in a shop full of historic weapons."

Interesting as Dmitriu's explanation was, Elizabeth's attention stuck on a minor point. "He's going for a sauna?" The being whom dirt particles avoided.

Dmitriu's lips curled. "It has been known. But I said it was an example. I might as well have said a sword on the hip of a suit-wearing businessman at a formal meeting." He began to walk away. "In the absence of solid information, feel free to make your own hypotheses."

Dmitriu, whatever his expressions of surprise when he'd first greeted them, had clearly been expecting them. From another room he produced cold fish, salad, cheese and bread, wine, orange juice, and water, and set it all out on the low table in front of the sofa.

Accepting with slightly bewildered thanks, Elizabeth and Josh ate, largely in silence. Once or twice, she thought Josh was about to speak, to ask her no doubt about Saloman and "Adam." But he never formed the words. Perhaps he was too tired to think straight, for almost immediately after he stopped eating, he lay back on the sofa and fell asleep.

Elizabeth watched him for a few minutes, wondering ruefully what all of this had done to the open, charming personality of her famous "cousin." She hoped it wouldn't sour him or change him at all, although surely that wasn't possible. She herself had changed. Some of it was good, she acknowledged. She had new confidence, was more able to take care of herself and other people. She understood more, was open to more. And yet she couldn't help wondering whether her parents would have approved of her as she was now. Would they even recognize her? Would the old friends who had once helped her nurse them and covered for her at school? Had the old Elizabeth had to die to make way for the new one?

She didn't like that idea. Restlessly, she stood up, pacing the large, empty room and wishing there were even one window she could see out of. Even in the dark, there might be something to distract her from unpalatable self-analysis.

Saloman, Saloman.

Shaking herself, she bent and began to pile up the used plates and food containers. She stood with them and walked across the room to the door through which Dmitriu had brought them earlier.

"Dmitriu?"

It seemed to be some kind of kitchen. At least, it had a sink and running water and a slightly rickety table at which Dmitriu sat, apparently staring into space.

He glanced up and gestured to the sink. "Thank you."

She dumped the dishes in the sink and shoved the containers to one side for later. It felt cool enough in here to be a fridge.

The taps worked too, running both hot and cold water over the plates and cups. Eventually, because she so much wanted to know, she asked, "Are you talking to him?"

Dmitriu smiled faintly, watching her lay the second washed cup on the draining board. "No. I was just thinking. About you, actually."

Elizabeth rinsed off a plate and balanced it, dripping, against the cups. "There's no point. I'd be bad for your digestion."

Dmitriu let out a surprised laugh. "Damned right," he said with feeling. "Saloman would turn me inside out."

"I'm not so easy to bite these days either," she said, unreasonably annoyed.

"So I hear. The Awakener's power is strong and growing stronger with every kill." At her involuntary twitch, he smiled. "Interesting. You still don't like that word. You don't enjoy killing my kind?"

"No," she said, low. She added the second plate to the draining crockery and for honesty added, "Sometimes I enjoy the fight." *Like at Travis's, with him behind me . . .*

Dmitriu's lip curled. "Like us."

Inside, she screamed in protest. It was what she had been avoiding ever since the conflict at Travis's, and she was damned if she'd think about it now in front of Dmitriu.

"It tears you up, doesn't it?" he observed with detached interest. "Being the hunters' best friend and Saloman's mistress. Being so much like us when we embody everything you hate."

Christ, he was nearly as bad as Saloman. She swung back to the sink. "I don't *want* to kill," she muttered, throwing down the bread knife with excessive force.

"And you have a pact with Saloman not to kill each other."

She glanced over her shoulder. "He told you that?" Slowly, she turned back and lowered herself onto the empty stool opposite Dmitriu.

"No," he admitted. "But you're still alive. And your love is as obvious as his."

Heat pounded through her body into her face. "He doesn't love me," she whispered. "He's thousands of years old and I pass a few nights for him." *Oh, fuck, did I really say that?*

But Dmitriu, it seemed, was not inclined to make fun. His eyes were unexpectedly serious as they met her desperate gaze. "You think that feeling is less intense for him because he's lived so long and felt it all before?"

It was so exactly what she did think that there seemed to be no point even in nodding. She continued to stare at him in bafflement.

He gave a half shrug. "It's true he lives very much in the moment, seeks out novelty in all its forms to keep himself entertained. I could see it amused him to sleep with his Awakener before he killed her—especially when she was as beautiful as you."

Elizabeth wrenched her gaze free and shoved back the stool until it ground unpleasantly on the floor. When the pain was bearable, she'd stand up and walk away.

"Only he didn't kill you, did he?" Dmitriu mused. "He let you walk away from him not once but twice. And damn me, here you are again, close enough to be joined at the hip."

Frowning, Elizabeth lifted her gaze to his.

"He even gave you power over the sword," Dmitriu observed.

"Is that what he did?" Involuntarily, she spread her hands on the table, palms upward. "It doesn't burn me anymore."

"It will protect you now," Dmitriu said carelessly, and Elizabeth lifted one shaking hand to rub her forehead free of the pain. "It can't have escaped your notice that, living each moment to the full as he does, he uses many of them to, er, plan future moments."

Her hand stilled. For an instant, she looked at Dmitriu through her fingers; then she let her hand drop back onto the table.

"With me?" she whispered. *Stop leading him, you idiot. How do you know why he's saying these things? He knows you want to hear them too much.*

Dmitriu smiled sardonically. "Of course. Among other plans, certainly, but yes, with you. I've seen him stay agonizingly celibate for you. I've seen him take other women without love to forget you, but still he brings you back. Is he monogamous by nature? I don't honestly know. But it's more than a few happy fucks he seeks with you. That much is obvious from watching him with you."

Her heart beat, and beat so hard she felt it would break out of her chest. "Then what does he want with me?" she whispered.

Dmitriu curled his lip. He might have been sneering, but she didn't think so. "Companionship," he said. "Whatever that means to him. Or to you."

Companionship. More than a one-night—or a two-night—stand, more than friendship. Like New York, only all the time.

She gasped, banishing the yearning that threatened to overwhelm her. "Like Tsigana?" she said harshly.

Dmitriu's eyebrows flew up. "Tsigana?" His eyes searched her face, dropped to her throat and breasts. "You don't look like her, if that's what you want to hear. And there is more to you, more beneath the surface—and, of course, you're more clever."

Alarm bells rang at that. Flattery. Was he testing her? Seeing what she would do if he convinced her of her emotional hold on Saloman?

"True or not," she said more briskly, "why, exactly, are you telling me all this?"

He shrugged. "Because I want him to have what he wants. And when he offers immortality, if not before, you have to be prepared. You have to know how far you're willing to go."

Elizabeth's lips fell slack. "When he offers . . . He didn't even offer that to Tsigana! Why would he even *think* of—"

"Because he never once looked at Tsigana as he looked at you over that sword."

Some wild, fierce emotion was trying to get out, to make her shout and run and burst with happiness, but she wouldn't let it. She wasn't so stupid.

"He killed his cousin for Tsigana! He killed Luk, whom he loved!"

"He killed Luk because Luk was insane."

Elizabeth shook her head. "You're lying. He told me he couldn't kill him for that. Until Tsigana went to Luk."

Dmitriu leaned forward, peering into her face. "Elizabeth, it wasn't *Tsigana*'s betrayal that hurt. Do you think he'd have taken her back if that were the case? Oh, Tsigana fascinated him with her caprice and her sheer weaknesses. She was one very flawed, selfish, charming little being; he cared for her, looked after her, forgave her. But her acts were never betrayal, because he never trusted her in the first place."

Elizabeth stared. "Then why *did* he attack Luk in the end?"

"He didn't attack Luk. Luk attacked *him*. That was the betrayal he couldn't forgive. That was why rage set in, and instead of disarming Luk, as he could have very easily by then, he killed him."

Elizabeth's hand crept to her throat. "My God," she whispered. "No wonder he—" She broke off, swamped suddenly by the memory of Saloman's agony as he told her the part of the tale he was prepared to. And even then he'd had to distract himself with lust, with fierce, deliberate, delicious sex, just to get the words out.

Her body flamed as her mind relived the strange scene, and she tried desperately not to believe, not even to want to believe, that his feeling for her was greater than for the flawed, beautiful, treacherous Tsigana.

"He's loved many women," she said, touching her hot cheeks with her fingertips. "But he didn't make any of them immortal. He told me he created only you and Maximilian."

Dmitriu inclined his head, still watching her with mingled curiosity and fascination. "That is true."

She stood up. "Well, for the record, Dmitriu, I don't want to be a vampire. I wouldn't accept immortality at any price." *But I would like to be offered it. . . . Just to know he cares. Just to be a little special.*

She walked out of the kitchen, her mind still spinning with Dmitriu's words and with her own tangled emotions, not least of which was self-loathing. There was an undeniable sweetness in the fantasy of being with Saloman and never growing old, but fantasy was all it was. The reality of so-called immortality was bestial murder, eternal darkness, and drinking human blood. In her heart she knew that accepting vampirism from Saloman, even through love, would be as great a sin as Dante taking it from Dmitriu or Travis or any other vampire he could convince. No, she wasn't even tempted.

And yet, she would like to be asked.

And to be with him for a little. *Even valid decisions can be changed.*

There was no sound from the sofa, no movement to tell her Josh was awake. She wished she could sleep too. She looked around for the sword. She wanted to handle it while Saloman wasn't here, to see if she could indeed hold it without burning. She wanted to touch something that was his, because this feeling was getting so out of control that—

Where's the bloody sword?

"Josh?" She spun around to the sofa. "Josh, wake up! Where did you put the—" She broke off, for Josh wasn't on the sofa. He wasn't anywhere in the room. Josh and the sword had vanished.

Chapter Sixteen

Struggling up from sleep, Josh felt wildly disoriented at first. The electric light stabbed at his eyes; the huge, wide space of the warehouse room made him blink before memory began to flood back. He sat up, shaking himself and rubbing his eyes. The sight of his father's sword, propped casually against the wall, made him pause, dropping his hands from his face.

They'd just left it there, alone with him. It was his, and they weren't even afraid he'd take it back. Because, presumably, they reckoned he was too afraid of vampires. When even Elizabeth Silk could kill them one-handed. All you needed was the right tool. And the knowledge not to be afraid.

Josh stood silently, listening to the distant sound of Elizabeth's voice, interspersed with the vampire Dmitriu's. Although he didn't quite understand her part in all of this, he acquitted her of malice. He was sure she'd done everything with the best of intentions, but vampires were freaky to say the least. Fucking scary was another description, but he was damned if he'd let fear keep his father's sword from him—fear of either the good vamps or the bad ones. If there really was a difference . . .

Walking silently across the room to where he'd dropped his travel bag, he took out the leather jacket, then spilled out a pile of shirts and pants to make some room. With the leather jacket over his hands for protection, he advanced on the sword and gingerly picked it up. Hastily, he flung it into the travel bag and zipped it. The hilt stuck out, so he disguised it with a shirt. Then, before either Elizabeth or the vampire came out to notice, he crept downstairs, shoes in one hand, bag in the other.

At each step, he expected to hear Elizabeth cry out, or the vampire to fly at him. His skin prickled and sweated with the effort to move with speed and silence. At the foot of the stairs, ignoring the pain of jagged stones and rubble in his soles, he raced across to the door, where he paused to stuff his sore feet in his sneakers, and then carefully eased open the door far enough to squeeze through. He didn't close it; he was too afraid the vampire would hear that and come after him. He jogged off into the night, still amazed he hadn't been heard. What in the world had Elizabeth been talking about with Dmitriu? She'd sounded intense and pained, while the vampire's tones were moderate and reasonable. But whatever they'd been discussing, he was grateful it had kept them distracted, because Elizabeth had told him after the Travis incident that vampires' senses were far more powerful than humans'.

When he reached the main road, he slowed to a walk, grinning to himself because he'd outsmarted everyone and gotten his sword back. Now he'd head back to the airport, get the first flight home to the States, and put the sword in a safe-deposit box. He wouldn't get to look at it much, but hey, he'd never done much of that anyway. At least it would still be his and he wouldn't have that nagging feeling of having let his father down.

His father, who'd believed in all of those things Josh had denied until this week. Dad had been right all along, and Josh entirely wrong to doubt him. He supposed, as he began striding along the road and scanning for taxis, that he should feel guilty, even ashamed of his determined skepticism, but in fact, what he chiefly felt was a pleased pride in his dad that made him grin.

He was still grinning when the car skidded to a halt with a screech of brakes just after passing him. An instant later it reversed at speed, narrowly avoiding the horn-blaring truck forced to swerve into the next lane. Josh didn't even feel the lurch of panic until Travis jumped out of the car and grabbed him.

Instinctively, Josh tried to shove him off, but the travel bag was wrenched out of his hands and flung inside the car. Josh yelled in fury, but a second later, he was flung after it, just as if he weighed no more than a tennis ball.

Dmitriu swore long and fluently in an impressive mixture of languages, finishing in English with, "Stupid little shit. I didn't even hear him leave. And now I have to go and find him before Saloman notices his bloody sword is missing again. Wait here."

"I'm coming with you," Elizabeth said grimly, grabbing up her jacket.

"You can't," he said irritably, already leaping down the stairwell in one jump. His voice floated back up to her as she ran down the steps. "I need to move too fast. Wait there."

Elizabeth forced herself to be sensible. Dmitriu was right. He could move faster without her; he certainly didn't need her to track Josh. So as the door banged shut behind him, she sat down on the dirty, broken steps and tried to think. Dmitriu wouldn't hurt Josh; Saloman had told him not to. There was no need to call in Saloman's protection now. In fact, Saloman might well be so pissed off at Josh's stealing the sword so soon after his getting it back that he could hurt Josh himself.

Maybe it would be better if Josh did escape with the sword; only, that left him alone and unprotected and the sword open to any evil being fast enough to grab it first. Elizabeth rested her elbows on her knees and her head in her hands, rubbing hard as if to restore her own powers of thought.

The trouble was, her heart wanted Saloman to have his cousin's sword. It was her head that knew he couldn't be allowed its power to add to his own. Could the hunters get to Josh before Dmitriu did? She doubted it, and yet now it seemed abundantly clear that the only safe place for either Josh or the sword was with the hunters.

She ran back upstairs for her phone, and got as far as scrolling down to Mihaela's number before she hurled it onto Dmitriu's leather sofa. "Oh, bloody, *bloody* hell! I can't have them running up against Saloman and Dmitriu and fighting over Josh like dogs with some particularly juicy bone! *I* need to find Josh."

Unlikely that she'd get to him before anyone else, but she certainly wouldn't if she just sat here and waited. Picking up the phone, she dialed Josh's number instead. Getting no answer, she stuffed it in her bag and ran back downstairs.

Elizabeth felt slightly numb as she left Budapest airport for the second time in twelve hours. She had been so sure Josh would either be there already or arrive soon after her. But she'd been here for nearly three hours, pacing the entrance hall, haunting the cafés and the American airline desks, and still there was no sign of him.

Outside, it was daylight. The sky was bright blue, building up for a fine summer day. Dmitriu would be back in his "penthouse," hopefully with Josh. She hoped without reservation now that Dmitriu had found him, because the alternative was unthinkable.

Walking toward the airport taxis, she wondered if she could actually direct the driver to where she wanted to go. She'd gotten here from the warehouse by a mixture of running and taxi, but Dmitriu's new home was not in a part of the city that she was very familiar with. She had no idea of districts or street names.

Elizabeth.

The voice in her head was electrifying. From a slightly numb dejection, she suddenly seemed to feel everything at once—the seductive effect of his voice, the joy of his presence that was pointless to deny, the wonder of Dmitriu's words to her last night. And hard on the heels of that, the knowledge that somehow she and Dmitriu had lost his sword, and that there were worse people than Saloman who could have it by now.

She halted, leaning one elbow against a railing. *Saloman. Where are you?*

I'm at Dmitriu's. Alone.

Oh, shite. She dragged her hand through her hair. *Josh ran off with the sword. Dmitriu and I went looking for him—he shouldn't have been able to get far in the time he had, but he's not at the airport, and if Dmitriu isn't back . . .*

Her hand fell back to her side. *Why isn't Dmitriu back? The sun is well up.*

Saloman was silent for so long that Elizabeth wondered if he'd actually broken the connection. There had been no trace of anger, or indeed of any expression at all in his brief greeting, but he could hardly have been pleased. Even Ancients must be subject to the odd temper tantrum.

Only, Saloman's tantrums killed people. Like his cousin.

Return to Dmitriu's, he said curtly. *Wait for me there.*

Elizabeth bristled at his tone of command. Did he imagine she was one of his minions? *Why, where are you going?* she demanded.

I have a takeover to finalize and some people to organize. In fact, I'm late.

Elizabeth turned away from a woman with a luggage trolley who was staring at her, presumably because of the appalled expression on her face. *You're going to a fucking business meeting? Saloman, Josh could be anywhere! Dante and probably Travis are here, to say nothing of the homegrown vampires who would love to drink his blood!*

My plans don't halt because you've mislaid your cousin.

I mislaid the sword too, she snapped. *Don't you even want that back?*

Oh, I'll get it back. Again. I'll even get your wretched Josh back. Later.

Saloman, couldn't you even— She broke off the thought, feeling it bounce back on her as if from a brick wall. *Saloman?*

He'd gone. In frustration, she kicked the bottom bar of the railing and called to him. There was nothing. He was blocking her. While continuing to take over the world.

"Elizabeth!" Mihaela threw her arms around her in such enthusiastic welcome that the café table shifted in noisy protest. Laughing, Elizabeth hugged her back and grinned over her shoulder at Konrad and István, who waited their turn to embrace her.

It almost felt like a homecoming, meeting at this street café where they'd drunk coffee together last year. The hunters' unabashed pleasure in seeing her again warmed her heart.

"So how come you're available at this time of the afternoon?" she asked as they sat down with their freshly ordered coffee. "Are you playing hooky?"

"We're just back from the mountains," Konrad said, wrinkling his nose. "Emergency clear-out of a troublesome fledgling commune. Messy business, but we have the rest of the day." Konrad winked. "Thanks for Severin. We owe you."

Mihaela nudged her. "Bloody well-done, Elizabeth. How did you manage it all by yourself?"

"Luck, largely," Elizabeth said deprecatingly. "That and the fact that I seem to be turning into a bit of a vampire magnet."

"You are an Awakener," István said seriously. "And stronger than any on record. Because Saloman hasn't killed you. Most Awakeners were killed very soon after the event."

Elizabeth closed her mouth. "I never thought of it quite like that before." Was this the potential Saloman had talked about? Her strength?

"Whatever, Konrad's right," Mihaela said. "We owe you for Severin."

"Well, if it makes you feel better, I was hoping you could help me find Josh. He followed me here and now I've lost him. He's got the sword."

Mihaela frowned. "Josh has the sword again? I thought you said Dante had it?"

Elizabeth took a mouthful of the excellent coffee to bolster her courage and set down her cup. "There have been a couple of developments since then. Dmitriu—your old mate Dmitriu—took the sword from Dante. Josh nicked it when his—and my—back was turned and made off into the night. Neither Dmitriu nor I could find him, and now I don't even know where Dmitriu is." She looked around at their stunned faces and gave a faint, sardonic smile. "In a nutshell," she finished.

Konrad let out a sigh that was half whistle as he sat back in his chair. "Okay . . . I think you've been misled. Dmitriu was never our ally, merely an erratic informant. I think he fed us tidbits of information from time to time to keep us off his back, but his loyalty, as I think was clear from his stance in St. Andrews last year, is still to Saloman."

"I know that," Elizabeth murmured.

"The likeliest scenario," István said heavily, "is that Dmitriu caught up with Josh and either killed him or took him back for Saloman to kill. In which case, Saloman has the sword too."

"No." Elizabeth glanced around the three surprised faces across the table. "I happen to know Saloman's still looking for it."

"How do you know this?" Mihaela demanded, leaning forward. "Elizabeth, what's going on here? If you're working with Dmitriu, you might as well be working with Saloman. If anything, Dmitriu used you, got what he wanted, and has now disappeared off your radar."

Elizabeth held up both hands in a gesture of acceptance before closing both of them around her coffee cup, despite the warmth of the afternoon. "I've made mistakes. We all know I'm not a real hunter. But the main thing is to find Josh. I've been thinking and I'm sure he's not dead."

"Why?" István asked.

Elizabeth shrugged a little uncomfortably. "It's an empathy thing. Maybe I'm kidding myself, but I sort of understand Josh, know what he's thinking when I'm with him, and I'm pretty sure I'd know if he were dead. I can still . . . feel him."

Mihaela and István exchanged hasty glances, but Konrad kept his gaze on Elizabeth. "You've discovered some kind of telepathy?"

"It's been growing," she said with odd reluctance. "Since last year."

Konrad nodded. "As you're getting stronger. I have it a little, though only with kills so far."

"The vampires you kill speak to you?"

Konrad's lips twisted. "Not for long. But occasionally I've heard them, yes. Is that what you hear?"

"No, but . . ." She hesitated, then took a deep breath. "I hear Saloman. When he chooses."

"Fuck," said Konrad with awe.

István pursed his lips in a soundless whistle.

"Does he choose often?" Mihaela asked, and some inflection of her voice made Elizabeth glance at her more warily. Her friend's dark, perceptive eyes gazed back at her with more concern than suspicion, and she had to fight the sudden urge to lay everything at Mihaela's feet.

But sharing the pain was a luxury she couldn't afford. It would distract from the main issue, which was to find Josh and stop Dante from using the sword to become undead.

"No, not often," she said steadily. *Not often enough.*

"Do you think he can read what's in your head?" István asked anxiously.

It was a good question and one she still wasn't quite sure of the answer to. "I don't *think* so," she said cautiously. "I think I have to . . . project? . . . for him to receive. It's a bit like a radio conversation." She glanced around them all. "Don't look at me like that. He doesn't ask me about you or tell me anything about what he's doing. He just does it to entertain himself, to keep me on edge. . . ." *To keep me in thrall.*

"When was the last time he contacted you this way?" Konrad asked.

"This morning," Elizabeth said steadily. "That's how I know he doesn't have the sword or Josh or even Dmitriu."

"He's as concerned as we are?" Konrad gave a short laugh. "Well, well, maybe we'll get the upper hand this time after all. So what's your theory, Elizabeth? Where are Josh and the sword?"

Elizabeth picked up her cup. "I think they're with Dante."

Konrad cast a quick glance around the nearby tables, which were filling up as the afternoon wore on. "Come on," he muttered. "Let's go somewhere more private."

As they drove across the city to Mihaela's bright, almost impersonal flat, Elizabeth explained her fear that Dante sought not just immortality, but instant power in the vampire world.

"Is that possible?" Mihaela said doubtfully, taking her eyes from the road to glance at Konrad in the passenger seat beside her. "Could he really become as powerful as Saloman just like that?"

"I don't know," Konrad admitted. "It depends what power this sword actually has. No one reliable has ever studied it; it's been effectively hidden since the eighteenth century, so we've no way of knowing how much of the legend is true. However, the fact that Saloman himself is looking for it probably tells us enough."

"You've seen it, Elizabeth," István said. "Did you feel or witness any special power?"

"It burned me when I touched it, threw up a vision of Saloman demanding its return. It did the same to Josh, but only after Saloman was awakened. I think it recognizes us as descendants. Which is worth your remembering, Konrad, if and when we find it. Don't touch it."

Konrad peered back between the front seats and nodded.

They drove the rest of the way in thoughtful silence, and István insisted on carrying her slightly battered traveling bag up to Mihaela's flat.

"Sometime," said Mihaela, opening the fridge door to find milk for her coffee, "we must meet without a crisis." She flicked her hand at the wine bottle, but only on her way to the milk. "I got a nice bottle of wine in, but I think we'd better leave it until this is dealt with."

"I think you're right," Elizabeth said ruefully.

Mihaela glanced at her. "You're looking well."

"Am I?" Elizabeth laughed. "Not sure how—I feel as if I haven't slept in the last week. Apart from on the plane over here."

Mihaela smiled faintly, sloshing milk into a jug and placing it on the tray beside the coffee and the cups. "I don't suppose that's because you and Josh . . . ?"

"Oh, no," Elizabeth said, and yet she felt herself blushing, because Mihaela had guessed so much of the truth, just with the wrong partner. "What about you?" she asked lightly. "Discovered any sexy lovers in between hunting expeditions?"

Mihaela wrinkled her nose. "No one I'd care to introduce to my grandmother. Or even to you." She tossed a packet of biscuits to Elizabeth, who caught it in one hand and raised her eyebrows quizzically until Mihaela sighed and let go of the tray she'd been about to lift. "I think I only go after unsuitable men so I don't feel bad about being unable to form a relationship with them. Who wants a bastard for a boyfriend?"

"There's a definite attraction in unattainability," Elizabeth agreed, feeling for the understated pain Mihaela didn't usually reveal at all. "To say nothing about badness." She raised the biscuit packet in a mock toast. "Here's to unsuitable lovers."

Mihaela laughed, her eyes just a little lighter for the understanding, and picked up the tray. Elizabeth followed her back into the living room.

Sitting down and waving at everyone to help themselves, Mihaela said, "We've been checking up on Dante too. Incidentally, I think we know now what his secret mission was the other night. His volunteer team remained pretty tight-lipped—presumably under instruction—but they came in the next morning well beaten-up."

"How?" Elizabeth asked in quick distress.

"Dmitriu," Mihaela said dryly. "Dante must have taken them to try to capture Dmitriu, taking along Saloman's sword for extra protection. Obviously it didn't work, because you say Dmitriu took the sword from him."

Elizabeth frowned. "But if he couldn't capture Dmitriu before, how come he can now?"

"We don't know that he has," Konrad pointed out. "You're just assuming it because you believe Dante came here for that purpose. Dmitriu could be anywhere; he could have taken himself back to Transylvania, or be trailing after Saloman somewhere else entirely."

Elizabeth opened her mouth to say that Saloman was definitely here in Budapest, and without Dmitriu, but, perhaps fortunately, Mihaela answered her original question.

"Perhaps because he's been studying enchantments."

"Don't be daft," István said, leaning forward from the sofa to pick up a cup. "Enchantments don't really work."

"Yes, they do," Elizabeth said, at exactly the same time as Mihaela said, "You don't know that."

Elizabeth waved her hand to give Mihaela the floor, and her friend took a sardonic bow.

"We only *think* enchantments are bunkum," Mihaela said, "because we never studied the material. I've noticed it on the shelves but we were never shown the books, never trained in it. What if it's a skill that's been lost to hunters in a more scientific age? What if vampires still use it? Besides," she added, by way of a clincher after she'd knocked back her coffee like medicine, "we all accept that our headquarters building is safe.

How can it be, without enchantments? Have you ever heard an alarm go off, or any vampire detector in the building? We say it's masked, as if it's disguised as something else, but come on, guys, would a sign saying, 'State Pensions Office,' or something really fool a vampire?"

István grunted, clearly unconvinced.

"István, we've had vampire prisoners in there! We've had visiting victims, sought-after descendants, even an Awakener!" Mihaela flung her hand out at Elizabeth. "No attacks, nothing. The vampires know we exist, just not where to find us."

"Vampires do use enchantments," Elizabeth volunteered. "And they use the word 'mask.' They can mask themselves or objects they choose to hide. I'm sure that's why you've never found Saloman's pal—lair," she corrected herself hurriedly, well aware that the other reason was that she herself had never chosen to take them there. "And I think there's some kind of mask on the Angel Club too."

The others gazed at her in some surprise, clearly thinking about it. Elizabeth looked at Mihaela. "What sort of enchantments has Dante been studying?"

"Powerful masking. Whatever that is. I got only a glimpse at his book pile before we got the emergency call to the mountains yesterday."

"The more powerful the vampire," Elizabeth said slowly, "the more powerful a mask would have to be to hide from him. He must be trying to hide from Saloman."

"Don't blame him," Konrad said with feeling. "If he's got the sword and Dmitriu, then Saloman's going to be in a towering rage. The question here is, do we want either Dante or Saloman to do our dirty work for us by taking the other out?"

"No!" Elizabeth said with spontaneous revulsion, and when everyone looked slightly taken aback by her vehemence, she managed to say by way of explanation, "Josh. Where would he come in any battle between Dante and Saloman? It seems to me our best hope is to find Josh and Dante before Saloman does. Rescue Josh and take the sword into safety at headquarters. About Dante himself, if we catch him before he's turned, simply grassing him up across the world hunter networks should clip his wings enough. On the paranormal front."

From her handbag, her phone made its out-of-charge bleep. Elizabeth bent to rummage for it and the charger.

"It might be enough," Konrad allowed. Elizabeth pulled her phone out, together with the charger that she wanted, plus a comb and her passport, which she didn't. They tumbled onto the floor and her forgotten American newspaper came too, springing free onto the carpet and unfolding itself at the picture of "Adam Simon."

Elizabeth dropped the phone to stuff everything quickly back in. But Mihaela's hand was before hers on the paper, and Elizabeth straightened, watching Mihaela's face.

"So that's the connection we've been looking for," Mihaela said slowly. "There's no hold over Adam Simon. He *is* Adam Simon." Her dark gaze lifted to Elizabeth. "Why didn't you tell me?"

"There's been no time," Elizabeth exclaimed. "I've been distracted with the sword and Josh's disappearance!" It was true, and yet she deserved all her uncomfortable feelings of guilt, for her instinct had been to cover up the paper before the hunters saw the photograph. In order to protect Saloman. She wondered when she would have told them—if she ever would.

Mihaela's gaze fell. "You're right, of course. And now that we know, we'll have more chance of dealing with him. Once we've dealt with Dante."

"Which is the issue," Elizabeth agreed. "How the hell do we find him?"

Chapter Seventeen

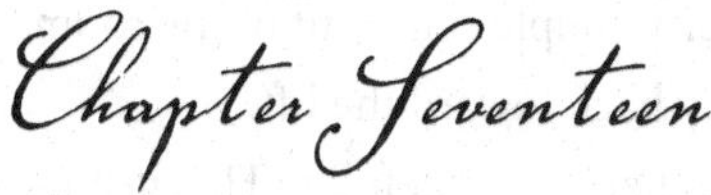

Finding him turned out to be easy. Thanks to the hunters' connections, they were given access to all the city's hotel registers. The only Dantes they discovered there were a visiting Italian family from Milan, but they did find an American "Grayson" at the Hilton in Buda.

Konrad went in alone to ask and was informed that Mr. Grayson wasn't in his room. However, since Konrad had managed to see the room number the receptionist contacted, Elizabeth and István wandered in next and walked straight up to room 242.

"It's true," Elizabeth murmured, after they'd both listened at the door for some time. "There's no one in there."

"Watch for me," István said, and to her amazement he picked the lock with a pin from his pocket and a credit card.

"How the . . . ?" she began as the door swung open.

István grinned. "Misspent youth. Go and look, but make it fast."

It was a single room, pretty modest by Dante's standards. The bed was neatly made up. Some tourist brochures about the castle and several unwritten postcards lay on the desk, promoting his cover, presumably. But otherwise, there was no clue as to his intentions or his whereabouts. After looking through every drawer and cupboard and checking the bathroom, Elizabeth crept out again. István closed the door just as an elderly couple came out of the room across the hall, and they walked smartly back toward the lift.

"Nothing," Elizabeth said ruefully. "He's using it as a base, nothing more. He might not even sleep there, for all I know."

"But it is your Dante?"

"Oh, yes. His passport's in there. It's in the name of Grayson, but the photograph is him."

"That guy must have some dodgy acquaintances for a senator."

"For anyone. Now what do we do?"

István shrugged. "Look around the area. If this is his base, then presumably he won't want to move too far away from it."

It was a long and frustrating evening. As darkness fell, the clouds gathered too and it began to rain. Elizabeth and the hunters split up in order to cover more ground individually, but since they had no idea what they were looking for, Elizabeth began to think it was a waste of time. Concentrating on an item could break through the masking enchantment, and Elizabeth's eyes and head ached from staring intently at everything from doorways to drain covers. All it took to miss something was one lapse at the wrong moment, and they could cover the entire city without finding what they were looking for.

"We're doing it wrong," Elizabeth said to Konrad. Sheltering in a café doorway, she held her phone to her ear and watched the passersby as she spoke. "This is just exhausting us. We need to watch his hotel and follow him when he leaves."

"Taken care of," Konrad said with just a trace of smugness. "And you're right. We need to rest, so I've organized another team to watch the hotel for us until morning. I've sent the others home already. Do you want a lift back to Mihaela's?"

"No, thanks, Konrad. I'll get a taxi."

Breaking the connection, she dropped the phone into her bag and stepped out into the rain, only to come face-to-face with Saloman.

He stood under the café light, dressed in black, with his hair loose around his shoulders, glistening with moisture. Raindrops trickled down his forehead, trembled on his full, sensual lips. Shadows lurked in the deep hollows of his cheeks. His opaque dark eyes held secrets she never wanted to learn. And many, so many, that she did.

"Saloman," she whispered. "Have you found him?"

"No," he said. "But I found you."

Because she couldn't help it, she let her forehead fall forward onto his damp shoulder. Tiredness consumed her, dragged at her limbs and her brain, and yet his arms around her gave her unreasoning hope and security. Whatever unacceptable powers the sword might give Saloman, she knew that Dante would certainly kill Josh, probably as his first undead meal. Another night was passing and Josh was in more danger with every minute.

"He's been studying enchantments," she blurted into Saloman's coat. "Powerful masking. And he's staying at the Hilton—the Castle Hilton. The hunters are watching it."

"I know."

She lifted her head to see if he meant it or if he was just making her feel better for revealing the hunters' knowledge. His eyes seemed to glitter as they gazed down into hers.

"Panic is unnecessary," he said mildly. "Dmitriu won't turn him."

"How can you be sure of that?"

"Because I told him not to."

Laughter caught at her throat and was quashed down. "You can't reach him, can you?"

"No. But I will. Go home to your hunter friend, and tomorrow we'll talk."

He kissed her mouth, a long, sweet kiss, thorough and sensual, but achingly gentle. Rain ran into her mouth; she could taste it on his lips, his tongue.

She didn't even see the taxi approach, let alone Saloman's summons, but when he released her, he simply handed her into the car and disappeared into the night.

Since the rain was obliging enough to keep going into the morning, Saloman found it easy to step out of his car under the protection of an umbrella and walk smartly around the corner to the Hilton entrance. He passed an oblivious hunter on the way in, but since the man was looking for Dante and not Saloman, masking was barely necessary.

Saloman let down his umbrella. He didn't go near the long, busy reception desk, simply strolled toward the stairs and followed his nose to Dante's room.

"Come in," the senator called at once to his knock, and Saloman did.

Dante, wearing slacks and a polo shirt, paused in the process of hanging up a jacket. He looked almost ludicrously surprised. Perhaps he'd been expecting housekeeping.

"Good morning, Senator," Saloman said smoothly. "I hope you don't mind my dropping in unannounced."

"Adam!" Dante recovered quickly, closing the wardrobe door and walking to meet him with hand outstretched. "Do you know I'd forgotten this was your home ground?" Saloman shook his hand, learning what he could.

Dante smelled of Travis. In fact, the scent of the American vampire lingered all over the room, as if he'd been here several times. But, more important, Dante had just come from his company, and that of several other vampires Saloman vaguely recalled from his brief visit to Travis in New York. Travis was here in force.

"You'll have to forgive me for not getting in touch," Dante said easily. "To be honest, I'm here on the quiet, for health reasons—incognito, you might say." The senator beamed, and Saloman smiled beatifically back. "In fact, I'm surprised you found me."

Suspicion lurked behind the genuine curiosity in Dante's eyes. Saloman dropped his hand. It hadn't touched Dmitriu, but that wasn't surprising. Dmitriu would have bitten it off.

"I just caught sight of you heading into the hotel and followed you up." It wasn't strictly true. He'd sensed Dante's presence very suddenly, almost as if he'd "teleported" into the city from nowhere, and tracked him here. Saloman wondered, vaguely, whether the hunter had seen him too, or if Dante had learned to mask himself from fellow humans.

The ability to enchant was a rare gift in humans, and Dante appeared to be a fast learner. There could be a reason for that—Dante could be of mixed race, descended from a union lost long ago in the mists of time between a human and one of Saloman's living people. He could be one of the few in whom the normally dormant gift—modern science would probably call it a gene—was active.

Saloman did not care for that idea. Lonely as he was as the last of his race—he didn't count modern hybrid vampires—he still would not welcome Dante as a member of it. If anything, the presence of the "gene" would make him even more dangerous to the world.

"Always charmed to meet up with an old friend," Dante said jovially. "We can do lunch, if you like—although I'd appreciate it if you kept my presence here to yourself."

"I'm afraid I can't," Saloman said. "I really just dropped by to thank you for Torrent Defense."

"Good little company," Dante said, missing the point. "Glad you came on board. I built it up myself from nothing, still own the largest share."

"Ah, not anymore," Saloman said. "I do. There'll be a few production changes. I see the future in electric-powered cars."

He smiled into Dante's eyes and for an instant felt the senator's sheer, unveiled fury. Dante had taken his eye off the ball, distracted as he was by his pursuit of immortality. And despite those higher concerns, it still rankled in a very human way that more of his business had fallen into his rival's hands.

But he recovered fast. He shrugged eloquently, even managed a short laugh. "Well, my friend, if you think electric cars will make you more money than state-of-the-art tanks, you go ahead. Thanks for letting me know."

"No problem. By the way, your friend Josh Alexander is in Budapest too. Did you know?"

Dante was hardly going to admit to knowing that. For Saloman, the question was merely a prompt, a matter of learning what he could as Josh entered the senator's mind. But Dante was good, not merely a politician and diplomat, used to hiding his thoughts and feelings, but also, it seemed, a Method actor.

Saloman caught only the tiniest glimpse, so faint and swift as to be almost unreadable, of a stone room, like a cellar of some kind, bare and damp, and Josh huddled in a corner, perhaps tied. The room was dimly lit, and dark shadows leapt up the walls, threatening. Vampire presence. And another shadow, the black shape of a man with his arms chained above his head—*Dmitriu.*

He felt the rush of Dmitriu's joy in the unexpected link, blotting out the terrible hunger. As he'd hoped, Dante's thought, although it barely included Dmitriu, had provided the boost he needed to reach his friend.

And then the instant was past. There was no time to send either comfort or information. Dante, banishing the inconvenient memory, was instead remembering Josh at his house party in Scotland, and the tenuous connection broke. No matter, it was enough for now, enough to give Dmitriu hope. Enough for Saloman to work on later, in peace. Now that the link was established, it would be easier to re-form, and from that, he should eventually find Dmitriu's location.

"Josh in Budapest? Really?" Dante marveled. "My, this is turning into a positive reunion." The smile in his eyes faded slightly. "You don't suppose he came because he discovered I was here, do you?"

"Why should he do that?"

"I have this feeling he still blames me for the theft of his sword in Scotland. He thinks *I've* got it!"

"Silly old Josh," said Saloman.

Perhaps it was Adam Simon's unexpected visit that had set him on edge, but Dante found the journey through the tunnel from the castle even more distasteful than usual. It was a long and uncomfortable walk, with him bent double for much of the way, with unspeakably grimy water dripping onto his neck at frequent yet never anticipated moments.

Worse than that, he was only too aware that their pretended work area, which covered the man-sized hole Travis had created between the tunnel and one of the castle's duller basement rooms, could not remain undiscovered for much longer. As it was, the ticket staff were beginning to recognize him. The man today had made a joke about the frequency of his visits and how much he must love the castle. Dante had been forced to play the stupid tourist, gushing about the wonderful history to be found in Europe as compared to the States.

The trouble was, the process shouldn't be taking this long. When Travis had discovered the tunnel and they'd first captured Dmitriu, Dante had never imagined having to keep him chained up for several days. The bastard was holding out for mere spite. He, Grayson Dante, should by now be immortal, gaining strength with every feed—and one of his early meals would be bloody Adam Simon. He should have been watching his shares, his companies, anticipating this—but honestly, what were the rest of the shareholders doing, allowing that fool to take over? To use the company's specialist skills to make electric cars, for God's sake!

Dante quashed the anger rising all over again and rounded the bend with some relief. There, in front of him, was the stone chamber with its iron door and locks duly repaired by Travis's henchmen. Dante suspected it had once been a hideaway for treasure, possibly built to hide arms and gold and religious treasures from the Turks. He liked to think the Hungarians succeeded in this, that when the Turks were eventually expelled over a century later, the Hungarians simply walked down here and removed the treasures again.

Whatever its original purpose, though, it suited Dante's perfectly. A thick stone chamber built within a junction of underground tunnels. Layers of stone and earth formed a natural mask, making protective enchantments both easier and more effective.

And according to Travis, no one had been in these tunnels for centuries.

"Why not?" Dante had asked. "I'd have thought vampires at least would have thrived down here."

Travis had shrugged. "There are other tunnels around here, full of tourists. And this part runs too near the river, probably. Most vampires don't care for running water."

Dante had listened to the faint lulling water rush of what had to be the river Danube close by. "Don't you mind?"

"No. I never yet heard of a vampire who drowned."

Dante knocked loudly on the iron door. It opened at once and closed behind him as soon as he'd slipped into the chamber.

Travis and his four vampire bodyguards, including the one who'd let him in, sat in a circle on the floor playing cards with the remainder of Dante's own men—he'd brought in two new ones to replace the dead. They all gambled together with a bizarre mixture of dollars and Hungarian forints, as if they had equal value.

"Is it dark yet?" Travis demanded. "I'm starving."

Dante glanced anxiously at Josh as he walked toward him, checking his neck for puncture marks. "You haven't touched him, have you?" he demanded.

"Fuck off," Josh snarled. It was bravado. He knew he would be

Dante's first meal. A descendant of an Ancient's killers would make a powerful first meal to follow his welcome drink from Dmitriu, the exchange of blood that would turn him.

"Three hours until sunset," Dante said, turning to face Dmitriu at last. Still in chains, hanging from the wall, he rested his head back against the stone as if he were asleep. His expression was tranquil, but Travis had already explained to him how the vampire's nerves would be jumping like a junkie's without a fix. Gaunt, pale as alabaster, Dmitriu resembled nothing more than a statue. A statue in a torn white shirt.

The tattered clothing, however, was the only sign he still bore of the vicious fight that had eventually captured him. The wounds of his beating had healed, the trailing blood and dried scabs reabsorbed into his body. Dante hadn't known whether to resent the inconvenient speed of his healing—since Travis had refused to take the trouble of beating him some more—or be impressed with such power, which would replicate in himself just as soon as Dmitriu gave in and agreed to turn him.

"Ready to exchange blood?" Dante said to him now, as he'd said many times over the last two days and nights.

"No," said Dmitriu without opening his eyes, as he'd answered every time.

"What are you doing there, Dmitriu? Conserving your energy?" Dante tried to provoke him. "What the hell for?"

"Killing you." The vampire's eyes opened, and in spite of himself Dante shivered in mingled fear and longing. "Without possibility of revival."

"How do you plan to do that?" Dante asked with mock interest, indicating the chains that held him. Dmitriu merely curled his lip. Dante knew an urge to go closer, to whisper in the vampire's ear and use the sheer force of his personality to persuade him as he'd persuaded so many others to his will. Vampires were not immune to strong humans, after all. But on the other hand, Travis had borne in on him the importance of keeping his distance, not just because of Dmitriu's speed and unpredictability, but because once out of the chamber and the tunnels, he'd betray the scent of everyone he touched to every watching vampire in the city.

And this, more than any other, was Saloman's city.

"I haven't decided yet," Dmitriu said with dignity.

"Come on, Dmitriu," Dante urged. "What do you have to lose? Do what I ask and you're free and clear of here. I'll even let you have a bite of Josh before you go, provided you leave the bulk and the kill to me. Then you can go on a spree."

"I don't recall asking your permission."

Dante smiled. Behind the muttered response he detected the dreadful, mind-numbing tiredness, the hunger that was tearing him apart. "Doesn't it drive you mad?" he said softly. "Just hanging there, smelling the blood in Josh? In me? Watching those guys come back every night, replete with blood, while you just continue to hang here like a piece of meat, starved of energy? It's easy, Dmitriu. Just turn me. Exchange your blood, the blood of Saloman, with me. . . ."

Dmitriu laughed. It was a weak sound that gave Dante hope despite the defiant words that followed. "If you want Saloman's blood so much, why don't you just ask him?"

"You're closer," Dante said with a quick, sneering gesture toward his chains.

"Not much."

Dante frowned. "What do you mean by that?" He took a hasty step closer, then, remembering Travis's advice, jerked back again. "Is Saloman in Budapest?"

"He's coming for you," Dmitriu mocked.

Travis, from his position on the floor, threw his cards down and said, "No, he isn't. I've met him, and I'd smell him if he was here."

"You?" Dmitriu sneered. "You couldn't smell your own grandmother if she were lying rotting beside you."

But Travis's words had caught Dante's attention for another reason. "You've met Saloman? When? Where?"

Travis shrugged. "In New York. You just missed him, in fact." He scratched and yawned, and Dante, used now to the American vampire's body language, knew he wasn't telling the whole truth. He couldn't quite work out how it mattered, though, and right now he had more pressing concerns.

Striding toward Travis, he said impatiently, "Can't we speed this up? We can't hang around here indefinitely, you know. Why don't you rough him up a little? Torture him or something?"

Travis shrugged and got to his feet, regarding Dmitriu with his head leaning to one side. "No point. The hunger is torture enough. If he can stand that, he can stand a few broken bones and bruises. Besides, he heals too fast for it to be worth the effort. If you want my opinion, he's never going to give in, so you might like to consider some other options so we can get the hell out of this fucking boring tomb. I've got business in the States."

"What other options?" Dante demanded.

Travis shoved his hands in his pockets and leaned against the door, his gaze on the sword that lay in the far corner, wrapped once again in Josh's father's old coat—more to keep it from tempting Travis's henchmen than to hide its presence. "*I* could turn you."

"Your blood is strong," Dante allowed curtly. "But it's not as strong as his. Saloman's child and Saloman's sword will enable me to face Saloman."

Travis said smoothly, "Except that you're giving the sword to me."

"I meant Saloman's sword in my turning, that's all. I haven't forgotten our deal."

"Good, because however strong he makes you, I can still enforce it."

"Point taken," Dante said steadily. "But you mentioned options. Plural."

Travis waved one impatient hand at Dmitriu and stuck it back in his pocket. "Just *make* the bastard drink from you."

Dante blinked. "Make him? Force him?"

"Sure. He's weakened with hunger. Two of my guys can hold him while I push his teeth onto your neck. Once your skin's pierced and he smells the blood, I doubt any force on earth could stop him from drinking."

Dante stared at him thoughtfully. "Why didn't you suggest this before?"

"Didn't think he'd be this stubborn." Travis sighed and took both hands out of his pockets as he straightened. "Also, it's not so certain, is it? We can ram your neck into his teeth, and while the next step—him drinking your escaping blood—is highly likely, it's not guaranteed. We'd just have to hope enough gets down his throat."

"How much is necessary?" Dante asked. It was a detail that hadn't seemed important enough to research until Dmitriu had proved so recalcitrant.

Travis shrugged. "Don't know. I've never come across a vampire reluctant to drink blood before."

Dante stared back at Dmitriu, who was pretending to be asleep once more. With uncharacteristic uncertainty, he tugged at his lower lip.

"All right," he said at last. "Let's give him tonight. And if he hasn't agreed by sunset tomorrow to the more certain method, we'll force him and hope for the best." Euphoria surged up with the decision. At last. At last, one way or another, he'd get this over with and achieve his goal.

Saloman discovered her at dusk, in the Matthias Church near the castle. She sat alone at the end of a middle pew, reminding Saloman of another church in which he'd found her and teased her because she'd amused and intrigued him even then. Now, her pale, anxious beauty moved him beyond words; her loneliness and her pain hurt him as if they were his own.

If I win, if I finally have her with me as my own, what will I do with her?

Although the church closed to tourists at six o'clock, neither the priests nor their helpers moving about the place seemed inclined to eject her. Perhaps they sensed her need.

Saloman moved silently to take the seat beside her. Her eyes closed, making it hard to determine whether his presence was welcome or not. In this city more than any other, her loyalties were divided, and Josh's danger was eating her up.

She said, "This is one of my three favorite churches in the world."

Saloman wasn't surprised. There was beauty and peace and rich memory in every stone. When it had first been built, back in the eleventh century, he'd considered it a monument to human artistry and ingenuity—and they'd managed it almost entirely without him. It had had a somewhat checkered career since then, going through expansions and remodels, a spell as a mosque, bombardment, and finally sensitive and appealing restoration. It was medieval colors that once again decorated its walls and vaulted ceilings. A large part of Saloman's life was reflected in this place, and he was glad she cared for it.

"What are the others?" he asked.

"St. Chapelle in Paris and St. Andrews Cathedral." After a moment, her hand slid over his on his thigh and threaded through his fingers. "I missed you," she whispered, and the ache of pleasure and hope began again.

He curled his fingers around hers. "Then come with me."

She opened her eyes and turned her face toward him. "Where? Have you found them?"

"I'm closer. Together, I think we can do it."

Chapter Eighteen

It had been six months since she'd been here, and Saloman's "palace" had gained a little more furniture, a few more paintings, and rich carpets underfoot. In the drawing room where he had once seduced her, preparatory to killing her, there were now a harp and a grand piano and a large mahogany bookcase full of books.

Elizabeth sank onto the velvet sofa and drank some bottled water before she opened the plastic container full of goulash and salad ordered from a take-away shop en route. Saloman sat gracefully on a cushion by her feet and watched her eat.

It was ridiculous, this happiness at just being with him, this feeling that now, because he sat by her side, the ills of her world would all be solved. Josh would return unharmed and Dante would be stopped and sent home to be a good senator. The sword would be safe. And she . . . What the hell would she do? Leave him again?

Everything in her ached for him, ached with the happiness of just looking at him, ached with the pain of some future parting she couldn't bear to contemplate. Warmth flooded her with secret joy as she remembered Dmitriu telling her how special she was to him. His companion.

She drew in her breath, trying to focus on the present. "I've been angry with Josh," she blurted, lifting a forkful of the tasty stew. "Angry with him for running away, for being so stupid as to get caught and have the sword taken from him *again*."

She chewed and swallowed before adding ruefully, "And then I'm angry with myself for not watching him, for distracting Dmitriu, for not convincing him, for being too involved with you to trouble understanding him."

"And then you're angry with me. I get it."

She glanced at him over a fresh forkful. "Are you really closer to knowing where they are?"

"I know they're underground, somewhere in the vicinity of the castle. I know Travis and his cohorts are there guarding them."

"How do you know this?"

Saloman shrugged. "I've felt Travis's presence since we arrived in Budapest. Off and on. Largely off since Josh and Dmitriu disappeared. But he makes odd brief appearances, as do his minions, largely in the Castle District. I sensed Dante too in that area, appearing there from nowhere and returning to his hotel close by. But wherever they're disappearing to in between times, wherever Josh and Dmitriu are, is well masked by enchantment as well as stone. I could sense them if I got close enough, but so far I haven't."

He paused. "Keep eating. You need to be strong."

Obediently, she shoveled some more goulash and reached for her bottle.

"Then, this morning," he continued, "I went to see Dante in his hotel. And in his mind I saw . . . this."

A bare, dank room full of darkness and threatening shadows, and Josh curled with cold in a corner. Elizabeth gasped at the sudden vision, and would have dropped the bottle if Saloman's hand hadn't closed around hers. She had grown used to his words and ideas in her mind, but never before had he sent her anything so startlingly visual. The experience as well as the content shocked her to the core.

"That's where we have to look," he said relentlessly.

"But how? That . . . dungeon could be anywhere!"

"The vision of it will strengthen our telepathic links, and together we boost each other's strength. At the time of Dante's thought I had an instant only to assure Dmitriu I was looking, but he'll be ready now, and with luck, so will Josh. He has the same latent telepathy as you do, and I think you can reach him."

Elizabeth set her bottle on the floor and gazed at him. It seemed a massive leap from the vague empathy with Josh she'd explained to the hunters to the kind of vivid telepathy she shared with Saloman. She'd always assumed it was Saloman's power that drove the connection between them, but perhaps he was merely more adept at manipulating it. Recently, she had reached him with more ease, so it was possible her telepathic powers were growing. Excitement rose, forcing her to catch her breath.

"With what purpose?" she asked. "How will that help?"

"They can tell us what they know of their position, and once the link is strongly established, we can follow it and find them."

"And then?" Her heart was beating fast. "You could get them out? Single-handedly?"

Saloman's lip quirked. "We could both go."

Fighting side by side as they had in New York . . .

But she realized he hadn't answered the question. Saloman had no need to go in single-handedly. He had a city full of vampires who could and would follow him. He'd probably already put out a shout for volunteers.

And he would take the sword.

As if he heard her thoughts, he said, "You're thinking too far ahead. First, we have to find out where they are. Have you finished eating?"

She nodded dumbly, and he took the container from her lap and set it beside the water bottle on the floor.

"Give me your hands." He held his out in peremptory fashion and she took them, sliding onto the floor opposite him. His eyes, gazing into hers, seemed to soften and flame at the same time, twisting through her heart to her core.

Unexpectedly, he lifted her hands to his lips, one after the other, reminding her unbearably of her seduction in this very room seven months ago. A battle to win her life and achieve a night of unprecedented sexual pleasure. She'd won both and been so in love after it that she hadn't been able to think straight since.

What the hell was she fighting for now?

Love . . . Was that her thought or his? It didn't matter.

He whispered, "I want to make love to you very badly. When this is over, you must come to me. We've tried it your way and it doesn't work."

She swallowed. "What is your way?"

His mouth hovered over hers. "All ways."

She couldn't be still as the lust shot through her, making her wriggle. She could make out the texture of his lips, every crease, every tiny, sexy movement, and she couldn't help brushing them with her own.

"Later, Saloman. When we've found them." *Now, oh, now, before we do anything else, just one quick, hard, delicious fuck . . .*

Shocked at herself, she let out a gasp that was half laugh and part sob, and drew back from him. "Show me your vision again," she said shakily, "and tell me how to reach him."

Elizabeth? Of course not, I'm dreaming. . . . Good dream, though, because I've been wanting to say sorry to you for running out like that. I should at least have said good-bye and thanks; and seeing the mess I'm in now, I know you were only trying to look out for me.

It had taken a long time, emptying her mind of every extraneous thought, even Saloman's disturbing presence, so that she could concentrate on Josh, particularly on Josh as seen in the nasty vision Saloman had extracted from Dante's head. The setting helped, as Saloman had said it would, had given her a context in which to put her thoughts and her call to him.

Several times she knew she reached him, knew she had entered his mind. But he ignored her. It wasn't like the calls to Saloman that bounced back when he blocked her. Josh wasn't blocking, merely unaware. He shook his head, as if trying to clear it of thoughts of her, making it doubly hard for her to stay in.

The work was exhausting, but with Saloman's strong, steady hands holding hers, she felt sustained and kept trying. However, Josh had fallen asleep before he finally answered her, and the excitement after such a long silence nearly startled her back out of his mind in the sudden desire to crow to Saloman of her cleverness.

Restraining herself, she calmed down and let Josh babble a little.

If they kill me, I'll be glad I've spoken to you.

They won't kill you, Josh, she said severely. *Not if we can find you. Tell me where you are.*

I don't want to think about where I am.

Then tell me how you got there, she said patiently.

They jumped out of a car, within spitting distance of that warehouse you took me to. Travis and his cronies. They grabbed me and drove me through the city.

Here, Elizabeth felt the fear swamp him again, and as it spread through her, she gripped Saloman's fingers so hard he should at least have winced.

Where to? she asked. *Where did they stop?*

Near the castle . . . They dragged me out of the car and then Dante drove off, leaving me with them, *and God help me, that was more terrifying than any of it. Dante was the boss, that was obvious, but at least he's the same species. . . .*

It's all right, Elizabeth soothed. *I understand. What happened then?*

I was terrified he—Travis—was going to bite me, kill me, but he didn't. He . . . he . . . jumped into the air with me, almost as if he were flying. Jesus Christ, I nearly wet myself.

Yes, I've been there, Elizabeth said ruefully. *Where did he jump to? Did you look?*

The height and the angle were dizzying, but through Josh's memory she saw the walls of Buda Castle in darkness, the sheer jump downward and the sickeningly fast run through courtyards and down pitch-black steps to a cordoned-off workman's tarp, pulled up to reveal a deep, dark hole—down which the vampire jumped, still carrying the screaming Josh.

Josh, you're wonderful, Elizabeth told him warmly, working hard to keep a lid on her excitement so that she didn't lose this connection.

Not very. I kept my eyes tight shut until they dumped me in here. And now even the terror of that first night seems better than the boredom of being here and the intermittent bouts of panic that I'm going to die.

Where are you now? Show me.

I can't. I'm asleep.

Open your eyes. You can still speak to me when you're awake if you just keep thinking of me. Think of me trying to reach you with my mind, and then we can reach you in reality.

There was a pause, then: *I'd rather be asleep.*

No, you wouldn't.

Shit!

Open your eyes; look around you, as if you're showing it to me. You are *showing it to me.*

The connection with him seemed to waver and she held on grimly, repeating his name, asking him to hold on, to keep talking as he hauled himself out of sleep. As if he spoke the words, she heard him wondering whether he'd been dreaming, felt his wave of desolation and loss, his sheer fear to be waking in such a place, in such a situation.

I'm still here, Josh. Show me.

Warmth, relief flooded him, making her smile as they seeped into her too. Then he began to look around him at the square, bare room Saloman had shown her earlier. This time, however, it was in much greater detail. She could see the dampness glistening and dripping off the walls, could make out the texture of the ancient stones nearest Josh. She saw the shadows, and she saw the huddle of men and vampires asleep or playing cards.

Dante lay alone on a blanket, asleep. No wonder she had the impression his bed at the hotel wasn't slept in. Josh's gaze switched back to the vampires, two of whom were quarreling over the cards. Josh clearly wasn't interested. He continued to look around the rest of the room, the familiar bundle of old coat where his eyes lingered. *The sword*, he said awkwardly in Elizabeth's head.

I see it.

His gaze moved on and she saw chains attached to the wall. Chains that held a man's arms on either side of his head. Not a man, a vampire. *Dmitriu.* His eyes must have been staring directly into Josh's, for he seemed to look right at her. She felt the shock of dark, knowing eyes full of pain and hunger and fury. And behind them she seemed to see the blacker, denser eyes of Saloman, who watched Josh through Dmitriu.

The vision shimmered and broke and she blinked to find Saloman's face so close to hers. He smiled.

"Saloman," she whispered, "I saw. . . ."

"I know." Without warning, he leapt to his feet, dragging her with him. There was a hug, brief and hard, and his lips pressed firmly to hers. "How clever you are," he said, half proud, half mocking. "Now we have something. Let's go."

Elizabeth barely had time to grab up her jacket before he dragged her by the hand, rushing downstairs and out into the night. Catching his exhilaration, she ran with him along the dark, empty street until his arm encircled her waist and he jumped.

As she flew upward in his hold, she seemed to leave her swirling stomach on the ground. She'd traveled with him this way before, but she'd forgotten the sheer terror in being lifted so high, in being hauled with him at impossible speed across impossible distances, at heights that should have made her scream. More than ever, she sympathized with Josh. But after a few moments of alternate running and leaping with him over rooftops and lampposts, she felt her instinctive panic die and she gave herself up to the thrill of it, to the excitement of the chase, because now, at last, they had clues to Josh's hidden prison.

"There *were* tunnels under the castle," Saloman said as he ran across the Danube Chain Bridge with Elizabeth in his arms. There was no traffic, and no one watching would have seen more than a blur, a passing shadow. "Much more than the so-called labyrinth that they show to tourists nowadays, although like those, they were meant to provide cellars as well as hiding places and escape routes, spreading down either side of the hill. Some are far older than the first castle. But most of them collapsed and fell into complete disuse long before I was staked."

"You think someone repaired those forgotten tunnels?"

"Let's see if they're there. Josh and Dmitriu could have been deliberately misled just in case I broke through to Dmitriu's thoughts."

Elizabeth's spirits plummeted. "Really? Is that likely?"

"It's possible. Travis is no fool."

"You almost sound as if you like him," Elizabeth said curiously.

"I might, given time."

They entered the castle, much as she'd seen in Josh's mind, by leaping over the walls and roofs and into the dark courtyards between.

"There's nothing left of the palaces I knew here," Saloman said. "It's all buried and covered up." Nevertheless, he seemed to know where he was going. Without obvious care about disturbing night watchmen or automatic alarms, he led Elizabeth to a sheltered indention at the base of the building and down some rough steps that had been blocked off with workmen's planks and Keep Out signs. Blundering in the pitch-blackness, Elizabeth drew a flashlight from her pocket to light the last few steps. There, at the bottom, on the bare, muddy floor below, was a cordoned-off tarpaulin.

Elizabeth's heart beat fast. "This is it, isn't it?"

Saloman stood very still, only his thin, delicate nostrils flaring. "They've been here. Dante. Travis, Travis's vampires, other humans who smell of Dante." He crouched on the ground, touching the earth, the tarpaulin. "I can't find a trace of Josh or Dmitriu, but that doesn't mean they weren't here. If they were carried, their presence would be long lost in the air."

His eyes became fixed on the tarpaulin as he concentrated deeply. His fingers curled in the muddy earth. "There *is* a tunnel. Very deep, but I can follow it." Straightening, he leapt up the steps so fast she barely saw him move, and by the time she trailed after him, he was gazing straight at the building as if his stare could burn its way through stone.

Without a word, he slid his arm around her waist and jumped. Free of the castle, he dragged her down streets and alleys, over the tops of other buildings and walls and gardens and along other streets. To Elizabeth, it was more like her blind, endless search with the hunters than following a trail, but Saloman did eventually stop between a broken fence and the high wall of a dark, unknown building.

"We're nearly at the river," he said. "But this tunnel has no end, no way out." He stared at the ground, and under Elizabeth's anxious gaze, he eventually smiled. "Got you," he said softly.

She hadn't known she was holding her breath until it rushed out in relief. "Really? Josh *and* Dmitriu?"

"With Dante and several other humans and vampires. And my sword."

"Can you get them out?"

"Probably," Saloman said without expression. He glanced at the sky, as if gauging the time. He didn't look daunted, let alone worried, but Elizabeth could tell by his stillness, by the steadiness of his cool, opaque eyes that he was deep in thought. He was planning, she realized with a sinking heart, not just how to rescue his friend and hers, but how to make this work for his larger plan. Slowly, his gaze came back to her and refocused. "First," he said, "we need to talk. Come."

"What's the matter?" Elizabeth asked breathlessly as he leapt with her over rooftops and the spaces between until she could see the distinctive terraced walls and towers of the Fishermen's Bastion. "Would Travis hear us? Sense us?"

"Not through my masking, if he can even sense through the stone. We just need space to think."

The space Saloman had in mind turned out to be one of the Bastion towers, all turrets, archways, and walkways. Catching her breath, Elizabeth gazed beyond the fairy-tale tower across the city. The Danube lay black and still in the darkness, with only a few glinting reflections from the bridges' lights; and beyond it stretched Pest, the newer half of the city. The view was magnificent, but Saloman chose to sit on the wall with his back to it, so that he could see only Elizabeth and the tower behind her.

"What are we thinking about?" she asked, just a little nervously. "How to rescue Josh and Dmitriu?"

"Of course. I could go in now and probably kill all those I need to. I can probably free Dmitriu to help, although he may be too weak to do more than watch my back. I'm fast, but I can't be sure I'll be fast enough to save the lives of our friends, should the vampires—or Dante's human thugs—have orders to kill them."

Elizabeth's stomach twisted. "I can fight. I'm stronger than in St. Andrews."

"Stronger even than in New York. I know." He reached out and touched her cheek, her lips. "But you can be killed by guns. Dmitriu says each of Dante's four thugs has one. I can't save you from all of them and take care of the vampires at the same time." His lips twitched. "Much as I'd love to fight back-to-back with you once more, this isn't that kind of fight."

"I think you've already made up your mind," she observed. "You want other vampires in there with you."

"Two, maybe three would be enough."

She swallowed. "Would you kill Dante?"

"Yes." For Dmitriu alone, that would be his justice. And he'd be saving the world from a dangerous threat. Dante as a vampire was too scary to contemplate. The breeze stirred his hair. Under the pale moonlight, his eyes were as steady and as open as she had ever seen them.

"And the other humans?" she asked hoarsely.

"If they stand in my way, I will kill them. I or my companions. Dante's men have stakes as well as guns. So does Travis."

Her stomach twisted, reminding her once more, if she needed reminding, of the huge gulf between her and the beautiful, lethal being who sat on the wall gazing at her. Happy to bring death in his wake to punish as well as to free his friend.

"But you would bring Josh out alive and unharmed?" she said anxiously.

His lips curved at one side. "Unharmed by myself and my vampires, you mean?"

There was no point in denying it. "Yes."

"Since you wish it."

She licked her dry lips. "And the sword?"

"I will take it, of course."

Of course.

He slid off the wall, which brought him too close to her. She couldn't think when every nerve was so aware of him, of what he could do to her. He said, "The argument against this plan is that it is probably too late to do it tonight. By the time I can bring Angyalka and the other vampires I'd prefer at my back, it will be too close to sunrise, and may be impossible to get out in safety."

"Do they *have* another night?" Elizabeth asked in growing despair.

"Oh, yes, I think so. They're feeding Josh, you know. Dante wants him healthy for when he drinks his blood. And Dmitriu can stand one more night unfed, since he knows I'm coming for him. But it will have to be quick. If Dmitriu doesn't agree to change him by then, Dante and Travis will force him."

"Force him? How the hell—" She broke off. "No, don't answer that." She stared at Saloman. "We need to be in place *by* sunset. Soon after may be too late."

"It may."

"Which makes it difficult for vampires."

"We can walk in the dusk. Or in shadow."

"Will that be enough?"

"I don't know."

"And you could be seen."

"You are too concerned with secrecy. Sooner or later the world must learn about vampires."

"That's another day's fight," Elizabeth said impatiently, and he inclined his head, still watching her. She drew in her breath, running her teeth across her lower lip. "I have another plan. We make the hunters our allies in this."

When his expression didn't change, she hurried on. "They don't care about sunsets or sunrises, and they can enter the castle when they choose without reference to official opening times."

"I can see you would be happier with human allies," Saloman said smoothly. "But they would not work with me, and I'm afraid I insist on being there."

To make sure Dmitriu lived, and to take the sword. "There's no choice," Elizabeth said in a voice that sounded hard even to her. "We need you there."

Again, he inclined his head, and Elizabeth had the bizarre, almost dizzying feeling that she'd just carried out his wishes. Was it possible he actually *wanted* the hunters there?

"The hunters must not kill Dmitriu," he warned. "And I still take the sword."

"No," Elizabeth said.

Still his eyes did not change and she knew her veto made no difference. He would take it anyway if she could not convince him. And God knew she didn't want to prod that particular wound. She gripped his arms, slid her fingers up to his shoulders.

"Saloman, I know what the sword means to you, but you must see that they can't allow you to have this added power. It doesn't matter to *you*; you're already more powerful than any other being! The hunters would keep it away from your enemies, from all other vampires and humans, and never use it themselves. Knowing that, would you not let them have it? I've been thinking about this so much, Saloman, and I believe it's the only possible solution."

For a moment, he was rigid under her hands, neither throwing her off nor embracing her as she made her plea from the heart. Then, at last, his eyes softened and he took her in his arms.

"Elizabeth, this is one request I won't grant." He kissed her protesting mouth, silencing her. "But if I tell you the sword's true power, I think you'll no longer ask it of me."

Elizabeth, trying to quell the leap of her body in response to his kiss, tightened her hold on his shoulders. Finally, she would learn the truth about the sword. She drew in her breath and said shakily, "Tell me."

Chapter Nineteen

"No," said Konrad, staunchly and predictably. "I think we've already proved that alliance with vampires, even to catch other vampires, is unreliable and counterproductive."

They had met her, as requested, in the underground station at Heroes' Square. The platform was quiet in the middle of the morning. A train had just been through, and now there was no one there but Elizabeth and the three hunters.

Elizabeth said, "Zoltán was never trustworthy."

"And Saloman is?" Konrad exclaimed. "Elizabeth, the bastard drank my blood!"

"But he didn't kill you," Elizabeth said quickly.

"Only because you were jumping up and down on his back at the time," Mihaela said dryly. "I saw you."

Elizabeth shrugged that off. "It's not really relevant anyway. The point is, Saloman has found Josh and is prepared to help us rescue him."

"If you know where he is too," István said reasonably, "then we don't need Saloman. We'll go in and get him now."

"We can't. There are too many of them. The American vampire Travis is protecting Dante, and he has three other vampires with him. Dante has four armed human thugs."

"So we need backup," Konrad said, reaching for his phone.

"Maybe," Elizabeth said urgently. "But some of us will still die. We have more chance if we make Saloman our backup. What's more, his speed has more chance of saving Josh. We're talking about a small tunnel, a small room already full of people. We can't take nine or ten more humans in there and expect them to be able to fight."

Two young men wandered onto the platform, both talking at once, and Elizabeth turned her back on them, facing the frowning hunters instead and lowering her voice. "Look, Saloman has an interest in the success of this. He wants Dmitriu alive."

"And the sword," Mihaela said in a hard voice.

Elizabeth glanced at her. "And the sword. But then, everyone wants that. My first priority is Josh, not the sword. My second priority is to prevent Dante from becoming a vampire. Aren't those things your duty too?"

"Oh, yes—along with killing vampires like Saloman and Dmitriu," Mihaela snapped. "What's gotten into you, Elizabeth? We've been hunting Saloman for more than six months. You've been in on at least two attempts to kill him, and now, suddenly, you want to take him along as your pet assassin? This is *Saloman*! Nobody's pet!"

Elizabeth bit her lip on the sharp retort already forming there. She couldn't help being hurt by Mihaela's attitude, because although theirs was an odd and erratic friendship, they had never actually quarreled. Apart from the time she'd stormed out of the hunters' library, but that had been aimed mostly at Konrad and initiated entirely by Elizabeth.

Gazing at Mihaela now, she recognized the desperate worry behind the anger flashing in her brown eyes. Mihaela knew there was something wrong, had known she was hiding things since she'd first arrived.

But then, she'd always hidden this from Mihaela. From all of them. It wasn't something she could speak about easily to anyone, but she knew, at last, that she couldn't and shouldn't keep the secret for much longer.

She drew in her breath. "Look, I know this seems strange to you. A bizarre, untrustworthy alliance. And I know you think it's weird that I'm even on speaking terms with Saloman. I'll explain all that to you later, if you want me to. For now, we need to make plans to rescue Josh."

She paused as a train raced out of the tunnel and came to a halt, silent until passengers had gotten on and off and the train pulled away again. Then, as footsteps faded away from their empty platform once more, she said, "Would it help to know that he wanted to take his vampires in and do the job without us? I persuaded him that you would be better allies for this job and he agreed—on condition you don't kill Dmitriu."

They were all frowning again. "Why did he agree to that?" Mihaela asked flatly. "He can't trust us any more than we trust him."

"Perhaps . . . because he wants you to believe he isn't the monster you think he is." The words came out with difficulty, and yet she was sure they were the truth.

"Is he?" István asked.

She felt the smile flicker and die on her lips without permission. "I don't know." She met his gaze, then shifted hers to Konrad and finally Mihaela. "But I think, at least in this case, we have to take the chance. For Josh."

Mihaela's breath came out in a rush. "I hope you're right."

Elizabeth smiled, knowing she'd won. Mihaela's faint responding curve of the lips felt like a reward. "So do I," she said fervently.

"We'll talk to him," Konrad said sternly. "I'm promising no more than that. We can't trust the evil bastard, and that's the bottom line."

Elizabeth raised her voice. "Saloman."

"Oh, shit," said Mihaela, and Saloman strolled out of the passage on the right.

Each of the hunters made an instinctive jerk toward pockets and bags, depending on where they kept their emergency stakes. They drew infinitesimally closer together too, keeping Elizabeth within their protective circle.

Saloman looked artistic and bohemian this morning, in dark trousers and a white silk shirt with wide sleeves. His hair was tied behind his head, and he carried the familiar leather coat over one shoulder. Although he must have seen the profound, if discreet impression his presence had made on the hunters, he gave no sign of it, merely halted a couple of feet away and inclined his head like a prince greeting his subjects.

Whatever the setting and whoever else was present, he always managed to look splendid and totally in command. And sexy.

Dragging her wayward thoughts away from that direction, Elizabeth murmured, "I doubt formal introductions are necessary."

"I don't believe so." Konrad stared directly at Saloman, perhaps to prove he wasn't afraid. "The last time we met, you bit me."

Again, Saloman inclined his head. "You tasted good," he said politely, as if giving a compliment.

Inappropriate laughter caught at Elizabeth's breath. Mihaela coughed, as if she too had to cover her reaction; then she said curtly, "What plan do you propose?"

"You must gain us entry to the castle before sunset. I'll take you to the tunnel where they're hidden and mask your presence until we break in." He shrugged eloquently. "After that, we fight to free our friends. I will agree to protect Josh if you agree to leave Dmitriu undead."

"Can they use the sword against us?" Konrad demanded.

"Not for long."

"The sword must remain with us," Konrad insisted.

"As long as I am with you."

Konrad opened his mouth to dispute that in no uncertain terms, so Elizabeth said hastily, "Perhaps we can deal with that issue once have our friends safe?"

"As you wish," said Saloman. He addressed Konrad, as the leader of the team. "Be in the castle grounds by seven thirty. Elizabeth will show you the way."

"Earlier would be better," Konrad challenged. "We can arrange to get you there safely."

"Shutting the castle to visitors and staff?"

"What?"

"Collateral damage," Saloman explained. "And too high a price. Seven thirty." He bowed his head once more and, turning, sauntered back along the platform, passing a woman with a buggy as he turned in to the exit passage.

As soon as he was out of sight, Konrad and István sprinted after him. Elizabeth and Mihaela watched in silence until they returned only seconds later.

István spread his hands wide. "Gone," he said helplessly.

"Is this about Josh?" Mihaela said abruptly.

Elizabeth looked up, blinking. "Of course it is!"

They had gone together back to Mihaela's flat, eaten a light meal, and were now preparing for the battle ahead. There had been no animosity apparent in Mihaela's attitude, although Elizabeth was grateful for the silences during which they each appeared to be thinking their own thoughts.

Mihaela's question had come out of the blue, as had her presence at the bedroom door as Elizabeth fastened her jeans.

Mihaela smiled faintly and leaned against the doorframe, watching Elizabeth clear out her bag. "No. I mean this alliance with Saloman. I understand your need to get Josh back at any price. My only worry is that your judgment has been impaired by . . . Josh."

Elizabeth placed her charged phone and her purse back in the bag and picked up the sharpened wooden stake before she answered. "You mean am I madly in love with Josh Alexander?"

"It crossed my mind. You were talking the other night about unsuitable lovers. I can't think of anyone less suitable to someone of deep loyalties than a movie star."

"Actually, I'd say Josh *is* pretty loyal," Elizabeth said judiciously. "But trust me, you've no need to worry on that score."

"I do," Mihaela said ruefully.

Elizabeth smiled. "Worry?"

"Trust you."

Elizabeth swallowed, blinking away the sudden tears. "Thank you," she whispered.

Mihaela came and put her arms around her. "Elizabeth . . ."

Elizabeth hugged her once, hard. "You're right to trust me, I promise you. And if I've kept things from you it was because I couldn't bear them myself. After tonight, I'll tell you everything, if you still want to hear it."

Mihaela drew back, gazing seriously into her face. "But you *are* all right?"

Elizabeth choked out a laugh. "In many ways I'm more all right than I've ever been. It's just all so complicated. . . ." She stepped back, dashing her hand impatiently across her face. "Are Konrad and István really okay with this?"

"They trust you too. Although Konrad has a theory that Saloman plans to shut us all in the tunnel while his vampires run loose over Budapest."

"He doesn't need to shut us in a tunnel for that to happen."

"That's what I said. Shall we go and meet our evil ally and kick some foreign vampire ass?"

Elizabeth picked up her bag. "Yes, please." She dropped her solitary stake into the bag and glanced up. "I don't suppose you have any more stakes, do you?"

"Cupboards full of them," Mihaela said largely, waving one hand toward the wardrobe. "Help yourself."

. . .

Travis was bored. He'd been shut up down here for three nights already, with only the shortest of breaks to hunt, and he was heartily sick of his companions, several of whom he had to prevent from killing one another from time to time. His vampires wanted to feed on Dante's men, who came and went more freely, but were always around at night when Dante was present. Travis didn't have a problem with using the thugs as a food supply, but Dante forbade it, and for the moment, at least, Travis went along with him. He suspected Dante was saving them for himself, for after Dmitriu eventually turned him. Dante was the sort who would want human slaves.

In fact, pacing the room, past the recumbent, miserable human, Josh, and his own half-asleep, half-playing vampires, Travis was conscious of his increasing distaste for this adventure. It was taking far too long and he was itching to get back to America to check on his own operation and gather up what was left of Severin's. If it weren't for the bloody sword and Saloman's wager, he'd have left Dante to stew. Hell, he wouldn't even *be* here.

Travis stopped his restless prowling next to the chained-up vampire Dmitriu. There were only a few hours until sundown. When Dante wasn't here, as now, Dmitriu's mask of serene disdain occasionally slipped. Travis could both see and feel his agony and that added to his distaste.

Travis wanted to go home and beat his own minions into order. He wanted to run his gambling operations and bite the favored few of his guests who never remembered. He didn't want to force this weakened yet powerful vampire—stronger than Travis, if the truth be told—to drink from Dante. In fact, Travis himself wasn't too keen on drinking from Dante anymore. And he was aware that once Dante was turned there would be a conflict for possession of the sword. It was a conflict Travis *thought* he could win, but he had no way of knowing how death via the sword would affect Dante as a vampire. In any case, once the sword was Travis's and he'd won his wager with Saloman, he really didn't want to swap one rival for another.

Travis didn't like many beings. Dante he was beginning to thoroughly dislike. Dmitriu, on the other hand, was at least interesting, if only because Travis had no idea what made him tick.

He hung there now, eyes closed, a frown on his blood-streaked brow. The hunger was making him sweat what blood he had left. And it would only get worse when the sun went down.

"Why don't you just do it?" Travis said abruptly. "Bite the bastard, kill him, let him drink from you. Who cares? We'll both be out of this shithole."

Dmitriu's brow smoothed; his eyes opened. Although he hid what he could of his pain, Travis could still see it. "I can't," Dmitriu said. "He smells bad. He'd taste worse."

"It's going to happen. Can't you just make it easier and quicker for all of us?" What Travis didn't want was a failed turning: for Dmitriu not to ingest enough of Dante's blood for the turning to "take." That would drag them back to square one, and another night in this stone coffin.

"No," said Dmitriu. He didn't even pretend to consider it.

Travis looked at him with curiosity. "Why not? What makes you so fucking stubborn?"

Dmitriu appeared to consider him. The veil of disdain lifted from his pain-filled eyes. "I will not abuse Saloman's sword nor leave it with *him*. On top of which, he's not worthy of immortality."

"*Worthy?*" Travis stared at him. "Am I worthy? Are you?"

Dmitriu paused again. Then he said, "You could be. I am sometimes, when I remember."

"You're delirious," Travis decided. "Unless you always talk such crap. Haven't you ever created an 'unworthy' vampire before?"

"No," said Dmitriu. "Have you?"

Travis hesitated. The truth was, he hadn't created any for a long time. He'd lost heart. At last he said, "I never got the chance to discover. They died as fledglings."

Dmitriu nodded, without sneering or accusing. "They didn't have the strength."

Travis frowned. "Is that what you mean by worthiness?"

"Part of it. Dante has that part. He's strong and would probably thrive."

"Then what's your problem?"

Dmitriu smiled. It was an oddly appealing, charming smile, and Travis knew a brief urge to entertain him at his New York club. "I don't like him. He is, er, a bad bastard."

Travis blinked. "So am I. And what the hell is Saloman?"

"Good question," Dmitriu said on the ghost of a laugh. "But if I had a choice of throwing in my lot with either Dante or Saloman, I know which one I'd choose."

"I won't 'throw in my lot' with anyone," Travis said disdainfully.

Dmitriu's eyes were serious. "Your choice," he said softly, and Travis turned away, unreasonably annoyed. It fucking well *was* his choice, and he'd made it, because Dante would be easier to beat than Saloman.

Halfway across to his eternally gambling vampires, he paused and looked back over his shoulder. "Where *is* Saloman?"

Dmitriu smiled and closed his eyes.

Huddled in the castle cellar room with the cordoned-off tarpaulin, the hunters looked at Elizabeth doubtfully. "Are you sure this is it?"

"I'm sure Saloman says it is."

A new flashlight beam descending the steps heralded the almost silent arrival of Konrad. Joining them by the tarpaulin, he reported quietly, "The alarms are off between here and the open exit. The night watchmen will cover the exit but they won't bother us." He glanced at Elizabeth. "Where is Saloman?"

"Here," said the deep, almost sepulchral voice that melted Elizabeth's bones. Beside her, Mihaela jumped and swore beneath her breath. Konrad and István swung around to face the steps, stakes drawn.

Saloman took the steps in one graceful jump, landing squarely in front of the hunters, which would have been taken as a threat had he not then stood perfectly still with his open hands by his sides.

"Good," he said, regarding the stakes. "You came prepared. Travis is a strong vampire for his age, and his bodyguards are cunning. If you deal with the latter, I will take care of Travis."

"How did you get past the watchman at the entrance?" Konrad demanded.

"He probably showed him his driving license," Elizabeth muttered, and Saloman bestowed a dazzling smile upon her, causing tense, hysterical laughter to try to fight its way out. Only the hunters' baffled expressions sobered her.

Saloman moved forward, ignoring the hunters' stakes as he brushed past them to crouch down and lift the tarpaulin. At first it looked just like the rest of the earth-strewn floor, even with a flashlight beam trained upon it.

"It's masked," Saloman said mildly, and then, as if the very notion banished the enchantment, Elizabeth could make out the deeper blackness, the gaping hole disappearing downward into nothing.

István held his detector at the edge. It could pick up normal vampire presence within a short distance, although Saloman's biochemistry passed it by. "Nothing," he said doubtfully.

Saloman said, "Dante passed here most recently. He's in the stone room now, with Travis. Three other vampires and four humans guard our friends."

"Can he know that?" Mihaela whispered in Elizabeth's ear.

Elizabeth nodded. He could if he was communicating with Dmitriu.

Dante uncovered the Sword of Saloman, throwing off the musty old coat and lifting up the weapon in both steady hands. Travis had to admit to a certain amount of awe. The sword was beautiful in the kind of way that called you to touch it, hold it, see what it could do.

He couldn't prevent the rush of excitement as he gazed upon it. This was his freedom from Saloman, his guarantee of continued power in America.

It was funny, but he hadn't realized how much this power meant to him until he faced the threat of losing it. He'd worked for centuries to build up his authority. And though he'd pinched some ideas from the late and unlamented Severin—all hail to the Awakener for that one—as to imposing his will on the maximum territory with minimum discipline, he knew he'd done it all bigger and better.

Travis didn't want to rule the world. But he had set his sights on leading the whole of North America and he was damned if he'd give up that aim, especially now that Severin was out of the picture at last.

"You see, Josh?" Dante said to the human captive. "This is why the sword never really belonged to you."

The human, who'd grown increasingly morose and uncommunicative as time passed, surprised Travis with a bitter burst of laughter. "Why is that, Senator? It couldn't belong to me because you wanted it?"

Dmitriu said provokingly, "It doesn't belong to either of you. It's Saloman's."

Dante ignored him. It was Travis who rose impatiently and stalked across to Saloman's "child." Ramming his face up close to Dmitriu's, he said low, "Is Saloman afraid of Dante? Is that why you won't turn him?"

Dmitriu said nothing.

Travis placed his lips very close to Dmitriu's ear. "Or are *you* afraid of Saloman?"

Drawing back to see the effect of his words, he was frustrated to see Dmitriu smile. "Only as much as I should be. It's you who should be truly afraid."

An instant longer he met Dmitriu's steady gaze. As unease twisted through him, he tried to force his way into the other vampire's mind, but even weakened as he was, Dmitriu held the door firmly closed.

Travis became aware that across the room, Josh was watching.

There had been little or no communication between the captives, which, in the circumstances, perhaps, wasn't surprising, but somehow it all added to Travis's unease.

Saloman. He was bound to be here in Budapest looking for the sword, maybe even looking for Dmitriu. And the sun would go down in minutes.

"Boss, can I go for a whiz?" asked one of Dante's men, interrupting the senator's love-in with the sword.

Dante waved it at him. "Hurry up, two at a time." His gaze, glittering and triumphant, swung around to Dmitriu. "We begin in ten minutes."

Chapter Twenty

István, ever the scientist, said, "Are these tunnels even older than the known labyrinth under old Buda?" He bumped his head and ducked down further, rubbing it in an irritated sort of way.

"Some of them," Saloman answered. "They're a mixture of what you would call prehistoric, dark age, and medieval. Some were once connected to the current labyrinth, but they've been blocked off."

He moved, stretching his hands over Mihaela's bent head to catch a falling piece of rubble crumbling from the ceiling. "As you can see, they're not terribly safe."

"Thanks," Mihaela muttered, and Elizabeth wondered if she'd rather have had the stone fall on her head. She didn't want to be beholden to Saloman; none of them did. Not yet. But Elizabeth was starting to see a way forward, a glimmer of the shadowy beginnings of something greater than antagonism and mutual murder.

She was starting to see Saloman's way forward, and it no longer looked quite so scary.

Saloman halted, both hands outstretched to stop István and Mihaela on either side of him. "Humans," he said softly, barely louder than Elizabeth's breath. "Two, coming this way."

Squinting past those in front, before the flashlights switched off, Elizabeth glimpsed the tunnel ahead. In a few more feet, the ceiling sloped higher so that most people would be able to stand. The tunnel then swung around a corner.

"We can't fight here," Konrad hissed. "Go forward!"

But Saloman was already moving, almost gliding ahead of Mihaela and István, who scuttled after him like huge crabs in the darkness. Elizabeth scrambled in their wake, suddenly claustrophobic.

Breaking free of the low tunnel and stretching, Elizabeth took a deep breath. Saloman stood at the curve in the wall, the hunters lined up behind. She ran silently to join them.

"Use your lights or you won't see," Saloman advised, and walked around the corner. Elizabeth and the hunters hastily spread out behind him.

"What the . . . ?" came an American voice from a few yards' distance, and Elizabeth made out two men with flashlights coming toward them. "Who the fuck's that?"

"Who the fuck cares?" was the immediate response, and the flashlights wavered as both men delved for their guns.

"Oh, shit," István said with a rueful glance at the crumbling ceiling, which he clearly feared would collapse in a firefight. He was probably right, but before Konrad, the only one of them with a firearm, could produce it, Saloman leapt forward.

Moving so fast he was a mere blur, he flew at the advancing men. They never even saw what hit them. A gun fired, but only the Americans fell, slammed into the ground by a force they never anticipated. Saloman leapt to his feet, quite as graceful as, and ten times more lethal than, a panther.

"Oh, God," Mihaela whispered, and Elizabeth gripped her hand hard as they ran forward. But there was no time to see to the fallen men. Ahead was what looked like a dead end, except that the stone suddenly shimmered into an opening iron door. It had been masked. This, then, was the stone room where Josh was imprisoned.

Someone—Travis—poked his head out of the door. The beams of several flashlights struck him in the eyes, just as Saloman leapt once more.

But Travis was fast. He slammed the door shut with a yell, and the screech of bolts and locks crashing into place echoed around the tunnel.

Konrad swore. "Now how the hell do we get in?" he raged.

"You could try knocking," Saloman suggested. "Or we could go in the way I always intended."

The gunshot in the tunnel clearly startled Dante from his complacence. He almost dropped the sword. As it was, the point made an echoing, clanking sound as he lowered it too quickly to the floor. Grimly, Travis pushed past him. Either one of Dante's fools had fired his weapon by accident, or . . .

Travis wrenched the door open and peered outside. Only feet away lay the recumbent forms of Dante's men, and looming over them, among others, the being he least wanted to see. The Ancient's eyes glittered; his whole body seemed to thrum with a power Travis had never before witnessed. It was terrifying in its magnitude, as if it had no boundary, no end. Lights flashed into Travis's eyes, almost blinding him as Saloman leapt.

Instinct preserved him. Throwing himself back inside the room, he slammed the door shut and knocked all the locks into place, swearing long and consistently.

"What is it? What's going on?" Dante demanded.

"I knew it," Travis snarled. "Bloody Saloman!" He turned on Dante. "To say nothing of the Awakener and other humans who stink of hunter." He allowed himself a vicious smile. "Well, who cares? Technically, I found the sword before him!"

He lunged for it, but Dante, with unexpected speed for a human, swung it out of his reach. "Oh, no!" Dante hissed. "You still have a part to play first!"

"Oh, for fuck's sake!" Travis raged. Hadn't the fool grasped what was out there? There came a dull thud on the iron door, as if someone had thrown himself at it. "See?"

"In any case, you've lost the wager," Dmitriu said to him calmly. "Saloman had the sword in his hands before you and Dante took it from Josh."

"Shut up," Travis muttered as the battering continued at the door. Was it time to change sides? Kill Dante—for good—grovel to Saloman, steal the sword when his back was turned, and pray it gave him the power to withstand the Ancient at some time in the future, safe back in New York City? The carnage of a fight was a good time to take off. . . .

"Bring him!" Dante commanded. "Bring Dmitriu and make him do it now!"

On the other hand, Saloman had blown his men across the room with one forceful exhale. How the hell was that done? Easy when a being had the power at his disposal that Travis had just sensed surrounding Saloman in the tunnel. Travis couldn't fool himself that the Ancient was likely to forgive him. He'd stuck this long with Dante; he might as well see it through and pray the sword and Dmitriu's blood would be enough to get them both out of this mess.

Travis jerked his head at his minions, who, already on their feet in response as much to the scents wafted in from the door as to the gunshot, began warily to unchain Dmitriu.

"I didn't plan to confront Saloman this early," Dante said anxiously. "You had better do this right, Travis, or we are both—not to put too fine a point on it—fucked."

"I know," Travis said grimly.

"Why couldn't that bastard just turn me when he was first brought here?" Dante demanded. "It would have been so much simpler and I'd be more ready—"

"Because Saloman told him not to," Travis said impatiently. He hadn't read it in Dmitriu's mind; he'd guessed it from his voice, his eyes, the same way he knew of the affection, the love that Dmitriu felt for his maker. Affection was not an emotion that Travis had much truck with these days, but he still recognized it when he saw it. In fact, damn the whole situation to hell, he realized he missed it.

I'm a three-hundred-year-old vampire, not a fucking teenager. "Get his feet," he snapped as Dmitriu struggled with his captors every step of the way. But they'd managed to get him in here when he was far stronger; the outcome was never in doubt.

They flung Dmitriu to his knees before Dante, who wordlessly passed Travis the sword. "I could fall on this myself," he warned. "Remember, I'm trusting you."

"Of course," said Travis ironically. There had never been the remotest trust between either of them. Just plain self-interest and the need of the sword.

And it would be a sweet thing to own, he acknowledged, admiring the grace and beauty of it in his hands. If he cut Dante's head off with it now, would it bring him enough strength, enough invulnerability to defeat Saloman with it too?

"The sword is Saloman's," Dmitriu said quietly. Was the bastard reading his mind? One of Travis's vampires had him by the hair, controlling his head, while the other two held him to the ground on his knees.

Travis tapped the sword meaningfully with one finger. "Possession," he pointed out to Dmitriu, and raised it with some satisfaction, aiming the point at Dante's chest.

"Keep it there," Dante reminded him, "while he drinks my blood and I take his. Do it quickly! Before Saloman breaks in the door."

But it turned out to be the humans trying to break in the door, and only, it transpired, to create a diversion. For, with a sudden crash that drowned out the banging, Saloman walked straight through the wall next to Josh in a cloud of thick, choking dust and falling stones.

"Adam?" Dante said hoarsely and inexplicably. He clutched his head in both hands. "Oh, shit. Adam Simon."

"I am Saloman," said the Ancient in tones that chilled Travis to his very bones. "Give me my sword."

Travis cried out as the sword tore free of his hand, ripping at the resisting muscle and bone and sinew. The sword flew through the air in a large, clear arc, only to land squarely in Saloman's grasping fist.

And then all hell broke loose. Three humans tumbled in through the door—how the hell had they managed to get in?—and were rushing at him with stakes. Using his arm to deflect the nearest, Travis sidestepped and lashed out with his feet. His minion, Al, rushing at Saloman, skidded to a halt and swung back as if to help him. It was his undoing, for the Awakener, who'd entered behind Saloman, staked him through the back and turned him to dust.

Travis had nothing left to lose. He launched himself forward as one of Dante's idiots fired his gun at Saloman. It didn't even slow the Ancient up. He disarmed his assailant with a flick of the sword that also cut off the man's finger, and then, through his scream, flew at the second human, knocking him cold with one kick.

Travis lost him after that, since the Awakener came at him with her lethal stake. She was good, too—agile and quick enough to dodge his blows without letting down her guard. No wonder she'd managed to kill Severin. And when Travis spun around her to bamboozle her into making a mistake, she did her best to follow. Still, Travis could have gotten her then, killed her and taken the power of the Awakener—no small prize in this or any other fight—except that suddenly the female hunter was there too, stake already plunging for the kill.

And now it was Travis caught catastrophically off guard. There was nowhere to go, no way to avoid it. In the weird speed of thought that accompanies such monumental events, he had time to think, *Shit. Now who'll look after my fools in America?*

And then, even before the stake point pierced the skin over his heart, the stake was ripped away. The hunter stared at him, as if she thought he'd done it himself. But it was Saloman, not even looking at Travis as he pointed the sword straight at Dante's throat, who held the stake by the sharp end. Blood spilled through the Ancient's fingers from the wound in his palm.

"Saloman!" the Awakener cried out with such peculiar anguish that Travis couldn't tell whether her concern was for the hunter or for the injured vampire.

Travis backed off in confusion. It didn't make sense. His enemy had just thrust his hand under the stake to save him.

Saloman spared the Awakener a glance, and Travis was sure some brief communication flashed between them. By rights, Saloman should have killed her months ago to gain the special strength of his Awakener, and yet here she still was, fighting by his side as she'd done in New York. Something weird was going on there.

Amid a spatter of blood, Saloman flung the stake to the ground, to be picked up by Dmitriu. Sitting on the floor, the starving vampire smiled and took aim for a throw at Travis's heart.

"Enough!" Saloman said thunderously, much as Travis had heard him say before. "It is finished!"

Travis looked around him. His vampires were all gone. One of Dante's bodyguards lay dead against the wall; another was out cold with his leg at a grotesque angle. With his free, wounded hand, Saloman gave Dante a casual shove that sent him flying back into the wall next to Josh. A bloody handprint now spoiled the senator's bright shirt. It was indeed over.

As the Awakener and the female hunter ran to free Josh, the men advanced upon Dante.

Saloman ignored all of them. Lifting the sword, he slid it into the scabbard Travis hadn't even noticed he was wearing. It was a curiously satisfied gesture, although there was nothing satisfied about his person as he swung around and marched toward Travis.

Ah. That's why I've been saved. I suppose it's an honor to be killed by Saloman.

But Saloman stalked right past him, turning his back to kneel by Dmitriu. Under Travis's bemused gaze, Saloman took the starving vampire in his arms. "You've done well, Dmitriu," he said softly. "Forgive the time I took."

"What time?" Dmitriu said weakly. "What's three days beside three hundred years?"

Three hundred years—the length of Saloman's death-sleep before he was awakened. Rumor said Dmitriu had sent the Awakener to him.

Travis shifted, from pure curiosity, so that he could see the Ancient smile. "I have another debt to pay," Saloman said, and drew Dmitriu's head down to his neck.

Dmitriu gasped, made some inarticulate protest that faded to silence when Saloman stroked his hair once. With a sob, Dmitriu fell on the Ancient's neck.

Piercing an Ancient's skin was not easy, so Travis had heard, but Dmitriu seemed to manage it. In fascination, Travis watched him feed, almost felt every swallow of the powerful, reviving blood, and suddenly he knew an upsurge of longing, not just to taste the sweetness, the sheer strength of that blood, but to know the strong arms that held him, the love that bound them. Friendship.

Slowly, Travis raised his gaze from Dmitriu's blissful face and found Saloman watching him.

Saloman's lips twitched. Inside Travis's head he said, *Anyone can make a mistake.*

Josh clung to Elizabeth, hugging her with trembling arms. "Am I dreaming? Are you in my mind again?"

Elizabeth hugged him back. "You're not dreaming," she assured him gently. "And I'm afraid the head stuff was real. You and I are telepathic, at least to some extent. Saloman helped us use that to find you." She drew back a little, scanning his face. "Are you all right? Are you hurt?"

"My ego mostly," Josh said ruefully. "I was petrified at first; then Dmitriu told me I was safe until he turned Dante, which he would never do. But they gave me food and drink, let me pee in the back tunnel, and didn't beat me. Shit, does that mean I was well treated?"

"For a kidnap victim, probably," Elizabeth said, smiling. "For a vampire's victim, definitely!"

"What the hell is he doing?" István asked, curious. Crouched over Dante, the hunter had been distracted by Saloman and Dmitriu on the other side of the room. Elizabeth felt her insides clench in a sudden rush of emotion, some of which she recognized as lust. Held to Saloman's throat, Dmitriu drank his blood.

"Dmitriu was kept chained and starved of blood," she said calmly. "To make him more eager to exchange blood with Dante. He needs blood badly. Saloman is giving him his."

"Shit," said Mihaela in awe. "I didn't know they did that."

Elizabeth didn't point out the trust and loyalty—traits that were regarded as peculiarly human—that went with the act. She let them speak for themselves.

"That Dmitriu," Josh said slowly, "is not a bad fellow. He suffered, but he never gave in. I don't think he even came close."

"He's a fool!" Dante burst out beside them. "He'd have had my undying gratitude—"

"What in God's name would he want with that?" Elizabeth said contemptuously. "When he has Saloman's?"

It was too much. Mihaela was staring at her and she had to look at Josh to avoid the question in her friend's eyes. She said quickly, "These are the hunters I was telling you about. Mihaela, Konrad, and István."

"I guess I owe all of you rather more than thanks," Josh said, with a winning smile. Already he was bouncing back, and that did Elizabeth's heart good.

"Nonsense," Mihaela said robustly. "Believe it or not, this is our job."

A movement across the room caught Elizabeth's attention, and she saw that Saloman and Dmitriu had risen to their feet and were advancing across the room. The hunters fell back, instinctively adopting a mutually defensive position. Elizabeth held her ground, for Saloman drew the sword from his scabbard once more and pointed it at Dante as he walked.

She noticed another curiosity. Beside and a little behind Dmitriu walked Travis. He should have fled through the open and unguarded door, but it seemed he was too intrigued. Saloman had saved his life when Mihaela would have killed him.

Clever bastard. Clever, clever bastard.

Thank you, Saloman said, apparently pleased with the compliment.

I suppose he's eating out of your hand now?

I have hopes that he will be very soon.

Another bloodless coup?

There was a faint pause. Then Saloman said, *If you don't count the three who died today. They would no doubt disagree, but I believe America is worth it.*

And the humans who died?

They died for Dante, not for me, and certainly not for America. Saloman came to a halt, the sword point at Dante's shoulder. "For Dmitriu's pain," he said aloud, "a little back." And he pushed the sword into Dante's flesh.

The senator cried out in surprise, but his eyes had begun to gleam again, and not with fear, or even pain.

Saloman smiled. "Of course, this is what you want, what all this ridiculous mayhem has been about. To have the sword pierce you while you die and are reborn an immortal."

Unbelievably, Dante's smile was back. He leaned forward into the sword with a wince of pain. Elizabeth felt sick. "Do it, Saloman," he said eagerly. "I'll be your most powerful slave."

"That's almost as ridiculous," Saloman mused, "as your first idea. What in the world makes you think the sword will give you any power?" He withdrew the blade as he spoke and held it up for Dmitriu to sniff. Dmitriu wrinkled his nose, and although Saloman couldn't have seen it, he smiled.

Blood oozed from Dante's shoulder, spreading another scarlet stain over his once crisp yellow shirt. Staring up at Saloman, he said intensely, "The sword *is* power. Everyone knows that, and the combination of Saloman and the sword is truly irresistible. I get that. I accept that. You can't blame me for trying, but now that I've met you, now that I know who you are, Adam Simon, and what you're capable of . . . I can face reality. You are the prince, and I, turned by you and the sword together, your most useful subject."

Saloman appeared to consider him while the hunters, Dmitriu, and Travis all looked from one to the other to see what would happen next. Elizabeth tensed as the hunters took surreptitious hold of their stakes. They wouldn't allow the creation of a new vampire under their very noses.

Saloman said, "That really *is* the most abject, pathetic piece of self-centered twaddle I have ever heard in my life."

Dante's eyes flashed. His hand moved to his wound as if it suddenly pained him.

"Shall I tell you the secret of the sword?" Saloman said conversationally. "Shall I tell Travis and my friends the vampire hunters too? Or perhaps I should simply show you. Sword," he commanded, "smite down my enemies."

Dante cringed; the hunters tensed; Travis took a circumspect step backward. But the sword stayed perfectly still in Saloman's loose grip. Elizabeth, who knew the reason, because he'd told her last night, watched every expression on his cold, arrogant face, watching for what he didn't say more than listening to what he did.

"Well, that doesn't work," Saloman observed. His gaze refocused on Dante. "It never did. None of it did. I enchanted the sword to make it easier to find if I was ever parted from it, because yes, the sword is valuable to me. What do you say? Sentimental value? Because it was given to me by my cousin Luk, whom I later killed."

Saloman spread his sardonic smile among the hunters. "The rest, I'm afraid, is unfounded legend, bunkum, rubbish spread about by people too ashamed to admit they'd been bested without magic. There *is* no magic, except what I put there—a conjuring trick to frighten thieves and murderers." His glance took in Josh and Elizabeth. "No offense," he added blandly.

"What are you saying?" Dante said hoarsely. "That the sword has no power?"

"None whatsoever."

"I don't believe you!"

Saloman laughed. It wasn't a pleasant sound. "Yes, you do. You just don't want to. All that for nothing." Now his glance embraced all of them: Josh, Travis, and the hunters. "It's worth nothing to any of you, with the possible exception of Josh. And there, on the sentimental value, I beat him by a few thousand years. You've been wasting your time, gentlemen. On which note, Senator, pray to whatever maker you believe in and prepare to die. Without rebirth."

He lowered the sword, holding it poised over Dante's heart. Justice. Execution. The greater good of the world. For all of those reasons, Saloman would kill Dante in cold blood and never see the crime.

Elizabeth forced her numb lips apart. "Saloman," she said hoarsely. He didn't even glance at her. All his attention was on Dante, whose appalled and terrified face finally bore the knowledge that he had lost. Not only had immortality eluded him; mortality was upon him far quicker than it should have been.

Urgently, Elizabeth seized Saloman's arm. "Don't," she pleaded. "Saloman, please don't kill him like this."

"How would you like me to kill him?"

"I don't want you to kill him at all!"

His cold, compassionless eyes moved, gazing at her instead. The sword stayed where it was. Repeating the argument she had often used to him, he said, "It isn't up to you."

Her breath caught. She stepped in front of Dante, knocking the sword aside. At the last moment, he let her, shifting it so that it didn't cut her.

"Yes," she said grimly, "it is. I won't let you do this, Saloman."

"Elizabeth, what are you doing?" Mihaela said urgently. Her voice was high with fright. "Step aside, for God's sake!"

"Get out of his way," Konrad commanded.

Elizabeth couldn't look at them. She had to hold Saloman's gaze, make him understand that there had already been too much killing. It did cross her mind that the hunters might do something really stupid to save her, like trying to stake Saloman, and then the bloodbath would be unthinkable. It also crossed her mind that Saloman would not delay his justice even for her.

I will never kill you, he'd said. But she'd never defied him when his blood was up, when he was aflame with anger. Except when he'd meant to kill her in St. Andrews and she'd confessed her love and kissed him. That had worked.

Before she could try it again, he reached out.

"Elizabeth, now!" Konrad exclaimed, and she felt the hunters move as one toward Saloman, with what intention she never found out, because Saloman only laid one hand on her shoulder and pulled her inexorably back against his body, where he held her, the sword again at Dante's chest. Baffled, the hunters skidded to a halt once more.

"You can't stop me, Elizabeth," Saloman said. "Not this time."

She twisted in his arm to look up into his face. “Then stop yourself. If it’s not up to me, it’s not just up to you either. It’s up to all of us. Isn’t that what you want? Eventually?”

Slowly, his gaze dropped to hers once more. “Why do you try so hard to save him? You’d have killed him yourself only minutes ago.”

“In a fight,” she acknowledged, “I might. This isn’t a fight. It’s murder. Please don’t do it. . . .”

“A strange distinction,” he observed, but she had the impression he spoke the words without thought. A faint frown marred his brow as he searched her eyes. “You *really* don’t want me to kill him.”

She couldn’t speak or even nod. It was as if all her energy were used in willing him to understand. And yet in all their dealings, she had never before recognized so clearly his difference from her and from everyone that she knew—his sheer, unpredictable *alienness*. Her arguments could not influence him; his justice was inhuman; there was simply nothing she could do. Words of persuasion, emotional pleas, all died on her lips unspoken. They could not save Dante.

Saloman lowered the sword.

Stunned, Elizabeth let her breath out in a rush. She closed her eyes in gratitude and profound relief, and slumped against him.

He said, “I have a feeling we’ll all regret this and I can say ‘I told you so.’ Until then, be gone before I change my mind.”

Dante, still not quite understanding that he was to be spared, had to be hauled to his feet by István, who pushed him toward the door, saying urgently, “Go, hurry. No one will save you next time.”

Saloman released Elizabeth and sauntered across the room. Only then, among the stares of the other hunters, did she see Mihaela’s expression. Not anger, or hurt. But pity.

Saloman paused, looking down at the old coat that had been Josh’s father’s and had covered the sword for all the time it had been in Josh’s possession. He bent and picked it up, then walked back to Josh. Konrad, standing in front of him, got out of Saloman’s way.

"Here," Saloman said, dropping the coat into the stunned Josh's lap. "It's as valuable as the sword. And no one will take it from you."

Then he turned once more and walked out of the room through the hole he'd made in the wall. Elizabeth's throat closed up. She wanted to weep, to hug him with pride.

Blinking, she caught Dmitriu steadily watching her, and remembered everything he'd said the night he'd been taken. Dmitriu's lips curved slightly. He made a bow that took in Elizabeth, Josh, and the hunters. It wasn't entirely ironic. Then he followed Saloman over the rubble into the tunnel.

Elizabeth took a deep breath and said, "Okay, we're going to need an ambulance. And what about the dead bodies?"

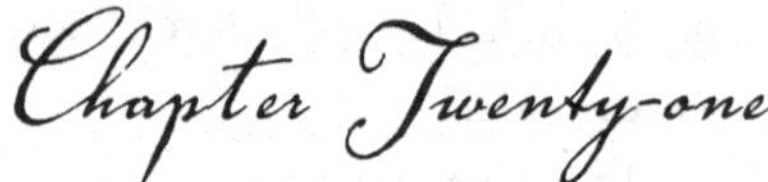

Chapter Twenty-one

The hunters' organization took care of the dead; the injured were taken to the hospital, apparently unsure what they'd seen or done. The hunters seemed to think any babbling about stakes and bodies turning to dust would be put down to head injury and trauma.

Josh refused to go to the hospital. His only injury appeared to be chafed wrists where he'd been tied. "I'd rather just go to a hotel," he said tiredly as they finally left his prison for the last time. He held up his slightly battered travel bag. "I still have this, complete with credit cards and passport—though I'd appreciate a lift."

"I think you should be in company," Elizabeth said anxiously, taking the bag from him. "At least for tonight."

"There are beds at headquarters," Konrad said. "I can take you there and someone would look in on you from time to time."

Josh wrinkled his nose. "Forgive me, it sounds just like a hospital. I'll take the hotel."

"You could stay with one of us," Mihaela said unexpectedly. "Except that the boys have grotty studios and I only have one spare room."

Elizabeth cast her a grateful glance. Mihaela's cool, comfortable flat with casual company was just what Josh needed for tonight. "I'd be happy on the sofa," she said. "Josh should have the bed. Or he can't come," she added, as he appeared to be about to protest.

Josh laughed, and in that way it was decided. As Elizabeth finally climbed the dark staircase from the tunnels into the dim shelter above, she found Mihaela waiting for her. Beyond her, in the predawn gray light, Josh was walking a little unsteadily between Konrad and István.

"You can give me the bag, if you want," Mihaela said.

"I can manage."

"Yes, but there's no point—you won't be on the sofa."

Elizabeth frowned. "Mihaela, Josh and I—"

"You might come back with us," Mihaela interrupted, "but you won't stay, will you?"

Elizabeth closed her mouth. Her whole heart, as well as her body, was crying out to be with Saloman. Mihaela had seen it all when she'd persuaded Saloman to spare Dante's life. Not just that there was something between them, but the depth of her feelings.

"Mihaela . . ."

"End it, Elizabeth," Mihaela said intensely. "If you must have tonight and you survive it, for God's sake end it."

"I can't," Elizabeth whispered, grateful for the darkness that hid her from Mihaela, that hid Mihaela's accusing eyes from her. "I've tried. I've tried so hard, but I can't."

"Oh, God, Elizabeth." Mihaela's hands gripped her shoulders, her eyes shining like lamps as they stared into her face. "This has been going on since the night he took you from the Angel, hasn't it? Jesus, no wonder you understood so easily about unsuitable lovers! But you *must* know this isn't a relationship. You can't have a relationship with a being who kills your people, who will kill you in the end."

I will never kill you. "He won't." Elizabeth gasped. "He won't kill me. And *you* must know he isn't insane, or even the unprincipled killer you thought he was. You must have seen that tonight."

"He's not exactly as we thought," Mihaela allowed. "I'll give you that." Her fingers gripped tighter. "But he isn't like us either. Whatever principles he has, they aren't yours or mine. He's a different species, stronger, more cerebral, perhaps, than the monsters we kill every day, but they are him too. Never forget that. You're alive only on his whim."

"Mihaela, it's not—"

Mihaela's grip changed, sliding up to Elizabeth's face, which she held hard between her hands. "There's more going on than you understand. There's prophecy; there's death and worse! God, even if he doesn't kill you, he'll kill your spirit. Look what he's done to you already."

Elizabeth stared at her. "What? What has he done?"

"Enslaved you," Mihaela said harshly. "As surely as Dmitriu or any one of his minions."

Elizabeth jerked back out of her hold. "Dmitriu isn't enslaved. He loves him."

Mihaela's arms dropped to her sides. "As you do?" she whispered. "You *love* him? Oh, Elizabeth, please, *please* end this. Because you mustn't, you really mustn't fool yourself about this. He doesn't love you. He can't."

The words twisted in Elizabeth's stomach like a knife, even while she denied them. She stumbled backward, away from the source of her pain, but Mihaela kept talking.

"Oh, maybe he's capable of passing affection of some kind, of loyalty, but that's not what you're looking for, is it? You've gone way beyond that, and you won't find it with a vampire."

"That's the trouble, Mihaela," she managed. "I have to look."

Mihaela stood very still in the darkness. The silence echoed in Elizabeth's ears. Mihaela twitched forward and Elizabeth tensed for the attack that Mihaela would perceive as for her own good. Elizabeth wouldn't fight back; she'd run.

Mihaela's breath caught on a sound that could have been anger or frustration. Her shoulders slumped. "Look, then," she said dully. "Look and leave and come back to us safe. Please."

Saloman was leaving it late. He could tell from the color of the sky, with the moon already gone, that the sun would not be long in rising. He had arranged to meet Elizabeth here on the Széchenyi Chain Bridge when it was over, and like a human boy on a date, he kept waiting just in case she still showed up.

He stared down into the depths of the Danube. The wide, seemingly endless river was just about all that was left of the city he remembered. He liked the new Budapest; he felt at home here. But sometimes it was good to be with the past. To remember past triumphs, past loves, past losses. To remind himself that everything passed.

There were many reasons for Elizabeth not to come, all of them valid. But it would have been good to stand here together, watching the river flow under them in the last of the night.

He had always known this would be difficult for her. When she was around the hunters, she was tugged both ways, and he rather thought the cat was out of the bag now, so far as the hunters were concerned.

Two more minutes to watch the Danube and the threatening light in the sky, to imagine her with him . . . to wish it so hard that in the end he wasn't even surprised when at last it became reality. He sensed her presence as she approached from the castle side of the bridge, breathless from running. He felt the warmth of her arm as she rested it on the wall next to his. He smelled her blood, sweet and strong and eternally alluring. The bridge was empty save for the two of them: no cars or pedestrians to disturb the illusion that they were the only two beings in the quiet city.

There seemed to be nothing to say, now that she'd come, so he simply let the moment absorb him, soaking up the gladness of her presence. After a minute, she took her phone from her bag and handed it to him.

He glanced down at the screen at a text message from someone called Richard. It contained only two words: "Dr. Silk."

He smiled. "You have your PhD."

She nodded, taking the phone back and dropping it into her bag.

"I'm glad. You worked hard on it and you wanted it so much."

"It was something I needed. Proof that I'm good at something. Almost like a justification of my existence." She gave a quick, apologetic smile. "I have confidence issues."

"Less so," Saloman said. One of his many delights in her was watching her grow.

She leaned her head on his arm, as if in gratitude. "The funny thing is, now that I have it, I'm not nearly as pleased as I thought I'd be. It doesn't seem as . . . important, in the light of . . ." She waved her arm, encompassing both sides of the city, and meaning, probably, the whole world and all she was discovering in it.

"And what will you do now?" he asked, turning to face her and leaning back on the wall. "Go home and celebrate?"

She nodded. "I suppose I will."

"And the hunters know you're with me tonight."

She swallowed, and he knew that whatever had passed when he left hadn't been easy for her. He felt a spurt of anger at the hunters for interfering, for trying to spoil what she had found with him. He could imagine what they said, knew some of it, at least, was true.

"Mihaela knows. I don't think the others are very sure what the hell's going on. Neither am I."

She raised her gaze from the river, turned up her face to look at him. Her eyes were clear and beautiful and heartbreakingly tragic. "I didn't mean to do this, Saloman. I couldn't help the love, but I didn't mean to deepen it; I didn't mean to understand you and care for your every thought and dream and . . ." She drew another shaky breath. "I didn't mean any of this, whatever it is."

He stirred, as if that would shift the pain. "Do you regret it?"

And her whole face softened into a smile that melted him. "I can't even do that. I can't stop and I don't want to."

He listened to the quick, strong beat of her heart, comparing it with the slower, steadier rhythm of his own. "Then don't. There is no need to make black-and-white choices. You have a life, a good life that you've made for yourself, a home that you care for. Just make yourself another home that is always welcoming."

A deeper gladness, of anticipation and excitement, made her eyes, her whole face, glow. "Where?" she asked.

"Wherever I am."

She lifted her arms around his neck, stood on tiptoe, and kissed him. Her breath in his mouth was sweet, almost like the blood of life as he crushed her to him. "Saloman, Saloman," she whispered against his lips, interspersing the words with wild, sensual kisses. "I am so far in love, it's out of control. . . ."

"That's the way I like you," he said huskily, and jumped. At any moment, the sun could singe him, and it would not be hotter than the desire burning inside him now. He wanted to take her as he ran, pausing against chimney stacks and balconies to caress her wildly eager little body, to kiss her and fuck her and hear her scream with joy before he jumped to the next stable surface and did it all again. But there was no time. He had to get out of the sun. And then to bed.

Immortality. She could see the charm of it as she fell naked on his silk-covered bed. Spending eternity like this, with Saloman. The thought made her smile, welcoming him as he loomed above her, fitting his pale, hard body over hers. She was wet for him already, had been since they'd stood embracing on the bridge, and the exhilaration of the race against the sun hadn't dampened the fire. He entered her immediately, as if he couldn't wait another instant, and only then, as she gasped at the familiar mingling of shock and pleasure, did he pause with a groan of satisfaction.

"At last," he whispered. "I have missed you, missed this."

"So have I."

The characteristic half smile formed and faded on his sensual lips before he kissed her. From instinct, she arched up into him, hugging him with her internal muscles, but still he didn't move inside her.

"Did you know that vampires experience more intense sexual pleasure than humans?"

"I believe you mentioned it," she said shakily, although right now, with him, she couldn't imagine how such a thing was possible.

His hand trailed down the side of her breast, then moved inward. One finger traced the dark circle around her nipple, teasing. "This is because all our physical senses are enhanced. And also because, telepathically, we can enjoy the pleasure of our partners and add it to our own. Would you like to feel my pleasure, Elizabeth?"

She stared into his profound, burning dark eyes, clouded with a fierce lust that was all the more exciting for being temporarily controlled. She swallowed. "Would it kill me?" she asked, not entirely joking.

"You have no faith," he said, bending his mouth to the nipple his finger was teasing, "in your body's capacity for pleasure." As he kissed her nipple, flicking it with his sensual, wicked tongue, he continued to trace arcs around it with his fingertip, and again her internal muscles contracted around him, urging him to thrust.

"What do I do?" she whispered with difficulty.

He lifted his head. "Open your mind to mine. As if you were talking to me. I'll let you in. And if you want to, you can allow me to feel with you."

"Don't you already?"

"Up to a point. I want it all."

She gasped. "I can't concentrate like this. . . ."

"Yes, you can. Concentrate on the pleasure." He moved once inside her, a long, caressing stroke that sent delight coursing through her whole body. *See?*

She smiled. *I see.*

The sensation opened like a flower. She could feel the tightness of her own wet, velvety warmth around him, feel what it did to him. *Oh, my. Oh, God . . .*

He began to move inside her, blasting her with his pleasure, which grew all the greater as he lowered his head and began to suck on her breast. She couldn't hold back. She'd told it all, everything that mattered, so she let him see it too, her body's abject enslavement as well as its unbearable joy in him, every spark of bliss, every wicked fantasy, because once her mind opened the box, she couldn't close it again, and didn't want to, because it fed her own pleasure like a rushing spring.

She saw which of her caresses affected him the most, as well as what he wanted to do to her, and it made her moan and cry out as she writhed frantically in the grip of a passion so fierce it was almost savage. But she couldn't stop. His lust, his ecstasy rampaged through her, dragging her body in its wake, and she hung on to him, glorying in it all, straining to give even more, to absorb everything that was flung at her.

It couldn't last at that pace, not for her, although she saw through him how it might be possible, how he made it go on and on and then began again. One day, perhaps. For now, there was only this wild, shattering orgasm spinning her violently over the precipice, dragging her with him in a writhing, straining heap. She no longer knew which pleasure was hers and which his, nor even which body belonged to whom, only that there had never been anything like this.

There was an instant when she thought she would lose consciousness, and was furious that she would miss any of this astounding experience. But as if he saw it, he let her come down slowly, withdrawing part of himself without breaking the connection entirely.

When she could see, she smiled, because he did and because she couldn't do anything else. She imagined she could still see herself through his eyes, familiar and yet not—an oddly beautiful and exciting stranger with her hair, her eyes, beads of perspiration on her forehead, purring, satisfied passion on her sensual lips.

"Is that how you see me?" she whispered.

"Some of how I see you. You're constantly new, constantly surprising me."

"You need novelty. Dmitriu told me."

"What else did Dmitriu tell you?"

She shied away from that. The connection was too close and another quarrel too far from what either of them wanted or needed. Instead, she said, "I thought you'd be angry because I stopped you from killing Dante."

His black, sculpted eyebrows twitched. "You couldn't have stopped me if I'd chosen to do it. For the rest, we are different. You insist on illogically preserving deeply flawed and dangerous humans. I drink blood to exist."

He rolled suddenly onto his back, and she moved her legs to straddle him.

"But then again, we are not so different," he said softly.

"What do you mean?" She thought of the fight in Travis's club, of the one in the castle tunnel, the reluctant yet undeniable joy of battle that was so shamefully close to the vampire love of killing, and realized finally that she could live with that too.

The smile in Saloman's eyes, hovering on his lips, was wicked, and so exciting that despite the unprecedented bliss he'd just given her, desire surged once more.

"I mean I've seen some of your fantasies," he said huskily. "And I'm hungry."

Her breath caught as he moved suggestively inside her. Then, without warning, he sat up and shifted across the bed to stand with her still held in his arms. He didn't break eye contact as he walked across the room with her. Then she realized a leather armchair was traveling toward them, and her lips parted in shock.

The chair stopped in front of a mahogany chest of drawers with a large, ornately framed mirror above it. Saloman shifted the position of her leg and sat down in the chair with her in his lap, so that they both faced the mirror. Nudging her hair out of the way, he touched the vein at the side of her neck.

The brief, almost forgotten fantasy sprang back into her mind. She'd wondered how sexy it would be to watch him as he drank from her. Moisture flooded from between her legs, soaking him as he moved lethargically inside her.

"It was a wicked thought," she whispered, twisting to look into his face rather than the mirror. "I was lonely."

"No excuses. Watch and enjoy. As I will."

He bent his head and his hair brushed her naked shoulder, spreading down her arm. His lips touched her skin, his tongue flickered over her vein, and she tensed, waiting for the pain. But he coaxed her, caressing her throat with his silken tongue, distracting her with his hands on her breasts, moving inside her. Only when she relaxed against him, lost again in the blinding desire, did he pierce her skin.

She cried out. Her closed eyes flew open and as he began to suck her blood, she watched the ecstasy replace the agony in her mirrored face. With a moan of bliss, she moved on him, relishing the rhythmic flow of her blood into his hungry mouth, and watched avidly to catch every movement of his lips on her skin. God, it was ultrasexy and wicked and weirdly, almost frighteningly beautiful to watch this being draw her lifeblood into himself while making love to her. It was like an endless cycle of life and pleasure, and when his eyelids lifted to meet her gaze in the mirror, she came in a long, drawn-out cry of bliss.

Still, she couldn't look away, saw his teeth detach from her bleeding skin and his tongue lick the wounds. When he lifted his head to kiss her mouth, the skin was already healing and she could taste her blood on his lips.

"Where is the evil in that?" he whispered. "There is only joy and life."

Curled into his shoulder with his arms around her, the silk sheets cool against her hot, sated body, she was almost asleep when her eyes sprang back open.

Dmitriu was wrong.

He hadn't offered her immortality.

The knowledge sliced through her haze of happiness like a knife. It didn't change anything. He still lay at her side, her lover, her companion. And she lay in his arms, like many who'd passed through his life before her. Like Tsigana.

No more than Tsigana.

Selfish, treacherous Tsigana, who might have been dazzled by him, might even have loved him in her own way, despite her faithlessness, but who had certainly tried to use him for her own ends. Tsigana, unworthy of immortality.

"Just like me," she whispered.

He moved, turning to see her face, which she hid in his shoulder, though she couldn't cover the wetness seeping from her eyes into his skin.

It didn't matter. She could no more become a vampire than she could kill herself or him. She'd already acknowledged that, and it remained the truth. But only now, when she realized the offer would never come, did she understand how much it meant to her to be asked. To be more to him than Tsigana.

For this moment, this night, Elizabeth, I love you, he'd said. Just this moment. Just this night, and a few more.

He said, "There is no one like you."

Slowly, she took her face away from his shoulder, ignoring her tears that he wiped with his fingertips, and stared at him.

He was right. There *was* no one like her. Somehow, she'd gotten uniquely under his skin. It crept upon her, not quite like a blinding light on the road to Damascus, but a revelation all the same. Whatever she was to him, or wasn't, he wanted her as his companion, for however many nights and days there were for them. Because of that, she had the opportunity to do something for the world. What that might be was very hazy and might even be very distant, but that was all right too. She had time.

And he was worth fighting for, this wonderful, mysterious, unpredictable being. However long or however difficult the struggle might be, she *could* make him hers in the end, as she was his.

Epilogue

Dante sat slumped in his hotel room's uncomfortable chair, watching the sun come up on a new day. From his window, he could still see the castle, the scene of his final defeat. His gambit for immortality had failed spectacularly, and with it, he knew, had gone his valuable position as Grand Master of the American Order of Vampire Hunters.

In an agony of loss and fury, Dante plucked at his shirt, pulling it loose from his neck. The bloodstain in the shape of Saloman's hand caught his eye, the symbol of everything that had gone wrong with his life. Saloman had crushed him and taken the sword in which he'd placed all his spurious, stupid hopes. The meaningless, pointless sword that turned out to have only sentimental value to the most powerful vampire of all time.

Because it was given to me by my cousin Luk, whom I later killed.

Dante froze, his hand still holding the shirt away from his body to reveal the bloodstain. Saloman's blood.

Elizabeth Silk had awakened Saloman, however unintentionally, with her blood, the blood of her ancestress Tsigana, who had "killed" him long ago. Saloman too had once killed an Ancient. And Saloman's blood was on Dante's shirt.

Springing to his feet, Dante found his phone on the dresser and scrolled rapidly down to the American hunter network before he pressed connect. Surely word would not yet have spread to remove him from his position as Grand Master. . . .

"Harry, it's me—how are you? I need a snippet of information from you. The Ancient vampire Luk, who was killed by his cousin Saloman in the seventeenth century—where is he buried?"

ABOUT THE AUTHOR

Marie Treanor lives in Scotland with her husband and three children. She has been writing stories since childhood and considers herself very privileged still to be doing so instead of working for her living. Her previous e-books include *Killing Joe*, which was an Amazon Kindle best-seller. In the Awakened by Blood novels, she is delighted to be able to bring together her long-standing loves of vampire stories, romance, and Gothic fantasy. To find out more, please visit www.MarieTreanor.com.

Keep reading for a sneak peek at the next thrilling romance in Marie Treanor's Awakened by Blood series,

Blood Eternal

Available in October 2011

When the earth moved, the vampire Saloman felt a surge of exquisite pleasure almost akin to sexual release. The tension in him snapped, broken by the rush of rare, intoxicating fear.

Dawn approached, and he was too close to the earthquake's center for safety, too isolated in these Peruvian mountains to be discovered should he become buried under an immovable fall of rock. Already he could hear the thunder of incipient avalanches and landslides, drowning out the lesser destruction of man-made edifices, but if he honed his supernatural hearing, he could just about make out the distinctive thuds of collapsing wood and masonry in the distant villages. The sounds of wreckage brought him a certain amount of satisfaction. The villages were already empty of life—he'd seen to that over the past couple of weeks.

Saloman was one of the very few able-bodied beings left on this mountain. Even the animals had fled, their instincts warning them that the Earth was angry. Unlike them, Saloman savored that anger, that knowledge of a unique power far superior to his own, a power before which even his strength could do nothing. And so he lay on his hard mountain ledge in the dark, reveling in his rare moment of helplessness, smiling up at the wavering black sky while the earth under him heaved and cracked, splitting rocks and trees, hurling down the flimsy village buildings.

He knew the risk, and he didn't want to end his existence or to return to the tortured sleep of death. He didn't want to leave this world. He didn't want to leave Elizabeth. And yet still he had come closer than he should to wait for the Earth to shake—partly because he wanted to feel the massive power of it, partly because, like the rebellious boy he'd once been, he wanted to dare the danger.

It was an indulgence he shouldn't have allowed himself. He acknowledged that as the ledge of rock split under his back, flinging him off the edge. At the last moment, he grasped onto the one stable corner, giving himself a modicum of control as he jumped the fifty feet or so onto the hard, jagged ground below—more from memory of the landscape than from sight, since the tumbling boulders and dust impaired his night vision.

By the time he'd found a flatter foothold, sheltered enough to prevent any more stones from landing on his head and shoulders, the quake had stopped. The mountain, however, hadn't. It continued to spit rocks down toward him, and below he could hear them gathering pace and volume. By morning, the mountain would have changed its shape.

Fear was good. He was glad he'd come up here to remember what it was like to be afraid. *Confront your fears*, his cousin Luk had told him, even before Saloman had died and been reborn as a vampire. Luk had turned him, and had taught him well, just as if he'd known that Saloman would be the last of their Ancient race. Saloman had learned to face soul-destroying loneliness; he'd fought and defeated everyone who threatened him. There was no one left who could invade his mind and find him wanting—which had been his first and most intense fear, the one that had formed his boyhood and never quite left him. And yet he could think of his father now without pain or hurt or terror, and he knew that if it had been possible for them to meet again, he would not be afraid. He had no reason to be.

Saloman lay down once more, gazing up at the steady sky while the mountain rearranged itself with noisy, dust-filled aggression. He smiled, because no one else could possibly have done what he just had. No one had ever done what he was doing now.

Watch me, Elizabeth. I will prevail. The world will do my bidding. You can't doubt it.

It was his own thought. He didn't send it to her. He wouldn't even tell her about this; he would let her find out for herself. Perhaps he'd even go to her, so he was with her when she made the discovery. Hunger tore through him. Blood and sex and Elizabeth. A reward before the next stage began.

He sat up, unable to be still any longer. His lesson in humility had, in the end, fed his self-belief. Only he could have survived the earthquake from here; he alone could unite and direct the world. No one could stop him. And as the world learned his power, who would want to? He'd find his way down the mountain and drink some human blood before he began his journey across the world to Scotland.

But as he rose, a scream of rage and terror slammed into his mind. Saloman let out an involuntary cry, grasping his head in both hands to prevent the pain, the anguish, instinctively trying to squeeze out the howling voice that should have been mere memory and yet felt as real as the rocks sliding and crashing their way down the mountainside. The flash of impossible presence surged and then vanished as swiftly as it had come, leaving Saloman to drop his hands slowly from his face.

Which is when he realized he had no time to analyze himself for sanity or injury. In a moment, he was going to be buried deep under an avalanche. Saloman hurled himself forward and leapt into the darkness.

. . .

Six thousand miles away, in a Scottish café, Elizabeth Silk caught her breath and shivered uncontrollably.

"What's the matter?" her friend Joanne demanded, placing two large mugs of coffee on the café table before resuming her seat beside Elizabeth.

"Oh, nothing," Elizabeth said evasively. *There's a vampire in my head. Or, at least there was for an instant.* What would Joanne make of that? "Someone walked over my grave."

The trouble was, it felt like Saloman, although her instant telepathic reach to him hit nothing. Not surprising. Although her abilities had grown by leaps and bounds in the past few months, she still operated best with peace to concentrate, even when Saloman chose to receive her. Something had happened, she was sure, though whether it involved physical danger or emotional upheaval, she had no way of knowing. Once, she would have denied the possibility of the latter. Now she knew him better, knew him as a being of profound feelings, even though they were often beyond her ability to understand. If something had occurred, if he needed her . . .

Thrusting her unease aside, she smiled and lifted her cup to her lips.

"I meant in general," Joanne said dryly. She was a short, eye-catching woman with purple-tinged frizzy hair and a razor-sharp mind. "You seem a bit glum."

"It's only ten in the morning and I was up until three."

"Doing what?" Joanne asked.

"Writing. I think I've finished the book based on my thesis. I'll send it off to your agent tomorrow."

"He'll be your agent too the day after," Joanne said with a confident grin.

"I hope so. I'm finally happy I've struck the right balance between academic and popular—which is pretty important with a subject like vampires and superstitions!"

"You're right there," Joanne said, raising her mug in a toast. "Hats off to you. So, that's out of the way—what now? Glasgow?"

"Ah. Maybe that's why I look glum. I didn't get the job in Glasgow." It had been a rare opportunity, a permanent, full-time post at Glasgow University. Elizabeth had applied, knowing she would have to be stupid not to, and yet her heart hadn't been in it. Perhaps this had come across at her interview.

"Idiots," Joanne said roundly.

Elizabeth gave her a lopsided smile. "Thanks for the support. I wasn't even certain I wanted it, so I've no right to whine about not getting it."

"I'm pretty sure there'll be a vacancy here at St. Andrews next year," Joanne said. "What else is still in the pipeline for now?"

Elizabeth shrugged. "Nothing truly inspiring. A college in London, part-time. And a maternity leave post at Aberdeen University."

She hesitated until Joanne nudged her and commanded, "Spill!"

Elizabeth laughed. "Well, there's a one-year appointment at the University of Budapest."

Joanne sat up straight. "Budapest!"

"It's more my thing, includes teaching a special course in the historic value of superstitions, and there'll be research opportunities in other areas. Also, I do speak the language, more or less. . . ."

"And your man's there," Joanne finished with unnecessary relish.

Elizabeth felt her skin color, and took a hasty gulp of coffee to try to cover it. "Only sometimes," she mumbled. "He travels a lot." Then, since Joanne continued to stare at her, she lowered the cup and sighed. "I don't want him to think I'm pursuing him."

"He might like that you are."

"But I'm not!"

Joanne blinked "Aren't you? I bloody would be."

Elizabeth couldn't help laughing at her friend's fervor. She still regarded the evening that she'd been obliged to introduce Joanne to her vampire lover as the weirdest moment of her increasingly bizarre life.

Saloman had arrived in her flat without warning two months ago, while she and Joanne had been putting the world to rights in the sitting room over a bottle of wine. He'd come through the kitchen window but neither he nor Elizabeth had corrected Joanne's assumption that he had his own key.

Joanne had watched their reunion with interest, clearly torn by conflicting desires to leave them alone and to discover more about Elizabeth's mysterious lover. She'd compromised by subjecting Saloman to a half hour of penetrating questions—which he'd answered or deflected with equal amusement as the notion took him—and then departing earlier than she normally would.

"Fuck me, he's gorgeous," she'd informed Elizabeth at the front door. "No wonder you're messed up."

At the time, Elizabeth had jeered at the term "messed up," for Saloman's arrival had filled her with the complete happiness only he had ever brought her. But now, in his absence, she acknowledged her friend's perception. She *was* messed up, and had been since she'd first met him. But if Joanne knew the truth—that Elizabeth's handsome and charming lover wasn't merely mysterious but the most powerful vampire who'd ever existed—she wouldn't put the cause down to his looks.

Joanne said, "So you're hesitating over whether to apply for the job? Apply now and worry later."

Elizabeth shifted in her seat. "Actually, I've already applied. They've offered me the post. I just have to decide whether to take it."

Joanne finished her coffee and set down her mug before rising. "Bite their hands off," she advised, swinging her bag off the floor and onto her shoulder, to the imminent danger of the mugs, which undoubtedly would have been knocked to the floor if Elizabeth hadn't seized them out of harm's way. Behind Joanne, a passing waiter stared at Elizabeth, wide-eyed. She must have moved too fast.

"I'll miss you, of course," Joanned added, oblivious to the entire incident.

"No, you won't. You'll come to visit me or I'll never speak to you again." Which was another point against accepting. In Budapest, Saloman's own city, there would be untold distractions from the world of academia—leaving love out of it, there were vampires and hunters and an inevitable conflict waiting to erupt that would place her squarely in the middle. Could she really hope to keep Joannc out of that?

But traipsing downstairs in her friend's wake, Elizabeth couldn't help feeling a secret leap of excitement at the prospect of moving to Hungary. Outside the Victoria Café it was raining, a fine, misty drizzle that seemed to exemplify the Scottish summer: dull.

"Well, back to the grindstone," Joanne said, happily enough. "What are you up to for the rest of the day?"

"I said I'd do a favor for a friend—visit this wounded soldier in Glasgow."

"Badly wounded?" Joanne asked sympathetically.

"Badly enough, but he's pretty well recovered physically. Apparently he's still traumatized."

"Sounds like a worthy but fraught day for you, then," Joanne observed, lifting her hand in farewell. She was clearly eager to get back to her books. Elizabeth watched her scuttle across Market Street with a feeling that came close to envy. Once, being lost in academia had been enough for Elizabeth too. And visiting an injured soldier would have aroused a much simpler compassion in her, without this guilty, nagging hope that because the British vampire hunters had asked her to go, he'd have something paranormally intriguing to say.

She was bored, she realized with some surprise. Achieving her doctorate had been satisfying; writing the book had been fun; research and teaching at some academic institution were still a necessary part of her ambitions, to say nothing about putting food on the table. Six months ago, desperately trying to keep her life stable and normal in the midst of unasked for and unwanted new responsibilities and dangers, she wouldn't have believed this was possible; yet now, perhaps influenced by her earlier shiver of anxiety, she actually *missed* the menacing world of darkness and vampires, a world in which her mind and body could both stretch without hindrance, and succeed.

She missed Saloman.

With the sound of the vampire's preternatural scream splitting his ears, Senator Grayson Dante knew it had all gone horribly wrong. Dante thought back to the accounts he'd read of Saloman's awakening, taken from Elizabeth Silk's testimony. She too had found an empty underground chamber, except it had turned out not to be so empty. She'd been bleeding from a thorn prick and surmised that it was the drops of her blood that had first made the dead Saloman visible to her. She'd mistaken him for a stone sarcophagus.

Dante crouched down and delved into his bag to retrieve the vial of blood. It was a tiny amount, distilled from the stain of Saloman's blood left on his shirt during their last violent encounter. He couldn't afford to waste any. He was sure this room was enchanted, as the outer cave had been, to deter visitors. But simply staring wouldn't break through this spell.

Dante unscrewed the lid with great care.

"What is that?" Mehmet, his Turkish guide, whispered.

It's the blood of the Ancient vampire Saloman, with which I hope to awaken his cousin and enemy, Luk, whom Saloman killed more than three hundred years ago. Would Mehmet run or laugh if he said such a thing aloud? Instinctively, Dante knew his need for Mehmet was almost over. But only almost. The Turk had one more purpose to fulfill.

Dante crept around the dark chamber. The beam from his flashlight bobbed eratically around the rough stone floors and walls, barely penetrating the profound blackness more than a couple of feet beyond his unsteady fingers. He hoped that if he couldn't see the body, at least he might feel it with his hands or feet. Even so, when his foot struck something that felt like stone, part of the floor's uneven surface, he almost paid it no attention. Then he paused and placed his finger over the phial opening before he shook it and removed his finger.

Drawing in his breath with a quick, silent prayer to no one in particular that it would be enough, he shook his hand out in front of him. His finger tingled as the tiny spatter of blood sprayed downward. And there in the darkness, without suddenness or shock, was what he'd been looking for all these weeks.

A stone table on which lay a sculpted body. Almost exactly like the one Elizabeth Silk had found a year earlier.

Mehmet's breath sounded like a wheeze. "My God, I almost didn't see it. I thought there was nothing. . . . Is this it? Is this your nobleman's tomb?"

"Almost certainly." Dante felt dizzy. His whole body trembled, not just as a reaction to his first glimpse of the deeply sinister figure illuminated by their flashlights, but as a result of the enormity of what he was doing. He found it difficult to get words out, and yet he had to concentrate, to ignore his sudden fears and stick to his plan. Mehmet had to continue to believe in the fiction that this was merely the lost tomb of a historic nobleman. And then, finally, Dante would reach his goal. Eternal life. Eternal power. Damnation, if it existed, was a small price to pay.

With carefully judged casualness, he passed the vial to Mehmet. "Here. I want to photograph this."

Even shining his flashlight on the tiny drop of dark liquid, Mehmet could have no idea what it was. He seemed happy that Dante had found what he sought—even if only so he could get back into the fresh air and climb down the mountain.

Dante produced his camera and pointed it at the tomb. "When I say 'now,'" he directed, "pour the contents of the vial over the carving."

"Why? What is it?"

"It'll make the tomb stand out more in the picture," Dante lied easily. He wasn't a politician for nothing. "Okay . . . now!"

Dante held his breath as Mehmet shook the tiny drops of liquid over the carved face. This was it, the moment of greatest risk and greatest hope, on which all Dante's ambitions rested. Religion, decency, nature itself—none of those things counted beside the huge power Dante was about to take.

At this point in the earlier awakening, Saloman had clamped his teeth into Elizabeth's neck. Dante had been torn over this part of his plan. The blood used in the awakening had to be Saloman's—Luk's killer's—or it wouldn't work, but Dante didn't know whether any of the mystical attributes of awakening would be bestowed on whoever did the pouring. No one had ever done it like this before, to his knowledge. If there was power to be had from awakening, he naturally wanted it for himself; but on the other hand, he needed Luk to be as strong as possible, which meant drinking the blood of his Awakener and killing him to absorb his life force. So far, Saloman had failed to kill Elizabeth, and therein lay his weakness. Dante did not intend Luk to make the same mistake.

It was a pity for Mehmet.

Dante shone his flashlight unwaveringly on Luk's dead face. It did indeed look like stone. He'd expected it to be more lifelike, to give some hint of his Ancient strength, a clue that he could be awakened. Despite the tiny droplets of blood splashed on Luk's cheek, nose, lips, and chin, nothing happened.

Oh, fuck. It isn't enough. After all this, I needed more blood. . . .

"Did you take it?" Mehmet asked.

"What? Oh, the photograph. Yes, I got it. Thanks." He took a step forward, meaning to take back the vial and see whether there was anything left in it. But before he could touch it, a sound like a faint groan issued from the carving.

Oh, yes. Hallelujah.

Under Dante's riveted gaze, the dead eyes of the sculpture opened and the lips parted. The skin moved, shifting slowly into an expression not of triumph but of shock. Even . . . fear. Luk sat up and Mehmet fell back with a low moan of terror. Luk's twisted mouth opened wider, revealing his long, terrifying incisors as he stared at Mehmet.

The vampire's scream started low, like a rattle in his throat, then rose quickly into the most horrific, gut-wrenching howl Dante had ever heard. Like all the pain of everyone in the world rolled into one pure, dreadful sound.

This isn't meant to happen, Dante thought in panic. *Something's gone terribly wrong. I must have got the wrong vampire. . . .*

Then in fury the creature who may or may not have been Luk swung himself off the stone table, and Dante stepped circumspectly behind Mehmet before giving the Turk a sharp shove into the reaching arms of whatever they'd awakened.

Printed in the United States
by Baker & Taylor Publisher Services